## Praise for the Ross Agency Mystery Series

"I've been a fan of SJ Rook since he first stepped foot into the Ross Agency and he just keeps getting better and better. I can't wait for the next book in this amazing series."

– **Kellye Garrett**, Anthony, Lefty, and
IPPY Award-winning author of the *Detective by Day Mysteries*

"Rook is a modern, hard-boiled antihero; as the story [LOST AND FOUND IN HARLEM] carries on, he demonstrates ability, humility, decency, and respect and concern for Harlem and its inhabitants… Pitts lovingly illustrates what life is like in a vibrant Harlem, showing people from different walks of life, nationalities, and socio-economic statuses. The neighborhood features prominently not only as a setting, but as a character all its own."

*–Kirkus Reviews*

"Her Ross Agency Mystery series is a whirlwind of quirky characters, dexterous writing, and imaginative subplots. Her black, male, protagonist, SJ Rook, is a determined and thoughtful PI with a penchant for the underdog reminiscent of the compassion of Easy Rawlins."

– **Cheryl A. Head**, Lambda Literary Award finalist and
GCLS Ann Bannon Award-winning author of the
*Charlie Mack Motown Mystery Series*

"Rook is a cross between Barack Obama – fearless, chivalrous, and fluent in both Harlem patois and standard English – and Humphrey Bogart – tough on the outside, but inside, a heart of gold. PAUPER AND PRINCE IN HARLEM is cinematic. Hollywood, are you listening?"

– **Robert W. Fuller**, author of *The Rowan Tree: A Novel* and *Dignity for All: How to Create a World Without Rankism*

"A great story with enough twists and turns to keep me on the edge of my seat. Pitts does a terrific job!"

– **Carolyn Marie Wilkins**, author of *Death at a Seance: A Carrie McFarland Psychic Mystery*

"Modern, vibrant noir. The [LOST AND FOUND IN HARLEM] plot was perfectly balanced, the writing illuminated the story, and the characters were drawn with witty sympathy. The relationship between them is especially refreshing."

– **Lisa Southard**, author of *The Small Histories of Anya Polgarrick*

"The setting is riveting, but what truly keeps you reading is characters and story. Rook, with his bum foot, cluttered apartment, and abiding (usually) faith in the human condition, is endearing, totally believable. This time [PAUPER AND PRINCE IN HARLEM] he's out to discover why the teen-ager he'd been playing checkers with in a park was gunned down by men in a van. As usual, Pitts' prose gives the greats of noir a run for their money."

– **John Burgess**, author of *A Woman of Angkor*

"From an all-too-common tragedy at the start of this fast-moving story [PAUPER AND PRINCE IN HARLEM] to the satisfying resolution, you'll not want to put this one down. PI Rook is a winner."

– **Tracy Clark**, Anthony, Lefty, and Shamus Award-nominated author of *The Chicago Mystery Series*

**By Delia C. Pitts**

*Lost and Found in Harlem*

*Practice the Jealous Arts*

*Black and Blue in Harlem*

*Pauper and Prince in Harlem*

# MURDER MY PAST

## A Ross Agency Mystery

# DELIA C. PITTS

Park Manor
Press

ISBN: 978-1-09833-503-8 (print)

ISBN: 978-1-09833-504-5 (ebook)

Author's Note: This book is a work of fiction. None of the characters, incidents, or locations are meant to resemble any real people, places, or events, now or in the past.

*For my Oberlin College friends – faithful, fun, and inspiring.*
*Dear Ones, we're still going strong!*

# CONTENTS

# CHAPTER
# ONE

Mountains of muscle lumbered behind us, closing the distance as we plunged through the warehouse door. I slammed home the bolt, locking the goons inside. They rattled the handle as we sprinted away. Like most door hinges in Harlem, these were rusted, but the iron bar was solid. The thugs were trapped. I hoped. They banged again, but the metal gate wouldn't budge. We galloped across the night-draped parking lot to the jumble of old cars, one hundred yards from the stubborn door.

Sabrina Ross flung open the trunk of a pink Pontiac and glared into the dusty interior. Bubblegum-colored rubber mats covered the floor.

"You remember that old movie with J-Lo and Clooney?" Brina said in a low voice. She was a detective, my boss, my boss's daughter, and a whole lot more in my life. When Brina Ross spoke, SJ Rook paid attention.

I jabbed at my cell phone and listened to the line ring on the other end. "Yeah, I never could figure out how two grown-ass adults fit into the trunk of a car."

"Unless they're dead," Brina muttered. She holstered her gun in the waistband of her jeans.

I hung up, then hit redial. Norment Ross, Brina's dad, wasn't answering. The cavalry was not on its way. I heard a noise and stole a glance at the warehouse.

Brina took off her denim jacket and threw it into the trunk. "Yeah, well unless you've got a better idea, I say we hide in here. We're running out of options." Shouts rose from the warehouse at the far end of the parking lot. "I'll get in first. Then you…Hey!"

I launched backwards into the trunk, grabbing her wrist as I fell. She landed hard on the rubber mats. I slammed the hood shut two seconds after she snatched her sandals inside. "I told you I'd get in first! What the hell is wrong with you?"

I jutted my chin into the soft braids on the top of her head. "Shut. Up. Now."

Male voices in multiple languages fanned through the parking lot. Spanish, Portuguese from Newark's Ironbound district, some kind of Slavic, and a Vietnamese-accented command voice. Crime in Harlem was an equal opportunity business.

My arms tightened around Brina's back and she pressed her face into my chest. Sunlit amber of forest paths pricked my nose, her fresh scent mingling with sweat and the tang of blood. Her lip was split, matching my eyebrow. We were in a fix.

Angry shouting swelled, the slits of light around the keyhole flickering as the men passed by. Then all fell silent. We waited several moments in the dark, listening to our breaths even out. I reached over her shoulder to push on the hood. It was locked. I muttered a curse into the thick rows of braids above her temple.

"Looks like we may be here for a while." Her voice rumbled through my chest, amused rather than pissed off. Which I definitely was. When I didn't answer, she chirped. "I thought you were calling Daddy."

"He didn't pick up." Her father was the head of our little neighborhood detective firm, the Ross Agency. Norment had sent us to collect against an overdue bill. Sixteen months without one dollar paid was too much even for Norment's over-generous soul. That job led to our confrontation with the multi-culti gang in the warehouse. And to our retreat to this goddamned pink car trunk.

"Well, call him again."

"The phone's somewhere in here. But with you taking up so much space, I can't move enough to find it." Dammit, was she smirking? "Roll over." I pushed her shoulder. "Maybe you can feel it."

She squirmed, shifting to face the trunk opening, and patted the floor mats. Grainy, sticky, wet, rubbery. But no phone. My knees pressed behind her thighs. She was tall, five eight to my six one, so I adjusted my shoulder to cover hers. Might as well make the best of the close situation, George Clooney style. She relaxed into me and I rested my hand on her hip. "Sorry, it's tight in here."

"I can't feel the phone." She shoved at the trunk lid. Maybe it would open by magic. Two sharp raps from her fist. Or by brute force. Nothing. We lay for what could have been minutes or only seconds.

My hand grew heavy on her hip. Not pressing, but firm and still. "A little privacy, a little quiet." I whispered across her ear, its rim warm under my lips.

"Look, we're cool and all that." She squeaked, a giggle bubbling inside the cheek next to mine. "But I'm not trying for any of *that* mess in the trunk of a frickin' car!"

"But it's got pink floor mats!" I chuckled. "Brina, relax. You're safe from funky flirtation." My stomach molded against her ass, my fingers increasing the pressure on her hip. Dipping my face to the soft bend between her shoulder and neck, I inhaled. "You smell good. Now, no talking."

She harrumphed and lowered her head to the grimy mat. I waited for more movement, her stillness spooking me. The slits around the key hole darkened. Night in August dropped late and sudden, like a heavy-weight boxer's knockout blow. I counted her heartbeats. Strong, slow, steady as a river they came, thudding against my chest until I lost track of time. I counted past one hundred, maybe one fifty.

I slipped my hand from her hip to rest it against her stomach. The t-shirt was damp with sweat, sticking to the spirals of her belly button. She softened under my touch. "We need to get out of here."

The cell buzzed, a rude hum against my ribs. I patted the grungy mat until I found the phone. I skated my fingers over the slick face to open the line, then fumbled the phone to my mouth. "Norment? That you? Where are you, man!"

"No. Not Norman. Or whatever you said." A silky female voice drawled through the electronic crackle. "Is that you, SJ?"

I knew that purr. Low, sandpaper tough, devious, enticing. My ex-wife's voice hadn't changed since high school. "Annie! Where are you?"

"No need to shout, SJ. I'm right here in New York."

"You're here? Where? How?" Stupid, but still better than croaking like a strangled frog.

"Continental Regent Hotel. For the week. Meet me tomorrow in the bar for drinks." An order, not an invitation.

"Sure, Annie. What time?"

"Seven-thirty too late?"

"No. Fine. I'll be there."

Annie hung up. Silence. No greeting, no explanation. No adios or good night. Silence. Payback for the last seven years of our mean marriage. And the three dark years since our divorce.

Brina jumped on the case. "Who was that? Didn't sound like a wrong number."

"Ex-wife. Anniesha Perry. She's in town for the week." My heart thumped against Brina's spine.

"She's from Texas, right?" Her voice was tight and higher than usual.

"No. Florida. Miami." I swallowed the groan rising from my gut. I wasn't having this conversation here. Or anywhere in the known universe. My past could stay past. For at least one more day. Or forever.

"We gotta get out of here. Now." Was that squawk really my voice?

She turned her head; moonlight seeped along the edges of the trunk's lid. Jutting from her cornrows, a slender metal hook grazed my face.

"Hey! You poked me in the eye with that idiot hairpin!" I sucked breath at the sudden idea. "Give it to me." With a few twists, I tugged the bobby pin from her braid. I hummed as I bent it. "Switch places with me."

Brina rolled under me. She snickered as I balanced on knuckles and toes over her. Not going to crush my boss. Unless absolutely necessary. Code of a gentleman, a soldier, and a private eye. I worked the hairpin into the key hole. After a few strokes, the lock yielded.

I eased from the trunk, unfolding the cramped muscles in my torso. I crouched beside the Pontiac to scan the parking lot. Clear. The goons were gone. Straightening, I grabbed Brina's hand and pulled her out. A smirk creased her face in the humid moonlight. She retrieved her jacket, stained with oil and sludge from the floor of the trunk. As she brushed transparent insect wings from her t-shirt, I punched Norment's number again. Success.

---

As I rattled ice in the heavy tumbler, memories washed through me. Out of the cloud-pink past, a woman ambled into a ritzy bar. A guy dropped his jaw, his wallet, his pants. Not necessarily in that order. Rollercoaster soared, swooped, crashed, and trundled on. I swallowed the soda's fizz. My mind rambled through our shared past, bracing for the ride to begin again.

Anniesha Perry, wife of my youth, was the woman. I was the guy. This swanky hotel saloon was the rollercoaster's latest stop. I wasn't the teenager who'd first met Anniesha or the young soldier who'd married her, but the thought of her could still send me to that fine summit where all the time and sex and money and laughter in the world were mine to take. The rollercoaster had crashed, of course. Several times before I reached forty. Our divorce was three years old, after seven years of married strife. But the carnival ride still circled. Not past enough.

Working as a private investigator in New York toughened me against the soaring and crashing. Right? Grew a turtle's horny shell for skin. And tied a knot of gristle where my heart used to beat. Sure. After two years tackling the grit and grief of neighborhood cases, Harlem sophistication dusted my shoulders. Right? Wrong.

The bar Annie picked was the jewel in a mid-town fortress of luxury I'd never enter on my own. The Continental Regent hotel was host to a week-long conference on twenty-first century entrepreneurship. Three thousand people jammed into the glittering pile for the meeting. Tuesday night after her call, I scanned the conference program online. Anniesha Perry was the convention's biggest deal: keynote speaker at the plenary session and a featured participant on several panels. In her photo, Annie wore a sunrise-pink blouse, a thin gold braided chain nestled in the notch of her throat. The bio under her glossy picture said she owned a Miami cleaning company which reeled in a million dollars a year.

*A million.* I was lucky to make three hundred dollars in a good week of detecting. Being a private eye was gratifying, but the rewards were non-financial. I liked solving puzzles, fixing problems, restoring order in the neighborhood. I was good at my job: tough on bad guys, sweet to old ladies, stingy with words, quick with fists. The combination played to my strengths. My business was long on danger and boredom, short on money. Since our high school days in San Marcos, Texas, I'd known Annie was out of my league. Now the black ink of her company's ledger offered proof positive.

Annie had said seven-thirty. At seven-ten I arrived at the Continental Regent to settle my nerves. I wanted to case the scene. Wednesday evenings in mid-August were slow; the saloon was stocked with tourists in mint green shorts, damp t-shirts, wrinkled shifts, and white sneakers. Posh regulars had bounced to the Hamptons or Martha's Vineyard. My own summer vacation had been less classy: Brina and I had spent ten days driving a mob hitwoman and her baby to a safe house in Florida. I'd survived that overheated road trip with sanity intact, but dignity and jeans in tatters. Now I kept my urban cred by wearing the same uniform of black trousers and black button-down shirt I always wore. My poverty could pass for elegance in these circumstances.

The damned black shirt. Brina had clocked it when she barged into my office at six that evening. Two buttons fastened, working on the rest. My fingers froze.

"Ex-wife gets a new shirt, hmm?" Her squint and abrupt tone pressed me into a stupid reply. I'd spent the afternoon lobbing single word answers to her questions about the date with Annie. She pried, I dodged. She steamed, I froze. She'd chewed off her lipstick in that exchange. Now she'd reapplied the loud red paint. Brina was looking for a fight.

So, I gave her one. "What makes you say that?" Standing behind my desk, I fumbled the third button and shifted from one foot to the other.

No answer needed. Brina shot her eyes toward the trash bin beside my desk. Crumpled cellophane and a flattened cardboard shirt box offered mute evidence of my purchase. She leaned over the desk and stabbed a finger into the wood. "Fancy linen. Never seen you wear that. And mother-of-pearl buttons dyed to match. It's expensive."

"You don't know what it costs."

"No. But I *do* know how much you earn, Mister Detective."

Brina was right. She knew my exact income. Because she made the weekly deposits. When we'd met two years ago, I was sunk in the trench of my personal collapse. A crippled bum turned out of my whore-house apartment by a fire. Meeting the Rosses gave me a job, a purpose. Saved my life. She had picked me from the mire of my private gutter. I'd become Brina's special rehab mission, her very own fix-it project. That was a past I'd never escape. What did Brina see of value in me? What did I bring her? In my years with Annie I'd been whole, a man bursting with potential. My strength and independence were hallmarks of those lost years. Now, the contrast with my present life of low wages, narrow expectations, and tight reins glared with dismal ferocity.

"Of course, you do. Down to the last penny." I pushed the final button through its hole and stuffed the shirt tails into my waistband. I snatched the belt to a tighter notch. The buckle slid home without a struggle. I pocketed my miserable wallet and smoothed the hair at my nape. I swept past Brina and out the door before we could exchange more bitter words.

Now, the collar of my black linen shirt felt crisp against my neck as I stepped from the bright lobby into the shadows of the Argent Bar. The hostess strutted around a podium, holding a menu at chest height like a shield. Her suit of silver sequins and navy velvet matched the décor of the lounge. Chrome, aluminum, and gray-stained oak floors chilled the room. Blue globe lamps hung from the ceiling like tear drops, shedding sad light. Some of the tear drops gelled into little blue tables scattered around the room. A long slab of blue marble anchored the bar to the right of the entrance. Indigo leather wrapped bar stools, chairs, booths, and benches.

The hostess was tall and white, with gingerbread hair divided by a severe part. She blinked her china-blue eyes fast, like she regretted my entrance. Regretted my existence, really. I showed my teeth, polished special for her. She steered me to a thumbtack-size table near the kitchen door. I walked past the insult, pointing to the biggest padded booth. The rear of the room had advantages: out of traffic lanes, easy to scan the space, hard to be taken by surprise.

The only other black guy in the place was the piano player. Simple to see why the hostess was uneasy: one black guy was okay; two black guys equaled a gang. If a third black guy arrived, we'd be a race riot. The hostess flinched. Where did I rate on her private scale of brown-people mayhem? Closer to Mahatma Gandhi or Osama bin Laden? Just north of César Chavez, but south of El Chapo? She measured me: neighborhood tall, not NBA giant. Lean, but solid enough for an alley fight. Paler than a paper bag, darker than a manila folder. I smiled. The hostess sucked her lower lip until it disappeared. She frowned, but led me to the booth I wanted.

As I marched past, the piano player slanted his chin in recognition of our membership in the fraternity. Straight-faced, I nodded. He strummed the first chords of the French national anthem for my tiny victory. Not gaudy, but loud enough to make the brandy snifter on the piano jiggle. The hostess flinched and retreated to her podium near the door.

A wide-hipped girl with buttery hair patrolled my zone of the lounge. She grinned approval of my seating choice, like she was lucky to be my waitress. I ordered a club soda; zero booze before Annie arrived. Sloshed was no way to start the meeting. Why'd Annie pick a goddamn bar for our reunion? Was the saloon a test? A threat? A dare?

This dry wait might kill me. Maybe that was Annie's goal: murder me with sobriety.

Sure, I wanted to see her. But I wanted a drink too. Straight and sober was good. But I also needed to calm my jangling head. The waitress sensed my jam. She prowled the aisle, shooting dewy glances at me, waving her pencil in my direction. As if her lush hips could lure me into ordering the bourbon she'd pour just for me. I could taste the dose, smoky and soothing against my tongue. But this time, things would be different. I wanted to be sober for Annie. This time. I shook off the luscious waitress.

Being blitzed had its upside. Easy for Annie to recognize me. Buzzed and familiar. Once a drunk, always a drunk. But I'd show her I'd changed. If she asked for a cocktail, I'd order my usual Beam on the rocks. If she laid off, I would too. Butter-Hair brought the club soda I requested. She dropped two coasters on the table, white paper squares with a blue circle around "Argent" scrawled in silver letters. On one coaster, a handwritten phone number beckoned. I appreciated the offer, but when she turned her back, I tore the coaster into five strips.

The club soda worked for a while. The clear fizz was pious, clean. The lemon's acid cut. But after fifteen minutes and three passes from the waitress, I craved a real drink. Something to smooth the edges and oil the rusty patches. Wet palms and anxious frown was a punk's look. But it was the only look I had. Too late to switch.

Then Annie stepped out of my past and into the bar, beautiful as ever. She wore a short pink dress and makeup in the right places. I always hated lipstick on her; she'd remembered. Her mouth was naked, the plum color of her flesh melting to rosy pink at the center of her lower lip. I sucked a long gulp from the club soda. All tension erased; all doubt cancelled, the ugly parts of our past null and void. As I swallowed, I held the glass at my lips. The coaster stuck to the bottom of the tumbler, a mask shielding my face.

The past had cheated me – of my health, my happiness, my future. Did Annie's arrival promise I'd win this time? Surefire cinch.

The coaster fell.

# CHAPTER
# TWO

Annie paused at the entrance, near the piano. My left brow pulsed; my ears throbbed. Liquid pooled under my tongue. She didn't see me, so I stared the way I wanted: a hard, raw, peel-the-paint exam. The stare was reward for the long dry wait in this bar. For three years of waiting.

Her body curved where it used to, a little hourglass wrapped in a tight dress the color of pink grapefruit juice. The tropical shade highlighted the deep brown of her bare shoulders and calves. Her skin shimmered as she turned to look for me. She'd pressed her black hair straight and long, pinning it in a bun on top of her head. A thick fringe of bangs hid her eyebrows, but revealed the familiar glint of her slanted black eyes.

As she moved, dangling earrings made of little coral pieces set in silver bounced against her dark cheeks. The orange stones should have clashed with the pink dress, but on Annie the combination looked smart, like money.

Twisting in the center of the bar, she didn't see me. *Had I changed so much in three years?* She slithered around two little tables. Pink fingernail polish winked at me from the gloom as she moved. She turned a 360, her eyes scraping each corner of the room. I should have risen so she could find me. I used to be that kind of gentleman. But I enjoyed seeing eagerness tag anxiety in a dance across her face. Watching Annie on the prowl was delicious. Plus, standing would reveal my hunger. She could guess about the rollercoaster, no need for my body to show and tell.

After two minutes, Annie found me. She beamed through the dim bar; my stomach clutched and surged. Strong teeth, uplifted jaw; a welcome-home grin. A smile to erase the past and cancel the future. I missed her. More than I knew; more than I should have.

Like a dream, she glided to my position. "Don't you stand to greet a lady anymore, SJ?" Annie's sass startled me from my trance. "Have you lost all your manners?"

I slid along the bench and stood. The familiar juxtaposition of my six foot one over her five four rushed at me. We still fit: tall over small, light on dark; as natural as my daily shaving routine. I placed a dry kiss on the cheek she angled to me. Her satin skin crinkled in a smile where my lips touched. She smelled rich, like candied cherries. "Good to see you, SJ."

*SJ, forever SJ.* Annie was one of a few people from my past who called me by my initials. Hearing them in her smoky voice made me laugh like a kid again. I would always be SJ to her, never the awkward Shelba Julio my sentimental mother had saddled me with. "Sorry, Annie, you caught me wool-gathering."

"As usual." No reprimand in her tone, just indulgence, home-style comfort.

"Yeah. As usual." From the top of the rollercoaster, everything she said was fresh and true.

Instead of taking a chair opposite, Annie scooted onto the curved bench next to me. The butter-haired waitress arrived to take our orders, a pout marring her face.

Annie knew what she wanted. "Bring me what he's drinking." Pink nails skated around the rim of my glass. "Double."

"You want *club soda*, Ma'am?" The waitress flipped her frown into a smirk.

Annie's eyes popped until white crescents showed below the pupils. "*That's* what you're drinking, SJ?" When I nodded, she grabbed my glass for a sniff. The worst confirmed, a sly smile lifted the left side of her mouth. "Not on *my* account, are you?" With a jerk of her wrist, Annie upended the tumbler. Ice cubes spilled onto the floor.

The waitress squealed – not loud enough to lose a tip – and danced from the puddle. I gasped.

Annie laughed at us both. "Bring me a margarita, sweetie. Crushed ice, in the biggest wading pool you have. With that pink salt on the rim. Just like last night." She raised her chin to show the tender skin at her jaw. "And bring my husband his bourbon. Jim Beam splashed over one big rock." She wrinkled her nose, her black eyes sliding to pin me. "That's what you're hoping for? Right, SJ?"

*Husband?* "Sure, Annie." Hooked, cooked, and served on a platter. *Husband.*

The piano man plunked a few jaunty notes explaining why the lady is a tramp. Then he switched to an Alicia Keys ballad and glided on.

———————

The drinks arrived fast and our conversation swung into rapid-fire recall. Old Texas friends and relatives passed through our speedy review.

We giggled about how we'd met as teens in San Marcos. Lab partnership in junior biology didn't lead to romance over the split frog carcasses, but we'd grown close. I grimaced at the painful memories. "You rescued me, for sure, Annie. I'd have flunked bio without you. Guaranteed."

"Well, I wouldn't have had to if you hadn't knocked the crap out of Tommy Hecht after school that day."

"He sliced the legs off my frog. And then he told Mr. Kaiser *I'd* done it. What was I supposed to do? Grin and let it ride?" I didn't say Tommy had bent my forefinger until the knuckle cracked the day before our knockdown. Sounded pathetic then, more so now.

"You broke Tommy's nose and knocked out two teeth."

"Only one." That old rage boiled through me. I studied the ice cube in my glass, hoping it would cool me by magic. "But yeah, I guess I overreacted."

"Two weeks suspension was pretty light, considering Tommy's dad was a pastor."

"And eighty hours of community service, don't forget. That tour at the city dump sorting bottles and cans gave me new respect for sanitation workers, I'll tell you what." I tested a thin smile, but tremors shook my voice. On the table between us, my fingers bent into a knot.

Annie's eyes widened. "Still mad at Tommy Hecht?"

"You bet. I'd have flunked bio that year, if you hadn't brought me the homework and lecture notes for all those classes I missed."

"We were lab partners, SJ. That's what partners do. Stick together." She pressed her hand over my fist. Her skin was cool and soft.

I sighed, spewing the steam of the old disgrace. I swilled a dose of the bourbon. Its heat stung my throat, but not as much as the angry memories. Thanks to Annie, I'd ground out a *B* minus in biology, while she polished off the *A*. That summer, I rejoined my post as a waiter at Frida's, the town's dullest cafe. Annie patronized the place more than the chicken-fried steak and smothered pork chops merited.

"You know I kept visiting Frida's for the chance to see you, right?" Her eyes glittered over the pink crust ringing her margarita.

"And here, I could have sworn it was the creamed corn and red-skin mashed potatoes brought you back." My laughter matched hers, full, deep, and open. She downed another long gulp, then licked the crystals from her upper lip.

I plunged into new territory: "It was you who keyed the giant daisy into the door of Greg Kahler's red pick-up, wasn't it?"

Annie stared straight at me for a beat, then winked. "That cheating bastard deserved it. I heard how he shorted you on your tips that weekend. No way I was going to let that go unpunished. I knew you wouldn't do it. You needed the job. But I would. And I did." Crimson dashed on the ridges of her cheeks as she snapped her mouth shut.

I raised my glass to her daring. "Greg howled like a barefoot pig on a griddle when he found those gouges in his brand-new Chevy. His face turned shiny as the wrecked paint job. And twice as red."

Annie's grin widened. "You figured it was me?"

"Yeah, it was a girl's stunt. A guy would've knifed the tires or slung a rock through the window. The daisy said female revenge. And you were the toughest girl in school, Annie. Nobody else could touch you."

She nodded at my logic, then cinched her lips into a pretty pout. "Yeah, revenge was my specialty. When you're tiny, you can get away with a lot."

"Like the time you dumped sugar into the purses of the girls on the JV cheer team?"

Annie sucked a quick gasp. "You knew?"

"I figured."

Her rant jumped to third gear: "Those color-struck yellow heifers dissed me. Said I didn't deserve the spot at the peak of the pyramid. Even if I was the smallest girl on the squad. They convinced Coach Willis to demote me to left flank. I was too dark, too nappy-headed, and too flat-chested to get top place. Those bitches called me 'coal dust' and 'ink spot.' So, I fixed them. A packet of Domino sugar in each purse did the trick. Ants trooped through those bags like a Mardi Gras parade!"

Panting, she came up for air. The whites of her eyes flashed as she blinked into the blue glare of the bar. She stroked the smooth hair behind her left ear. "How'd you know it was me?"

"You wailed about the ants like the rest of the girls." I lowered my voice until she leaned against my shoulder. "But the next day, you were the only one who didn't switch purses."

"You paid that much attention to me, SJ?"

"Always." I held her gaze for a beat. She lowered her lashes into a dark fan across the hollows under her eyes.

We skipped over the dismal days of army and divorce. She remembered the anger; I recalled the shame. No need to dig into that mire again.

But I wanted to solve one little puzzle. "How'd you get my phone number?"

"From Big Lolita." The senior cousin on my mother's side championed our marriage long after everyone else bailed. "When I knew I was coming to New York, I called her and she gave me your number. She still loves me. In spite of everything."

"Yeah, in spite of everything." I blew a long gust down my glass.

Annie was determined to recall our shared past. "Remember that backyard party Big Lolita threw?"

"The barbecue where I met you? How can I forget?"

I'd met Annie the summer before junior year of high school. My cousin Dolores was a hairdresser. We called her Big Lolita because her daughter was also Lolita. Big Lolita hosted a family cook-out every year and that August she invited a new client, Annie's mother. Annie came too.

"You sure you remember me, SJ? Or you remember that party because of how you decked that boy out behind the garage?"

"You keep a list of all my fights, do you?"

"No, only the coolest ones." She softened the quip with a smile, but I winced anyway. "What was that one about?"

I dragged a hand over my face in a poor attempt to hide. But she'd asked a direct question, so I owed a clean answer. "Chuy Alvarez kept teasing me. While the adults were out of earshot wolfing ribs, he kept calling me names. Finally, I told Chuy to meet me behind the garage." The kid lived at the end of my cousin's street, where pavement dwindled into dirt road. His family lived in a trailer piled on cinderblocks and his hand-me-down pants were always too short. But none of that stopped Chuy from jabbing me with the sharpest insult he could find. "He called me a bastard."

Chuy's actual term of art was "nigger bastard." But I didn't repeat that for Annie. I was indeed a bastard. My long-gone father Sheldon Rook was a darkly handsome rascal, according to my mother, Alba Julia. He'd disappeared months before my birth, leaving her with unruly memories and a baby several shades browner than her milky skin. Her consolation was inventing a fanciful blend of their names for me: Shelba Julio Rook. No denying the bastard part. But I'd fight the other at every chance.

"So, you clocked this Chuy. Three punches to the belly. He went down like a sack of onions, as I recall."

"You recall correctly." I tipped my glass at her.

"Hard to forget that fight. You were scary furious. Chuy was bigger than you. On the varsity wrestling team too. But you were mad as hornets in heat. Took him out quick and good."

"You were impressed?"

"I was." Annie squeezed her lids, then shook her head. "Day one of fall semester, I saw you in biology. I sat next to you at the lab bench."

"On purpose?"

"Of course, SJ!" Laughter floated from her lips, tinkling and bright. "How do you think we ended up as lab partners?"

"You didn't mind the anger?"

She twisted her lips to the side. "No. Not at first. I thought I could handle it. I was crushing hard on you." She ducked her head, then picked at a salt crystal on the stem of her giant glass. "And I was so damn teen stupid."

I puffed until bourbon rippled over the ice like uneasy memories.

———————

The present was safer ground, I could regain my balance there.

"Annie, I read you're heading a multi-million-dollar operation. How do you do it? You look fresh as a baby in a cradle." Laid on thick, south Texas cornpone slathered over the compliments. "You ought to bottle that care-free potion and sell it to these New York City women. Stress and distress are the name of the game. Up here, if you're not anxious, you're not really trying. That's how they see it."

She detected the BS. "Aw, poor thing! New York City ladies not treating you nice like you're used to?" She tossed her head until the brown column of her neck shimmied with laughter.

"I'm doing all right in that department. Don't worry your pretty little head." Bravado rang stupid, but I tried it anyway. Thoughts of

17

Brina jittered through my mind: her smiling face, her warm eyes, the intensity of her focus as we unraveled a puzzle together.

Annie's brow lifted, satisfaction tilting her full lips. "You got yourself a fancy New York City girl, do you, SJ? Tell me about her."

I hadn't meant to mention Brina, but with the subject raised, coy didn't fly. "We work together in a detective agency. She's my boss."

I ducked my eyes, studying the ice in my glass. That flat declaration made things seem simple between Brina and me. They weren't. Not by a long shot. Heat prickled my neck, the blotches giving Annie the clue she needed. Under pressure, my ears turned dusky red, the reaction both predictable and amusing.

Annie's eyebrows arched in skepticism. "And dating the boss doesn't land you in trouble?"

"None so far. She's fair, honest, tough. She helps people. I help people. She gets me and we have each other's backs. That's what matters." This was the most I'd ever said to a third party about what Brina meant to me.

Annie still had that talent for slicing through me like a goddamn can opener. Her smile widened. "And I bet she's stunning too."

I nodded but didn't offer details on how beautiful Brina was. Annie knew me; elaboration on that score wasn't necessary.

"Sounds good, SJ. You sound *real* good. I'm glad. You had me worried a few years back. But seeing you now–solid, steady, clear like this—makes me feel we went through all those troubles for a reason. So the both of us could land in a better place." We touched glasses and took slugs from our drinks as this new-found peace settled over the table.

But since she'd split me open, I had clearance to return the shot. "And you? Anyone special in your life right now?"

"I'm not solitary, if that's what you're asking. I've got my little amusements. But right now, the company is my baby, my family, my everything."

"Tell me about your company."

She launched into corporate titan mode, her eyes glittering. "I have two hundred and fifty-five employees operating out of four locations in Dade County. We do everything from residential and commercial cleaning to janitorial services in major hotels, restaurants, hospitals, and entertainment venues." Her breath came fast and hard as she spoke. "The thing I'm proudest of is almost all of those two hundred and fifty-five are women. We have a few men scattered here and there, but mostly it's us ladies who get the job done, day in, day out."

I thought about how Brina ran the financial side of our little detective agency. Her meticulous attention to every penny spent or earned saved us from disaster each month. Brina wasn't in charge of a multi-million-dollar firm, but with her drive and smarts, she could pull it off, no doubt.

"How did you get started?" When Annie left me, she'd had less than four thousand dollars in the bank. She'd built her company from nothing in the strictest sense of the term.

"I started by doing the work myself. Me and another girl, we rented a vacuum cleaner, bought some pails and mops, and went door-to-door drumming up business. I always tell my employees I know exactly how hard they're working, because I scrubbed the same floors they do. I washed the same windows and I scraped out the same ovens and refrigerators too."

"They must love working for you, Annie."

"I don't know about love. I'm a tough boss. But the people who work for me know I respect them, and they return that respect to me."

"And you bring in the big bucks."

"We do pretty well, all told."

The modesty was fake, but seductive. I wanted her to keep talking with me like this all night. Balancing at the rollercoaster's peak was exhilarating. More softball questions kept her going. "And what's your company called? Perry Cleaning Solutions?"

Annie hesitated for the first time. Her eyes drifted toward her lap and she bit her lower lip. "No. Actually, it's called Rook Cleaning Services."

"It's named after me? Why?" I swallowed deep to calm my racing heart.

"Not after *you*, SJ. When I started the business, I was called Rook too, remember? And then I didn't get around to changing it as time went on. We grew big so fast. We got known by that name, so I kept it. Even when I changed myself back to Perry."

Every day she went to the office, Annie was forced to think of me, of my ugly temper, and our terrible parting. I shifted in my chair, leaning from the table. "I don't know about that, Annie. It doesn't sit right somehow."

"Yeah, I know. But figure it this way: If you hadn't married me, I never would have escaped south Texas. And if you hadn't wrecked our marriage, I never would have founded my company. I'm a big old business success thanks to you, SJ."

I suspected there was a touch of Annie-style revenge in the name game too. But I let it slide. "So, Rook Cleaning Services is all on me?" I dragged a hand over my mouth, but a smile peeked out.

"Yep, all on you, wise guy. And to think, you never even wiped a countertop the whole time we were married!"

"I did so. Remember that weekend you were sick and I made you a cake from scratch? From my mother's favorite recipe. Yellow cake with chocolate icing." I grinned when Annie hummed and licked her lips. "And after, I washed every bowl, pan, and spatula. When I was done, that kitchen was spotless."

"I'll give you that, SJ. You really put your foot into that cake!"

Guilt fluttered in my gut, a twinge, no more. I'd never baked a cake for Brina. Maybe I should.

———————

Annie and I talked on. I wanted us to continue like this all night. Catch up, heal those little wounds that still festered. Laugh the way we did in our early days together. This evening proved those memories weren't my idle fantasies. Our talk showed we'd been foolish, misguided, juvenile. But we weren't wrong about the fundamentals. I wanted more time with Annie. More time to repair, to explore. More hours to bury the past. More days to imagine a future.

Annie wanted more too. She sketched a fingernail along the braided metal of her necklace, lifting it from her throat. Wires in three shades of gold twisted together, yellow, white, and rose. She pressed her thigh against mine. A firm touch, not hard. But enough to spin the rollercoaster.

"You ever think about us, SJ?"

"All the time." A stretch. But the core truth croaked over my dry tongue.

"We *were* good together, you and me."

"Sometimes." More truth; I swallowed the last of the bourbon.

"Miami's a nice town." Her fingers twitched over my leg, just above the knee.

"So I hear. Nice beach, nice ocean."

"You ever think about moving?"

"You inviting, Annie?" The train tottered on the greased tracks, high above the carnival midway.

She winked, black eyes slick with tropical heat. "Depends."

Depends? My stomach lurched under my heart.

Annie slid her eyes left, black pupils filling the slanted corners. I waited for another wink, but she stilled her gaze. I rubbed damp palms over my pockets, my fingers near hers on my thigh.

She said nothing more, scattering me in a thousand directions. Depends on what? Phases of the moon? The tides? If the sun rises tomorrow? What?

I never found out. Strangers invaded. Barbarians occupied our booth. The present erased our past with a bold swipe.

And the next day, two bullets deleted our future.

# CHAPTER
# THREE

By the time I found Annie the next day, she was dead.

At four in the afternoon, I rode the elevator to the eighteenth floor with the Continental's manager, Brock Stevens. He plowed around several turns of dark oriental carpeting and beige walls, until we arrived at the door to 1823, Annie's room. Stevens slid his key card into the slot and pushed the door. Sweat popped along my collar as he fiddled with the latch. I stepped forward, but it was his hotel. I let him enter first.

Stevens was a big man, rolls of blubber shimmying over his belt. He charged across the threshold with his head down like a bull. I was a step behind, my view blocked by his broad back. His cry pierced me. He howled like a baby stuck by his first vaccine: shrill, intense, mournful. As if the entire world had betrayed his trust. He froze in his tracks, one arm stretched forward, index finger pointing.

I shoved Stevens aside. Annie sprawled on the floor next to the bed, bare legs ajar like an abandoned door. A pink kimono embroidered with orange flowers and pale pink butterflies draped over her body. A bullet had carved a hole through her left breast. Another bullet punctured the flesh below her ribcage. The singed dots blemished her velvet skin. The braided gold necklace draped on her throat, grazing her earlobes. Her long hair fanned around her shoulders like a black cape. Splayed hands rested on either side of her head. A maroon-and-gold quilt hung off the end of the king bed. The cream sheets were rumpled, pillows mounded against the mahogany headboard. On the side table, the lamp was lit and the phone's red message button pulsed—an exercise in futility.

Beside the bed, gore spread over the carpet, camouflaged by the rug's maroon tufts. Blood unfurled in dull red wings on both sides of Annie's body. So much blood, still damp when I touched it. The air conditioner blasted arctic winds across the room, lifting her candied fruit perfume from the sheets. Stench of musk and burnt iron polluted the air; the room reeked of gun smoke and sex. Annie's face was mild, pink lips slack. Like sleep had taken her on a gentle flight. Her forehead was smooth, her cheeks shiny below half-open lids. Like she wasn't lost to me forever, only napping. If I kissed her, she'd wake and call me SJ. And we'd laugh at this crude joke.

The manager jutted a finger into Annie's cheek. He too wanted to awaken her from this brutal sleep. I jerked his arm. This stranger had no right to touch her. Crouching, I lifted the hem of her robe and covered her bare hip with pink butterflies. My finger stroked her thigh as I settled the kimono. The dark skin was dense as glass: smooth, firm, and cool.

I barked over the air conditioner's drone: "Call 911. This is a crime scene. Don't disturb anything." Stevens stared at the bed, paralyzed. "Call the police and notify your house security. Now."

I sounded professional, masterful in the face of grotesque violence. Like murder was my beat. Like I witnessed a hundred deaths each year. Like my wife's killing was one more statistic jotted in my notepad. Like my past and maybe my future hadn't been hacked to ribbons. Like all the tears dammed inside my heart would rush out sometime. Like I'd survive this horror.

I stood and walked backwards through the door and took a seat in the corridor.

From my place on the hall bench I watched Stevens pace. He punched at his phone. Sweat beaded in the folds of his brow and dripped beside the blunt curve of his mouth. Anger had overtaken his initial shock: crime wasn't permitted in his hotel. Especially murders; so disruptive, so messy.

I wanted to see Annie one more time. I needed time to cradle her head and stroke her cheek and arrange her hair in a flattering style before more strangers had a chance to view her. I wanted to tell her I was sorry I hadn't been able to give her the life she desired. Tell her I was glad she'd created the fulfilling life she deserved. That I'd wonder forever about the marriage we should have had. Always mourn the unexplored self I might have been with her. If only we'd had the time. I needed time to tell her everything before letting her go. I needed time to see Annie again.

But instead I sat on a stiff velvet upholstered bench in the hall near room 1823. Maybe I stayed because anguish trapped me. Or because Annie was my wife. Or because I was a material witness to her murder. Or maybe I had nowhere else to go.

I slumped on that bench a long time. Twenty minutes, an hour. Maybe a week. In the hazy distance, clanking announced the arrival of police, emergency medical personnel, technicians, official photographers. They reeked of male sweat and chemical solvents. A fog of sterile skepticism settled over the room and the corridor. The bustling and commotion droned around me, a backdrop to my dry sorrow.

———————

"Rook, how long you been here?" A low voice rolled through the fog, as heavy as the hand gripping my shoulder. I shrugged, but the thick fingers held firm. "It's time. You can go home now."

I leaned to escape the intruder without abandoning the bench. But Archie Lin crowded next to me anyway.

Detective Archibald Lin's job on the NYPD Homicide Special Task Force brought him to crime scenes around the city. Sometimes he ran across me in the vicinity of one of his cases and drafted me into the effort. Most days, he was a welcome friend and partner. But peering into Archie Lin's flat face now didn't bring me any joy. His cheeks were ashy and sunken. Worry smeared gray film over his black eyes. Seeing Archie was awful. But the shock did jerk me from the cloud of blame where I'd floated since finding Annie's body.

"Archie, I don't need this. Leave me alone."

His rumble was official, strong. "We already took a statement from the manager, Stevens. He's first on the scene, so we got his positive ID and what he saw when he entered the room. You don't have to hang around here."

I rubbed the back of my head. Pain pulsed in a shallow rhythm between the cords at my nape. When I said nothing, Archie's voice dwindled to a whisper. "Tell me, Rook. Tell me what this means. What do you know about this?" I stayed silent, so Archie took a different tack to pry me from the investigation. "Gavin's the lead on this case. He's got his men canvassing this floor. They'll interview every guest, maid, and bell boy on the wing. I told him we'd get your statement tomorrow. When you're up to it."

Heat surged behind my eyes. "She's my wife, Archie."

He gasped, wet gurgling in his thick chest. He pressed back into the cushion, his shoulders rising toward his ears as if to shield them from the unwelcome news. A dull flush rolled from his cheekbones to his throat. Archie knew I'd been married. I guess he imagined that connection was in the forgotten past, a relic I'd discarded when I started a new life in Harlem. A life with Brina. Now I'd jolted Archie by calling Annie my wife and his eyes burned like coals as he looked at me.

"Don't cut me out of the investigation," I growled. "And don't handle me. I don't need it. I don't want it, understand?" Anger blasted through the pain at the base of my skull. This wasn't my case yet, but I wanted it to be. For Annie. For what we'd been together. For the man I'd been with her and the man I'd become since we parted. I wanted to find her killer.

Archie squeezed my forearm. "Okay. I get it. I hear you." The squeeze turned into patting. "Then you can tell me what happened. Just us talking." Thump. "You and me." Thump. "There's nothing more we can do here, either one of us." Thump, thump.

I pushed his hand away. "Is she… is she still in there?"

He shifted his bulk on the bench. "Yeah, they haven't brought her out yet. It'll be a while." Archie reverted to the cool, practical tones of a professional colleague. "You know the drill. The techs get a first look. Photos, measurements, samples, prints. The usual. Then off to the medical examiner for a complete work up." This was better than the soft murmuring he'd started with. Good. No coddling needed.

A dry distant voice skidded over the gravel in my throat. "I'll stay with her. Until they take her away. She's alone in there, Arch. With strangers. I don't want her to be alone."

He nodded his heavy head, black eyes glimmering. "I get that. You're right, we'll stay." He loosened the knot in his ugly red tie and rolled up tan shirt sleeves. He mimicked my position: torso caved, elbows on knees, head down. A solid friend.

"Tell me what happened, Rook. All of it."

So, I told him the story of last night. Almost all of it.

# CHAPTER
# FOUR

"Miami's a nice town."

Annie's fingers had twitched over my leg, just at the knee. Blue lights in the Argent Bar had shimmered above our booth. At nearby tables, the tourist droning sank into silence. She leaned closer.

I punted: "So I hear. Nice beach, nice ocean."

"You ever think about moving?" She licked a salt crystal from her pink lips.

"You inviting, Annie?"

She winked, tropical vapors hot in black eyes. "Depends."

With her Miami question hovering in the air, Annie drew her hand from my thigh. She waved it like a flag at a man posing in the bar's entrance. "Ricky! Over here!"

*The hell?* Annie had invited colleagues from the conference to join us. Maybe she'd done it as insurance against the possibility our reunion might turn disastrous. Like a girl on a blind date arranging to have her best friend call half-way through the evening. An escape route in case the date turns out to be a serial killer. Or boring. Or a boring serial killer. Like that, our private conversation was cancelled, and the evening swerved in a different direction.

"Here we are, Ricky!" His rodent face was smooth and tan, but boyish the way women prefer. The creep's long incisors glittered at Annie when he caught her movements.

"Scoot over, SJ. Ricky can sit next to me." She patted the tufted bench and the rat scurried to the seat on her left.

Annie introduced him as Ricardo Luna, her vice president for marketing and sales. Was this how all her executive meetings started? Two wet kisses to the temples and a third on the mouth? Luna had patent-leather hair, Hollywood teeth, and petroleum-black eyes. Everything about him grated on my nerves. His thick eyelashes and dense cologne, the way he stuck his chewing gum under the table when his rum-and-coke arrived. Everything. He was younger than we were, thirty-two max from the look of his slick cheeks, unlined neck, and narrow waist. I pictured Luna's tan Cuban fingers twisted in Annie's hair. His trim body hovering over hers. Had this baby vice president delivered a personal sales pitch she found irresistible? I raised my finger for another bourbon.

"Mr. Rook, it is such a pleasure to meet the namesake of our company at long last. I've heard many nice things about you." His voice was creamy, lite-jazz smooth.

No way Annie's pillow talk included compliments about me. And this joker had zero standing to call me Mister, like I was a senior citizen in a rocking chair. Tight smile, bright voice: "Call me Rook. Annie tells me your company's going gang-busters."

"Yes! We were named one of the region's top ten minority-owned businesses last year by the Miami *Herald*. Our contracts surpassed one million for the third straight year. We're developing a fifth location to open in Hialeah by next spring. Anniesha has built something terrific out of Rook Cleaning Services. It's a privilege to work with her!"

Ricky's elevator spiel was convincing. His youthful exuberance almost persuaded me to invest in the company. But my name was contribution enough. To stop Luna from gushing more, Annie placed her hand on his forearm. Looking deep into his eyes, she squeezed. Twice. Lovers for certain. Was this boy one of the "little amusements" she'd mentioned earlier?

I dropped the smile. "Tell me, Ricky. What brings you to New York?" Annie's eyes narrowed. She recognized the danger behind my clenched teeth.

Her infant VP babbled on unawares. "Supporting Anniesha, of course. Getting invited to give the keynote address at a conference as big as this is quite an honor. Everyone at the company is so proud of Anniesha. So, we wanted to show the flag and demonstrate how much we support her leadership at Rook."

And take care of business in the sack too. A snarl rose at the back of my throat, scratching to escape through the tight smile on my lips.

Annie intervened in Luna's defense. "I asked Rick to assemble the analytics for my presentations this week. And when he saw how busy I was preparing the Power Point slides for tomorrow's presentation, he prepared the slides for the keynote for me. Since he did such wonderful work, it was only fair Rick come along for the trip too."

Fingers beside my pocket curled into a fist. If I sucker-punched him, I'd confirm the hostess's race bias. So, I clutched, gritted, and laid low.

An explosion would have been earned—a burst to gut our fake civilized cheer. A snap to make the snooty hostess renew her membership in the KKK. *Ignition, lift-off.* I opened my mouth to drop a snide quip, but Annie blocked me. She waved in the direction of the bar's entrance. Again. She half-rose from the bench to signal our location to two more intruders. *Had she invited the whole damn convention to join us for drinks?* The newcomers teetered over to our table with wide grins and fluttering fingers. They shook hands, thrusting dry palms against my damp one.

"Are we late, darlings? Did we miss anything juicy?" The male invader spoke first. He planted a kiss beside each of Annie's eyes, then dropped an open-mouthed smack on her lips for punctuation.

The female unfurled a violent side-eye at this moist greeting. Resentment pursed her lips, but she said nothing except a chilly hello to me. Why blame *me* for the slippery intimacy between her companion and Annie? The duo fell into chairs and scooted forward. I studied them through lowered lashes.

Annie introduced the pair with quivering exclamation points. Gerald Keith! was a professor of anthropology! at Alexander University! His companion Sarah Anastos, a post-doctoral fellow at New York University! was also an anthropologist! He was handsome in a brainy way: Woody Allen without the creep factor. And she was sexy in a downtown elfin style, long face, nice figure. This academic odd couple seemed out of place in a conference of hard-charging entrepreneurs. What did Annie see in these trespassing snobs?

Dr. Keith dressed like Indiana Jones just returned from dusting sand off the Ark of the Covenant. He wore a multi-pocketed khaki vest over a thin white shirt with no collar and well-cut gray slacks. His four silver rings featured coral and turquoise nuggets. Had he scored them after shrewd bargaining with a desert caravan merchant? Smugness bent his lips; maybe he'd sold the Ark to the highest bidder.

In contrast, Dr. Anastos was dressed in the black uniform required of all true New Yorkers. Her loose trousers were gathered at the ankle like harem pants, highlighting four-inch heeled silver sandals. A skinny black undershirt showed off her gleaming white breasts and wiry arms. Giant hoop earrings with coral chunks were her nod to evening wear. Both anthropologists kept their curly red hair cropped in identical fashion–high on top, close over the ears. Maybe to underline their tribal connection. Anastos's hair was darker, like Cherry Coke. Keith finished his look with a goatee, its reddish growth flecked with white.

"Anniesha, how *marvelous* to see you again!" Keith beamed and clapped in a theatrical manner, calling attention to his rings and thin elegant hands.

"Don't be ridiculous, Gerry. We just saw each other this morning at that godawful panel on youth sports merchandising. *And* we saw each other last night at the reception after my keynote."

Annie's rejection of Keith's BS was gentle, and teasing, the way old friends–or lovers–interact. Though they were seated on opposite sides of the table, the connection between them was obvious. Too warm.

"Ah, always the anti-romantic, aren't you, my pet?" Keith beamed at Annie, ignoring the rest of us as if we were paddling down the Amazon river with slotted spoons. "I simply meant it's damn good to see you. As always."

She chuckled at him. That low, rich laugh, combined with the "my pet" endearment, sent hot sweat dripping along my spine. Was Gerry Keith another of Annie's "little amusements?" Kiddie Ricky Luna, Genial Gerry Keith. How many more men was she sleeping with at this convention?

Sarah Anastos and Rick Luna both frowned at this exchange. I was as irritated as they were by the flirtatious banter between Keith and Annie.

Anastos turned on me as the stranger to steer the conversation to safer shores. "When she invited us, Anniesha said you're a private investigator, Mr. Rook. What exactly do you investigate?" She sipped her frothy Cosmo and licked her lips at me.

Again, with the Mister. Did being a decade older earn me senior citizen status? Was I wearing a blue handicapped parking tag around my neck? "Call me Rook. Like the Cleaning Service."

They didn't care about my work with the Ross Agency; lowered lids and puffed cheeks signaled boredom. But I gave a thumbnail sketch anyway. If I answered their questions first, I'd have free rein to drill into their backgrounds as the night wore on. I told them Norment Ross founded the agency over thirty years ago to provide services to people in our hard-knock Harlem neighborhood. We looked into those puzzles, disputes, and missteps that fell below the radar of the police. As free-range detectives, we offered security, confidence, protection, and peace-of-mind to clients whose lives often lacked those basic comforts.

When I finished, Anastos blinked as if rising from a swoon. She piped at me through tight lips. "Where do you carry your gun, Rook? Slung on your belt? Strapped under your arm? Ankle holster?"

"I don't carry a weapon." Flat, cool, and dry. If she imagined a hard-boiled detective would talk this way, then I'd deliver.

Keith's voice vaulted in disbelief. "That *can't* be true! You're a private eye. You *have* to carry a gun."

Annie rested her chin on a palm and leaned toward me, her black eyes sparkling. She was having fun.

To her unasked question, I shaped a reply several words longer than my standard answer: "I end fights with fists, not bullets. Chances of surviving are higher if I leave guns out of the conflict."

Annie nodded. She knew about my bad war: the dead army buddy, the destroyed toes on my left foot. This slow head bob meant she got me. Opposite her Keith snickered, a delicate ripple.

But a hoggish snort burst from Sally Anastos's pixie lips. "A private dick without a gun! Sounds like a play by Edward Albee. Lots of existential angst, castration metaphors, and fragile masculinity galore."

She laughed so hard a glob of Cosmo bubbled at the corner of her mouth. Keith patted his protégé's forearm until her fit subsided. "Now, Sally, be kind."

Then he returned to patronizing me. "I find this *absolutely* fascinating, Rook. You delve under the facade to ferret out tensions roiling in the community and use that insight to solve problems. Like an anthropologist *manqué*. I'd love to learn more about your work sometime."

Probably the stiff Tom Collins talking, but Gerry Keith sounded almost sincere. Maybe he recognized in me a fellow student of the human condition. Or perhaps he thought flattering me would get him into Annie's pants. Again. Maybe the gambit worked; she ordered another round of drinks to prolong the evening.

When the waitress arrived with her loaded tray, it was my turn to ask the questions. Irritation made me curt, booze made me loud. "So, Gerry, what's the link between anthropology and enterprise? Why are you at this conference?"

"Always digging for the core, hmm, Rook? Well, in fact, I owe much of my academic success to the delightful Miss Perry here."

He tipped an imaginary hat in Annie's direction. She winked back. Goddamn him.

"Several years ago, I decided I'd had enough of field work in Pondicherry. That's in India, you know. The heat, the flies, the dust, the dysentery. Mind and body, I needed a respite. So, I looked for a way to apply the principles and techniques of anthropological research to a topic nearer to home."

As he warmed to his subject, a blush rose under his tan. Keith tugged the vest and glanced around the table to make sure we were following his lecture.

"I've always contended that anthropology needn't revel in its racist past and colonial roots by confining its work to the study of so-called 'primitive' peoples in exotic locales. I got into some trouble with the more tradition-minded members of my discipline, the Malinowski-and-Margaret Mead crowd, you know. But screw them. I knew I was on the right track and my research in working-class Miami neighborhoods proved it."

Keith's lecture style was compelling, even if over-the-top for cocktail hour in a hotel bar. With his blazing green eyes and melodious voice, Gerry Keith was a born entertainer.

"But you know my greatest work depended on the insights provided by my favorite project, Sally Anastos here. *Doctor* Anastos, as I should say now."

He shifted his smile to her and her hazel eyes glittered with happiness. She didn't mind being called a "project." In fact, she seemed blitzed by her professor. As Keith continued his praise of her work, she preened and squirmed. She'd start purring at any moment. Maybe flip on her back for a stomach scratch.

"Sally was the one who worked for a year as a maid in Anniesha's company, conducting Spanish and English language interviews with hundreds of domestic workers across Miami. You might think Sally was a spy of sorts. But really this was top-notch field work. We call it participant observation. She lived right among the people she was studying. She adopted their clothing, customs, language, rituals, and cultural constructs as part of her everyday existence."

The project sounded showy and patronizing. Cultural tourism at its worst. But I hoped Keith would go on, and he did without prompting.

"The vast amount of data Sally collected from her informants shaped my most important new publication. Perhaps you've heard of it? It's called, *The Dirty and the Clean: Authenticity Among Miami's Underclass.*"

"No, I can't say I have. Sounds fascinating, Gerry." I flashed my molars. He was pompous and vain, seasoned with a big dose of cultural appropriation. But he liked my grin, so he aped it.

I glanced at Annie. Did she agree with my unspoken appraisal? She kept her expression neutral and ducked my gaze. Her forehead was smooth and her mouth opened in a slight smile. She looked indulgent, not resentful. Maybe she really did admire this jerk. Rick Luna's sneer suggested he was gearing up to mock Keith. Good for him.

But Sally Anastos chimed in with formal accolades before Ricky could burst the prick's balloon. "Gerry's book won the top prize from the American Anthropological Association last year. Its originality and sweeping scope were cited in reviews in all the important scholarly journals. They said he'd elaborated a theoretical framework that blazed a new direction for the entire discipline."

Sally's speech sounded like a pitch for a movie biography of the great man. Or maybe the first draft of his obituary. She was definitely fluffing Keith's resumé.

"Gerry's work looks at the intersection of culture as it's being re-made by immigrants confronting the loss and reassertion of identity in their new homes. Those peer reviews demonstrated how the most creative minds in the field appreciate Gerry's work." Her eyes burned with a fanatic's gleam. The conviction of a true believer cancelled any objections we uninitiated little people might raise. "Gerry was at the top already, of course. But *The Dirty and The Clean* confirmed him as a superstar. Even that idiot dean, Galaxy Pindar, was forced to admit how important Gerry is."

Keith sighed and waved an elegant hand. "Galaxy Pindar is a fool, Sally, that's for sure. But we have to give her obeisance. She's Alexander's dean of arts and humanities, after all. A fine example of the power of affirmative action, to be sure." His little cheerleader grinned at the slur and rolled her eyes.

This festival of mush required a refill, so I raised a finger at the wide-beamed waitress. As she glided over with a fresh bourbon, I wondered again if Sally liked being called "my favorite project" by her mentor. Brina would have pulled a gun on him for that piggish BS. Maybe Sally considered the term a compliment. Or maybe she was used to the insult after so many years working beside him. Academic women are hard to read.

Instead of basking in the glory alone, Gerry reflected it at Sally like a sun beaming its brightest rays on a pale orbiting moon. "But really, Sally deserves all the credit in the world. I got a publication out of it. And a little acclaim too."

Downcast eyes and pursed lips signaled his phony modesty. To save my bourbon, I glanced away from the sickening show.

Gerry sailed on. "But Sally's dissertation on the Miami maids earned her a post-doc fellowship at NYU. It's highly competitive, you know. And our Sally triumphed over the best of the best to get that fellowship. She's truly an academic star in the making."

Keith raised his glass to his disciple and drained the Tom Collins. The high praise flushed Sally's cheeks, the pretty pink flowing to her lips and throat. She took another sip from the Cosmo to cover her pleasure.

I coughed to break up the sentimental moment. "So, what exactly are you two doing here?" I wanted my original question on the table, since neither Keith nor Anastos had answered yet. So much mutual stroking, so little time.

Gerry rode to the rescue with a simple response. "Since our work is based on field research in Anniesha's company, we were invited to offer papers about the intersection of scholarship and entrepreneurship." The link seemed obvious when he said it like that, which is what made him a great professor. "Sally gave her presentation on the first day of the conference. And I'm on a panel tomorrow morning. Do stop by, if you're able, Rook. You'd be most welcome."

Annie, who'd been quiet during the Keith-Anastos vaudeville, tilted her head toward me.

"Yes, SJ. Make a day of it. Come for Gerry's panel in the morning and then catch my session at three. I'm presenting with a colleague of mine, Pearl Byrne. Pearl runs a cleaning service in Poughkeepsie that has taken off in the last couple of years, just like mine has. So, we thought we'd combine forces to make a presentation together."

Keith's red eyebrows collided above his noble nose. Below the frown, his voice scratched. "Funny you working with that Byrne woman." Gerry's growl didn't seem amused. "I can't imagine what you see in her."

Ice in Annie's glass tapped her teeth. "Pearl's a friend. And a leading businesswoman in our field, Gerry. Why so bent?" Annie wrinkled her nose, like she knew the answer, but enjoyed needling her boyfriend. Or whatever he was.

Keith tossed his head and pouted like a club kid. I figured he didn't appreciate being surprised. Not by Annie. Not by anyone. "Pearl's company was the other one we used for our research for the book. We wanted to interview workers at a cleaning service of comparable size to yours, but one that employed predominantly white workers in a northern city. A control group for your workers, Anniesha."

"Yeah, we figured that out, Pearl and me. To disguise the identities of our companies in your book, you invented names so we'd remain anonymous."

Annie looked straight at me, so interpreting her next remark was easy. "You called my company, 'Brownie Cleaning Services.' And Pearl's was 'Blondie Cleaning Services.' Very clever. Who came up with that? You or Sally?"

Keith and Anastos shared a glance, not sure how to read Annie's tone. Was she outraged, amused, or disgusted? After considering for ten seconds, he decided a straightforward answer was the safest. "I think it was me, but to be honest, I've forgotten how we determined those names." Keith dropped his lecture hall boom. "I went with simple phrases to avoid confusion. I hope you weren't offended, Annie. Were you?"

"No, no. Not a problem, Gerry. I know just how you meant it." Annie flashed a radiant grin to suggest all was forgiven, if not forgotten. I remembered that look from the old days. Her cold voice sent tiny needles racing along my shoulders. "In fact, I hope you all can come by my presentation tomorrow. It should be quite a show."

Apple polisher Luna chirped: "Why's that, Annie? What've you got planned?" Annie said Rick had prepared the slides for her other speeches. But he was in the dark about her final presentation.

"Oh, it's a blockbuster! Pearl and I are going to pull back the curtains covering up the business. Reveal how it's done from an insider's perspective. Expose the dirty underside of the cleaning business."

I could wrangle metaphors too: "Lift the rug and show the filth hidden underneath?"

Annie grinned my way. The third margarita had unleashed her tangy, loose side. "Exactly right, SJ. Not everything written about our industry has been on the up-and-up. A lot is fraud. Fake people dealing cover-ups and lies. But we know all the good stuff. The truth. We'll expose the dirt tomorrow afternoon. You ought to stop by. It should be quite a show."

Echoing her own words, Annie sounded pleased with herself, proud and defiant in anticipation of the trouble she intended to cause. This was the sexy, confident girl who'd fascinated me from day one. Gerry and Sally again exchanged glances of concern. Annie's mysterious boast worried them. Or maybe they were just baffled by her pronouncements.

Luna spoke for all of us: "Oh, come on, Annie." He looked around the table for support. "You can't leave us hanging like that. It's cruel. I've got to go to make a business call right now. Can't you give us a little hint?"

Annie smirked like a cat and darted her tongue across her lips. "Nope, you get nothing from me now. Make it to the presentation tomorrow and you'll hear enough to blow your minds." She curled her fingers into a fist, then thrust them wide like an explosion. Her high peals were the only laughter at the table.

A few minutes later, with handshakes all around, Rick Luna scurried to his errand. As he stood from the table, he said he hoped to be gone a few hours at most. He promised to catch up with Annie for dessert in the hotel restaurant. "And we're still on for breakfast at seven, right?" A wink, a kiss on her temple, and Rick disappeared.

Maybe the red-headed dynamic duo would quit too, go get dinner somewhere else. Find a jungle tribe to harass. Leave us the hell alone. Instead, Keith ordered another round of drinks. I declined; I had a long train ride to Harlem ahead.

But Annie seemed determined to match them glass for glass. "One of the few benefits of staying at the over-decorated, overpriced conference hotel is you don't have to worry about driving home drunk." She downed a gulp then lapped the pink salt from the cup's rim.

Keith roared as if Annie had uttered a profound observation. "That's why I decided to book a room at the Continental for the night. It was pretty easy to persuade the department to foot the bill." Another laugh, louder than the first.

When I frowned, Anastos explained: "Gerry's the chair of anthropology, that's why the department approved the expense." She chuckled and wiped the corners of her mouth with a thumb. "He only had to persuade himself."

"Must be nice." I shook my head. Who knew being a tenured faculty member at a major university was such a cushy job? No one but God and an oblivious dean to look over your shoulder. "In my second life, I'm coming back as a full professor."

Red curls bristled on Sally's crown as she defended her chosen profession: "It's more hard work and grief than you'd imagine, Rook. They don't hand anything to you. Nothing. In academia, you've got to fight and scratch for every last thing you get. Fellowships, publications, grants, promotions, awards, recognitions. No handouts or free lunches anywhere."

Sally wasn't three sheets to the wind yet, but she was zipping past sail number two. Rather than dulling her senses, wallowing in the alcoholic slush sharpened her tongue. "You know what the motto of any academic is?" She didn't wait for my prompt, offering her own Cosmo-fueled answer: "'What's in it for me?' That's the guiding principle behind every faculty member's decision or action. Five little words: 'What's. In. It. For. Me?'"

That slogan was more cynical than anything I'd encountered as a private investigator. Hard-boiled or not, we dealt in solving problems and rescuing hope. Maybe in my next life I'd stick with the Ross Agency.

Keith tossed a smarmy smile at his top fan. "Oh, Sally, dear Sally. You're giving our new friend here a jaundiced view of the ivy tower…

I mean, *Ivory* Tower." A slurp from his Tom Collins lubricated Keith's words. "Don't believe a word she says, Rook."

I'd had a snout full of intellectual posturing. "I'll try not to, Prof."

With that, I was out of there. I shook hands with Gerry Keith and Sally Anastos. I promised to look for them if I made it to the conference the next morning. That chance hovered midway between fat and none, but I didn't tell them that. They didn't know and I didn't care.

Maneuvering through the clutch of tables to reach the exit took extra concentration after three bourbons, but I had help. Annie walked me to the door of the bar, her hand in the crook of my elbow.

Alone again, I let loose: "They're pure horse crap, Annie. How can you stomach them?"

"Oh, they're not all bad. Selfish, maybe. Stuck-up bigots, sure. But they're smart and connected. Amusing."

"Conceited shits, is what they are." I stubbed my foot against a chair and Annie squeezed my arm. My unsteadiness was due to the alcohol, but my wobbly gait reminded her of other infirmities.

"How's your foot, SJ? I meant to ask earlier, but didn't get the chance."

"Still there. Some days worse, some days better."

As we passed the piano, I stuck a rolled twenty-dollar bill in the brandy glass on its ebony surface. Brother piano man nodded thanks. In farewell, he tickled a few bars of "Smoke Gets in Your Eyes." Caution, jeer, or empathy? Who knows what he meant?

Annie had escorted me through the hotel entrance to the street. Our evening had ended there. That's all Archie Lin needed to know and that's all I told him. The rest of the story was private, buried forever inside my heart's deepest chamber.

---

When Annie and I'd reached the sidewalk, we paused, our eyes raised to the pink-frosted gray clouds rushing overhead. The bent wand of the crescent moon cast its pale beams between the mid-town spires. Traffic rumbled in a dark tide around us. Taxis dropped clients; bellboys hustled brass luggage carts from the curb through the revolving doors. We stood in the surging flood of pedestrians, oblivious to their grumbling. Someone bumped Annie and I caught her shoulder. Her skin was supple and firm under my fingers, muscles yielding to my grip.

Then she surprised me. We'd used all our words, so she did the only thing left. She ran her hand along the back of my neck, pulling me down for a kiss. Her lips were warm and soft under mine, the way they always had been. Deepening the kiss beyond a token embrace wasn't my idea. But my head wasn't in charge and it happened. Her mouth tasted salty tart from the margaritas. And sweet from all the past we shared. Her tongue stroked mine, sending sparks from ears to groin. I raised my hands to angle her face in the old style. Any objections I had, any thoughts pleading for attention, everything evaporated in the familiar sensation of returning to her body. Returning home. Kissing her promised everything. I wanted more. More of everything we'd shared. Everything I'd lost.

Annie pulled back, laying a hand against my cheek, her fingers cool on my heated skin.

"I… Annie, I mean…" The jumble of sounds bumped against my teeth.

A tiny twitch of her mouth replaced a smile. Her simple interruption stopped me from crushing the moment with foolish words. "Thanks for meeting me, SJ. See you tomorrow. Think about what I said about Miami."

Then she vanished. And I was lost.

The burst of fresh Harlem air as I emerged from the subway cleared my head. The moon shone grand and clean between the project towers as I walked home. No need to rush; casing the past, plotting my future took time. One kiss had changed my mind: attending the conference was essential now. It might have changed the direction of my life too. Was I ready for another ride on the rollercoaster?

# CHAPTER
# FIVE

I blinked, the muted stripes of the hotel corridor wavering before my tear-clouded eyes. I rubbed a thumb under my lower lip. I swallowed to capture the sigh bubbling in my chest.

Archie Lin bumped his thick shoulder into mine. The bench trembled under his weight. A uniformed officer fiddling with an iPad raised an eyebrow at Archie, then slipped along the quiet hall and into Annie's room.

Wrinkles flared near Archie's eyes. "Yeah, I get it: crowded hotel lobby, dizzy subway ride home." He slid a pudgy hand across his mouth, tugging it into a frown. "So, go on, what happened this morning?"

If he found my recap casual or spotty, Archie wasn't saying. Not yet. He knew better than to interrupt a crime scene witness, even a friend, in mid-testimony. I swiped a finger under my nose, and continued.

---

Carting a jumbo-sized hangover, I had rattled in the morning train to mid-town. I'd traded my black shirt for a light blue number straight from the dry cleaners. I'd dragged a brush through my hair, patting down the curls on top, touching a bud of pomade to smooth the edges above my ears. I slapped two drops of cologne on my chest. The warm scent smelled clean, like driftwood I collected on long-ago beach vacations with my uncle Luis at South Padre Island. My mirror said I looked okay, but I ran a cloth over my belt and shoes to make sure they shone.

No point in arriving at seven to interrupt Annie's breakfast with Rick Luna. Whatever they'd done together the previous night was none of my business. Yet. The possibilities writhed in my imagination; I'd handle the Rick situation if needed. Ten o'clock was early enough for my purpose.

In the bright sunlight, the Continental Regent sparkled, as if a power-washing had cleaned the structure of last night's grime. Buzzing with good cheer, convention delegates swarmed through the halls of the hotel. The lobby seemed bigger than it was last night; crossing required my full attention. Bell boys seemed half the age of their teammates from last night; their wolf eyes assessed how much folding money I might have in my pocket. I trooped under crystal chandeliers that seemed shinier than before. I shivered past air conditioners on full blast in the long halls. I plowed wide corridors flanking Cinderella ballrooms; the halls led to a hive of smaller conference rooms divided by temporary partitions. Simultaneous sessions with hyphenated titles demanded my attention, but I tramped past.

I trudged through this maze for eleven minutes before finding the room I wanted. Gerry Keith's name was printed in large red letters on a signboard at the entrance. Five minutes late for the start of the presentation, I pressed into a corner near the exit. He'd attracted an overflow crowd of female admirers. Sally Anastos might be the head priestess, but she wasn't the only member of the Keith cult.

His talk was informal but lofty, full of magnificent ideas for how business could intersect with academia. He outlined the prospect of sexy profits all around. The audience tittered and clapped in appreciation of his insights and worldly quips. People took notes and snapped photos for the insatiable Internet. His knack with words was inspiring and alluring. He lightened the burden of the theorizing that was his claim to fame. Keith brought a large rolling briefcase stuffed with books.

When the session was over, he spent thirty minutes autographing copies of *The Dirty and The Clean* for his gushing fans.

"See, I told you he's a rock star." Sally Anastos slipped next to me, her shoulder against the wall.

We watched the line snaking toward Keith's table. She wore black again, this time a thin t-shirt, skin-tight jeans, and flat sandals. Little silver disks replaced the coral hoop earrings of the night before. In daylight, the springy red curls framed her bright eyes in an appealing way. I looked for tell-tale purple shadows along her lids, but saw none. She was a better drinker than me.

Bouncy, almost bubbly, Sally pulsed with nervous energy. Maybe I really was getting old, if the arrival of a keen young woman with nice breasts could scatter the remnants of my hangover. A veil of perspiration shone on her upper lip and her pink nostrils twitched around heavy sniffs. She seemed excited, and satisfied, like she'd accomplished something big. A secret thing of great significance. Four times her eyes darted from my face, scouring the room for a glimpse of her mentor. Gerry Keith was the reason for her vital delight, not me.

Giving in to her was my only move. "Sure, Sally. Gerry's a star."

Had she spent the night in Keith's room at the Continental? Was she glittering like this because of him? Maybe she got her kicks some other way, but her satisfied vibe murmured sex. It wouldn't be the first time a professor extended his collaboration with an eager grad student from the classroom to the bedroom.

Sally studied me with an indulgent air, combining youthful pity with amusement. "Come on, you look like you could use another cup of coffee. Gerry'll meet us at the snack station at the end of the hall."

She took my elbow the way Annie had the night before. With a firm grip, she steered me through Keith's fan club. By the time we'd tapped the coffee urns and selected strawberry Danishes from the mountain of pastries at the snack bar, Gerry arrived.

"Rook, my man! I'm delighted you could make it this morning." Keith pumped my arm like a handle on a rusty faucet. If the coffee didn't wake me, his assault would. "I saw you at the back of the room, amigo. You got the last square foot of space on the floor. Lucky man!"

Gerry was preening like a peacock in mating season; having me witness his latest triumph brought a glow to his already ruddy cheeks. He'd traded the desert explorer garb for a sharp charcoal suit with a tweed vest in shades of blue and green. He looked smug, confident his place in the universe was secure. The crowd's applause, the acclaimed book, the attention of the beautiful Sally Anastos, everything fit. The man who stared at him in the mirror each morning was indeed as powerful and deserving as he thought.

"You were right, Sally, I could have sold *twice* as many books. I should have brought more copies like you said."

She smiled and leaned toward her mentor, picking an invisible speck of dust from his sapphire-striped tie, then straightened it to lie flat below his throat. The veil of sex draped over them. If they weren't lovers, then the world was truly turned upside down.

---

I ate lunch with Gerry and Sally in the hotel's sleek restaurant. High ceilings dotted with starburst light fixtures, yellow-and-gray checkerboard wallpaper, caramel upholstery on the tufted chairs, silver embossing splashed across the heavy menus. The room was casual posh, the guests were elegant in bleached jeans, jewel-toned silk shirts, and four-inch heels. In my off-brand look, I didn't fit at all, but I could play my role: audience for the triumph of Gerry and Sally.

Our conversation, an expanded lecture by Gerry footnoted by Sally, was interrupted several times by fawning women. If they owned copies of *The Dirty and The Clean*, Gerry signed them with good cheer. If they asked for selfies with the superstar, he obliged with a show of auburn eyelash fluttering to indicate modesty. I was irritated with the performances, but happy to let the prof cover the tab. The Alexander University anthropology department could afford my bacon cheeseburger.

I only wanted one thing: to find Annie. In answer to my question, Gerry and Sally said they hadn't spotted her that morning. Rick Luna was also a no show. They didn't display any worry about these absences.

Gerry rolled his shoulders in a broad shrug. "I'm sure she'll turn up eventually, Rook."

"Yeah, she had a long night, like the rest of us," Sally chimed in. Her voice was casual, the notes tripping along the scale like a carefree melody as she glanced toward the roving waitress. "Don't worry about it, Rook. She'll be along later."

Gerry topped Sally's idea with professional clarification. "She's probably in her room preparing for her presentation. Collecting her thoughts, reviewing her notes, practicing in front of the mirror, rehearsing her best lines."

Sally squinted as she recalled the previous night's conversation. "When she left the bar, Anniesha said she wanted to go over her PowerPoint slides with Rick last night, didn't she, Gerry? Or was it this morning?"

I didn't give her the satisfaction of a flinch.

"Yes, she sure did." They didn't shrug, but their shared body language suggested disdain and indifference were their chief emotions. Neither academic planned to attend Annie's panel at three.

"I promised a colleague from NYU I'd look over his draft grant application this afternoon," Sally said, sounding preoccupied but determined. She glanced at Gerry. "You remember Colin Spiegel, don't you?"

"Colin Spiegel? No, you absolutely cannot snub him, Sally. Despite what they say, it isn't love but professional courtesy makes the academic world go 'round."

"You know it. Colin will scream bloody murder if I don't show in his office this afternoon. He'd kill me." She topped this cheery complaint with a violent eye roll. "And where are you going, Gerry?"

"I've got an appointment with one of the deans at Alexander this afternoon. Galaxy Pindar is dim as a foggy mirror, poor thing. But she has a big budget and limited imagination about how to spend it. I promised to lend the tragic girl a few of my ideas."

This pledge sent showers of laughter across the table. Their chummy self-absorption tore my last nerve. I crumpled the cloth napkin and stuffed it between the sweating glass of diluted cola and my plate. When I stood from the table, both academics widened their eyes. I thanked

Gerry for the lunch, shook hands with two quick pumps, then turned for the exit before they finished their showy farewells. The lunch felt oppressive and I needed a break.

To escape, I stretched my legs with a walk around the neighborhood beyond the Continental Regent. In the dense August heat, I angled my shoulders to plow through the crowds.

I'd left Brina a quick phone message as I waited on the train plat-form for the ride to mid-town. I wondered what she made of my vague phrases. Was she peeved or worried? Without mentioning Annie, I'd said I was returning to the conference hotel. Had that caused yester-day's jealousy to flare again? A murmur of guilt brushed my mind. I pictured her in the reception area of our office, staring at invoices from creditors. Or shouting over the clanking air conditioner to pry details from a potential new client. Or rolling her eyes at another long surveil-lance tale from her father. Or blowing sweaty curls from her forehead as she reviewed my latest razor-thin case report. Brina made our agency work. More than just function, she made it prosper. And she did the same for me.

I dragged fingers over my mouth, tasting the salty perspiration drip-ping from my nose. Last night's kiss shimmered like a desert mirage. What did it mean to Annie? Was it a mistake? A nostalgic trip to a past we were lucky to escape? Or was this a glimpse of the life we might have led, if fortune had run our way? Could we still rewrite our story? Confusion wrestled with desire: maybe the past could be revised.

Heat from the pavement pounded through the soles of my shoes to my head. When I shoved through the hotel's revolving door, the lobby's stale chill air slapped my face. I blinked to repel sweat, but the drops stung my eyes. I slipped through the crowd, headed for the escalators. I took the stairs two at a time, racing around drowsy conventioneers carrying shopping bags full of treasure. From the second-floor landing, I trotted down the broad corridor toward the meeting room where I hoped to find Annie. If I hurried, I'd catch her before the session started.

I didn't know what I wanted, but I was eager to see Annie again. Maybe her face would clear my mind and settle my heart's direction.

I hitched a sigh and shifted on the hall bench. I ducked Archie's soggy glance. That inside stuff wasn't for his ears. Not yet. Not ever. But the rest of the story was. Archie bobbed his head and I continued.

# CHAPTER
# SIX

By the time I had found the meeting room for Annie's program, I was sweaty and exhausted. And no nearer an understanding of what I hoped to say when I saw her again. I was early and the rows of folding chairs weren't filled. I chose a seat near the air conditioning vent to enjoy its cool breeze while I waited.

At ten minutes to three, a tall older woman with a cap of blonde hair took a seat behind the long table at the front of the room. Odd, Annie hadn't appeared. She was always a meticulous planner; she'd arrive early to prepare for the presentation. I had come to the session ahead of time hoping to speak with her before the formal program began. But maybe we could arrange for another drink after the session. Or dinner tonight. Or a rollercoaster trip to the future. Together.

The blonde woman shuffled papers, consulting her laptop and then her phone. This must be Annie's collaborator, Pearl Byrne. She was dressed like an off-duty nun in a stack of navy-blue boxes: a broad-shouldered suit jacket on top of a square skirt hemmed to an inch below her knees. Her convent-ready shoes were dark blue with squat block heels. Above them, her sturdy legs were pale as sea foam. The woman smiled and nodded at several people in the audience as we waited. She ignored me. I was one of only three men in the crowd and, as the room filled, that remained true.

At twenty-five minutes past the hour, Annie was still missing. A sheepish representative of the convention organizing committee announced the session was cancelled. Complaints rumbled from the crowd as it lumbered toward the door. I stayed in my seat as the grumbling women shuffled around me. Head down, I eyed my phone for another call to Annie.

I didn't catch the movement in my row until the blonde woman from the front sat in a chair beside me. "You're Mr. Rook, aren't you?"

She shook my hand with a firm grasp. Her palm was calloused, the knuckles leathery and thick. My raised eyebrows drew an explanation. "There weren't many men in the audience. And you're just like Anniesha described you: tall, rangy, good-looking."

She smiled, showing small teeth in lots of gum. "I'm Pearl Byrne. Anniesha and I were supposed to do this session together." A frown drew two lines between her milky blue eyes. "I'm surprised she didn't show. She was so excited about it when we talked yesterday afternoon. Jumping out of her skin, she was. I can't figure out what happened. Have you heard from her?"

"Not since last night. We had drinks together in the bar downstairs." I swallowed hard, then fidgeted with the phone. "She invited me to come to the session this afternoon. I haven't spoken to her today. Have you?"

"No. This isn't like Anniesha. She's all business. Responsibility personified. I can't imagine what kept her from getting here on time."

I glanced at my phone again. "I tried her room several times. No answer. Maybe the hotel manager can help."

Pearl and I wove our way through the congested halls and down the escalator to the hotel's main entrance. Scanning the lobby, I glimpsed a patent-leather head spurt from the revolving door and into the crowd. Maybe Rick Luna. I was too distracted to follow the darting figure in a pastel suit.

At the front desk, we explained our concern. I asked for someone to go to Annie's room. The clerk was cordial as she glanced at my fists flexing on the counter. Our request was above her pay grade. She referred us to the manager, Mr. Stevens, who tried four times to contact Annie by house phone.

Brock Stevens was a sweaty loaf of bread squeezed into a red vest. His black pants were shiny in the knees and torn at the left pocket. He twisted his fingers like a school girl as he resisted our pleas for action. Stevens asked why we thought Annie was still in her room. Couldn't she be out shopping? Or meeting a friend for lunch? Maybe she had tickets for a Broadway matinée. Due diligence was his motto, tact and discretion defined his method. His mild common sense drove me crazy. I blinked three times to stifle my rage. The flickering made Stevens look shifty, but that wasn't his fault.

Delay sent alarm bells clanging in the back of my head, at the exact spot where the hangover headache had hit four hours earlier. For each second we hesitated, another thump pounded my skull. As I fumed, Pearl kept cool. She spoke in the sing-song cadence of a nun facing a class of mulish sixth graders: explain, point, smile, repeat. She described the aborted presentation and our attempts to call Annie. Three times she covered the same ground. After each verse, Stevens balked.

I rotated my shoulders to blunt the returning headache. And bumped into the phony grin of Little Ricky Luna. His daytime outfit of lime shirt and powder blue suit emphasized the luggage-tan color of his throat. A thirsty woman in a navy dress with white polka-dots stared along the counter at him. He looked that good.

Luna's greeting wasn't warm. "You still hanging around, Rook?" The noisy crowd at the registration desk jostled him into my face. He'd had fish tacos for lunch.

"Yeah. You too?" Sunlight picked threads of gold in his black hair. If possible, I hated him more on second viewing.

"I'm registered here. Spent the night and everything." He grinned like he'd won the Megabillions sweepstakes.

Wrangling with this junior pest wasn't my aim. Unless pushed. "I'm looking for Anniesha. You see her?"

"None of your business if I did." More teeth, black eyebrows hopping.

"I'm making it my business. Ricky."

He smirked and puffed his glossy chest, a bantam on display for the admiring chickens. He thrust his chin at me. "She told me about the divorce, Rook. She got lucky when she dumped you."

"That what she said?" Heat raced from my collar to my hairline. My belt and shoes tightened as I rocked forward.

Luna's grin twisted with juicy intimacy. "Use your imagination, cowboy."

"Use *this*." I slapped his chiseled left cheekbone. Pearl Byrne turned her head at the thwack of palm against skin. The lustful woman in polka-dots bugged her eyes, thick tongue darting over lower lip. No one else noticed.

Luna whined through a smirk. "Now I see why Annie called you a fucking animal." He touched his face. Pink jumped under the twelve o'clock shadow on his left cheek. "Only Annie spelled it *P-I-G*."

I slapped him on the right. "Don't say her name again, asshole." Luna gasped, his palm fluttering in front of his mouth. I curled my fingers into a fist. Was the lounge hostess around to witness her race riot fears coming true? I didn't care: Rick Luna needed clarity. I'd deliver it. Before I could raise my hand again, Rick flipped the hem of his baby blue coat. Jammed into his belt was a small pistol, gleaming black against the white patent leather.

His lips peeled from his teeth in a snarl. "Go ahead. Try me."

Pearl Byrne stepped between us, heavy fingers on my forearm, a worried Mother Superior breaking up a school yard squabble. "Please, Mr. Rook, let's go. The manager will take us to Anniesha's room now."

Pearl herded me away from Luna. He yipped and fussed like a lap dog until we reached the elevator bank. Ricky lucked out; gun or no gun, I'd settle him later, after I found Annie.

———

Stevens fiddled with the key card to unlock the door to Annie's room. I let Stevens enter the room first. I angled my elbow to block Pearl's view from the hall. I saw Annie; her blank face and naked legs told me she was dead. She'd been dumped in a heap on the floor. Erased, stolen from me. There was nothing I could do to reclaim her. My orders to the gaping manager spewed with professional ease, my voice brittle as the first ice of winter. As he fumbled for his phone, I retreated toward the door, shoes dragging over the spongy carpet, my eyes on Annie's sprawled body.

Thinking over those scenes as I unspooled them for Archie, my mind clouded. Details that should have been certain crumbled into dust. Facts I should have gripped for close examination dissolved and blew away as I talked. I tried to capture the scene in the murder room. I wanted to remember everything. But the effort boxed me; the facts fled.

I remembered how Pearl barreled into my back at the entrance. But she must have glimpsed Annie. Her shrieks wrenched Stevens from his daze. On my instructions, he shouted into his phone, louder with each command. As if he could whip chaos into order with a raised voice.

In the hall, Pearl's face stiffened, flat and gray as pavement. The blue in her eyes flashed, then sank under a wave of tears. I wrapped Pearl in my arms. The folds of my shirt muffled her cries. Soap fumes mixed with warm vanilla on the pale skin of her neck. After the initial wave of sobs, Pearl wrestled her hand between our bodies. She touched her fingers to the four points of the cross as she mumbled prayers of remorse. Useless gestures, empty words.

I wanted to return and do something useful for Annie: straighten the foul bed covers; unplug the harsh table lamp; throw a blanket over the destruction. Anything important, anything for my wife. But Pearl needed me. So, I stayed in the corridor, my arm across her heaving shoulders. She dropped her head on my chest, the yellow petals of her hair fanned over my blue shirt. Freckles floated under her translucent skin, like flakes of rust in soapy water.

The cops landed in battalions, rustling with official purpose. The first surge of police seized the hotel room and established their beach head. A second wave arrived: the caring squad. A female officer crumpled a tissue into my hand and offered me a bottle of water. I shook my head and stuffed the Kleenex into my breast pocket beneath Pearl's tears. Another woman patted Pearl on the arm, and led her away. Without

Pearl's sudsy warmth beside me, the damp spots on my shirt chilled my chest.

Hollowed out, I had waited on the bench until Archie Lin came and listened.

When I ended my story, Archie stayed on that bench. It took an hour for the cops to finish the ugly business of cataloging the details of Annie's death. Strangers zipped plastic bags on both hands, preserving evidence. A plastic cap snapped over her hair. Other strangers threw a white sheet over her pink kimono. Another pair hoisted her by the shoulders and ankles onto a stretcher. They jerked the gurney over the door frame, jostling her tiny body.

I didn't have a title or a claim on her. Our time was up. Our past murdered. I watched, drained and silent, as strangers swept Annie down the corridor away from me forever.

Archie walked me through the hotel lobby, his nails gripping my elbow. On the street, I turned toward the subway entrance, but Archie called a hired car. I rode the empty miles to Harlem above ground.

# CHAPTER
# SEVEN

In the hours after Annie's murder, I walked. A lot. Misery dogged me, but I kept walking.

My Harlem streets were choked with pink fog that night. Not the flushed haze of forgiveness that blankets memory in a warm mist. The other kind of vapor – a vile rosy pollution, putrid and sticky. Remorse's lurid pink smoke spotlighted every past fault, every misstep, every wrong turn of my life in a sickly glow.

The morning after Annie died, I walked to my office. Pink haze still draped each lamp post. But my gray metal cabinets and aluminum blinds corralled their dingy files and dim light without new demands. Those dusty surfaces lent a familiarity that played like comfort. I deleted eighty-five messages from the spam file on my laptop: those Nigerian princes, political wizards, and male enhancement peddlers could live without me. I took phone calls from people who'd misplaced their necklaces or their pension checks. I downed coffee and dry cornflakes at my desk.

I read online news reports of Annie's death. Seeing her picture, the one from the convention program, jolted the numbness from my heart. Her face reminded me of the job I had to do. The news stories were short and jumbled. Maybe the reporters were eager to move on to another, sexier, incident. Maybe the murder of a black executive from a small maid service didn't hit enough juicy notes. Too minor, too obscure, too Florida for above-the-fold coverage in the Big Apple.

But she was my wife; that made her death my case. I gulped more coffee and wrote notes on yellow legal pads. I covered four pages with my scribbles. I wanted to remember everything from my last conversation with Annie. As I reread my notes, I etched black arrows next to two names. Then I walked home.

Brina dropped by my studio that evening to bring sandwiches and feed the cat. Herb ate, I didn't. The cat grated. Selfish, unfeeling, and greedy, Herb didn't care about me, so I returned the sentiment. Didn't matter if he ate or starved. I wanted nothing to do with him.

After washing two dishes and three glasses, Brina plated the sandwiches she'd brought. "I wasn't sure what you'd want, so I made roast beef on pumpernickel and tuna on rye." She pushed the plate across the kitchen peninsula toward me.

I grunted and slumped deeper into the arm chair.

"Or I've got cheddar, sliced thick the way you like." She held up the cheese square like a snapshot. I lifted my head but didn't say anything. She shifted her jaw right, then left. I looked away before the tears in her eyes had a chance to fall.

I shook off the comfort food. The sandwiches went into the fridge untouched.

When Brina retreated to the bathroom, I stood in front of the picture window to let the yellow city lights and white stars dazzle my aching eyes. I heard scrabbling noises from behind the bathroom door. I thought she must be rummaging under the sink. After a moment of silence, water rushed in a muted torrent. Scraping sounds, then more liquid gushes. She was scrubbing the bathroom.

I didn't have the heart to stop her. She wanted to comfort me, take care of me. A wave of guilt surged through my chest. I'd thought of leaving Brina. I'd imagined building a life without her. A future built on promises the past had failed to deliver. Even with Annie gone, I still thought about it.

Brina returned to the main room ten minutes later, her knuckles striped with red scratches that matched the red along her eyelids. When she smiled, I could see where she'd chewed flakes of skin from her lower lip.

She waved her arm around the apartment, as if it were a grand ballroom. "You shouldn't stay here by yourself tonight." When I opened my mouth to object, she interrupted, "I won't let you. And that's final." She folded back the quilt and sat on the bed, defiance mixed with hope flitting across her face.

I didn't want comfort food and I didn't want pity sex. While she undressed, I turned again to the window, as if we were modest college roommates. The sky had darkened to somber shades of purple; pink-tipped clouds first choked the amber moon, then swallowed it. Brina slept in my bed; I sank into the high-backed chair, watching airplanes streak past the window. After staring for ninety minutes, I charted the floorboards, trudging from the kitchen peninsula to the bathroom door, past the oak table, the chair, the chest-of-drawers, and around again to the refrigerator. I stumbled once on the blue-gray rug, then remembered to skirt it on the next twenty trips across the room. I didn't touch the cat. I didn't touch Brina. I didn't sleep.

Saturday, the second day after Annie's death, Archie Lin dragged me to the Continental, claiming he needed help scouring the hotel room for clues. He was lying, but I went along with the charade anyway. I wanted to inspect the room and Archie was my official ticket.

Room 1823 looked barren and smelled stale. Despite the air conditioning, a hint of Annie's candy perfume remained, even after forty-eight hours behind crime scene yellow tape. We snapped on blue plastic gloves for our inspection. Archie moved clockwise around the perimeter of the room, while I churned in the opposite direction. After ten minutes, we met at the foot of the bed and sat on the bench, shoulder to shoulder.

Archie dropped some general news first. "Her brothers come to pick up the body tomorrow. Said the funeral would be back home in Texas. You going?"

"No."

Her family didn't like me before we got married. I'd brought a duffle-load of trouble with my mixed races and my double-take on languages and my disappearing act of a father. Too many borders, too few boundaries. Her brothers threw a party when we divorced. Annie's people couldn't stand me then. They didn't want me now. And I didn't need the pain. But Archie could guess whatever he liked. I wasn't talking.

Switching to the job, he probed further. "You think of anything else since?" He knew me, knew I'd taken on this murder as my own case.

"Mr. Stevens the manager is going to have a helluva time getting that blood stain out of the carpet." I tipped my head toward the floor. "What do you think he'll use? Bleach won't do the trick."

Archie stared at me. He let the bitterness evaporate for twenty seconds, then tried again. "You got any new ideas about the murder?"

"Yeah, I think the convention's over and the guy who did it got away."

"There were three thousand people in this hotel at the time. We couldn't hold them. Or interview every one of them without a solid lead or at least a flimsy hint."

"Nobody saw anybody come to her room that night?"

"Nobody that's admitting anything."

"But you got evidence of somebody in the room?"

"Rook, don't go there."

I lowered my lids and stared straight at him. "Go where? I saw the bedsheets too."

"Don't push."

"Archie, if you have relevant information about Anniesha, spill it."

He puffed a sigh, a little peep which sounded comical coming from his big body. His eyes scrunched into slits as he looked away. "Forensics found evidence she wasn't alone all night."

"Obviously. Somebody shot her."

"That's not what I mean."

I got his drift, but I waited ten seconds until the words felt right on my tongue. "Somebody was in bed with her? Had sex with her? Is that what your crack team of genius scientists found?"

"Yeah. I'm sorry."

"Sorry for what? You match the DNA to suspects, you got a possible killer." When I stopped talking, Archie stopped breathing. I filled in the gap, so neither of us would die on the spot. Too much death in this room already. "And you want to know if the lucky mystery guy was me. Right?"

He lifted his hands from his knees and spread the fingers wide, like they were fat supplicants begging my forgiveness. "Yeah. I mean, I'm not blaming you or nothing. It wouldn't be the first time a reunion with the ex got a little more intense than the parties originally planned. You know, for old times' sake. What's past is past. Let bygone be bygones. You know how it goes."

"I know how it goes, Archie. But that's not how it went with me and Annie. Nothing like that happened."

"Well, I needed to ask direct." He paused a beat. "Cause we had reports from a couple of bellboys and a desk clerk they saw a woman matching Anniesha's description kissing hot and heavy with a man who looked a lot like you."

My words darted with enough venom to make Archie gasp: "There're lots of men who look like me." Shielding this remnant of our privacy mattered. "Plenty of men."

"Not really. Tall, lanky, light-skin African American. Gimpy foot. It was you, Rook." He huffed at the insult to his intelligence. "Or are you saying you didn't make out with her that night?"

I folded. "We kissed." His shoulders sagged in misery, so I went on. "She walked me from the bar to the hotel entrance, like I told you. Then she kissed me. And I kissed her. That was it. Took the subway home. Came back to the hotel the next morning. Found her dead, just like I told you. I never saw Annie alive again after we kissed goodnight."

I snapped my mouth shut. A sticky silence fell between us. Archie wasn't to blame; he was doing his job. He could have hauled me to the precinct for questioning. Made me repeat every sentence I'd already given him. I'd have to submit to a formal interrogation eventually. Soon I'd write it all down on police note pads, check it for accuracy, sign on the bottom line. But Archie'd stood up for me. He'd run interference with his brother cops to keep me off the list of suspects in Annie's murder.

For the time being. I didn't know how much that intervention cost him, but it wasn't without consequences. I didn't want to get him in trouble.

I softened my tone. "You need a DNA sample? For comparison. To rule me out."

"Nah, I got your statement. That's good enough for me."

I barked in disbelief. "Good enough for you. But not your lieutenant. Take the sample, Archie. Keep us both in the clear."

He shrugged, reluctance tensing his face. Sweat drops beaded in his skimpy eyebrows. Archie was embarrassed. But my friend was a good detective. He pulled a slender plastic vial from an inside pocket of his jacket. He had the kit on him. He'd intended to get an elimination sample from me all along. The cotton bud tickled when he wiped it around my gums and inner cheek. He popped the damp swab into the tube, sealed it, scribbled my name on a label, and pressed it on the tube. Official. With the date and case number and his initials. Tough part over, the rest of the interview was a downhill tumble.

"You got any ideas who this guy could be?" Archie lobbed questions into the sweet air. "I mean, when you were reminiscing and catching up, did she talk about any other man in her life?"

"Did she confess her steamy bedroom secrets to me? No, Annie didn't say anything like that. But then, she wouldn't, would she?"

Archie leaned back on his elbows, crumpling the bed quilt. He kept his eyes on the mirror over the desk in front of us. "We don't figure this was some rando she found in the lobby. I guess it could be. Some women are like that." A beat to convey an apology. "Do you think she'd do something like that? Pick up a stranger from the hotel bar and have sex with him on the spur of the moment?"

"No, that's not like her." Present tense. Still. "Not the Annie I know." Not the Annie I loved and maybe was ready to love again. Digging fingernails into my palms buried the thought for a while.

When my pause stretched toward agony, Archie pushed on. "So, what was your gut telling you that night? Did you get a hint about who she was seeing? Who she'd hook up with? We're at a dead end here. We got nothing."

"I do."

"You do what?"

"Have suspects for you."

"Like who?"

My guesses were strong hunches, fueled by suspicion. But Archie was being straight with me. I owed him my best judgment. Even if the ideas were laced with bitterness and jealousy. "Like the two men we had drinks with the night she died."

"Who?" Archie stiffened, his bull neck starting from his collar.

"Ricardo Luna, a whiz kid exec in Annie's company. He was buzzing around her, sloppy and excited like he owned the golden ticket that night." No need to mention my slap-down of Luna in the lobby the next day. Petty and irrelevant. If Ricky whined, I'd explain.

"And who else?"

"Gerald Keith. Professor at Alexander. Anthropology."

"Some university egghead? Sounds unlikely."

"He got his data from research at Annie's company."

"And how do you figure collecting anthropology data turns into an affair?"

I raised my fingers to tick the elements of the equation. "Intense interaction. Add flattery. Multiply by long hours. Equals sex. Happens all the time." Brina and I had started that way, the formula was pretty standard.

"Like an office romance?"

"Yes. Minus the cubicles and copy machines." I raised my eyebrows and Archie smirked.

"So, you like either Professor Keith or this Luna kid for the murder?"

"Maybe. Luna carries a gun. I saw it on him. No idea of the model."

"It's a place to start. We'll check on it." His eyes turned wet, like a homesick Labrador retriever. "I know that wasn't easy."

I didn't have room for the sentimental BS Archie wanted to shovel. I expanded my description of the contenders. I had nothing to lose. And I wanted to catch my wife's killer.

"Rick Luna's a hotshot number-cruncher who grabbed her attention. A mouthy suck-up. Slick and easy on the eyes, if you like the teen movie idol type. Annie does." Tasted filthy saying that out loud so I rubbed my tongue around inside my lips. After a quick rinse, I spit out the next description. "Gerry Keith has the high-power brains, status, flashy looks, and bulging ego to keep her interested. Both men were staying at the hotel, so they're top contenders in the Who-killed-Annie sweepstakes."

"Thanks. Those leads could help. We'll run DNA tests on these jokers. Miami-Dade police can help with Luna." A damp sigh rushed from Archie's chest, blowing minty air across the room. "I'm sorry to drag you through that, Rook. But we got to explore as many angles as we can. Whoever had sex with her might have gotten into some kind of dispute afterwards and shot her."

"Yes, I figure the same. They fought, he left. Then he returned to settle the beef with a couple of bullets."

Archie rose from the bench and glided toward the door. His body swayed and he curved his arms around his torso. "This is how it must have gone down. She hears a knock, pushes back the covers, gets up from the bed, walks to the door." He paused, twisted the knob, and pulled open the door. "She steps aside to let in the visitor." He shoved the door closed, then pivoted to face the room. "They move toward the bed. Anniesha in front, the visitor behind."

Archie's knees bumped the mattress. He looked at me then turned toward the invisible figure in the room. "They speak for a minute, maybe Anniesha sits on the bed." Archie fit his movements to the scenario, the mattress sagging under his weight.

"The talk turns rough, Anniesha stands, points at the door. Maybe she closes the distance between them, trying to force the visitor from the room. The gun is pulled from a pocket, two shots fired point-blank. Anniesha falls next to the bed." Archie stood on the stained spot where I'd found Annie's body. "I figure that's how it happened."

"Maybe."

"You got anything else?"

"Annie wasn't asleep in bed when the visitor knocked."

"How do you know that?"

"Her hair. When she sleeps, she wraps her hair in a silk cloth. To keep it smooth. But when I found her, her hair wasn't wrapped. It was spread across the floor. Loose. That means she was still awake, not yet ready for sleep. Maybe she was sitting up in bed or at the desk working when the shooter knocked."

"Or maybe she shed the scarf before she opened the door."

"Then she would have dropped it on the chair when she walked to the door. Or tossed it on the desk. Or draped it on the bathroom door-knob. The scarf wasn't anywhere around. Still stashed in her suitcase, I bet."

"Okay, say you're right. She was still awake, still working." Archie nodded.

I expanded my scenario: "And if she was working, maybe she was putting the finishing touches on her presentation. Which means she would have been typing on her laptop." I raked my gaze across the room. "I don't remember seeing it when I found her. But I was distracted. Did your crime scene gurus find her computer?"

"I don't remember it in the report. I'll check."

"Question the manager Stevens again. He might have seen the laptop, even if I missed it. Worth looking into."

"You got it, pal."

From the bench at the foot of bed, I looked sideways at the blonde oak dresser opposite. I caught the glint of something red. On my knees, I swept an arm under the dresser. I snagged a little stone from the dark sheared carpet: a nugget of coral, filaments of glue holding dust to its roughened edges. The tear-shaped stone had fallen from a jewel-er's setting and rolled under the dresser. I thrust the coral chunk into my pants pocket before Archie saw my movements. Annie had worn silver earrings with coral. Gerry Keith and Sally Anastos had decorated themselves with coral jewelry too. This stone chip might be a clue. Or it might be a coincidence. I would find out on my own. No need for police interference or help. This was my case now.

"See anything under there? We stopped housekeeping from clean-ing. Our boys are pretty thorough. But we didn't want to disturb the scene until we were ready to let it go."

"Nothing. Just lint rolled into a ball."

I picked at a frayed thread on the cuff of my black shirt sleeve. I clamped my lids shut, but my mind churned over the past. Annie and I had known each other for two decades, together for ten, hitched for seven. I spent three of those years in Iraq and three more AWOL from our marriage. When Annie finally quit me, it felt like a curse and a blessing at the same time. I contributed zero to her business success, except for a solid reason to strike out on her own.

The thought torrent dammed shut and I blinked twice. Then again. My dry lids stretched over scratchy pupils. Archie tipped his square head so his eyes caught mine. He shifted an inch closer on the bench until I could feel the heat coursing through his suit jacket and into my shoulder.

"We'll find him, pal. Don't doubt it. We'll find him." His assurance was hollow, but comforting all the same.

Words came before I could stop them. "I hadn't heard from her since I arrived in Harlem three years ago. I've been pretty lucky since then, you know that. But this reunion was a high stakes play."

"You told Brina this?"

"No."

"You should. She can help."

"Maybe." I shrugged and clamped shut. Archie was right. It didn't happen often; he missed nine times out of ten, which is why he kept me around. This time he was right.

Brina'd hear from me. But I wanted to be ready before we talked. Ready to unpack the truth: I'd thought about taking up with Annie. Wanted to sleep with her. If I'd had my wish that night, Annie might still be alive. And maybe I'd be on a plane to Miami. To a new future. I'd been close to trashing my present for a chance at resurrecting the past. But with two shots, someone had murdered my past and slaughtered my future.

We walked to the door. I stood alone for a minute in the murder room, taking it in one last time. To give me privacy, Archie stepped along the corridor so I couldn't see him through the open door. I glanced in the full-length mirror near the closet. My face was gray and blurred, as if I'd walked through cobwebs and not bothered to wipe away the film.

This revelation to Brina might be the ugly story which ripped us apart. Maybe she'd give up on this forlorn fix-it project she'd made of me and continue her life hurt but unburdened. Brina would hear from me. But not yet. First, I wanted to catch a killer.

I scrubbed my face until heat returned to my jaw. In the hall, I trailed Archie through the maze of thick carpeting to the brass elevators. When he stood aside, I punched the down button with the butt of my fist.

# CHAPTER
# EIGHT

I picked at the crusts of Brina's sandwiches for breakfast and lunch Sunday. Herb's smug feline support helped lift the gloom, as did a slow march around the neighborhood. The sun scalded the pavement until a pink haze shimmied from under the feet of trudging drifters. Odors of sweaty shoe leather, onions, and carbon monoxide thickened the air as I walked. I wanted a pause in the misery, a breech in the grim fog. My ramble took me to the door of the Emerald Garden restaurant, just below our agency office. I spotted Norment Ross inside. I didn't duck; I wanted the help he could give me. The old man grinned, then waved me in. To escape the blues, I needed good kicks in the ass and the head. Norment Ross supplied both. Late Sunday afternoon, he unpacked his tool kit.

We parked at a table in the rear of the deli. Loud, bawdy, charming, and tough in equal measure, Norment set his checkered driving cap on reviving me. His method was the spoken word, his instrument a smooth voice inflected with Southern charisma. He bombarded me with stories, legends, and fables about his past. He spoke of his childhood and teen years on the wild side of stately Charleston, his early days running numbers in New York.

Mei Young, the owner of the Emerald Garden, was also our land-lady. After Norment talked at me for eight minutes, she brought two big bowls of savory noodles. To spark my shriveled appetite, she'd dug deep into her Chinese repertoire instead of serving the standard deli sandwiches the restaurant offered.

Norment's long frame, wrapped in a brass-colored sharkskin suit and a chocolate brown collarless shirt, was stretched under our table. His ankle bumped a casual rhythm against my chair leg as he talked. Norment often took lunch at this table with Mei Young. The two enjoyed a reliable, but mysterious relationship. They slept together, sure. But I didn't know what she was to him. Was Mei a fierce defender of domestic order like Sherlock's Mrs. Hudson? Or a wily control offi-cer in Norment's neighborhood secret service? Was she pal, mistress, guide, or matron? As I looked across the red Formica table at my boss, I wondered what fired their bond, which seemed as flat and unchang-ing as the western prairie.

It was after four, Norment usually ate at twelve thirty. But three days of frustration pushed our hostess to extraordinary efforts in the cause of making me eat. The tall bottles of San Miguel beer Mei sat beside the bowls combined with the smoky spices of the noodle sauce to make my mouth water. Her temptation worked; my stomach growled in approval. I grabbed a fork and nodded at Norment to continue his stories. He did, with gusto.

He talked about starting a private security agency in Harlem because he'd never gather enough money to go to law school and his past as a numbers runner meant he couldn't enter the police academy.

But there was something missing from these tales. I picked at the sore spot. "You never talk about *her*, Norment."

"Who's that?" He knew, but he made me say it.

"You never talk about your wife. Why?"

"Didn't think you wanted to know. That's why."

"I do now."

He peered into my eyes, squinting to judge if I was sincere. "Now? That what you want. Right now? For sure?"

"Yes. Tell me."

"I'll do better than that, son." He straight-armed the table, causing the chair joints to squeak. "I'll show you. Come on."

Norment moved fast for an old man. By the time I'd gulped the last of my beer and scrambled through the restaurant door, he was tapping his toe on the curb at the crosswalk. I hurried to join him. I'd seen him zip through the boulevard's traffic many times; but now he waited at the corner for the light in deference to my gimpy foot.

"Where're we going, Norment?"

"You'll see. Keep your eyes peeled."

Our journey was short. At the opposite corner we passed Zarita's bar, a favorite hang-out I'd skipped since Annie's death. At first, I thought my boss wanted to treat me to a therapeutic round of brown liquor in my preferred den. But he led me past the saloon. We stopped at the next entrance, a doorframe shuttered with crude boards. Remnants of advertising posters fluttered where glass used to be. Norment bent a plywood square next to the knob, reached inside, and fiddled until the door yielded. We stepped inside. The foyer was narrow; I stretched my arms full-length and touched the walls on either side. A steep staircase rose from the penny tile floor of the vestibule.

"This used to be old Doc Rogers's office. Best dentist in the neighborhood." Norment swept his hand upward like a steward on a cruise ship. "Second floor. Watch where you step. Some of the slats are missing."

"You know this place?"

"Sure, anybody with teeth in their head knew Doc Rogers, back in the day." He continued speaking, the voice drifting and spurting as we trudged up the stairs. "I had a tooth ache like you wouldn't believe. I thought about just pulling out the damned tooth myself. You know, tie a string around it, attach the other end to a door knob, rear back and slam that sucker shut so hard it pulls out the tooth, root and all."

We reached the second-floor landing. Norment paused like a Shakespearean actor, casting dark glowing eyes my way to see if his story had me hooked.

"I'd watched my old daddy do it when I was a little snapper. I'll never forget seeing that bloody tooth hanging off the string on the bedroom door, while he hopped around on one foot, howling like a banshee.

I thought I could do it. I was bound and determined to do it. I even bought some string and tied a knot around my poor screaming tooth."

To show the technique, Norment rattled the knob of the door facing us. After two seconds of twisting, it clattered to the floor leaving a hole in the frame. We pushed into the office suite. An old fire had damaged every surface in the space. Plumes of smoke, dust, and rot rose around our shoes. The place smelled of cinders, burnt leather and decayed animal guts. I coughed and squeezed my nose; Norment smiled at the familiar surroundings.

"But when it came right down to it, I was a coward, Rook. Not even half the man my daddy was. I just couldn't pull the trigger. Couldn't bite the bullet. Couldn't slam that door."

He stroked his fingers through the dust-clogged air, then turned a full circle. "So, I went to the dentist office like the tame little city critter I'd become. To this office right here." The waiting room was almost empty, only a three-legged green vinyl sofa and a steel coat rack remained. Both were tattooed with fire's black marks.

"I rolled in one fine day, my jaw swoled out to there." Norment curved his hand in an arc from chin to shoulder to illustrate the monstrous swelling. He pointed to the far wall, where a five-foot opening was topped by an arch to the ceiling. Beyond the grimy metal counter was another room with three abandoned work stations. Mounds of ash decorated the center of each metal desk. Feathery streaks of soot climbed the wall; flames had eaten gaps in the plasterboard, exposing charred insulation and blackened lumber.

"And what did I see behind that reception counter, but the prettiest, freshest, finest little thing you'd ever hope to find. 'Jayla Dream' was written on the plastic name card stuck on her pink uniform. But what I read was, 'Norment's Wife.' I knew it from the first second, clear as day. This girl had to be mine."

He stopped to fan dust motes drifting in front of his eyes. I moved to the lame sofa, which tottered under my weight as I sat. "So, Jayla Dream was a dream, hunh, Norment?"

"Oh, no, sir. She wasn't no dream, not on your life. That girl was real, solid, indisputable, actual *and* factual. I asked her out on a date right then, before I even climbed into the dentist's chair. She said no, of course. Turned me down flat. Who'd want dinner with a man with half his face blown clear past his shoulder?"

Norment waved me toward a door to the right of the arched wall. It was hanging by a single hinge, so we ducked as we passed. We walked down a hall; I wasn't sure of the strength of the charred linoleum tiles below our feet, so I stepped in the spots Norment did. We passed two closed doors and then slipped into an examination room. A mint-green reclining chair lounged next to a gaping circular hole in the floor. The chair's guts exploded from its cushion in a black spray of stuffing. A water standpipe and dead cables sprouted where a dentist's sink and power equipment had once stood. Ghostly images of drills, high voltage lights, suction tubes, spit cups, aluminum instrument trays, and bloody gauze made me shiver. Pale sunbeams filtered through the grease and dirt on a window beyond the chair.

My escort laughed. "Doc Rogers jerked that blasted tooth with one lurch." Norment wiped his white-flecked goatee, then laughed some more. "Packed me off in twenty minutes with four aspirin and a bill the size of Brooklyn. Dreamie didn't even say good-by when I left."

If he could smile, I would too. "No date. But at least the tooth was gone."

"True. But I came back the next week. And the next week. And the week after that. I had to pay my bill to Doc Rodgers. That was my excuse for the visits. But I kept paying in smaller and smaller amounts each time so I'd have a reason to come see Dreamie. If she hadn't broke down and agreed to go to dinner with me, I might still be paying off that dentist bill to this day."

His bald head shone like an incandescent bulb. His joy at telling this story was so infectious, I chuckled too. Norment pulled a giant white handkerchief from his back pocket. He rubbed the seat and arm rests of the green chair, wiping around clumps of singed stuffing. He dragged a finger across the crackled cushion to be sure it was clean, then sat.

I leaned against the fire-ravaged wall, caught in the web of ancient history. "But you closed the deal, didn't you?"

The tale of Jayla Dream unfolded. "You *know* I did. She was so beautiful, you won't believe me when I tell you. You can see a lot of it in Sabrina, she's got her mother's face and sassy spirit, that's for sure. But Dreamie was something special: short, fair-skinned, apple-bottomed, with big almond-shaped eyes and a smile to snatch your breath away."

He closed his eyes and inhaled a giant gust. "I loved the way that woman smelled. Like a warm deep forest of spices and flowers." He rolled the words over his tongue, tasting the joy of those first months with Dreamie. "Courting, dating, hooking up, whatever you want to call it. We got there fast. So fast in fact, if you count the days with a fine-tuned calculator, you'll figure out Brina was born five months after we got married." His laughter rumbled across the room, sexy and bold, a warm wave of pride curling around me.

I wanted more about Brina. I rotated a finger to encourage him. Norment, being Norment, didn't need the boost. A few nods, hums, and whistles of approval were enough to prime his storytelling pump.

"When Brina was born, Dreamie quit her job at the dentist office. I thought she'd go back after a while, but she never did. Said she wanted to strike out on her own, see what she could do with her artistic side. She loved to draw, sketch, water colors too. She'd go to the park with little Brina in a stroller and sketch the birds she saw. Robins, finches, jays, even pigeons looked special when she'd finished with 'em."

Norment stretched in the chair to rummage in his wallet. Maybe he carried one of Dreamie's bird sketches. Instead, he drew out a small photo. I crossed the room to study the photo cradled in his palm. It was a faded portrait of the family triangle: Norment in a green open-collar shirt grinning behind Dreamie who squeezed little Sabrina. The young mother wore a canary sweater dotted with fluffy white clouds. Her jeans were gathered with a braided leather belt. Her squirmy toddler was swamped in matching yellow corduroy overalls. Norment's huge hands pressed on his wife's shoulders. He stooped to put his head at the same level as hers. I picked up the brittle slip of paper to study it. They looked ordinary, innocent, happy.

When I returned the photo, Norment resumed his story. "Dreamie tried selling some of her drawings. She set a folding table on the boulevard, laid out her sketches, and sold a few. People liked how she captured those common critters in uncommon ways." He looked toward the dirt-streaked window, as if searching for the animals captured in Dreamie's art.

"She wasn't bringing in much money, and I wasn't either in those early days. Starting up a private investigation business is damn tough at the outset. Folks don't know you, don't trust you, won't give you their honest earned money to look after their property or their troubles. I expected it would be rough going. But Dreamie took it hard."

He wiped his mouth and nose with the handkerchief, rubbing at the long-ago embarrassment. "It wasn't like she wanted to spend and spend. But she wanted things, nice things, like most women do. I couldn't hardly rub two nickels together and her bird pictures only brought in a few pennies. We fought and scratched and argued so much, it just scoured the polish right off our marriage. Dulled its shine. Til there wasn't nothing left but the raw and the rough."

Norment's voice dwindled to nothing, as if remembering made each breath painful. "Dreamie drank a little, I drank a little too. And she tasted the other stuff, which I never did. She went in for coke mostly. I knew it was a terrible cycle: we'd argue about the dope; she'd go out and get some more. Then we'd argue some more, then she'd get strung out again. Some weeks after a fight, she'd take off and leave us for a day and a night. I never knew where she went. Just figured she hung on a street corner or in a park 'til she got straight enough to come home."

The flowing words shuddered to a halt, as if memory squeezed them into little pebbles that blocked his mouth. He jerked his eyes to meet mine and started again.

"Once she went missing for three whole days. She got clean after that. Not completely straight, but not strung out neither. Never disappeared for a long stretch like that again. A little girl needs her mother. Dreamie knew that; knew she shouldn't take off and leave Sabrina like that."

This was the hard part of the story. Over the years I'd known them, I'd heard bits of it from Brina and from Norment too. So, I let him advance at his own pace through these jagged shards of the life Dreamie had shattered almost three decades ago. His words crept slow and dense, with a mournful tempo that dropped night's black canvas over the dentist's office.

"One day, we argued pretty fierce, worse than before. When I came home, I found Brina crying in her room, her soft little cheek red from where Dreamie had hit her. Not hard, not rough. But still a slap no mother ought never give her child. I asked Brina what it was about. But all I could get from her was some story about a silver fish and some earrings."

I'd seen the beautiful silver fish earrings and heard Brina's side of the story. It was a baffling moment which still festered in her imagination. What I'd learned didn't alter his story, so I kept quiet.

The past, jumbled and treacherous, carried Norment on. "When I asked Dreamie what happened, she couldn't say anything clear neither. The whole story was a muddle. But I didn't care what the fight was about. I told Dreamie she would never hit our daughter again. Not as long as I drew breath would she ever hit my baby girl again." Norment stopped. His lips flattened over the phrase. I held my breath until he continued.

"Things returned to normal then. Off-kilter, but normal the way we knew it. A few weeks later, Dreamie walked out the apartment one evening. Walked out into the dark and the rain. I never saw her again. She took off, never said a word, never left an address, or tried to get in touch. Nothing at all. Just abandoned us."

The rawness of this long-ago moment clawed at us. Norment dabbed a pinkie to the corner of each eye. He sniffed through reddened nostrils.

To save him from picking at the sore spot once again, I took up his story. "You said you looked for Dreamie. Looked all over the city, then the state. Police missing-person reports, friends and neighbors, private contacts and clients, even some of your former pals in the mob."

Norment nodded his heavy head and blinked twice. Permission granted, I continued. "You enlisted everyone in the search, but nothing turned up. You did everything you could, Norment. You know it. I know it. Most important, Sabrina knows it. She knows you tried your damnedest. Dreamie's gone. Just vanished and that's all there is to it."

The old man plucked at frayed stitching on the arm of the dental chair. "Yeah. She's lost because she didn't want to be found. That's how I figure it. At first, the cops grilled me. Suspected me of foul play in the disappearance. But after a while, the plain truth settled over all of us. Dreamie quit us and made a life for herself somewhere else. She didn't want to be found. Not by me. Not by Sabrina. Not by anybody around here. I've made peace with the past. Took me a while, but I did it. I just hope Sabrina has too."

"Norment, I think she has. She's come to that peace too." I was nowhere near as positive as I sounded. But I wanted it to be true. The disappearance of Dreamie was a mystery we couldn't solve here. But I had a simpler question. "What happened to the dentist?"

"Doc Rogers? Office fire. Took him and his files with it. That was over twenty years ago. Nobody wanted to rent the space since. Fools claimed there was ghosts haunting the rooms." Norment turned his head in a deliberate arc. As he rose from the chair, he slapped his palms together to erase the dust. "Best dentist in the neighborhood. Never been none like him since."

At the top of the steps, we peered into the black stairwell. I moved in front of the old man, firing the flashlight on my cell phone. Dust, like smoldering pink fumes, circled through the beam of light over the stairs below. Norment clapped his hand on my left shoulder, long fingers digging under my collar bone. We descended to the entrance that way, me leading, Norment following.

In the vestibule, we stopped before the outer door. We stood for a minute, shoulder to shoulder. Darkness hid our faces and carried our voices.

"Which tooth was it, Norment?"

"The one got pulled? Lower right molar, in the back."

"You come here often?"

"I get that old twinge in my jaw every three, four months. Throbbing like that ghost tooth still aching to be jerked out. The past is like a hot pulse beating some secret rhythm in my head. When it hits, I stop here for a tune up. Rest in the dentist chair a while. Think on the past, on the missing and the lost. After a while, the pain retreats and I get to work again. Rook, that ache don't never disappear altogether. Don't figure it ever will. But I can handle it now. You will too. After a while."

"Thank you." I raised my chin, though he couldn't see the gesture in the dark. "For bringing me here. For sharing your past. For sharing Dreamie." Maybe he could feel the ruffle of air as I exhaled. "It helps."

# CHAPTER
# NINE

The next day, I took the train to mid-town. Sweaty subway commuters griped and shoved, but even their grousing couldn't push the Continental Regent out of my brain. Maybe another morning scouring the halls, alcoves, and meeting rooms of the giant hotel would bring some new insight into Annie's murder. Or at least lift the fog clogging my senses.

After a trudge along the hushed corridors of the eighteenth floor, I tackled the grand meeting rooms on the second floor. They were crammed with a fresh set of convention-goers. Giddy with the freedom of new contacts in a strange city, these visitors congratulated themselves on their good fortune. Lots of back slapping, cheek kissing, and shoulder clutching lubricated the festive crowd. They didn't look different from the people who'd attended Annie's conference of entrepreneurs a week ago; maybe it was my jaded eye that made them seem so unwholesome.

I hit the escalator in search of the hotel manager's office. I wanted to pick his memory to prime my own. When I reached the foot of the stairs, I spotted Brock Stevens, crouched over a computer behind the maroon marble counter. He was jabbing at the monitor screen, giving instructions to a girl with long shiny hair and a tight red suit. I dodged heavy foot traffic to cross the lobby.

Stevens recognized me before I leaned against the counter. His eyes wobbled toward the ceiling, then settled on my face. "Mr. Rook, I was... I wondered... well, I'm glad to see you again." I doubted that was true. But his hospitality training won out over more ghoulish instincts.

"Just thought I'd make another pass through. See if I'd missed anything." I hadn't invented an excuse for my visit, so the gulp of anguish in my voice was real. I scratched an index finger through a tangle above my left ear and shifted from side to side, studying the maroon-and-gray swirls in the carpet.

I wanted him to invite me to his office, but Stevens took pity on me. "Could I entice you to join me for a cup of coffee, Mr. Rook?" Or maybe he didn't want to be caught alone in a small office with me.

"Sure, I could go for that."

"Arlene, I'll be back in fifteen minutes. Chuck can help you sort out that glitch in Mrs. Rosenblum's reservation."

By the time we'd eased into a wide booth in the shop off the main lobby and ordered black coffees, my stomach had settled. Stevens used a soft voice, the chirpy one he might deploy in a nursery school. Or with unhappy customers. He wanted to soothe me, defuse any leftover anger. Maybe he feared I'd lodge a law suit against the hotel for wrongful death. Did he think I could claim millions in a gaudy court case pitting a grieving relative against a heartless corporation? Stevens wanted me calmed and comforted. I wanted something too. Information that might give new insights into the hours before Annie died. When the two white mugs of brew arrived, I steered from the mushy chit-chat.

"Stevens, I'm not here as a tourist and I'm not with the police. I'm here on my own account."

He cringed, fearing a legal gambit. "Yes, the police told me you were connected to that poor woman. Her husband, they said."

"Former husband."

"I'm so sorry for your loss. That has to have been such a devastating experience, finding her like that."

"Thank you. Yeah, it was." I paused a beat, while he slurped coffee to cover the quiver in his lower lip. "I wanted to check your memory of the night before the death. Did anything stand out to you. Did you see anything that struck you as strange or uncomfortable?"

Stevens turned the mug 360 degrees, examining the Continental Regent logo. "It's funny you raise that. The police asked me about the day itself, the day she died. Everything I remembered: where I'd been; who I'd seen. All that. But they didn't ask about the day before." He shrugged at the mysterious ways of cops.

"Something stood out to you? Something different about the day before the murder?" Using the blunt word made Stevens's eyes jiggle. He stopped their dance with a tap to his eyelid.

"Yes, not a big something. Probably not important."

"What was it? No telling what's important and what's not."

"Well, I remember seeing your wife–ex-wife–talking at the entrance to the gift shop. Around two when I took my afternoon break. She was with a tall man with a red beard and curly red hair."

Gerry Keith. "How do you know it was Annie and not another woman?"

"Your wife is–was–a striking woman, Mr. Rook. And, well, um… there weren't many people of her description in attendance at that conference…" He drifted over the obvious.

"You mean, she was one of the few African Americans in the crowd. Right?"

"Right. Just a handful." He gulped as embarrassment flushed his jowls. "And she was so beautiful, she was hard to miss. Or forget."

"How did they look, Annie and the red-headed man? Friendly, angry, distant, professional, cozy?"

"They looked cheerful. Lots of smiles. Like old classmates at a reunion."

"Kissing, hugging? Like that?" The words gritted between my teeth and I raised the coffee mug toward my face.

"No, nothing like that. Just heads thrown back, wide eyes, easy laughs. I couldn't hear what they were saying, of course. But they seemed comfortable, happy. Until *she* showed up."

"She?" I figured the little sprite Sarah Anastos had broken into the enchanted scene between Annie and her suitor, Gerry.

"Yes, a new lady arrived at the gift shop and spoke to them. I don't know what she said, but your wife and her friend pulled apart, like they'd been disciplined by the principle for rowdy behavior in the school cafeteria."

"What did this new woman look like?"

"A white lady. Older than your wife. By ten, maybe fifteen years. Plain face, no make-up. With blonde hair chopped in spikes around her head. She wore a shiny blue pants suit and a white blouse with a frill at the neck and buttons down the front." Stevens touched his own tight collar and strained shirt placket to illustrate the look.

Images of Pearl Byrne's prim, dated style jumped in my mind. This was the new information I was after. The payoff for this painful interview with Stevens. Maybe Pearl knew something or saw something that might help me crack this case. What had she said to Annie? To Gerry Keith? "You were too far away to make out their conversation, I guess."

"No, I couldn't hear anything. I was across the lobby. Maybe 150 yards away. It was like a silent movie. The whole encounter took a minute, three max. I wouldn't have remembered it at all, except that same blonde lady was with you the next afternoon, insisting I take you both up to Room 1823. To find out why your wife wasn't answering the phone. Some strange coincidence, right?"

"Yeah, strange." I studied the dregs of my coffee until the tears dried under my lids. "One more question. When you entered the room, when we found… found the body. Did you see a laptop or tablet anywhere?"

"No." He squinted as he recalled the scene. "I didn't see a computer of any kind. Is your wife's missing?"

"Yes, I think so."

"I don't know what to say. I can ask the cleaning staff if they know anything about a laptop." Stevens glanced at his watch, then tucked his arm below the table, as if the impatient gesture was rude.

I took pity on the harried manager. "Time for me to shove off. You've been more than generous with your time." I handed him my business card.

"I hope I was some help. I don't think I was… but, maybe…"
"You helped. I don't know how much yet. But you helped."

---

The next morning's commuter train ride to Poughkeepsie demanded little: stay vertical and focus on my questions for Pearl Byrne. I wanted to find out what she'd said to Annie in that encounter outside the hotel gift shop. I hoped she might tell me about Annie's planned presentation, the one derailed by her murder. If Pearl could offer insights into Annie's relationships with Gerry Keith and Rick Luna, I might find more evidence pointing to their involvement in her death. I didn't think Pearl was the killer. She'd led me to Annie's room. And her horrified reaction to the discovery there seemed genuine. Pearl would have to be an ice-cold psycho to pull off that level of deception. My gut said Pearl was in the clear. But this visit could let me rule her out. And rule in someone else.

Riding against the commuter horde gave me room to sprawl across two seats for the trip north. Outside the hustling train, the scenery was industrial: flat gray buildings trimmed in amber brick; a shroud of parched August brown weighing on the canopy of trees escorting us from the city. The streets slogged like streams of black tar beside the train tracks.

I'd phoned for an appointment, but ducked telling Pearl why I wanted to see her. When she agreed to meet, the crack in her voice said she thought we needed a round of mutual comfort. Maybe we did. So, I'd dressed for the pity party: black trousers, fresh from the cleaners, and a summer-weight shirt, also black. No tie, but to lift the gloom, my socks sported white baseballs on a field of blue, Pearl's favorite color.

The taxi driver had no trouble finding the offices of Maid for You, Pearl Byrne's cleaning service. Four blocks down the main drag, three-quarters around the traffic circle, another three blocks to a dingy remodeled garage on a quiet side street. I could have walked from the train station, but sacrificing the cash to avoid the sweat was worth it. No reason to start our talk with a lathered collar and a screaming foot.

Two powder-blue station wagons were angled on the cement apron in front of the building. The company name was painted on the side of each vehicle: sunny yellow letters dabbed over the crossed handles of a broom and a mop above a foaming bucket of suds. The same logo swung on an oval sign above the entrance. I was in the right place, a certainty reinforced by a cheery girl with blonde ringlets who stood from a metal desk to greet me when I pushed through the glass door. She said she was Pamela and Ms. Pearl was looking forward to my arrival. Three women in pale blue mechanic's overalls, their ponytails tied with yellow bandannas, lounged on metal folding chairs in front of Pam's desk. Rolled sleeves exposed the women's bunchy biceps and red wrists. Their cuffs floated above bare ankles and Converse sneakers. I guessed they were the squad waiting for their next assignment. The three shifted on their squeaky chairs and stared at me; no smiles, just harvesting data. Shoes, belt, buttons on my shirt. Pam giggled and twiddled a curl behind her ear. I pinned eyes on the door beyond Pam's desk.

Pearl Byrne flung open the door. "Oh, you are *scary* prompt! I like that, Mr. Rook. Please come in." She blocked the entrance, so I had no choice but to step into her arms. Sinking into her doughy embrace felt good, like a reunion. The soapy scent rising from her neck was as I remembered from that grim day in the Continental Regent hotel: clean and warm with vanilla. Tangled with the sweetness was a new smell, powdery ash. We hugged for a ten-count. Then she snuffled against my neck, patted my back, and pulled away. She pointed toward four upholstered arm chairs enclosing a low round table. The furniture sprawled in front of her aircraft carrier-size desk.

I didn't know whether to call her Pearl or Ms. Byrne. Death made our connection as intimate as it gets. But I hardly knew her. In the dismal circumstances, I stuck with a narrow smile and skipped using a name. "Thank you for making time to see me. I know you're busy."

"Everyone's busy. I'm not special." Pearl wore a blue-and-white striped shirt stuck into the elastic waist of dark pants that bagged at the knees. Hiding her beautiful legs like that was sad, but I coped.

When I'd dropped into the flowery brocade of a chair, Pearl walked toward a cabinet pressed against the high window beside the desk. Two large white crocheted doilies protected the counter's wooden surface. More lacy circles festooned the low table at my knees. On one of the doilies was a clear glass ashtray. Gray cinders pyramided in the hollowed block.

Pearl caught me staring at the ashtray. She smiled in thin apology: "Picked up that bad habit in high school. During my days as a teen terror."

"I did too. The tough guy stance looked cool."

"But you ditched it?"

"After Iraq."

She tapped a bone from a pack of Camels on the desk. "Smart." A match flickered toward the cigarette dangling from her mouth. "I'm not much of a coffee drinker. I can ask Pammy to bring you some if you'd like." She lifted a large army green thermos from the doily and tipped it toward me. "Or you can try some of my fresh lemonade. Icy cold, squeezed this morning, laced with local honey and dabbed with strawberries for color."

"You had me at icy cold. Thank you." A splash of rye for an improvised whiskey sour would have been nice, but I didn't ask and Pearl didn't offer.

After I murmured phrases of awe and gratitude for the virgin lemonade, she recited the recipe. Then we savaged the brutal August heat for a few more sentences. I needed to get to the point of my visit, but couldn't come up with a graceful transition. So, after a third gulp of lemonade, I dived in without elegance.

"I wanted to check your memory on a few facts about the hours and days before Annie died." My longest sentence of the visit ended on a rough note.

I didn't know how she'd take the change of subject. To my surprise, Pearl's mouth curved upward, her eyes crinkling in gratitude. "You know, the police were so curt, so matter-of-fact about those horrible things. I never got the chance to talk about it. And of course, no one up here wanted details of a death. My neighbors, workers, friends from church. Not even the priest. No one wants to hear about death." A plume of smoke curled toward the ceiling. She knocked her cigarette against the ashtray. "I can't blame them, really. You feel as though you're infecting them, spreading a curse if you keep talking, don't you? Everyone wants you to lay those thoughts to rest, leave them in the past, bury them where they belong."

I watched a drop of condensation skid past the pink liquid in my glass. I swirled the tumbler once, then set it on the low table. "When was the last time you saw Annie? Do you remember?"

"I do." Pearl sat forward until her knees bumped against the table. "She was so bright then, gleaming and polished, like a shiny ornament on a Christmas tree or the figurine on the hood of a fancy car." A gasp halted her memory. "Oh, that doesn't sound right at all. As if Anniesha was some engraved idol or fetish. She wasn't. A totem, I mean. Or an abstraction. Anniesha was the liveliest person I've ever known."

Tears streamed over splotches of red on her white cheeks. My gut was right: Pearl was no killer. She stubbed out the cigarette, then struggled from her chair. She circled the desk to retrieve a tissue box from a lower drawer. Dropping the box on the table, she swiped a wad of Kleenex over her eyes. "You asked when I'd seen her last?"

"Yes. Was it in the hotel?" I could have specified the gift shop. But I kept the question open-ended to avoid steering the response.

"We'd made plans to meet at two on the afternoon before our presentation. We wanted to review a script we'd drafted, run through the division of labor, and sketch answers to questions we thought the audience might pose."

"Where were you going to meet?"

"Neither of us knew the neighborhood at all. Never been at the Continental Regent before, so we didn't know any restaurants or cafés nearby. We decided it would be easiest to meet in front of the gift shop in the hotel lobby."

"And did you see Annie there?"

"Yes, she was already at the gift shop when I arrived." Pearl glanced toward the window, avoiding my eyes.

"Alone?"

"No. Not alone."

"Who was with Annie?"

"She was talking with that professor, Gerald Keith." A deep sigh, as if the man's name caused aches to ping in her chest. Pearl pressed her lips into a line bisecting her round face. "I guess it doesn't matter if I tell you: I don't like him much."

Stern damnation from this gentle woman. Blazing hellfire in a few measured words. Teamsters unloading their filthiest terms couldn't match her ferocity. I nodded and rubbed my damp palms against the rough cloth of the arm chair. "You'd met Professor Keith before?"

"Yes, he'd visited me here at my office. Brought that little girl with him too."

"Sarah Anastos?"

"Yes, that's the one. Scrawny red-headed thing. Stuck on Professor Keith like a chickenpox blister, she was." Dissing Sally Anastos returned a spark to Pearl's bleary eyes.

I tilted my head at the neat disease imagery, but kept Pearl on track. "When you saw Annie and Keith at the gift shop, how did they seem? Cool? Chummy? All business?" Repeating the questions I'd posed yesterday to hotel manager Brock Stevens kept me from grinding my teeth in rage.

"Oh, they were friendly alright. Plenty cozy. Leaning close into each other, his hands hovering over her shoulders, her fingers fluttering above his vest. If you want to call that chummy, you'd be right on the mark." As she snapped the last word, her tone was cool and tart; the honey stayed in the lemonade.

"What did they do when they saw you?"

"Jumped like I'd caught them plotting some grand intrigue. I laughed; the shock on their faces was just that funny."

"Shock? How do you mean?"

"Surprise mixed with guilt. Once upon a time, when I was twenty years younger and fifty pounds thinner, I used to teach seventh graders in a parochial school. I'd see that same look on the sweaty faces of those little cherubs at least once a day. A portion of shame, mixed with a bit of wonder, topped with a frosting of pride. Children are funny creatures. Adults too, I guess."

"That's how Professor Keith looked? With Annie?" I stuffed my hands into the crevices next to the chair's plush cushions. Hidden, the fingers curved into fists.

Pearl stroked her glance over my face, then pushed the box of tissues to my side of the table. "I'm sorry. I didn't mean to upset you, Mr. Rook."

"You didn't."

Pearl absorbed my lie without challenge. She refilled my glass from her thermos bottle. "I'd like to show you something, if I might."

"Sure." A change of subject was good. As welcome as the cool lemonade drizzling down my throat.

Pearl fished a small laptop from the center drawer of her desk and set it on the table between us. "You know how Anniesha and I worked on our presentation before we arrived in New York?"

I shook my head. The movement spiked the pain that had been gathering at the base of my skull. I jabbed fingers into tight muscles along my shoulders, but the ache spiraled.

"We did it over video conference calls. You know, those apps where both parties log in. Like Zoom. Split screens allowed us to exchange documents, review tables, draft PowerPoint slides together. It was exciting. Her in Miami, me here, but we were working together as if we were in the same room. Made me feel modern and tech savvy working online with Anniesha like that." Pearl tapped the keyboard then swung the screen in my direction. "I recorded our meetings."

On the screen Annie's face sprang to life. She wore a pink polo shirt with a green palm tree stitched on the collar. Glistening skin, rosy gloss on her lips and cheeks. Bright teeth, slanted black eyes brimming with humor under those thick bangs. She'd brushed her hair into a loose ponytail which draped over her left shoulder. Pearl poked at a key to lift the mute. Annie's voice seared my veins. Seeing her, hearing her like this, was a fresh reminder of how Annie had been my home, my energy, my strength when I was young and whole. She laughed into the camera, teasing about some grammatical error on a slide: "And you're supposed to be the English teacher? Shame on you, Miss Pearl!"

The two women chirped for a week. I didn't hear a word of the exchange. Watching Annie's face was all I could manage. A buzz invaded my ears, humming until their conversation dwindled to a drone. My fingers cooled, vague pains pricking under the nails. A dark halo squeezed the edges of the screen, then collapsed like the pupil of a sun-blinded eye. The unexpected encounter with Annie's vibrant, living form had driven from my mind all the questions I had planned to ask Pearl.

The buzzing stopped when Pearl patted my forearm. "You alright, Mr. Rook?" Her fingertips tapped my sweaty skin from wrist to elbow.

"Yeah, I'm fine." Another lie, but her smile deserved the effort. "Thank you for sharing that."

"I thought you'd want to see her again. To remember Anniesha the way she was. Before..."

"Yes. Thank you."

"Did you notice where she was in that conference call?"

"No."

"That was her office in Miami. You could see the green shelves, the shiny white tiles on the walls. And that poster framed in bright pink behind her. A picture of an art deco hotel, I think it was."

"Sure. Art deco." I had no idea if that was right, but echoing Pearl was a safe step while I regained my bearings.

Pearl slipped to her desk again, this time opening a shallow side drawer. When she returned to the table, she balanced a small box on her palm. The carton was square, covered in eddies of cream and pink. On one side, lustrous green script read: "*Rêves de la Plage.*"

I took the box and opened it. I lifted out a clear glass bottle, the size and shape of a tulip bulb. A faceted crystal stopped the bottle's neck. The stopper's surface was smoky pink, swirled with clouds, like a large marble. Inside, golden liquid shimmered as I tilted the bottle. "What's this?"

"A gift from Anniesha. The perfume she always wore. She gave it to me when we first met. Isn't it beautiful?" Pearl's eyes shone, a soft smile bending her lips. "Go on, open it."

I tugged the pink marble until it yielded. Annie's scent drifted across my face, tangy like cherries glazed in burnt sugar. I stoppered the bottle and glanced toward the windows. Unblinking, I stared into the sun until its glare justified the mist in my eyes. "What's the name mean? Do you know?"

"Anniesha told me 'Rêves de la Plage' is French for 'Dreams of the Beach.' Pretty, right?"

"Yes. Lovely," I said.

I balanced the bottle on my fingertips. I remembered our last night and Annie's sweet voice: *Miami's a nice town.* How Annie's fingers had grazed my knee. How I'd choked: *So I hear. Nice beach, nice ocean.*

I slipped the bottle into the box. I felt raw, exposed, but grateful too. "'Rêves de la Plage' fits her. Thank you for sharing with me." I handed the box to Pearl. "Will you wear it?"

"I don't think so. I don't see how I could now. Knowing what it means. That scent will always remind me of Anniesha. Always. How could I ever wear it, Mr. Rook?" A pledge more than a question, the wail carried Pearl to her desk. She returned the perfume box to the drawer and pressed it closed.

When she sat next to me again, the tenderness of the moment had faded along with Annie's scent. "Mr. Rook, I have a suggestion."

"Sure, shoot." A lousy turn of phrase, but I couldn't take it back.

"Have you considered phoning Anniesha's vice president, Rick Luna?"

"What for?" Did Pearl guess I'd tapped Luna as a potential murderer? What could she hope I'd gain from talking with him?

"I'm sure he'd like to hear from you. From anyone who knew her."

Pearl had introduced the topic, so I could probe further. "Did you see the two of them together at the conference?"

"Only twice. On the first day of the conference, Annie introduced us. She'd mentioned Rick when we talked online, so it was nice to finally put a face to the name. We talked for maybe five minutes, not more. Just general stuff. He seemed bubbly and eager to please. Like a puppy dog. Then, the day before she… before she died. I saw Rick talking with her at a little table in a corner of the lobby. He was leaning close, hanging on every word she spoke. Intense."

I wanted to ask Pearl if she thought Annie and Rick were lovers. Talking about sex with an ex-nun wasn't my idea of joy, so I hoped by offering a vague phrase or two she'd get my meaning. "Did you form the impression they were more than just close colleagues? Did it go further with them, do you think?"

She sighed and rolled her shoulders. "You mean, did I think they were sleeping together? Yes, that crossed my mind. He seemed more than warm. Passionate, I'd say. And she was sparkly and excited." Pearl raised her eyes to catch mine, like she knew what she had to say might hurt. But she was determined to get it out anyway. "I never saw them kiss, but there were enough touches and long gazes to convince me they were more than just friends."

"Okay." This information confirmed Rick could have slept with Annie the night of her murder. I wouldn't scratch him off my list of suspects yet. "I've got the picture."

"Will you call him?" She was persistent. A nun on a mission. Who did Pearl believe would benefit from the phone call she proposed, me or Rick? Or was she hoping to salve her own feelings?

I snapped. "I'm supposed to comfort that worm? Make *him* feel better? No chance." I stood, moving toward the door. This interview needed to close before it swamped me.

"I spoke with Rick two days ago. He's suffering, Mr. Rook. He lost someone too. Someone close. Maybe not like you did, but I think your call could help." We'd reached the door. Pearl squeezed the knob, but didn't turn it. "Compassion is what I'm suggesting. Or understanding. I don't expect you to forgive someone you believe trespassed against you. Mercy is the toughest quality for any of us to achieve." She twisted her fingers together until they shone waxy white. "But I believe it's our obligation to strive for compassion. Can you see things from Rick's perspective? Your marriage was over. As far as he knew, your relationship with Annie was a thing of the past. He had no reason to believe anything else. He merits forgiveness now. And I believe you will find mercy flows in both directions, Mr. Rook. Rick could use a little and so might you. Just give it a thought, would you?"

Pearl chuckled, eyes crinkling until the blue disappeared. "And thus, ends today's homily." Then her voice lowered and she patted my hand. "If you can't see your way clear to speaking with Rick, that's okay. I understand."

"I'll think about it." I swallowed the gravel from my voice with a heavy gulp. Should I have asked Pearl flat out if she suspected Rick had murdered Annie? Maybe. But I couldn't bring myself to dish the question. Her plea for empathy for him suggested she believed he was innocent. Besides, talking sex with a nun was one thing, speculating about murder with her was a line I couldn't cross.

Pearl's moist kindness wafted over me as I stood in the reception room, waiting for the taxi to arrive. We shook hands under the bubbly gaze of Pam the secretary, who walked me to the curb. Clouds of Pearl's sympathy dampened the atmosphere of the train ride to the city. By the time I reached my apartment, I'd folded. Pearl won. A phone call to slick Ricky Luna might serve more than one purpose. Maybe I'd learn enough to knock him from my suspects list. And maybe I'd feel better too. I'd do it. But not yet.

# CHAPTER
# TEN

Norment Ross's generous heart and the avalanche of stories he told me over those days worked. Even so, beyond my personal trips to the Continental Regent and to Poughkeepsie, I wasn't ready to step into the work world again. Still bruised and tender, I hesitated. Norment called me "street-shy." But Brina and her practical bluntness dragged me into the arena.

"See, here's how it works, Rook. This is a *detective* agency. Not a *defective* agency. You need to pull your weight around here. Or we run short of money and go out of business. Got it?"

After that first futile attempt at consoling me, she'd spent the next nights at her own apartment. She'd given me space to recover. Maybe this new brisk tone signaled her sympathy had run its course, replaced by exasperation mixed with a residue of jealousy. Usually, my gut served me well in reading people. More often than not, I appreciated their intentions and goals, sometimes before they even recognized their own desires. I relied on sound instincts and accurate hunches to see me through rough cases. I got people, that was my private eye super power. But with Brina, I was stumped. Maybe with her, I was too close. Or maybe just heart-blind. Whatever the cause, reading her feelings was the hardest challenge I'd faced in a lifetime of tests and trials.

Now, she tugged at the handle of the window in my office, her black coils bouncing as she tried to exchange the muggy interior air for equally humid outside air. After a minute watching her grapple with the stuck window, I took pity and joined the effort. With our combined force, we unjammed the swollen frame and lifted the sash upwards. A gust of steam poured into the room, ruffling the papers on my desk.

"Right, boss. You got anything interesting for me?" I'd get back in the saddle again. But only if that saddle posed a challenging puzzle. I was her fix-it project, so Brina made it her priority to know what medicine I needed and when to patch me up. Sorrow mixed with boredom could be disastrous. I wasn't moving on. Five days after her murder, Annie's death remained my top case, but I needed another job.

Brina delivered the dose. "I don't know if you'll find this interesting. But it is urgent. One of Daddy's old army buddies from Vietnam, Allard Swann, operates a small nursing home about ten blocks from here near Striver's Row. He called this afternoon to ask for our help in locating a patient who's run away from the premises."

Brina pushed damp curls from her forehead and puffed upwards to cool her flushed face. She'd rolled the sleeves of her lavender t-shirt past the joint of her shoulders and untucked it from her denim skirt. As she continued the account, she raised the hem of her shirt to expose three inches of gleaming brown skin to the breeze wafting from the open window.

"Mr. Swann says the old lady has taken off before, but only for an hour or less each time. Mostly she wanders around the block and returns by herself. But today she's been gone for six hours and counting. They don't know where she is and they're getting frantic. Think you can help out?"

That sounded like an order, not a hope. As we turned from the window, I bumped shoulders with Brina, punctuation to our bantering. "I can try, boss. Give me the address and I'll start from there."

A small job, clean, simple, and healthy. I was ready.

The Swann Memory Center occupied an elegant house on a block distinguished by its hushed calm and the heavy shade of its trees. The pink brick façade shimmered in the late August heat. A deep front porch shadowed the residence. The building's unusual spot in the congested city was underlined by the parking space ten steps from the Center's front door. I planned to cruise the neighborhood in search of the runaway patient. So, Brina leant me her Honda for the afternoon.

Allard Swann greeted me when I rang the doorbell. His office might have been the library in the building's past life as a private home. It was lined with fat books in mahogany shelves, plump upholstered chairs crowded every corner. Lucky I'd worn a white dress shirt rather than my usual black one; the Swann Center looked like a funeral home, no need to add to the gloomy impression. Wine red leather chairs in front of his desk and deep tufted sofas along two walls struck a note of traditional elegance and reliability. A black steel safe sealed with a dial lock squatted beside one sofa. Swann's business depended on assuring anxious families that their loved ones would be well cared for under his supervision. Corralling wayward dementia patients was his core mission. Losing one to the uncertain streets of Harlem was a blow Allard Swann couldn't afford.

A male attendant brought iced tea on a silver platter. Swann, tight smile plastered in place, was sweating like the drinks glasses when we sat in front of his desk. His three-piece suit of light-weight gray wool was oppressive at the end of summer. But he refused to shed the uniform no matter the temperature. Swann was five inches shorter than me, but carried sixty pounds more, in the form of a pot belly suspended above long legs. Dark skin tinged with a hint of red and a full head of black hair completed the picture. If Allard Swann was as old as Norment Ross, his barber's expert dye job kept the years at bay.

"Thank you for coming so promptly, Mr. Rook. Sabrina assured me she was sending her best man for our little job. I'm glad you were able to make the time to take on this assignment."

The endorsement felt good, even if Brina had exaggerated the size of our agency by several magnitudes. "Glad to be of service. Dr. Swann." A nameplate on his gigantic carved desk said he had a medical degree. And a Ph.D. "Tell me as much as you can about the situation, and we'll see what we can do."

Swann gulped half the tea and launched. "I'll begin at the beginning. I founded the Swann Memory Center eighteen years ago as a solution for families in the community seeking a comfortable residence for their loved ones stricken by dementia, memory loss, and other aspects of senility."

He droned like a sales brochure come to life. I fidgeted in my seat. If the old lady was on the lam, we needed to cut to the chase. "How many elderly do you keep here, Doctor?"

Swann frowned at my phrasing, delicate lines wrinkling his brow. "We usually have fifteen to eighteen patients in residence at any one time. As you can imagine, several of our residents pass on every year. Many of them are at the end stages of Alzheimer's or other degenerative brain diseases. For centuries, Black families have shouldered the responsibility of caring for our aging parents. We see protecting our elders as a sacred duty. But for many of us, the toll is overwhelming. The Swann Center provides Harlem families with confidence that their loved ones will be well cared for by attentive, carefully trained staff. For the final chapter of their lives, our center offers residents a home-like atmosphere that is quiet, familiar, and safe."

Swann delivered this sales pitch with such practiced and soothing tones, I almost signed myself into the center. I could use a long rest in a comfy rocking chair. "Tell me about the missing lady, Dr. Swann. You told Brina she's escaped several times in the past."

Swann scowled at my choice of verb, but let it ride. At this point the professional reputation of his business was more important than a little bruising to his ego. "Yes, Carolyn Wiley has been with us for almost two years. She's seventy-six years old, a life-long New Yorker. Except for the signs of advanced dementia she exhibits, Mrs. Wiley is in excellent physical health for her age. She has bouts of anger and depression from time to time, but those are off-set by periods of good cheer and cooperativeness. She seems to enjoy the food, the company, and our staff a great deal."

"Yet, she wanders off? Why do you think that is, Dr. Swann?"

"I don't know. And from my conversations with her, I don't think she has any idea either."

"Do you know where she goes when she disappears?"

"No, I don't. In the past, she has gone off shortly after we serve a snack around four in the afternoon. We think she slips out the back door, down the alley, and away. No one sees her go and we don't even know in which direction she walks."

Swann didn't run a tight ship. Mutiny roiled the ranks and now he wanted me to solve the untidy case. "Does she ever speak about her ramblings. Does she tell anyone here where she goes?"

His neck stiffened as my questions expanded. "Not to my knowledge. The staff are all as mystified as I am, Mr. Rook. And if Mrs. Wiley speaks about it to another patient, it's unlikely the friend would retain any understanding of what she has shared anyway."

"What does her family say? Are they near-by? Maybe she's looking for one of them?"

"Oh, no. That isn't possible. Mrs. Wiley is a widow. She has only the one son, Carl Wiley. There are no other surviving members of her family. And her son lives in Seattle. Obviously, she's not visiting him on her walks around the neighborhood." Swann spelled it out in case I was losing my marbles too. Letting insults slide was the best policy.

"How about friends? Is there anybody Mrs. Wiley might try to see? A pastor or sorority sister? A friend from work, maybe?"

"I can give you a list of contacts we have for Mrs. Wiley here in the city. She worked for thirty-seven years in the neighborhood libraries. But none of those contacts are near-by. And none say they've seen her today. But if you want to check with them again, please do." Like he didn't trust me to do my job, but feared I might uncover he hadn't done his.

"When did you notice Mrs. Wiley missing this morning?"

"About six. We do a bed check several times a night on all our patients and when we looked in on Mrs. Wiley this morning she wasn't in bed or in the bathroom or in the kitchen or anywhere on the premises. I ordered two of our staff to search for her. We assumed she'd come back in an hour as she has done in the past. But by noon she hadn't returned and we got worried." Swann twisted a large ring on his right hand, turning it until the hefty medallion disappeared against his palm. "That's when I called Norment's agency for help. It's hot today, and without food and water, I don't know how long she can last. Can you do anything to find her, Mr. Rook?"

"Give me the list of her contacts, a recent photo, and her previous addresses, too. I'll check them as fast as possible. We'll do our best to find her."

I plunked the half-full glass on the table. I wouldn't make promises I couldn't keep, so my assurances stayed vague. But I was itching to get on the street to start the hunt for Mrs. Carolyn Wiley.

———————

For two hours, I drove to the church, office, restaurants, dry cleaners, library, and movie theatre Carolyn Wiley used to frequent. Nothing new. I phoned contacts I couldn't reach in person and cruised every street in a five-block radius of the center. How far could an old woman, even one as healthy as Mrs. Wiley, walk in six hours? Had she taken a taxi somewhere? I'd forgotten to ask Swann if she had any money on her or had access to a debit card, either her own or someone else's.

I returned to the center to give Swann a status update and ask for information about Mrs. Wiley's finances. The shady spot wasn't open when I arrived, so I double parked and hoped the meter maids would be kind. Armed with new information and more names after a flash stop in Swann's office, I raced for the porch steps.

A sharp voice arrested my exit. "You that nice young man looking for my friend Carolyn?"

A woman, her face crumpled like a waxy paper bag, sat in a glider to the right of the main door. Her silver-laced hair was braided in six plaits hanging from her head like a little girl's do.

"Yes, ma'am. I am." I sprinkled a frosting of Texas sugar on my words.

She measured me, a slow trip down my body, her eyes clouded with cataracts, but still sparkling like river water. "I can tell you where you should look. If you want to know, that is."

"Yes, I do want to know. Mrs. ..."

"I'm Queen Esther Monroe. You can call me Queen. Been a long time since I needed the Missus anymore."

"Queen, anything you can share would be much appreciated."

"Well, come and sit here on the glider and I'll tell you what Carolyn told me." She patted the green cushion next to her thigh and I sat down. The two-seater was a tight squeeze, but we managed. Queen pushed the glider as we talked. Slow and easy, like the rhythm of her speech.

"Carolyn told me she's been walking around to visit her old house. The one she lived in before she got stashed away in the center here. I don't think it's too far from here. So that's where you ought to check. If you want to find her. That's where she'll be. If she wants to be found."

Queen patted my knee to make sure I'd understood her message. I thanked her for sharing these insights. This would be a big help in finding her friend, I said.

The old woman's nose crinkled in disgust. She spit on the cement floor of the porch. "Oh, Carolyn Wiley's not my friend. Not since they brought her in here and trimmed off that stringy braid. Hair twisted down past her waist when she arrived here. But they showed her. The conceited high-yaller cow. They took her and cut off that braid the first day. Now she's got short hair like the rest of us. No, Carolyn Wiley's not my friend. Not the least little bit. What gave you that fool notion? I can't stand the stuck-up bitch."

The sudden shift startled me; I hiked my shoulders to fend off a quarrel. As I did, Queen fingered the top button of her dress, then pushed it through the button hole. Below pink roses dotted on the blue dress, the scalloped neck of her white slip lay over her flat chest and collar bones. "Hot enough out here for you, young man?" Then the next button was undone, revealing a fine dusting of white talcum powder on her coal black skin.

I stood from the glider and thanked Queen again for her help. As I slipped down the stairs to the car, a blue uniformed attendant appeared on the porch to bring the scattered old woman an iced drink and rebutton her dress.

———————————

I'd twice driven down the street Carolyn Wiley had lived on and not spotted her either time. But on Queen's advice, I tried a third run, this time on foot. I parked at the corner and walked toward the address in the middle of the block. A white panel van and a muscular pick-up truck were stationed in front of the house. My view of the steps was blocked.

I crossed to a few yards from the house. At the top of the tall run of steps, I saw a hunched figure, her thin arms clasped around her knees. She wore a pale pink seersucker shirtdress with red piping along the collar and short-sleeve cuffs. Pearly buttons matched her white mop of hair. Her skin was burlap-colored over sharp cheekbones and a pointed chin. With her narrow eyes and cracked pink lips, Carolyn Wiley looked like her photograph. I slowed, approaching her the way I'd walk to an anxious mare in an open field. I held my hands loose at my sides and fixed a mild expression on my face. I needn't have been so careful.

Mrs. Wiley greeted me with a radiant smile. "Carl, is that you? What kept you so long? I've been waiting forever for you to get home from work."

Her grin bloomed into a laugh as her black eyes jumped with delight. I was her absent son returned from a day in the office. I fit myself into her storyline and returned the wide smile. No use challenging her story or denying it. Maybe I'd learn something useful. At the least, I'd avoid hurting her.

"Sorry for the delay. Traffic was horrible. All that construction downtown tied it in knots." I kept my comments generic. I knew nothing about her son, so offering too many specifics might spoil our developing relationship. "Have you been waiting here long?"

I wiped my brow and looked up from the foot of the staircase. She shook her head and waved knobby fingers at me. "Come on and sit a while, Carl. I'll tell you all about my day."

I joined Mrs. Wiley on the step and she grasped my fingers in hers. Her grip was strong. But her hands felt bony and cold, like touching an injured bird's wing.

"So good to see you, Carl. I missed you, dear. So much. I can't tell you how much. But I've been watching these boys working on the house. They're doing a good job, I'll tell you that. Real sharp, these boys, real sharp." Her watery eyes focused on my face. She whispered: "They're nice boys, but they've hidden my beautiful braid. I've come to find it. But they've hidden it someplace inside the house." She stroked fingers along her nape, fluttering the short spikes of silver hair.

As if summoned by her complaint, four Black men emerged from the basement apartment. Three solid types in overalls followed a wiry man in a khaki shirt and jeans into the sunshine. The crew leaned against the red pick-up truck, chatting in low tones and looking at me. After they reached some consensus, Khaki-shirt stepped forward and signaled for me to come to the curb.

Though we were well out of earshot of Carolyn Wiley, the man spoke in a whisper. He cast anxious eyes at her with each sentence. "You related to her or something?" His dark face tensed with worry.

"No. I'm a friend. I've come to take her home. Has she been here long?"

"Yeah, today was the longest. She comes around here quite a bit, sometimes twice a week. Usually sits for fifteen minutes on the front steps like she's doing now. Never says nothing much, just hello and like that. But today she was here for an hour, then went away, then came back again. Just sitting the way she is now."

Carolyn's connection to the house sparked my curiosity. Why did she insist on returning to the site week after week? What was its hold over her? "I hope she hasn't been a nuisance to you fellas. You know, she used to live here, decades ago."

"Yeah, she told us that. With her son Carl, she said. We were hoping you might be Carl." Lines on his forehead eased and his mouth opened wide. "No, no problem for us. We're just worried about her. Real nice old lady. Always polite-spoken and friendly. If she comes at lunch time, we give her a sandwich and a can of Coke. She said she prefers the bottles but she always finishes off the can anyway. Just pecks at the sandwich, but she loves her some Coca-Cola." He looked over his shoulder at Carolyn and shook his head. He seemed more miserable than Allard Swann when confronting the dilemma of caring for this distracted and willful old woman.

He offered a hand and I gripped it. "Thank you for looking out for her," I said. "She's Mrs. Wiley, by the way. As you can tell, she's not all there. She lives in a nursing center a few blocks away. But every once in a while, she gets the urge to go home. And that's when she shows up here."

Carolyn Wiley's mental incapacity was none of his business. But he'd helped, so I owed him an explanation. Offering facts was a good way of getting more. This man could tell something about the house that Carolyn still thought of as home. I wanted to learn why this place continued to draw her to it after so many years.

"What're you all doing here? Remodeling?" Not a huge leap, but the easiest way to get a man talking is to ask about his expertise. Professional pride defeats privacy every time.

"Yeah, it's a complete renovation of the basement. Used to be a space for the kids, I guess. Like a playroom or rec room. Ping Pong table's still down there. But it's already got direct access to the street. Right under the front stairs, see?"

He pointed toward the black iron picket fence separating the lower entrance from the sidewalk. Next to a small window with bars across it, a red door below the main staircase led to the basement. "Now the family wants to make it into a full apartment. Separate like, so they can rent it out."

"You're gutting the space?"

"Yep, demolition down to the studs." He unfolded a grimy red hand-kerchief and rubbed it over his brow. "We're knocking out non-struc-tural walls, opening up the rooms as much as possible. Lowering the floor a couple inches. New kitchen, bathroom, hardwoods, sheetrock, wiring, plumbing, HVAC, paint, everything. It's gonna be real nice when we get finished."

"And the family that owns this place? Where're they?"

"Boss said they are off in Martha's Vineyard or Block Island. Or some other fancy place like that until mid-September. Must be nice." He laughed and wiped the handkerchief over his nose until the cloth was dark with sweat. "They take off for the summer and then when they get back, the work is done. Like magic."

"No muss, no fuss." I spanked my hands together and brushed them, whisking away all renovation worries in a flash.

"Yeah. For *them*. We got all the muss and fuss we can handle," he said. We chuckled in working-stiff solidarity.

"I appreciate you looking out for my friend. If Mrs. Wiley comes around again give me a call and I'll come get her as soon as I can." I pulled a Ross Agency business card from my wallet and scribbled my cell number on the back.

He took the card and scanned the front. The glossy black surface with its staring eyeball outlined in red and green always got plenty of attention.

"You a detective or something?" His downward grimace and wide eyes said he was impressed.

"Yes. We help people who get in trouble. Like Mrs. Wiley here."

"Well, sure hope I don't have to call you again, Mr. Rook. But I'll hang onto this just in case."

He stowed the card in his breast pocket, buttoning it closed. "I'm Darrell Peete, project foreman. Just so's you know."

"Nice to meet you, Darrell. Call me Rook."

We shook hands again, an alliance in the making. Later, I wondered why I hadn't given Darrell the phone number of the Swann Center so he could contact them if Carolyn showed up again. I knew the answer: I'd done it for her. By taking Carl Wiley's identity, even for a few minutes of play-acting, I'd taken charge of his mother's welfare. I wouldn't surrender that duty without good reason. She was my case now, my third: Annie's murder; Dreamie's disappearance, Carolyn's fog-enveloped secrets. The lives of these three women braided together in my imagination, their troubled pasts heavy with loss and mystery. These were my cases to crack, mine to fix.

I climbed the stairs and took Carolyn Wiley by the fragile knob of her elbow. She fluttered a wave at Darrell and his boys from my car on our ride to the Swann Center. They waved back, like she was the Homecoming Queen.

# CHAPTER
# ELEVEN

The next morning, I sprawled in bed, staring at the harsh white sky blistering Manhattan. A few birds with open beaks sailed by the window, panting in desperate search for a shady ledge. As I tracked their flight, a sheen of sweat rose on my chest.

I should have rolled into the office, typed a paragraph on my rescue of Carolyn Wiley, and scrounged through the agency's pending files for another assignment. Brina the girlfriend was willing to give me space to grieve. But Boss Brina expected me to resume the routine of our detective life. *Saddle up, strap in, move on, man up.* She wouldn't blast all those macho phrases for cutting the cords of past traumas. But I could hear the words in her voice, low and warm like a brutal rhyme. Campaign slogans whose power came from repetition: *Saddle up, move on. Come on, how long?* Not happening, not yet. I wasn't there.

I padded to the kitchenette and shook the last crumbs of cornflakes into one bowl. Into the second, I scraped a lump of canned hash for the cat. Herb flattened his ears to protest my morning laziness. Then he switched his thick yellow tail in warning: Herb wanted me out the door too. He expected to claim the chair next to the window for his own lounging agenda. But after I poured milk for us both, he okayed the new set up. I told him I had to make several phone calls. I needed the privacy of my apartment for the next one on my list. I didn't want the pitying ears of Brina and Norment Ross eavesdropping on my conversation with the hotshot of Miami, Ricardo Luna.

Repeating my last name greased the telephone hop through the administrative maze of Rook Cleaning Services. After the third dazzled secretary gasped and cooed at the chance to speak with the real Mister Rook, I reached the vice president for marketing and sales.

The last time we'd met, I slapped his mug into center field. But if Rick Luna was expecting an apology, he didn't sound pissed when I failed to deliver one. "Thank you for checking on us, Rook. Things were really rough here last week. I'm not going to lie. The first days without Anniesha were rocky."

"I'm not surprised, Rick." I smoothed my voice to match his creamy Caribbean vibe. Pearl Byrne's words flooded my mind. She'd urged me to strive for compassion. To see things from Rick's perspective. You'll find mercy flows in both directions, she promised. Her observations pushed me to consider erasing Rick from my suspects list. I wasn't there yet. But I was open to changing my mind. Even if he was cleared, Rick still might have useful information for my case. I wanted to know what he remembered of Annie's last days at the hotel.

Luna continued, gushing. "Everyone loved her. The girls thought of her as a mother, a leader, and a role model. We can't imagine how we'll go on without her." He blew his nose, then snuffled, sipping the air to regain his composure.

Clichés dribbled from my tongue. "Annie was a star, that's for sure. But she'd want you to carry on, keep the business thriving. The company is her legacy and she'd count on you to keep it going."

He gurgled like a ballad. "It's so kind of you to say that. I'll let everyone know you called to express your condolences. It will mean the world to our girls."

I felt better for doling the sympathy, as Pearl Byrne had expected. The warmth spreading in my gut wasn't caused by the blazing temperatures. Maybe I'd thank her someday. But, now that I'd tapped the empathy vat, I had other aims in mind. "Rick, do me a favor."

"Sure, anything you need, just ask."

"Tell me about that last day at the hotel. The night before Annie died."

"I told everything to the New York police when they phoned last week. Then I did a second round with Miami-Dade cops two days ago. Can you believe, they even took a DNA sample, filthy freakin' bastards!"

"I know. But I'm trying to fit together the details. Learning as much as I can about that night will give me peace of mind." This was truer than I'd ever reveal to Rick Luna. With the phone and eight hundred miles between us, I could freely wipe my eyes as long as I stifled the tears in my voice. I didn't tell him I was investigating the murder. I wanted him focused on his memories, not my reasons for asking.

With my prompt, Luna sketched the events leading to our evening of drinks in the Argent Bar. He'd hit several famous department stores on Fifth Avenue, window-shopped the small boutiques in between, and slipped into the shadowed nave of Saint Patrick's cathedral to cool off. I didn't care about the upkeep of his wardrobe or his soul. But I let Luna's self-involved narrative skitter along for three minutes without interrupting. Until he returned to the Continental Regent hotel. That was the story I wanted.

"Did you see anyone noteworthy in the lobby when you got back?"

"Noteworthy? You mean, like famous? Like a celebrity?"

"Like people you or I know."

"Oh." He deflated, then dug up the reply. "I did see that awful thing from the university. You know, the girl with the shrieking red hair."

"Sarah Anastos?"

"Yeah, that's the one. When she turned up an hour later to meet us in the bar, I was shocked."

"Why shocked?"

"Because she looked totally different."

"How?"

"When I saw her at six in the hotel lobby, she was dressed like a street orphan. Filthy black t-shirt with threads dangling over her stomach. Torn black leggings for that spider-on-a-web look. And those godawful black sandals with thick cork soles and two leather straps. You know, the clunky ones teachers and hippies wear. The girl looked pathetic."

"But when she joined us in the bar, she wore silver spike heels and fancy satin pants," I said.

"I know! Right? High glam! How she found the time to clean up her act, I can't imagine. But thank God, she did!"

I figured Sally Anastos had pulled the quick-change stunt with clothes stashed in the hotel. Had she stored an overnight bag with a friend at the convention? I nominated her idol Gerry Keith for the honor, but didn't share my guess with Rick. If Sally was sharing a room with Keith, did that eliminate the possibility he had slept with Annie before she died?

Wound up about the Anastos clothing disaster, Luna rattled on. "I suppose the man she was talking with in the lobby didn't care what she looked like. He seemed totally into her even if she dressed like the inside of a trash can."

"Who was Sally talking to?"

"How do I know? Never saw the poor fool before or since."

"What did he look like?"

"Look like? He was another academic type, like her. Short, pale, and spotty. Wire-rim glasses, stringy brown hair, and a poser beard."

For sure, not the elegant Gerry Keith. "Could you catch what they were saying?"

"Catch? As easy as catching the clap in high school. They were shouting. Not screaming, but almost. He wanted her to come with him. She wanted to stay at the hotel. He grabbed her wrist; she jerked away. He grabbed again. She pushed."

"Any names?"

"I heard her say, 'Piss off, Colin.' But that's all."

During our lunch after Keith's brilliant lecture, Sally had mentioned plans to meet a colleague named Colin Spiegel. Could there be two academics in New York with that hybrid name? Had to be the same man.

As Rick Luna wound down, his doubts revved up. "Why are you so interested in that chick? She's like the dictionary definition of loser. Steer clear, dude."

I laughed at his theory. "I have zero designs in that direction, Rick. None."

"Glad to hear it. You deserve better. You'll get better. Hang in there." He coughed; I coughed. My bruised heart was off limits, so he switched subjects. "We've got a full plate for the next few months. Including opening that new office in Hialeah. Lots to plan, lots to coordinate."

I signed off thirty seconds later, sending sympathy and good wishes to everyone at Rook Cleaning Services. I'd meant to ask him if he'd slept with Annie. Pin down exactly how much he'd stolen from me. But I let it slide. If Rick Luna could pardon my slap, I could forgive his loving Annie. I felt better. Mercy flowing in two directions, just like Pearl predicted.

———————

A shower and a roast beef sandwich fueled my mental script for the call to Colin Spiegel. Disguise was essential to my plan, so I scrounged in the junk drawer next to the sink for an old burner phone. The cell had belonged to Andre the pickpocket. When I blocked his most recent heist, I boosted the phone. Andre didn't complain about the theft; I like to think he appreciated the irony.

The NYU website revealed Spiegel's office phone number after eight minutes of searching. He answered on the second ring.

I pictured him crouched over his desk waiting for the antique landline to connect him with the outside world. Books and journals dangled from dusty cases piled to the ceiling. Stacks of papers, charts, binders, newspapers, envelopes, and shredded magazines clogged the surface of a tiny desk. Crusty mugs crammed with pencils, pens, letter openers, and lip balm anchored each corner of the desk. More towers of books teetered on either side of the door. Maybe Colin Spiegel was a sleek modernist, his office a bare temple to efficiency. But that's not how I imagined him.

My intro was syrupy, thick with a Texas twang I'd abandoned when I left the army. "Dr. Spiegel, I'm so pleased to reach you. I need a few minutes of your time this afternoon. I serve on a selection committee for an important academic fellowship and I'm delighted to inform you your name is on the long list for final consideration. At this stage, we are undertaking preliminary phone interviews with the candidates, confirming basic data that will be used as we narrow our search. Do you have a few minutes?"

I rushed through several more paragraphs of multisyllable words after Colin agreed to the interview. As I'd figured, the thrill of being selected for a money-bearing honor pushed practical questions from his brain. He never asked me for the name of the grant. Or even for my name. The night we met, Sally Anastos had said the slogan of every academic was, "What's in it for me?" That cynical motto certainly applied to her friend Colin Spiegel.

After we'd established that he'd been born in New Haven and raised by a single mother who worked as a secretary at Yale, Colin listed his educational credentials. Wesleyan, great. Columbia, terrific. I hummed in admiration, making sure the scratch of my pencil could be heard through the phone.

Then I pressed for home: "You have several impressive recommendations in your file, Dr. Spiegel. In one of the strongest, the author describes her collaboration with you on several research projects."

"Oh, that must be Sarah Anastos. We've worked together quite a bit over the past few years."

Bingo. Got him in one. "You understand, I'm not supposed to reveal the names of the writers of these recommendations. Confidentiality rules are important to our process. But I won't deny your guess."

"Sarah is a wonderful girl. A great colleague. I'm not surprised to learn she's plugging for me."

"How do you know Dr. Anastos? If I might ask."

"Shared Connecticut background to begin with. Hardscrabble like me."

"She grew up in New Haven with you?"

"No, her dad ran a Greek restaurant in Bridgeport. Four kids: three girls, one boy. Sarah was the first in her family to finish college. Her baby brother's just started at Alexander this fall."

"An admirable achievement indeed."

"Sure was. With her doctoral studies underway, Sarah had it made. The word 'superstar' was invented to describe someone with her talent and drive. The whole world was hers, like a highway blazing before her, no barriers in sight..." Spiegel's voice drifted into a sigh.

"What happened? A roadblock?"

"Yeah, she met a diversion, a detour. That's what."

I figured he meant Gerry Keith, but I wouldn't offer the name. No leading the witness. My prompt stayed vague: "Sarah changed?"

"You better believe it. When I first met her, she was this sweet kid from the sticks. Affectionate, lively. Hard-charging for sure, but compelling. She had a firecracker mind sparking with creativity and wit. She was fun, the brightest woman I'd ever known. Then she chopped her hair." His voice darkened over the last phrase. "And everything changed."

"Her hair?"

No chance to stop his rant now. Not that I wanted to. "Yeah. Sarah had this gorgeous brown hair, dark waves down her back. I used to tease that she could tuck the braid into the waistband of her jeans, that's how long it was. Then one day she cut it off. All of it. Down to a few curls and some stubble around the ears. And dyed it a hideous shade of red. She was so proud of the new look, said it was an expression of her true self, the self she'd suppressed all these years."

"That's quite a turn around."

"No kidding. The new red-headed Sarah wanted nothing to do with her old friends. Especially, not me. Even last week we argued about it again. I met her for coffee at a hotel. She was attending a conference there, so she fit me in between sessions. I asked her why she was wasting time and money on a fancy conference when it wasn't even an academic meeting. Just a bunch of pretentious capitalist fat cats. She wasn't presenting an academic research paper or moderating a panel. There was no professional pay-off for her. Sarah said she didn't care what I thought, this conference was her break-out moment and she wanted to savor it."

"She certainly had changed, as you put it."

"I don't... I don't know why I'm telling you all this. It's not relevant to anything. I've really gotten off topic. You're an excellent listener. What did you say your field was?" I could hear a fingernail scraping over his beard as he scrambled to salvage our conversation.

"One of the best parts of this job is getting to know the brightest young lights in the field." I laid it on thick, but maybe my flattery would calm his worries.

"I hope this doesn't sway your report to the grant committee. The committee's views of me or of Sarah's letter shouldn't be affected by this. I hope this private communication stays between us."

"You have my word on it, Dr. Spiegel. I won't share what you've said with anyone."

"Thank you for your understanding, Doctor…um, what did you say your name was?"

"Thomas Dray. *D.R.A.Y.*" I counted on his ignorance of hip-hop's storied past to carry me over this hump.

"Thank you, Dr. Dray. It's been a pleasure speaking with you." No teeth gritted in sarcasm. His voice rose in non-ironic waves of gratitude. "I wish the committee well as its deliberations move forward. What's your timetable for announcing the grant awards?"

"We expect to wrap up deliberations in a few weeks. The board insists we deliver our selections before the end of the semester."

"An ambitious schedule, for sure. Well, good luck, Dr. Dray."

"Thank you. We'll need it."

I hung up and stroked my right cheek, then the left. Bullshitting on such a massive scale was exhausting. My jaw ached from the stress; shards of pain skittered along my neck to collide between my shoulder blades. I rotated each tense arm, fists poking the air above my head. Walking to the kitchen, I flexed both biceps, then unleashed a flurry of punches into an imaginary speed bag in front of the fridge. I reheated a cup of coffee in the microwave and downed the muck in two gulps.

My talk with love-sick Colin Spiegel left me dry and dispirited. But I'd gotten what I wanted. The information about Sally Anastos's transformation from dutiful drudge to high priestess in the cult of Keith was useful. Figuring out how this fit together would require a one-on-one match with Sally.

# CHAPTER
# TWELVE

Dr. Swann paid the Ross Agency for my first rescue of Carolyn Wiley. A hefty sum, according to Brina. But he didn't pay for the next two. Those rescues were on my own tab. Darrell Peete called me twice. On the first afternoon trip to Carolyn's former house, I found her perched at the top of the stairs, bony fingers drumming her knees, restless eyes sweeping the sidewalk. A full-blown family reunion, she greeted me with unbridled joy. I was her prodigal son, Carl, home from a slog at the law firm.

The second time Darrell called, change roughened his voice. "Sorry to bug you again, Rook." He hacked deep in his throat, then blurted the rest. "But I thought you'd want to know about this."

"Is it Mrs. Wiley? Has she wandered to the house again? Give me a minute to borrow a car and I'll pick her up as soon as I can."

I gulped the bourbon I'd ordered at Zarita's Bar, my weekday afternoon haunt. I dropped a ten on the counter to cover this drink and the one I'd have tomorrow. Trotting toward the door, I pressed the phone to my ear. Darrell Peete's hesitation garbled his words.

"No, no. It's...well, this time we found her inside the apartment we been remodeling. I mean... well, I don't much like talking about it on the phone. When you get here, you can see for yourself."

Carolyn was nowhere in sight when I jumped from the Honda. Darrell waved me to a spot behind his white van. "Thanks for coming, Rook. We didn't know how to handle this."

He led me to the curb side of the panel truck and snatched open the sliding door. Inside, Carolyn Wiley crouched on the middle bench, fingers clamped around her knees. She wore the same pink seersucker dress as when we first met. Her hair stood from the crown of her head like a rooster's comb. Black soot singed the tips of the white spikes. Brick red smeared from her cheekbone to the corner of her mouth. Her hands were covered in the same brick dust.

I set a calm cadence, as if we'd met for a picnic in the park. "Mrs. Wiley, good to see you again." Slow drawl, bright smile. I leaned into the van until my face pressed close to hers.

Though I'd used her title, she reverted to her old name for me. "Carl, you took so long today." Reproach snapped at my conscience. "I expected you to help me look."

"Look for what?" I couldn't call her mother, or mama, or mom. Whatever endearment Carl may have used stuck in my craw. I wouldn't push the theatre that far.

Darrell tugged on my sleeve. I stood next to the open vehicle, my eyes on Carolyn. The foreman whispered behind a calloused hand. "We found her inside the basement. On her knees, scraping at the floor next to the brick wall. Pulling flakes of paint from the brick."

"Did she say why?" The image of the old woman scrabbling in the debris sent shivers racing along my shoulders. "What was she looking for?"

"Never got that much sense out of her. Took two of the boys to haul her out of there." Darrell polished sweat from his forehead with his bare hand. "Never figured a skinny little bird like that had so much fight in her."

"Fight?"

"That's just how it happened. She opened a nasty rip in Jermaine's cheek." He pointed to the pick-up where his crew huddled. A slash of scarlet glared against a young man's brown skin. "We finally wrestled her into the van and fastened the seat belt around her. She quieted down then." The foreman shook his head and scratched the wool under his helmet. "That's when I called you. She's been muttering to herself ever since."

"Let me talk to her. Then I'll take her home." I nodded at Peete, then turned toward the vehicle's open door.

I leaned in again, left foot on the ground, right knee on the van's floor next to the bench. I squeezed Carolyn's bony ankle to get her attention. She lifted her head like it was a cannon ball. When her bleary eyes focused on mine, I relaunched our theatre. "Where you looking for something in there? Can I help you find it?"

The grin glowed from her battered face. "Yes, Carl. That's what I've been trying to tell you. I lost my bracelet in there. My braid's in there too." She stroked the short feathers at the back of her head. "But it's the bracelet I need. I must have it back. You can help, I know you can."

"I can try. Tell me what it looks like." Imaginary, but if I played along, she'd stay docile.

"You remember it, Carl. Fancy Byzantine links in silver with a small lobster clasp. Your father gave it to me for our fifteenth wedding anniversary, just after your twelfth birthday. Beautiful thing. I said it was too heavy, too ornate. But he insisted I wear it."

The detail of her description threw me. The jewelry sounded real. "And now you've lost the bracelet?"

"Yes, down in the basement. Look next to the brick wall. It's bound to be there."

"Let's get you home."

"But the bracelet…"

"I'll look for it after you're settled in your room." I stiffened my voice to a command register. "I can't start looking for the bracelet until you're safe at home."

"It won't be hard to find, Carl. You'll see it."

"The more we delay here, the longer it'll be until I can return to search." I unfastened the seat belt from her sunken waist and she raised her arms to my neck. I carried her to my car and drove to the Swann Center.

———————

Soothing the nerves of the skittish center staff took thirty minutes. I spent forty-five more listening to Dr. Swann babble about the security measures he intended to establish next week. More nurses and attendants, a night guard, new electronic locks, bars on the windows and iron grills on the doors. High style prison décor. By the time I escaped it was past eight. I steered the Honda four times around the block of the Wiley house before I made up my mind.

There was something worth looking for in the neglected rubble of that basement. Something shrouded in Carolyn Wiley's addled mind. Maybe a fancy silver bracelet. Maybe a plaited rope of white hair. Maybe something more significant. I'd find it. For Carolyn. For myself.

# CHAPTER
# THIRTEEN

Shadows from dusty trees cooled the street. Darrell Peete and his team had retired for the night, leaving a spot for me where their white van had stood. I sat for ten minutes until the last gossiping neighbors retreated indoors and I had the block to myself.

Exploring this house pulled at a dangerous streak in me. For several days, I'd wanted to see inside Carolyn Wiley's obsession. What drew her to this old pile, years after she and her family moved away? She couldn't invite me in, she didn't own the place anymore. But her eager story of the vanished bracelet gave me an opening. Maybe she had lost jewelry in this basement. If I could find her precious bangle, maybe I'd restore calm to her agitated mind. This was breaking and entering, no doubt. But it was crime for a good cause. Backed by Dr. Swann's support, I hoped, I'd square it with the cops if necessary.

The rusty hinges of the iron picket fence creaked as I opened the gate. I crept down two steps to the brick patio in front of the basement windows. A black-and-white tuxedo cat hissed from the stone threshold under the main staircase, then slunk away as I took its place. Shadows canopied the basement door, turning its berry red paint to burgundy. Pedestrians at street level wouldn't see me work the flimsy latch. I didn't own a regulation pick-lock kit, but my metal nail file and debit card met the task. With the apartment empty, neither the owners nor the construction crew had bothered to install a serious bolt against burglars.

Inside the basement, I paused at the shoulder-height windows to survey the room. The floor plan was simple: an unobstructed space running from the front living area to what would be the kitchen. Frail moonbeams filtered past oily glass and iron bars printing a stark pattern on the floor. Rubble -- wood laths, plaster, brick, wire, and rebar -- stretched in irregular clumps from the entrance to the rear wall. The air was dense, still, and cool, like stepping into a bank vault. White plasterboard covered three vertical surfaces–the wall behind me, the long wall to the left, and the far wall where a short run of steps rose to the backyard. On the right, the white sheetrock had been stripped to reveal a brick wall.

According to Darrell the foreman, Carolyn Wiley had been digging at the base of this brick wall. Ruddy powder smeared her hands and face when I spoke with her in the van. That brick wall was the place she'd looked for her bracelet. So that's where I started my search.

The wall was fourteen feet long but its texture changed two-thirds of the way down its run. The majority of the brick was fixed ceiling to floor with mortar. I tapped my file against a few junctures to test their soundness; they held, no chips or flakes fell. I side-stepped along the wall, tapping until I located a quirk. A five-foot stretch was built from bricks stacked without mortar. In this section, the bricks balanced against each other, their weight alone holding them in place. I studied the floor next to this section. Red dust and paint flakes swirled among stray bricks at the base of this wall. Smudged indentations in the dust could be knee prints. Maybe this was where Carolyn had knelt to scrabble for her bracelet.

I crouched beside the wall, poking at the bricks. The first six held tight. The seventh moved. I pushed until it yielded, falling inward to a hidden space. I heaved bricks until I'd punched a hole fourteen inches square. Black behind the wall revealed nothing. I switched on my phone's flashlight. I shoved my right hand through the opening, waving the beam. I pressed one eye to the hole, scanning the light's arc. Silver flashed, then disappeared. I steadied my hand and looked again. The cool metal wink of silver repeated. This was what I wanted: Carolyn's lost bracelet.

I slipped the phone into my pocket and dislodged six more bricks, laying them on the floor at my toes. I knelt to press my chest against the wall, plunging arm and shoulder through the hole. The moldy stench of decay crept past my sleeve. My fingers touched more debris. I felt crumbled brick, gritty cloth, plasterboard slabs, powder. The sharp edge of a tool, maybe a spade or trowel. No bracelet. I withdrew my arm and looked again. The glint of silver teased from the left quadrant of the black space. I knew where to fish. I bent the metal prong from my ballpoint pen into a hook and thrust my arm again. Four blind casts until the hook caught. Metal clinked against metal. I had the bracelet.

I tugged; the hook slid, then jammed. Another pull, the bracelet budged. A third yank broke the resistance. My feet skidded. I fell back; my arm jerked through the hole in the wall. Another arm – all bones – flew toward me. A skeletal wrist cuffed with a silver band. White bones dangled from my fist. I lay flat on my back. Puffs of dust swirled above my mouth. The bones swung over my face. I saw little fingers with delicate knuckles; tendons of plaster linked these slender pickets to the fragile wrist. Above that joint, white bones ended in a jagged break. The hand hovered on my chest, a birdcage balanced on white claws. I flinched; the cage collapsed. Chalk dashed against my black t-shirt. The bracelet skittered to rest over my heart. It was a simple silver bangle, smooth under its film of powder. Not the complicated chain of Carolyn Wiley's distorted memory.

I knelt at the wall again. I pressed my face to the opening to scan the dark tomb beyond the bricks.

---

Police arrived six minutes after I dialed 911. Reporting discovery of a human skeleton sets a fire under the cops. Eight minutes later four squad cars were angled next to Brina's Honda, their blue lights flashing across the shadowed trees lining the street. An ambulance straddled the sidewalk, its open rear door rammed against the iron picket fence in front of the basement apartment.

I couldn't fade from the drama or play fake curious neighbor. I told the first officer on the scene what I'd found. "Yes. The skeleton was behind the brick wall... Curled like a sleeping child in the crawl space... I pulled out just enough bricks that I could see it—I didn't want to disturb it further. No, it wasn't a body... A skeleton...just bones with clothing. That's how I knew it was human. From the clothes." My lips hitched over my teeth, the basement funk still sour in my nostrils.

Eyebrows raised, he looked a question. No words could tamp the dense stink of that closet. Or block the mildewed fumes invading my eyes. I shook my head, tongue stuck to the roof of my mouth.

Sweat plastered the cop's forelock on his face. Below green eyes, more sweat smeared on his upper lip. "You only got a look, but any ideas on who that skeleton might be? Anything you could tell from the clothing? Any jewelry or wallet or ID?"

"I couldn't see a wallet. The only jewelry was a silver bracelet on the wrist. The skeleton was wearing a yellow sweater and blue jeans. There was a braided leather belt too. The yellow sweater had a pattern on it. Maybe ducks or clouds."

His eyes popped. "You figure it might be a woman or a girl? Don't know any real man would wear a fruity sweater like that."

"Maybe."

Carolyn Wiley was incidental to the story, an old lady I tried to help recover lost jewelry. I kept her name out of my account. My case, not his business. He didn't ask the basic question of why I was snooping in the vacant apartment. If he was too spooked by my discovery to ask the fundamentals, I wasn't going to volunteer information. When he'd finished jotting in his notebook, I gave the officer my card. I took a spot on the curb opposite the house. Concerned, cooperative, but under the radar was my role.

Whispering neighbors stood in clutches of three and four along the curb. A man sidled toward me. He wore a soiled undershirt, baggy track pants, and blue bandanna knotted over his scalp. "Hey, bro, what's going on? You got any idea?"

120

"Not much. They found a body in the basement. The crawl space."
I skipped my role in the story.

"You mean, like a junkie or something? Too many of them bums and bangers infesting our neighborhood."

"Don't know. It was a skeleton, not a fresh body."

The man shook his head to erase the grim images of death and decay scampering across his mind. "Bad news. I figure no way a person could be in that crawl space for legit reasons. Had to be some business on the wrong side of the law, any way you cut it. The owners are still up in Martha's Vineyard or wherever, on vacation. I guess the cops'll get around to calling 'em."

As the man finished his speculation, metallic scraping and rough shouts drew our attention to the death house. A gaggle of police technicians in dark blue wrangled a gurney through the basement door. They hauled it up the two steps to the street. A lump on the stretcher was zipped into a black body bag.

The swollen bump was small and misshapen, like a chimp or a broken doll. Nothing human left. These forlorn remains, the gurney, the police swarm, everything reminded me of Annie. Five days gone now. Even as they'd shuttled her corpse from the hotel, she'd retained the warmth, contours, and substance of the living woman. Annie smelled like Annie, even in death. But this skeleton was a jumble of bones, less a person than scattered fragments of an idea. Where was the humanity in this pile's diminished and undignified form? A shudder rippled across my neck.

My nosy sidekick turned, worry etched on his face. "You okay, bro? This city supposed to be tough and hard. But seeing a dead body's always gonna shock, right?"

"Yes, always." Murder wasn't my beat. Never would be. No explanation, just fact.

The man glanced at me, then passed his hand over his nose, like I exhaled plague. To cover, he pointed at the uniformed parade across the street. Each officer carried a clear plastic sack of clothing. One evidence bag caught the eye of my new pal. "Lookit that! Them's a nice pair of black high-top sneakers. You know, old-school cool kicks, Nikes maybe. How much you wanna bet those shoes never make it to the precinct. End up on the feet of some cop's kid. Trust and believe. They gonna be stole."

I tipped my chin, but didn't take the cynical bet. There was nothing more I could gather at this somber scene. And nothing more I could give. The police would question the home owners and neighbors. They'd check dental records and descriptions from missing persons reports. They'd dig up cold case murder files, open investigations, and inquiries from other jurisdictions.

The coroner's report would give an indication of time and cause of death. Forensic reconstruction would yield the gender, age, and physical description of the dead person. The cops might float background scraps to reporters. A news story could generate clues from a curious public to help identify the skeleton. Harvesting current gossip for intel on past crimes was a trick the cops played to perfection. I'd leave them to their scavenger hunt.

I had two hunches I wanted to pursue beyond police scrutiny. Carolyn Wiley knew the house, maybe she knew something relevant to this strange death. Through the haze of damaged memory, she accepted me as her trusted son. Our fragile connection might let me push further than obtuse cops could. I'd inform them about Carolyn if necessary. Otherwise, I wanted to keep her out of the investigation.

First, I had to probe the awful meaning of the skeleton's yellow sweater. Norment Ross's old photo of his family held the clue. I knew he could identify the lost woman in the wall. I dreaded burrowing into Norment's past again. He'd shared his painful stories to help me. More prying now seemed grisly. But I needed those answers before launching a dangerous expedition to dig up Carolyn Wiley's buried memories.

# CHAPTER
# FOURTEEN

My hunch played as I'd feared.

The morning after the police unearthed the mystery skeleton, I shared my insights with Norment Ross in his office. I described the house and reminded him of my connection to it through the wandering Mrs. Wiley. Not wanting to lead Norment to false conclusions, I didn't volunteer a description of the skeleton. I dropped an open-ended question, hoping the facts wouldn't match my gruesome discovery: "What do you remember about the clothes Dreamie wore the last time you saw her?"

He leaned forward, elbows planted on his desk. "Well, that'd be more than twenty-five years ago. But here's what I recall. Dreamie liked to wear blue jeans. I'd always tease her and call them 'dungarees,' like we do in Charleston. She claimed they were in style, but they looked kinda low-class to me." Fond smiles flickered across his face. "Anyway, that's what she was wearing the last time I saw her, blue jeans and her braided leather belt. And I know she had a sweater, 'cause of the cool weather. Probably yellow, 'cause she favored that color. She had so many tops and blouses in yellow. I told her that shade of bright yellow made her face glow like the sun." More smiles and a pause. I figured he was trying to delay asking why I was so interested in the clothing. "I guess that's why she wore so much of it. I wouldn't swear to it, but I think she was wearing a sweater like the one in that photo I showed you. That's all I got, Rook. Blue jeans and a yellow sweater. Does that mean something to you?"

"Yes, it does." No sugar-coating the truth. He deserved to learn what I knew. "Norment, did Dreamie wear a silver bracelet?"

"Always. I gave it to her the day after Sabrina was born. Nothing fancy. Plain silver was all I could afford. But Dreamie wore that bangle every day. Why?"

"I think the woman they found is Dreamie."

He sighed, two gut-deep torrents of sorrow, but he didn't weep. His eyes narrowed, the dark lids clamping over pulsing strings of red around the pupils. I held my breath, wanting my guess to be wrong.

When he spoke, Norment sounded more surprised than pained. "So that's where she's been all these years. Holed up in a house ten blocks from me. All these years of searching and fretting. Wishing and hoping. Come to find out she's been just ten blocks away the whole time."

Tears came later. Norment asked me to accompany him to the coroner's office downtown to identify the remains and view the clothing. He didn't call her Dreamie. Or his wife. Just "that poor woman." Maybe he hoped if he didn't say the name out loud, the truth would stay buried. He didn't want Brina to go with him. Digging up the past was a man's job, not a daughter's, he said. These first moments with his lost wife belonged to him alone. He'd break the news to Brina at a better time and place.

———

We sat side-by-side at a metal table in a small conference room with beige walls and scuffed linoleum tiles. A clear plastic bag lay flattened in front of us. A young white cop, R. Salton according to his name tag, sat opposite, his square fingers drumming the table. The cop shoved the bag toward Norment. Salton glanced past our shoulders toward the two-way mirror behind us. This interrogation room was designed to extract the truth and we were subjects of the latest experiments. They were using the soft approach on us. Salton's doughy face folded in a half-smile. His pity thickened into soup around us.

The ziplocked sack contained jeans and a yellow sweater, white tube socks, flowered panties, and a white bra. Black blotches stained the braided belt. Tiny bites frayed its leather. As predicted, the black Nike sneakers hadn't made it to the evidence lock-up. No silver bracelet either. The cop removed the items one by one. Brown, green, and gray mildew stains marred each piece. Rodents had gnawed everywhere. The moldy clothing reeked of neglect or absence. Each item had been folded with care. The package wasn't bulky once the bag was punched down and the rank cellar air expelled.

In answer to Salton's questions, Norment identified the clothing as belonging to his wife, Jayla Dream Ross. The cop led him through a point-by-point recital of that painful history. Norment outlined the last day he'd seen his wife: the breakfast they'd eaten, his drive to the office, his return home in the evening. He described what Dreamie looked like, how tall she was, what she'd worn that last morning. He explained how he'd searched for her and how he'd given up hope. As Norment talked, the cop grunted over a narrow spiral pad, scribbling notes with a leaky ballpoint. Ink blotches soiled the words. Finished with questions, Salton planted his fist on a yellow legal pad and shoved it across the table. He pushed the pen with his fingernail. Salton said Norment had to write his story, then sign to make everything official. Torture prolonged. I objected, but Norment seized the legal pad and produced his own ballpoint. He took up the task without complaint. Clean words on a clean page mattered.

When he was done writing, Norment asked if he could take home his wife's clothing. The officer shook his head; it was evidence in an on-going investigation into a suspicious death and had to remain in police custody. Salton's voice was flat and slow, as if this routine bored him. As if he'd spent every day of his brief career telling dim-witted husbands their lost wives were dead. Norment could have demanded professional courtesy, cop to PI, crime-fighter to detective, neighbor to neighbor. Something to smooth over this saw-toothed indifference. But he held his tongue and grimaced sideways to shut me up.

Norment's last question was the simplest: had Dreamie been murdered? Sticking to the rules, Salton declined to characterize the death beyond calling it suspicious. The cop clomped from the room, leaving us alone with the evidence bag. Maybe he went behind the two-way mirror, spying to make sure our grief was real.

I refolded each item into neat squares and slipped them into the plastic bag. Panties, bra, sunny yellow sweater, shredded jeans. Pathetic little souvenirs from a lost life. As I moved my fingers over the clothing, a spray of confetti fell from the dank creases. The minute flakes were dark blue and rigid, like flecks of paint. Two of the shavings stuck to the moisture on the tip of my index finger. The lacquer was shiny and thick. Maybe these flakes were residue from wall paint. Maybe from another source. Had the walls of the basement room where Dreamie was buried been painted blue? I angled my body so the movements of my right hand were hidden from the spying cops behind the two-way mirror. I scooped a sample of the blue confetti under my nail and transferred that hand to my pocket where I flicked the shavings into the collection of lint and stray dimes. I collected three samples of the blue flakes. They glittered like iridescent scales from a tiny tropical fish. I wanted to know what these chips meant.

When I'd finished returning the folded things to the evidence bag, I pushed it toward Norment. He pressed both hands on the bag covering his wife's clothes. Then he laid his head on the plastic and kissed its cold surface. The plastic crackled under his touch, air hissing from a hidden hole. As I rubbed his shoulders, Norment wept for his Dreamie, gone twenty-five years. Annie had been dead six days.

Our return train ride to Harlem was the longest forty minutes I'd ever endured.

# CHAPTER
# FIFTEEN

I was bad at receiving comfort and not much better at giving it.

I tried to console Brina in the hours after Norment broke the news to her of the discovery of her mother's body. My afternoon phone call caught her in the car. "You going to be at home tonight? I can drop by. If you want."

"That's okay. Thanks." I heard the sniffle as she gunned the engine. "I'm heading to Daddy's place now. Probably spend the night on his couch."

"You'll be together then. That's good." I hesitated as she coughed. Plunging on was the best I could do. "If you want anything. Call me. Anything." I didn't know how to fit into her life. Or if she even needed me to. And she wasn't offering clues.

"Sure. I'll call." Traffic noises surged over her words. I heard car horns, screeching brakes, and angry curses shouted in the silence between us. She muttered, not loud enough for me to catch what she said.

"Brina, is everything okay? What's going on?"

"Some fool in roller skates and gold spandex tried to break the law of gravity in the middle of the intersection."

"You okay?"

"Yeah, he's fine. Two Band-aids will patch him up."

"No. You. Are *you* okay?"

"Sure. I'm doing fine." Briskness returned to her voice, erasing any falter or opening for me to share a consoling word. "Catch you later," she said. She clicked off before I could ask more.

The next morning, rather than dissolving in misery, Brina burrowed into work. Perhaps too much time had elapsed for sorrow to catch hold of her. That motherless past was half her childhood, all her teen and adult years. Or maybe Brina's memories of Dreamie were so faded it was difficult to summon any overt mourning. When I'd met her two years ago, Brina recited the agency's informal motto: "Lots of people go missing in Harlem. We find the ones who want to be found. The rest, well, they stay lost." Maybe that forlorn observation applied to memories as much as people. Perhaps for Brina her mother, and the past they'd shared, was meant to stay lost.

Brina worked with subtle determination to keep her father occupied and distracted. She ate more meals with him, invited him to join our trips around the neighborhood more frequently. She directed more cases toward Norment, even the strenuous tasks she ordinarily would have assigned to me. I couldn't know what father and daughter said to each other in private. Maybe there were more tears behind closed doors. I knew one thing for sure: without a satisfactory resolution to the mystery of how Dreamie ended up buried in that house, the case and the sorrow might be past, but it would never be over. I wanted to deliver that resolution.

———

The second day on the job after the discovery of Dreamie's body began like the one before: bleak and silent.

I sat in my office, fiddling with old files, scratching words on creased index cards. I thumbed through email to delete time-share pleas, online gambling opportunities, and offers to save my immortal soul with vegan supplements. Greasy smells from the restaurant below seeped through the floorboards to blend with the exhaust fumes from the street beyond the window. Squeaking of a desk drawer announced Brina's arrival in the outer office. She didn't stick her head in to greet me. I let her be.

After an hour, the silence grew oppressive, like the vague drone of distant lawn mowers. I left my office carrying a mug to pretend I was in search of more coffee. Brina wasn't at her desk near the front door. When I reached the break room, I heard the rush of water in the bathroom. The roar was dull but furious, not a drip from the sink or the urgent whirl of the toilet. The shower was gushing in breakneck clamor.

I could have burst in, but uncertainty made me waver. When the water stopped, I leaned against the wall opposite the bathroom door. Brina would dress, emerge in a few minutes, and we'd talk then. I gripped my mug, ready with a joke and an excuse. After three minutes, she didn't come out; another minute and she still hadn't moved inside the bathroom. Long enough. I knocked once, then shoved into the answering silence.

Clothes were heaped on the floor below the white porcelain pedestal sink. Her black bra and panties draped over the closed lid of the toilet seat. I sat the cup on the edge of the sink and flung aside the white plastic curtain. Brina was standing naked in the shower stall.

"You okay?" I could see she wasn't, but I asked anyway. As if this was an ordinary exchange rather than an invasion. Or an intervention.

She didn't answer. Below dripping lashes, her eyes narrowed, then caught mine. They sparked bright, but as purposeless as the ocean surf. I reached for her hand and pulled. She had to step across the raised lip of the stall to keep her balance.

When she squared before me, I tried again. "Let me help, Brina."

Water cascaded down her body onto the black-and-white penny tiles. She shivered, sending drops from her shoulders to my shirt front.

"I don't know what to do." The voice squeezed through her teeth in a whimper. "What am I supposed to do for Daddy now?"

I grabbed four green towels from a stack on the wire shelf beside the sink. They were skimpy and rough, only hand sized. Good enough. I patted water from her face and neck, taking care to run a corner of the first towel into the angles beside both eyes. The next two towels I dragged down her breasts and stomach, then her legs. I dropped the cloths on the floor to soak up the puddle. Another towel to dry her back. But water from her drenched hair continued to stream down the canal of her spine.

"There, all dry now, Brina." Kindergarten teacher language. Or nurse-style baby talk. "Let's get you dressed."

She snatched a look in the mirror over the sink. The crease flickering between her brows registered puzzlement, not alarm. As if she wasn't supposed to be here, wet and naked. Gripping my biceps, she balanced on one foot then the other to pull her panties over her hips. She snapped on the bra without help. I picked up her loose cream-colored pants. They had a paisley pattern in yellow and black. To put those on, she sat on the covered toilet seat. She crumpled the yellow t-shirt into a ball in her lap. Bold yellow; Dreamie's favorite color.

"I'm too wet." A wail shuddered through her words. "Wet all over."

"Okay, let me help." I edged around until I was behind her. I raked my fingers through the mop of her hair, untangling curls as I went. I dabbed a towel in a circle around her head from ear to ear, then from brow to nape. I finger-combed again, laying the black mass over her shoulders. Water dampened her bra straps. In that moment, I'd have surrendered my life to ease her suffering. "Baby, it's alright. You're alright. You're safe. I got you."

She shivered again, the words falling in a torrent: "I didn't think I'd miss Dreamie. I hardly remember her. She's just a vague profile from the past. A departed shadow. That's what I thought. But now I know she's dead, I can't stop thinking about her." Her lips pulled away from her teeth, a spasm that carved deep lines around her mouth. Her eyelids froze over huge pupils.

"That's okay, Brina. You should think about her. She's your mother." I wanted comfort to slide from my puny words into her heart.

White flared around the pupils; the whites of her molars blazed too. "But I never really knew her. We just had a few years. So long ago it shouldn't even count, right?"

Brina shivered again. Maybe from cold, maybe from the past crowding into the little room with us. Pops spouted from her lips. She wanted to talk. I stood behind her, a hand on her head, as she continued. "I never had anyone to look toward as a model. To learn how to be a woman. Not really. I'm pretty good at being a daughter by now." She laughed, the bitter croak reverberating against the tiled walls. "I stayed in this job, being a good daughter to Norment long past the expiration date. But it's all I know how to do. So, I stuck with it. Never moved on."

I didn't have words for relief, or explanation, or understanding. Nothing came. I pressed my palm against her scalp. She pushed her head into my hand, the way a cat does when it wants you to go on petting it.

I kept stroking as she talked. "If I knew how to be a daughter, maybe I could have figured the right way to be a grown woman too. Maybe even a mother, when the time came. But I never had the chance to learn." A sigh curbed the rant. Then, with a shudder, she continued. "You know, Dreamie never wanted me. She didn't choose me. I was a mistake, an accident. I was a slip-up. I just arrived. Plagued her every day for ten years. Then Dreamie disappeared. I sent her away and she disappeared."

That was wrong. I wanted her to see how mistaken she was. I gripped both shoulders to seize her focus: "No, Brina. You didn't cause Dreamie to go away."

Brina shook her head, then stroked her cheek. "I did it. She slapped me, hurt my face. And my feelings. She didn't choose me. So, I wanted her gone. Wished for it. Prayed for it. And two months later–*poof*–she vanished." She flicked water into the air. A few droplets brushed my face.

"You were only ten, Brina. Just a little girl. Kids think in magical terms. Imagine they have special powers. But you didn't cause your mother to leave. She did it on her own."

I wasn't sure Dreamie's disappearance was voluntary, but I said it anyway. I wanted Brina to understand she wasn't to blame for the loss of her mother. I raked my fingers through her hair again, stroking the damp coils into patterns against her scalp. She raised her right arm. A red elastic band squeezed her wrist. I twisted the elastic around her hair, making a loose ponytail at her nape. She drew the yellow t-shirt over her head and finished dressing. Sun yellow, Dreamie's color, the shade of optimism and happy times. The shirt beamed its cheery glow toward Brina's face. She stood before me, looking at her reflection in the mirror over the sink.

I pressed my mouth onto the wet top of her head and hugged her tight to my chest. A brief smile tickled the corners of her lips. Then she patted my hands where they lay on her stomach and pulled away. Another few seconds of silence to gather the wet towels, wipe down the sink and toilet cover. We returned to our desks.

I waited for Brina to join me, ask a question, give an instruction, start a new case. After five minutes of foot-tapping, I crept from my office again. She was sitting at her desk, hands frozen on the keyboard. I went to the breakroom and found a red mug. After filling it from the bathroom sink, I set the water to boil in the microwave. One minute was enough. A dig through cartons in a cabinet yielded a packet of instant oatmeal. Cinnamon and brown sugar. I let the oatmeal flakes drift into the hot water, spoon stirring with a slow beat until the cereal thickened. I splashed French vanilla coffee creamer into the mug. Not milk, but it looked alright.

Brina said nothing when I sat the mug on her desk. She pulled the cup across the blotter, then shifted the spoon in a circle once around the oatmeal. She nodded, then lifted a thumbnail portion of the mush to her lips. Maybe I hadn't baked Brina that fancy layer cake she deserved. But I could do something for her, if she'd let me. Maybe I was more than a dented wreck she'd found crumpled in a ditch, a fix-it project she'd taken on years ago and couldn't find the heart to junk. Maybe in some small, but real way, the shower proved I could matter in her life.

After Brina swallowed a second spoonful of oatmeal, I slipped back to my office. I opened the laptop to see if she'd shoot me a message. Nothing. After three quiet minutes, I pulled a pen knife from the shallow center drawer and attacked the innocent desk top. I scratched at a new letter in my name, working the knife deep into serif flourishes on the B in Shelba. When I was nine, I'd learned the rainy-day basics of carving from my uncle Luis. I had a ways to go before I carved the whole tag into my desk. But my name was emerging from the wood. I flicked the shavings with a thumb, then blew dust from the raw scar to reveal its new curves.

Like the lines of my cobbled name, these two cases from the past would emerge with careful digging. If I was the detective I claimed to be, Dreamie's death was my puzzle to solve. For Brina and her father, this strange death wasn't a derelict notion buried under decades of neglect. Dreamie mattered now. Like Annie.

Now I had a second case from the past. Not abstractions or puzzles, solving these cases could determine my own future. Two women dead, two wives lost. Pieces missing, clues buried. My job was clear: I wanted answers and I'd dig for the results. Even if revealing those shrouded truths caused pain.

I jabbed the tip of my knife into the stained wood again. There was a third woman, living but trapped by her past. I needed answers from Carolyn Wiley too. I thrust the blade against the grain; a new splinter, fresh and pale, jumped across the desk.

# CHAPTER
# SIXTEEN

I'd promised Carolyn Wiley I'd join her for dinner that evening at the Swann Memory Center. I would have cancelled if Brina had asked. But she said no, repeating her quip: "We're a *detective* agency, not a *defective* agency." Coddling, crying, and pity parties were out of bounds.

She drove, dropping me in front of the Striver's Row mansion at five-thirty. Balanced on the drain grate, I bent toward the open window. I meant to offer to stop by her apartment later. But before I could speak, she peeled from the curb. Sometimes our boss-lackey relationship worked like a charm, warding off awkward feelings and smoothing touchy situations. Sometimes the professional distance hurt like a bitch. This evening, it hurt.

I'd hoped my date with Mrs. Wiley would yield a few clues about her past life and current predicament. Maybe even about the skeleton in the basement. I wanted to ask for details about her missing bracelet. And if I could find a graceful way, I wanted to ask how Dreamie might have died in her house. But my plans were derailed.

We were joined at the front desk by her sometime friend, Queen Esther Monroe. I escorted the women into the dining room, both elbows getting a workout holding the ladies upright as we staggered to our table. Carolyn wore a variation on her uniform: this time the shirtdress was turquoise, accented with white pearl buttons. Her subdued outfit gave Queen center stage. She wore red from toe to top: scarlet sweater, pants, and shoes with gold heels. The red baseball cap crammed over her wiry braids was dotted with stars picked out in gold sequins.

Queen was the most exciting feature in the dining room. By far. Ten square tables covered in white linen were set in straight rows around the parquet floor. Only half the tables were occupied. Residents sat in pairs or quartets, some of the men wore three-piece suits, others sported striped pajamas. All the ladies had dressed for dinner like they were going to a prom or a night club. They wore dangling earrings, crimson lips, and slack muscles.

The oak-paneled room was stuffy, no open windows allowed, no air conditioning units in sight. Though the ceiling was high, the two overhead fans dumped hot air onto our scalps in sizeable scoops. After a few minutes I was gasping like a hooked fish flopping on a wooden pier. In sweaty desperation, I undid the top two buttons of my shirt. This drew an approving nod from Queen Esther. She fingered the neck of her red sweater. I was sure she'd have popped a button or two for me if she'd had any.

"Hot enough in here for you, young man?" Queen asked.

"Yes, ma'am. Plenty hot." I swiped perspiration from my hairline. And just for Queen, I fluttered my shirt front to fan air onto my chest. The movement didn't cool either of us.

"Nice! I like that, young man." She batted her sparse eyelashes and tilted closer. Aromas of peony and mothballs rose from her neck.

"Don't start up your nasty teasing again, Queen." Mrs. Wiley used a hatchet-voice to guard the civility of our table. "I didn't invite my guest here for any of your fool nonsense."

Mrs. Wiley had called me Carl when she greeted me in the front hall. As she took my hand and leaned close, she'd twice whispered his name on clove-scented breath: "You came, Carl. I wasn't sure you would. But you came. I'm so happy to see you again, Carl."

But after those first moments, she avoided using her son's name. In Queen's company, I was a favored guest, not a long-absent child. Did Carolyn realize she'd made this switch? Had she suppressed memories of

Carl on purpose? Or were these instinctive impulses that rose to guard her fragile stability? She smiled at me, then tilted her head toward a table near the bowed window dominating the dining room. Like a veteran cardsharp, Carolyn sat with her back to the window, the classic defensive position. She nodded me toward the chair in the middle. Facing the window, Queen squinted in the sunset glare, turning her head from side to side in search of relief. Carolyn smiled as I sat. The arrangement seemed to suit her just fine.

Despite Queen's flirty style, our three-way conversation was as dull as the dinner offering. The bland menu was fixed by a dietician whose previous gig might have been Sing Sing prison. Every food item was gray: charcoal (meat loaf), gravel (mashed potatoes), steel (string beans) or lead (biscuits). All nutritious, all balanced, all dull. Serving restaurant style, two waiters in black and white loomed over our table. Crepe shoes made their movements silent; but their presence felt oppressive.

After thirty minutes of chatter about the weather, flu shots, arthritis, diabetes, heart murmurs, and shingles, I was ready to call it quits. I pushed my chair from the table and planted a hand on either side of the bowl of cement-colored pudding. Sensing my intention, Queen intervened.

"I wonder why *she* spent this entire dinner in the parlor?" Though the question was vague, Queen looked me in the eye. "The least *she* could have done was join us for dessert, don't you think?"

Carolyn crumpled her eyebrows. "Whoever do you mean?"

"I mean his *wife*, of course." Queen jerked her head toward the front hall. "She's been waiting out there in the other room all this time."

Before I could derail the inane conversation, Carolyn grabbed the question. "Yes, dear, what's your wife's name?"

"Annie." I blurted the truth rather than join an argument I'd never win.

"Oh, what a lovely name!" Queen's gummy smile gaped in delight. "A fine, old-fashioned name."

Not to be outdone, Carolyn added, "Yes, I had a cousin named Annie. It's a charming name. Why didn't your wife join us for dinner? We saved a spot for her." She fluttered her thin fingers over the unused fourth place setting at the table. Her keen gaze demanded an answer from me. The right answer.

"Annie said she would wait." I gulped a quarter of the ice water in my glass.

Queen narrowed her eyes and hunched forward. She whispered a juicier breakdown of the situation: "They had a fight, you know. That's why his Annie refuses to come." She sighed at my imagined marital troubles. Heat tingled the ridge of my collarbones, aiming for my ears.

Carolyn rushed to my defense. "All young couples have their squabbles. You know that, Queen. No need to embarrass him over a thing like that." She chirped and cooed as she patted my knuckles. My ears got hotter.

"Well, I hope he knows what to do to set things right." Queen jigged her eyebrows until the bill of her cap bounced.

"Of course, he does, Queen. He's a grown man."

"Grown, maybe. But that don't mean he's educated in the ways of women. Too many men think all they need to make a marriage flower is that spade they got tucked below their belt." Queen smirked, her glance stroking my shirt front, headed south. "I been married forty-four years. And I'm here to say there's some other tools a handyman better use if he wants to do his gardening right."

Carolyn snapped her lips into a tight purse. "Queen, we don't need any of your nasty advice now."

"Not nasty, just practical." The imp glanced at my ears, grinning. "Look at him. Don't he have the prettiest blush? He's a handyman. Knows his way around a lady's garden, don't he? He knows exactly what I'm talking about."

I stuck my hands below the tablecloth and gripped the hem to avoid touching my earlobes.

Carolyn's voice was soothing. "I'm sure he and Annie will make up as soon as they get home tonight."

Queen licked her bottom lip. "You better believe that's true. My grandma always told me, never go to bed angry. But I say, go to bed angry and then rise up satisfied next morning. Satisfaction is what's due. Right, handyman?" With a slurp, she pulled her lip from her gums. And winked.

As our talk skidded into the gutter, Carolyn bent her head toward me, trying to elevate the tone. "You'll look for Annie as soon as we finish dinner, won't you, dear?"

"Yes."

"And you'll settle your squabble?"

"Yes."

"You'll go back to Annie, won't you?"

"Yes." I never meant to admit that out loud. But there it was: in some fantasy alternate time line of my life, I might have gone back to Annie. I closed my eyes as thoughts of Brina in the shower swept through me.

"And you two'll fix your quarrel and everything will be perfect again." Carolyn stated her hope as a certainty. Her blue-flecked lids quivered, coral rushing onto her cheeks as she waited for my answer.

"Yes, it will." At least I'd made her happy.

Carolyn clasped her thin hands and shivered, the shimmy sending tremors across the shoulders of her dress. A fine lace of goosebumps pricked the fawn skin on her arms. She was cold.

Glad for the diversion, I unleashed my manners. "Mrs. Wiley, you're chilled. Can I get you a sweater?"

"Such a gentleman! Yes, please bring my blue cardigan, if you'd be so kind."

"From your room? Sure. Which one is it?"

"Second floor. Room 9. On the left at the top of the stairs. You can't miss it."

I didn't wait for further instructions from Carolyn or an objection from Queen. I jumped from the table. Stretching my legs was good, snooping was required. I was relieved to escape the prying. And the truth-telling. The waiter approaching to clear the dessert dishes might intervene. If he offered to fetch the sweater himself, I'd be blocked. I hustled for the entrance hall and took the wide stairs two at a time.

As Carolyn predicted, finding her room was simple. The upper stories of the mansion were not as gracious in size or appearance as the ground floor. Ceilings were ten feet, no more. All the rooms were angled in cock-eyed fashion. The spaces had been subdivided by a builder driven by profit, not logic or elegance. Short corridors veered around unsettling corners, forest green carpets underfoot, muddy beige walls on all sides. The funhouse effect was amplified by mirrors placed between the doors. Maybe these constant reflections gave residents reinforcement of their identities. See your face, remember your name, recapture your past. The parade of mirrors gave me the willies.

No locks, so I entered Room 9 and closed the door behind me. Carolyn Wiley's furniture was as simple as her dress style. A twin bed with a pink coverlet of tufted cotton. A nightstand with a white-shaded lamp. An oak rocking chair upholstered with a padded seat cushion covered in light blue checks. A shallow closet where she hung her shirt-waist dresses, and a lightweight navy-blue coat, but no sweaters. My mother always said you should fold your knitwear, not hang it, so I looked into the dresser for the cardigans. I found five – pink, navy, green, white, and robin's egg blue.

A white cotton runner covered the dresser. On top of it were family photos. I picked up each silver-framed picture and studied its subjects. At the back of the array was a dim photo of a young couple in formal clothing. Eagle-eyed Carolyn wore her black hair braided into a crown around her head. She was leaning her shoulder into the chest of a stout man with brown curls and light burlap-colored skin to match his wife's. Philip Wiley wasn't smiling, but his cheeks pleated around his eyes and his dark full lips compressed in a sensuous pucker.

In front of this photo were more recent shots. Pictures of the sole product of the Wiley union, the missing son Carl. There was middle-school Carl in a football uniform, chubby and pale, kneeling alone in front of empty stadium seats. Carl in a chocolate brown academic gown for high school graduation. In a maroon gown for college commence-ment, with his foot braced on the bumper of a smoke-blue Buick. And in the crimson gown of the country's most prestigious law school. In this march of accomplishment, Carl never smiled, never unpursed the full dark lips he had inherited from his handsome father.

I picked up another photo of Carl, this time in a family cluster. His weight had congealed into sloppy fat, his scowl into an icy mask.

He was standing in front of a blue Buick. To his left slouched a white woman with curtains of licorice-black hair falling beside her face. In front were their two children: a chubby boy with curly brown hair and a regal stalk of a girl with long legs, sharp cheekbones, and intense eyes. Carl's daughter was an exact replica of her elegant grandmother, Carolyn Wiley.

Scratched on the back of the photo were names: Carl, Maddie, Thornton, Athena. And a date: Seattle, July 2014. The family was stationed in the street on the driver's side of their car. Behind the sleek Buick was a hideous pile of concrete blocks; it looked like Carl Wiley had built his house of frozen cottage cheese.

I turned away from the pictures. If I was going to snoop, I was going to be thorough. I slid open the shallow top drawer of the dresser, the place where women keep their most personal items. I found four plastic laminated IDs Carolyn had used when she served as a librarian and two New York state drivers' licenses. I laid the two cards on the cloth runner next to the silver framed photos. The license with Carolyn's picture had expired in 2001; her son's license had expired in 1994.

Inside the drawer, a thick plait of silver hair coiled in a pink flowered saucer. Carolyn's severed braid looked like a snake at rest. Nestled in the smooth strands was a large silver key. Teeth bristled from both sides of the bold shaft. Silver letters on the leather key fob read "Buick" above the car dealer's name and address. The black tag was frayed on all four sides, the edges curled from wear and stained from sweat. I picked up the key and let the fob dangle against my palm.

Why would Carolyn Wiley treasure this old key? Why did she keep it? She didn't have a car any more, wouldn't be permitted to drive even if she still owned one. Had this Buick belonged to her dead husband? Or was it one Carl had abandoned when he moved west? The car in his Seattle photo was also a Buick. A smoke-blue Buick.

Men have a type, an ideal woman we keep hidden from decent people once we reach voting age. This preferred girl drifts through that interior slide show we flash when our eyes glaze during a day dream. Or a lecture. Or a dinner party. Or when we sleep. Or when we love. She may be tall, thick, short, scrawny, dark, pale, sassy or sensual, friendly or kittenish or dangerous. The specs of this favored girl never vary. That's the one we want. Always. Same goes for autos: we have a type. A preferred car which grabs our feverish imagination at a young age and never lets go. Carl Wiley had a preference, a type. A car he craved through the years. He stuck with the car he wanted no matter what. These photos revealed he loved smoky blue Buicks. Maybe they made him feel safe. Or big, or important, or desirable. Or just adult. Who knows why, but Carl loved his blue Buicks.

This old Buick key meant something special to his mother. Something precious, something she didn't want to forget. I couldn't steal it. I wanted to. My gut told me this was a clue I needed to keep until I solved the puzzle. But removing an old lady's memories wasn't something I could stomach. I took a photo of the key and its tattered old fob. Then I grabbed the robin's egg blue cardigan from the dresser drawer and ran downstairs to shelter Mrs. Wiley from the cold.

---

Dinner over, we three walked to the front hall of the dark mansion. Queen tugged on my shirtfront until I bent for a kiss on the cheek. As the bill of her red cap butted my eyebrow, she giggled against my jaw. Then she scampered toward the staircase, a uniformed attendant in hot pursuit.

Carolyn Wiley watched her friend mount the steps. "I'm so happy you came, Carl." She pressed my hand to the dancing pulse in her chest, then kissed my fingers. "It's been so long since we had dinner together."

"Yes, I'm glad we found the time." I dabbed my lips to her powdery cheek then squeezed her shoulder. The bony knob shifted as she leaned into my touch. "I'll be going now," I said. She sighed and nodded in resignation.

As I walked away from the grand old house, I reflected on what I'd learned. Despite Queen's addled intervention, the visit had been salvaged by my discoveries in Carolyn's room. The car key and photos I'd found were clues to solving my case. I couldn't ask Carolyn a direct question about the blue Buick, either as myself or as Carl. Not yet. Her son's car held a hidden meaning, a link to forgotten events in Carolyn's past. I was sure of that. But before I confronted her, I wanted to unknot the kinks in my theory. I needed an auto expert to uncover the ties between this befuddled old lady and the dead wife buried in her basement.

# CHAPTER
# SEVENTEEN

I was the first one in the office again the next day. When Norment and Brina might arrive was a dreary guess. After fumbling my way through the dim reception area to my own office I flung aside the door. I meant to sling my jacket on the couch and head to the break room to start the coffee machine.

A cackle stopped me. A thick silhouette squatted behind my desk. "So, you're the new muscle around here, hmm? Rook, right? Nice to put a mug to the name."

Flicking on the overhead spotlighted the stranger sprawled in my chair. His face was familiar, but I refused to give that away.

"You seem comfortable at my desk," I said. An even tone, a few registers lower than my normal delivery, not that he'd realize it. I didn't carry a gun, but I could talk like I did. I kept my right hand in my jacket pocket to uphold the implication of armed threat. I issued simple orders. "Keep your hands flat on the desk. Get up. Slow. Move to me."

He did as I'd asked. I patted both flanks of his black windbreaker and along the loose folds of his dark gray slacks.

He was unarmed. And amused. "Kid, you're good. Real good." A chuckle warmed his words. "Old Man Ross picked a winner in you."

A sardonic smile tilted the bushy black moustache. Creases radiated across the dark contours of his face. He wore a pink mesh driving cap on his close-cropped head. Rose-colored aviator sunglasses, combined with black leather high tops to give him a youthful air, but I put his age at mid-fifties. Under the jacket, a knit shirt with pink-and-gray stripes hugged his chest. He had plenty of muscle, but pads of flesh pillowed his waist.

"Alright, tell me who you are."

"Can I sit down first, kid? Or do you want to keep pretending you got a gun in your pocket?"

"Sit on the couch. And keep your hands where I can see them."

Grinning, he sank into the middle of the leather sofa and relaxed both hands on his blocky thighs. I leaned against the edge of my desk facing him and crossed my arms over my chest. I raised my eyebrows but didn't say anything more.

"Don't you want to ask who I am and why I'm in here?" His tone was genial and hearty, like a long-absent uncle come uninvited to Thanksgiving dinner.

Rather than acting like the scolding aunt at this reunion, I'd play the curious cousin. I nodded for him to continue. "Start with your name. I'll see if I want more after that."

"John Burris, but only my mama and a few old boys from the South Side call me Jackie. Everyone else calls me 'Smoke.'"

He leaned forward to offer his hand, but I kept mine folded under my arm. I knew the name; I'd seen his picture. Smoke Burris was a former employee of the Ross Agency. Norment had given me scanty details of Burris's tenure: he was rough, honest, a wild-cat prone to following his own instincts. Four months ago, I'd needed an out-of-town hideaway for a threatened kid in my care. Brina suggested I send him to stay with Burris in Chicago. Norment made the arrangements. I'd exchanged texts with Burris but we never talked. He'd done me a solid favor. But gratitude didn't make me inclined toward instant friendship. The man was still an invader.

"I'm not your mama, John. So 'Smoke' it is." My spine relaxed. A little. "And what makes you think you can sit at my desk, Smoke? In my office. Without my permission?"

"*Your* office now. *My* office back in the day. I used to work here, kid. Didn't Old Man Ross ever tell you who come before you in this job?" Burris removed his sunglasses, the grin still stretching his lips.

I knew the bare facts. But hearing his story would give me the advantage. So, I lied. "No, never did."

"And little Sabrina never mentioned my name, neither?" Smoke shook his head, his brown eyes dancing a zig-zag pattern across my face.

"No, she didn't."

"Not a mumbling word from either of them. Well, look at that. All those texts and not a chirp. Ain't the past a funny old thing. After all those years, all those good times we had. You'd think they'd fill you in about me."

"You'd think so, wouldn't you?" I hitched myself onto the desk. I wanted to ease pressure off my bum foot, but stay several inches higher than Smoke.

"And you sent the kid to me without asking any questions? "

"I trusted Norment's judgment on that one," I said. "So, tell me, when did you work here?"

"I guess I started here about ten, twelve years ago."

"You guess? You're not sure?"

"Things that far in the past get hazy, you know." He grinned some more, like we were old chums reminiscing about cruising the streets together.

"Go on. What did you do for the Agency?"

"Man, what *didn't* I do? They had me running every which way, mostly security assignments. Guarding offices, homes, private parties, things like that. Anywhere somebody needed muscle, brains, a sharp eye, and a zipped lip. That's where they sent me."

I nodded; this outline of the Ross Agency's core business sounded familiar. I'd tackled the same assignments dozens of times.

But then Smoke took the description in an unexpected direction. "Every once in a while, one of Ross's friends needed a bodyguard to escort some of his money across town. I did some of that. I learned real fast not to ask too many questions about who the client was and where the money came from. Not everything was on the up and up. You get the picture, dontcha?"

I did and it made me uneasy. Had Norment maintained his connection with local mob figures, running errands for them as recently as a decade ago? Why had neither of the Rosses ever said anything about this to me? Concern must have streaked across my face, because Smoke continued as if I'd asked questions out loud.

"This is how it worked back then. The agency had two sides to it: The legit side, which little Sabrina ran. And the not-so-legit side which Ross kept in his own back pocket. How much each half of the operation brought in varied from month to month. Sometimes it was Sabrina bringing in the lion's share with all those neighborhood cases and security gigs. Other times it was Norment with an important haul he kept off the agency books. Cash-in-hand kind of operation."

"Brina never knew about these other transactions?"

"No, she never did. Not to my knowledge. Norment ran with a pretty rough crowd when he first come up to Harlem as a youngblood. Long before Sabrina was born. You ever heard of Martin Colón? Sometime you want some good stories, ask Norment about numbers running for Colón's bank." Smoke rubbed his hands on his thighs as if to warm them. He smiled, an inward-looking expression fogging his eyes with memories of delinquencies past.

Norment had described to me and Brina his short early career as a numbers runner for the up-and-coming mobster Martin Colón. I'd first met Colón face to face when I served as a guard for his granddaughter's birthday party. Then my ties to the gangster tightened when his thugs threatened a boy in my care. I'd sent that kid to Smoke in Chicago to escape the Colón mob. He must know some of this history. He was keeping secrets from me just as I was from him. Norment had put those old mob connections far behind him. The past was dead and buried. In the two years since I'd joined the agency, I'd had no reason to think otherwise. But I didn't intend to share these insights with this stranger.

All this reminiscing turned Smoke's thoughts in another direction. My silence gave him a chance to quiz me. "So, how's sweet Sabrina doing? Married yet?"

"No, not married."

"No? Still single? Man, what's *wrong* with the brothers in this city? Chicago dude would've nailed that down long ago. But you East Coast boys, you talk a good hustle, but you just not up to the job, right? Can't close the deal, if you get my drift." He grabbed his left elbow, then straightened the forearm, thrusting the clenched fist toward me twice in a crude gesture.

"I mean, that is one *fine* looking young sister. I know you know it too. Coming in to work every day was pure pleasure with her in the office. I mean, the legs, the ass, the whole package. What a way to kick-start the morning! Mmmm, I tell you *what*! That girl could set a man up for the whole day, am I right?" He smacked his lips, then rubbed his chin as his eyes clouded with happy memories. "She used to wear this particular mini-skirt, shortest in Harlem. White with blue pinstripes, like ticking on a mattress. I tell you, that little skirt could make unlawful thoughts last a whole week. No lie."

I knew that skirt. Brina hadn't worn it in over a year. Not since we'd been together. Smoke's rambling was meant to provoke me. He wanted to see if I'd take the bait and challenge him out of chivalry or jealousy. To cut off his jovial disrespect, I glared at him until he shut his trap. He'd guess about me and Brina soon enough. I wasn't going to give him the satisfaction of getting bent out of shape off his rude remarks.

When he didn't get the rise he wanted, Smoke stopped the blather, considering me with a narrowed eye. "Sabrina lost her charms since I left? Or she just not your cup of tea, kid?"

"My cup of tea is none of your business, Smoke."

"True, true." He laughed as if I'd made one helluva joke. When I flattened my lips and deadened my gaze, he continued in a different vein. "Say, I was hoping to see Norment and Sabrina before I left. They coming in soon?"

"They should be here in a while. Were they expecting you?" I sounded like a secretary taking a phone message. Formality kept Smoke at the distance he deserved.

"No, I'm just in town for a gig. Thought I'd drop in and shoot the breeze before the job begins. Catch up on old times, you know."

Smoke and I chatted for twenty minutes. Him, expansive and blustery, me terse and cloudy. He told me a few stories about the young kid I'd sent to him. Whip was doing fine, studying hard in school, helping around the office, keeping out of trouble. I wanted to minimize what I revealed while prying the max from him. I needed to know as much as possible about the Rosses, given the complicated nature of my personal and professional relationships with them. But Smoke had zero need to learn anything more from me than he already knew.

The agency's past mattered to me, especially when it landed on my desk uninvited. The rule of threes said bad news came in bunches: first Annie, then Dreamie. Did Smoke make three? This universal law had wound itself into a nub of sorrow. My job was to untangle it and kick the past behind us. I was looking for a thread to pull apart this sad knot. So, I nodded and hummed while Smoke jabbered.

Brina blew into the office at ten, easing the atmosphere. She was wearing turquoise trousers and a red peasant blouse tied under a navy blazer. No striped mini-skirt, no unlawful thoughts for Smoke to wallow in. She greeted him with a squeal and a hug, then planted a kiss on my cheek. I twitched at the unexpected contact. She never broadcast our relationship, not in the office, not on the street. Public displays of affection were out with us. Smoke scooted on the sofa to make room, but she pushed aside files to sit on my desk. Next to me. Shoulders touching. Smoke was a savvy detective. The hop in his left eyebrow said he got the message about our connection.

"Sabrina, girl, it does this old man's heart good to see you again. You're as beautiful as the day I left. Maybe more. These New York City boys treating you alright, I can see that."

He winked at me; his lips dropped into a leer that vanished after a few seconds. I focused on a spot in the center of his moustache. No response needed from me: Brina was off-limits. After routine chit-chat, she pushed the talk to the visitor's current occupation.

"Smoke, you're a blast from the past, for sure! What brings you to Harlem? I heard you'd landed in L.A., then Chicago. Are you out west again?"

"Nah, I gave up that west coast scene a few years ago. Too freaky for me. You know me, I'm a simple boy at heart. Traditional values, home cooking, and all that."

"All that bull, you mean. You've never been simple or a boy. And home is wherever you drop your latest pair of overpriced sneakers." Brina's eyes crinkled with smiles and laughter rippled from her throat as she turned to me. "You know why they call him 'Smoke?'"

As I sighed, she continued: "Because he's as hard to pin down as smoke. Shows up one day, fades the next. Reliable as exhaust fumes and just as impossible to hold. The original man of mystery, that's Smoke."

"That why you got rid of me, Sabrina? Because I was unreliable?"

Before she could answer, he turned to give me more history. "Never could get Sabrina to go out with me. Not dinner. Not a concert. Not a club. Not even a movie. Goose eggs every time." He shook his heavy head as he added up the zeros. "Oh, I tried, believe me, I tried. But she was having none of my nonsense. Not one bit. Sabrina's got rules, and heaven help the dude that breaks even a single, solitary one. Man, I'm telling you, I got no mercy from this beautiful lady. None whatsoever."

Rather than feeling depressed by this story of past frustrations, Smoke seemed in high spirits. Twinkling eyes, curving lips, shiny cheeks, the works. According to him, sentiments on both sides never progressed beyond vague flirtation. Smoke was signaling the field was clear. Brina hadn't been involved with him. He might be a player, but Smoke was generous and fair too. I tipped my chin to let him know I got his message.

Brina rolled her eyes, picking up on the message too. Her honesty forced a reverse to a previous comment. "Just so we're clear, Smoke. I never said unreliability was why you left the agency. You'll have to sort that out with Daddy. That's between you and him. I had nothing to do with it. As you well know."

"Sure, I know. Just enjoy hearing it from you direct." Smoke's eyes shut over a broad smile. "When's the old man arrive?"

My cue to start the long-delayed pot of coffee. While I was in the break room, Brina could fill him in on the recent discovery of Dreamie's body and the misery swirling around her father. I knew she wouldn't mention Annie; that was my loss alone. We didn't have trays to carry mugs and I wasn't a secretary. So, when the coffee was brewed, I shouted the invitation. Smoke followed Brina to the break room and filled up on black coffee. The three of us, fortified with high-test brew, took seats around the small conference table to continue the catch-up talk.

"So, Smoke, you never did answer my question: what brings you to town?" Brina in bull-dog mode was a sight to behold: keen eyes, fearsome red pout, jabbing finger. "And where've you been since you left the agency, anyway? What's up with Comet Security?"

"Like I said, I tried L.A. for a few years, but it didn't suit me. So, I rolled home to Chicago to see what I could scare up in the way of business. I took after your daddy's trade and started a little security company. The Comet Agency. Small-time gigs at first. But enough to get me noticed. First in Park Manor, Englewood, Chatham. Then all around the city. Two years ago, I landed a gig as personal bodyguard to an up-and-coming young musician. Local concerts, clubs, small venues on the South Side. Good work, not too demanding. Until the brother hit the big-time. Then, boom! Watch out! Maybe you heard of him: 2-Ryght?"

Brina squealed. Coffee sloshed over the lip of her mug. Once again, I was stuck in the outermost rings of pop culture ignorance. I'd never heard of this young rapper. But Brina gushed. Then she swooned. Then she babbled. When she recovered her voice, she spelled the name for me: 2-Ryght with a Y.

"Is he English?" My question was dumb enough to wrinkle Smoke's dusky brow. "I mean, the name and all. Like a Brit phrase."

"What the hell you talking about? English? Boy's a South Side dude, like me." Smoke bugged his eyes at Brina to check if I was kidding. Or truly as stupid as I sounded. She shrugged, unwilling to defend me.

Brina explained 2-Ryght was the hottest thing to hit music in the past ten years. Cool, blistering, sorrowful with a justified touch of violence. The ultra-fresh 2-Ryght told the story of the streets from a new angle. According to Brina's glowing report, politics wasn't divorced from everyday life for 2-Ryght. Culture and class were core parts of how everybody lived and died. From the young bloods to the cops, from the angel babies to the do-wrong women, from the gangstas to the pastors, 2-Ryght's lyrics captured the rich array of life on the rough side of town. His first album, "Ryghteous," went triple platinum. And rumors that 2-Ryght was on the verge of dropping a second album had the whole world ablaze. Or at least, a part of the world I didn't inhabit.

Ignorant, I asked basic questions that would have embarrassed a hipper person. "Does he have a real name, or is 2-Ryght what his mother called him at birth?"

Brina's scrunched nose indicated I was a hopeless geezer. She looked to the expert for details.

Smoke answered without an edge to his voice. "Now I *know* you pulling my leg, man! Nobody can be *that* ignorant. Name is Dwayne Reynolds. Sweet kid. A baby really. Takes care of anybody needs help. But don't let that get out. It'd spoil his street cred if people found out 2-Ryght isn't a borderline psycho with a long rap sheet."

Lines drooped beside Brina's lips at this disappointing glimpse of the real 2-Ryght. Tame and timid is nobody's ticket to fame. But she recovered to ask about Smoke's assignment in New York City.

Smoke puffed his chest. "You probably heard 2-Ryght is diversifying his business opportunities. He's not kicking music to the side. But he's looking to find other ways to bring his outlook and personality to the public."

"Cashing in on his fifteen minutes of fame?" Cynical was my role in this conversation, so I delivered.

"Yeah, you could look at it that way." Smoke was in a forgiving mood. And he was showing off for Brina. His arm almost broke as he patted himself on the back. "Dwayne's developed a new line of sneakers with a major company. They'll have his 2-Ryght signature on the side and he picked out the color combinations and leathers too."

Smoke lifted his left foot to table height so we could admire the prototype: smooth black leather uppers with chocolate suede caps and red laces with scarlet patent leather tips. An inch of white foam swooped over black rubber outsoles. Corrugated heels made the shoe look dangerous, like high tops Satan would wear for a night of clubbing in Hades. The rapper's name was scrawled in green patent loops along the ankle.

"Comes in red with yellow suede and an all-white snakeskin version too, with a pink sole. Nice, hunh?"

Brina gushed over 2-Ryght's edgy design choices. Then Smoke returned to the story of young Dwayne's business plans. "Today is the big launch of the new sneaker line. A collab with the biggest shoe manufacturer in the biz. They call the line, 'Science Class,' 'cause 2-Ryght's taking everybody to school. And they're dropping here in Harlem. You know that shoe store up the boulevard at West 145th? That's where it's all going down. Four this afternoon. You all need to come, check it out."

I cut through the bull. "You mean, you want us for back-up and crowd control? That's what you're looking for, right, Smoke?"

He frowned at my jab. But he didn't deny the truth of my guess when he turned to Brina. "I'm not asking for nothing for free, Sabrina. Paper's no problem. You know 2-Ryght is good for it. You'll get a solid payday. I just need to make sure everything goes smooth this afternoon. Bringing in local security from the Ross Agency is the way to make sure the whole event goes off without a hitch."

Smoke laid out his case, stroking agency ego and curiosity at the same time. Brina's bright eyes said she was hooked before he'd completed the pitch. She let him finish anyway.

"I know you got a better handle on local troublemakers now than I do. If it comes down to it, you can spot a neighborhood thug looking to make a name for himself by busting up the ceremony in front of the cameras. Staging a beef with somebody big like 2-Ryght could be some stupid joker's idea of a ticket to fame. I need to stay on top of that and I'd sure appreciated help from you all. That is, if you're available, Sabrina."

Brina's eyes glowed with excitement, her voice piping high and sweet. "Sure, we're available. I'll check with Daddy when he comes in. But far as I know, we're clear for the afternoon. Right, Rook?"

Yes was my only option, as she well knew. The twist to Smoke's moustache said he enjoyed seeing her play me.

But he had other plans for my time. "Actually, Rook, I got something else I want to run by you. A little case my cousin tossed at me night before last. She knew I was coming to town and hoped I could stop by and look into it for her. But obviously, I'm tied up pretty tight with the shoe launch today. And I'm outta here tomorrow morning. We got a meeting in L.A. with some producers 2-Ryght's discussing a movie part with. That boy is red-hot, I'm telling you. Multi-talented threat."

Before Smoke could launch into another hyped-up cheer for his celebrity client, I asked about his cousin's case. "Is this a for-real cousin, or a little something-something you got going on the side? Just checking before I decide to look into the case for you. Pardon my skepticism, but I just met you, and…"

"Yeah, it's okay. You have to test and verify. I get that." He stretched his pudgy fingers towards me, smoothing the air between us. "No, Galaxy is my actual, for-real cousin. Straight up. Her mother and my mother were sisters. We came up together in Englewood, on the South Side. But took different paths, I guess you could say. Galaxy is a professor with a degree from Northwestern in some flubber-jubber about Africa. She's here at Alexander University now. A dean of whatchama-callit over there."

Smoke's concern seemed authentic, if vague. I pulled Brina into my office for a consultation. I needed her approval before I took this side gig for her former colleague. We agreed she would bring her father to cover the shoe launch. Brina was happy for the chance to give Norment another distracting task. Pile on the work, put Dreamie in the rearview mirror. That was the plan.

After Smoke and I shook on the job, I phoned the office of Dean Galaxy Pindar for an appointment. I recognized the unusual name. This dean was at the top of Professor Gerald Keith's list of campus enemies.

He and the devoted Sally Anastos had spent lots of energy slamming Dean Pindar the night before Annie's murder.

That afternoon, I scanned the Internet for details about Galaxy Pindar, scholar in trouble. I hoped Brina was right: the fastest exit from mourning was work. Annie was eight days dead. Forgetting wasn't an option; revenge topped my agenda. This visit to Alexander University might yield new information about Gerry Keith and his research project. Even new insight into his relationship with my wife. Rather than a detour, this trip to campus could forge my path to payback. I wanted to kill two academic birds with one stone.

# CHAPTER
# EIGHTEEN

The twenty-minute taxi ride to Alexander University's uptown campus gave me time to review the information I'd gathered about Smoke's cousin.

Dr. Galaxy Pindar was Dean of Arts and Humanities at the university, a position she'd held for six years. She was also Distinguished Professor of African History and past chair of the history department. Her resumé listed books, articles, presentations, awards, and even an art exhibit she'd curated on West African textiles. Smoke said Galaxy was a few years older than him, putting her in the late fifties. In her formal photo on the Arts and Humanities website she looked a decade younger. Maybe academic life really was a splash in the fountain of youth. Now my destiny was lock-sure: when I reincarnated for a cushy second crack at life, it would be as a tenured full professor.

Smoke said his cousin was worried about a threat to her personal safety. But he couldn't get more specific than that. Galaxy sounded spooked by some trouble in the office or at home, he wasn't sure which. She knew he was in private security, so she'd brought the issue to him. Smoke said even though he didn't know me well, the Ross Agency stamp of approval was good enough for him. He was sure I could handle whatever problem cousin Galaxy threw my way. I was happy for a jaunt through the leafy quadrangles of Alexander University. Better than join-ing the mob at the shoe store. Standing on a street corner swamped by the surging hormones of fans of 2-Ryght the Rapper was my idea of hell.

Concrete barrels decorated with purple creeping vines and golden mums blocked vehicle access to the campus. The cab dropped me in front of the library, and I strolled fifteen minutes to Randolph Hall, the location of Dean Pindar's office.

I could have made the walk in less time. But the warm September sun inspired undergrad women to make one final glorious display in cut-off jeans. Long legs, long hair, sultry pouts, steamy gazes. Every girl lounging under the lofty trees seemed mesmerized by a phone, tablet, or iced latté. Expanses of skin shone vanilla, margarine, almond, meringue, and buttermilk in the sunlight. I looked them over; they looked me over. I nodded; they smirked. I blinked; they fluttered. We agreed to be agree-able. Only a few boys joined the basking girls. I wondered if one of the boys might be Sally Anastos's kid brother, enjoying his first semester of college. Banners in violet, white, and gold flapped over the pretty scene declaring the longevity of Alexander University. The scrolled motto on the pennants was brief: *Labor in the sun, learn in its light.* That brutal tour in ninth grade Latin with Sister Margaret Agnes finally paid off.

The festive academic atmosphere put me in a good mood, which was punctured by the arrival of a campus cop.

"You looking for something in particular, mister? Or just sightseeing?"

Stuffed into a navy uniform that was too tight across the chest and too baggy at the knees, his scowl screamed killjoy. The offer of guid-ance was proper, but the cop's tone foamed with suspicion. I was two decades older and two shades darker than the students draped across sunny patches of grass. In black trousers and black button-down shirt, I looked like a stranger. His challenge was expected.

Still, it set the hairs dancing at the back of my neck. Getting profiled was never fun. "Thank you, officer. I have a three o'clock appointment with Dean Pindar in Randolph Hall. Is it that way?"

I pointed down the dappled gravel path in the direction I was going. I'd studied an online map, so I knew the campus layout. I didn't need his help, but playing a confused visitor was best in this situation. Better than the purse-snatcher or rapist of his imagination.

"Yeah, straight ahead, then through the arch on the left. Big, gray, lots of stone. You can't miss it." He settled a pudgy hand over the radio at his waist. Which was crammed next to the gun on his utility belt.

"Thank you for the help. Officer."

I toddled away, exaggerating my limp to give him a sense of physical superiority: I was tall, but no threat; muscular, but I meant no harm; good-looking, but innocent anyway. Without turning my head, I could feel Officer Friendly fall into line behind me. We proceeded in single file until I reached the stone arch separating the quadrangles. As I made my left turn and passed under the massive gate, I waved at my personal bodyguard. He halted, looked both ways to see who might be watching. Then he waved back. Another victory for town-gown relations.

Try as he might, the campus cop hadn't discouraged me. I hoped Galaxy Pindar's problem wouldn't deflate my spirits either.

Despite my dawdling stroll, I arrived five minutes early at the dean's office. Her administrative assistant radiated good cheer when I pushed into the suite. According to the nameplate on the desk, this was the Nathalie Kwan I had spoken with on the phone. She had soft brown eyes under a matching mop of wavy bangs. Her outfit of white t-shirt and gray slacks seemed informal; the denim jacket and purple paisley scarf slung over the back of her chair increased the casual effect.

"Nice to meet you, Mr. Rook. Dean Pindar's in a meeting. But she should be done any minute now. Can I get you some coffee or cold water while you wait?"

"Water would be great. Thanks."

Nathalie disappeared into a kitchenette beyond a large display case. When she brought a dripping bottle, I pressed the icy plastic against my forehead and neck. Her grin heated the room, but I cooled off anyway.

I took one of four violet-and-white striped arm chairs at the far end of the office suite. In front of me was a stuffed book case; framed photographs hung on the wall above it. As the minutes dragged on, I had time to study the display.

I thumbed through brochures stacked on the bookcase. The exhibit celebrated the recent publications of three professors who were finalists for the Blackistone Prize, the university's highest award for scholarly achievement. The first academic in the running turned out to be someone I knew: the anthropologist Gerald Keith. Lucky me. Copies of his new book on Annie's cleaning company, *The Dirty and the Clean: Authenticity Among Miami's Underclass,* were piled in a pyramid on the top shelf right below a flattering picture of the great man himself.

Anger, fierce and unexpected, pounded behind my eyes. Gerry Keith seemed every bit as smug in this still photo as he had in real life the night we met. I wondered again about the nature of his connection to Annie. How had he reacted to her death? Did he even care that she'd been killed? I ran a finger over the nugget of coral in my pocket. Had it fallen from Keith's ring when he visited Annie in her hotel room that night? Had it broken off in a struggle before he shot her?

"I apologize for the wait, Mr. Rook. Can I get you another bottle of water?" Nathalie's voice wavered across the room. "I'm sure Dean Pindar will be with you in just a moment more."

The brittle crackle of plastic in my hand jerked me to consciousness. I set the crushed water bottle on the side table. Scaring the secretary was a lousy move. "Sorry. I got carried away by some bad memories. Nothing to do with you."

Nathalie brought a fistful of paper napkins from the kitchenette. We knelt on the grimy carpet to dab the puddle. The water turned the napkins muddy brown as we worked.

Cheery Nathalie made the most of the situation. "Maybe this way we can get a bit of the dirt out of this grungy rug. It used to be pretty swirls of lilac, now it's just ugly. I've been trying to persuade Dean Pindar to have it replaced for months."

She laughed, I smiled. Handing her my wad of soaked paper, I repeated my mantra: "Sorry for the mess. I got distracted."

No need to scare her by reporting Gerry Keith's self-satisfied mug had sparked my angry spasm. To divert the sharp-eyed assistant, I unspooled my softest voice: "I'm hoping to visit the anthropology department next. What's the quickest way there?"

160

"Did you pass under the arch at the center of campus?"

"Yes." I stood, brushing my hands together.

"Then walk back the way you came. But at the arch continue north for a block to the Barstall Building. You can't miss it. Giant glass cube with ugly metal ducts in red and purple laced around it. Anthropology is on the third floor."

"Thanks. I'll find it."

I returned to my chair and Nathalie went to her desk. To cool my temper, I examined the photo of the second contender for the Blackistone Prize. James Nakamura was a professor of American Studies. He looked somber in gray tweeds and violet-striped tie. The title of his book, *Hot Plate, Hot Type*, was far more intriguing than his wan face and blank stare. Maybe Nakamura's work covered some sizzling topic that would steam the judges' lenses. Hope sprang eternal.

The third nominee was Smoke's cousin, the accomplished Galaxy Pindar. The dean's book was called *The Navel of the World*. Its back cover said she'd written a comprehensive history of the Nigerian town of Ile-Ife, which Yoruba people consider the birthplace of humankind. I scanned the dense text on the cover and inside flap, learning more about African history than I'd ever known before. In her photograph, Pindar's unsmiling face was pale and plump, framed by a mass of light-brown dreadlocks that snaked across her shoulders. She looked nothing like her hip-hop cousin Smoke.

"What's this prize all about?" I waved the brochure in the air. Nathalie might think I was unhinged; maybe my question would assure her I was tame.

She was eager to describe the competition. "The Blackistone is the top prize for professors at Alexander. It's worth fifty thousand dollars to the winner. Can you imagine that?"

"No, I can't." I leaned forward in the plush chair.

"Each year the three finalists say the same thing: the prestige and recognition are all that matters. Maybe so. But you better believe the money comes in handy even for them making full professor salaries."

"I guess it's an honor just to be nominated in such distinguished company, right? Like the Oscars."

Nathalie wrinkled her snub nose. She wasn't buying the appeal to academic modesty. "Sure, it's an honor. No doubt about it, Mr. Rook. But I guarantee you the chance of winning all that money sets their oversized brains on fire too." A cynic after my own heart: sweet, sassy, and realistic.

I didn't tell Nathalie I knew Gerry Keith. And I couldn't bear to read how Keith had written his research into Annie's company: too close, far too soon. I didn't let on I wanted to visit his office when I was done with Dean Pindar. So, as the wait dragged, I resigned myself to a sprint through James Nakamura's book.

I'd just cracked a copy, when the door to Dean Pindar's office swished and the man himself rushed out. Nakamura was compact and muscular, neatly dressed in dark slacks and a purple pullover. Giant tortoiseshell-framed glasses covered the middle of his face. His straight black hair was streaked with white at the temples; this dashing look probably earned him a clutch of female devotees. Brina once used the term, "silver fox," to describe a graying senior she admired in a restaurant. She would put Nakamura into that glamorous category. In contrast to his staid portrait, the American Studies professor brimmed with vigor. Red flashing along high cheekbones underlined his energy.

Professor Nakamura threw a brilliant smile in Nathalie's direction. She giggled. Then he sped across the reception area before I could rise from my chair. With that exit, the admin assistant waved me into Dean Pindar's private office.

———————

I often fall for women on the spot. I'm a sucker, sue me. Galaxy Pindar was not "my type" of woman. But I fell for her anyway.

The dean was short and round as a basketball. Layers of fabric curtained her figure from shoulder to ankle. She wore black leggings and short boots under a tunic in wheat-and-gray stripes. On top of the tunic, she piled a long vest featuring the inevitable violet required of all loyal Alexander University staff. Eyeglasses in red frames dangled from a purple cord around her neck. The smooth face above this drapery flushed in pretty shades of gold and rose. The pink flooding her cheeks mirrored the red streaks on James Nakamura's face moments ago. Maybe a coincidence, maybe not. Her light brown eyes, though shrewd, were inviting. Their directness was seductive: I was hooked. And the dreadlocks, which had seemed stiff and forbidding in her formal portrait, danced across her shoulders like loops of honey. Forty reduced to thirteen again, I longed to curl her locks around my fingers. With effort I suppressed the impulse. The dean wrapped my hand in hers, preventing me from assaulting her gorgeous hair.

"Please excuse the delay, Mr. Rook. You were kind enough to come to campus and I was rude enough to keep you waiting. Bad job on my part. James and I had things to discuss and we just didn't seem to get to the end of it."

"No need for apologies, Dean Pindar. James is Doctor Nakamura?"

"Yes, chair of American Studies and a dear old friend of mine."

"And your rival for that big prize, right?"

Her smile, which had been formal, burst into full bloom. Laughter bubbled from her deep bosom. My crush raged on.

"Heh, yes. You saw that display out there? I cringe every time I walk past it. An ugly show of ego. If you haven't already figured it out, self-satisfaction is the cardinal attribute of our little academic world."

The scholar huffed and turned down her mouth in a sardonic grimace, inviting me to join the disapproval. "I told Nathalie that display looks like I'm stuck on myself. Garish. But she said it was the job of the dean's office to celebrate our faculty and it just so happened this year the Blackistone committee picked me as a finalist."

She sighed, tossing the ropes of light brown hair away from her face. Her modesty seemed real. In my smitten state, I was ready to award her first prize. Especially given her other opponent. "Professor Gerald Keith is also in the running," I said.

Galaxy snorted. Not the polite simper of a well-bred socialite. Or the coy titter of a shy undergrad. The dean grunted like a pro linebacker. "Gerry Keith may be my rival, but he's never going to be my equal."

"You know him?"

"Of course. Gerry is the biggest of big shots at Alexander. Just ask him. We've entertained our colleagues for years with disputes over tenure, core curriculum, faculty appointments, departmental budgets, and diversity. You name the issue, Gerry and I have fought about it. At least twice a year he questions my academic credentials in a faculty senate meeting. He calls me an affirmative action fraud, but in the most elegant terms imaginable. And that's just the overt crap. He takes micro-aggression to a whole nother level."

"You two don't get on." Understatement was my game.

The dean hoisted her eyebrows and sighed. "Gerry is a self-regarding piece of shit. But he's got the best student evals of any professor in the School. And he's adored by experts in his field. His rock star status is entirely justified. I've read his book. It's solid and innovative research. He deserves to be considered for the Blackistone Prize."

"When do they announce the winner?"

"Next Friday, thank God. I don't expect to win. I'm just looking forward to getting the whole thing behind us. And dismantling that snotty display."

This was the kind of character detail about Keith I'd come to campus to collect. I wanted to build a portrait of the man based on the observations of his colleagues. Dean Pindar was doing me a solid. But if I was going to have time to catch Keith in his office, I needed to turn this conversation to the original purpose of my visit. I smoothed imaginary wrinkles from my collar. "Dean Pindar, your cousin said you had a concern you hoped I could help you with."

"Oh, please, call me Galaxy. That dean stuff is for tenure battles and trustee meetings." She waved her fingers as if shooing away flies. "How is Smoke anyway? I haven't seen him since a family reunion in Chicago a few years back." She swept her hand in the direction of a round table in a corner of the office. I took one of the four seats. She sat in the chair opposite me, her elbows planted on a vibrant yellow table cloth.

"I can't really say. I met him for the first time this morning when he took over my desk. Like he owned it."

"Yeah, sounds like Smoke. Jackie was the bad boy in the family, always running the streets. Broke a few windows, lifted a few beat boxes, stole a few cars, hustled a little weed, got a girl pregnant in high school. Everything dangerous, mischievous, or illegal, Smoke did it. And got away with it. You know why they called him 'Smoke?'"

"No, why?" Brina had already told me a version of his street handle, but I wanted to hear the family take.

"Because he always got away. Always. *Poof!* That boy managed to vanish before the chickens came home to roost. Every damn time. Forced me to play the good girl in the family. I always did resent Smoke for that." The chuckle and head shake suggested no lasting bitterness toward her delinquent cousin. Bygones were past, if not forgotten.

Galaxy stretched her spine, tipping back her chair. "Maybe he told you. Our mothers were sisters. Mine worked in the admissions office at the University of Chicago, which is how she met my dad, who was an accountant in the bursar's office. Bringing home a white boy in the early sixties wasn't cool. At all. So, my mom got plenty of grief inside and outside the family. But they stuck together through it all. Auntie Delphine, Smoke's mother, always stood up for her baby sister, no matter what. My mother was no angel, but Delphine sure was."

As she spoke, I scanned her spacious office. Three books were stacked between us, holding down the yellow tapestry table cloth. Sagging book cases lined two walls of the square space. The third wall featured a massive window looking out over the quadrangles of the campus. In front of the window were three pedestals supporting wooden sculptures: carved figures of a warrior on horseback, a mother holding a child at her breast, and a crowned head with deep scars across both cheeks. These souvenirs of her work half-way around the world were visible reminders of how Africa touched her life.

"Well, Rook, now you know way more about my family than you ever wanted to learn." Her soft drawl and informal use of my name drew me back to our conversation. "But your patience is a good sign. You're a private detective, aren't you? Your work must be like field research: it requires tolerance for human foibles, a sense of humor, and a truckload of patience to do it well. Sensitive snowflakes and wimps with attitude need not apply."

Gerry Keith had tried that same form of flattery. He set my teeth on edge. But this time it worked. Comparing my job to hers, Galaxy made me an ally. What can I say? I'm a sucker. "I don't know about that. People who know me say anger, not patience, is my main trait. But I'm trying to turn that anger into positive drive."

"That's all anybody can do, right? Work on it." She beamed until my throat warmed and I gulped. Then a cloud drifted across her eyes, dimming the smile. "Speaking of anger, let me show you why I need your help today."

Galaxy moved to her desk. She opened the bottom drawer with a tiny key and pulled out a yellow folder. When she returned to the table, she pushed the folder to me with the tip of her index finger, as if the paper itself was poisoned.

"Pardon the drama of the locked drawer and all. But I don't want this stuff to get out across the campus." She propped her glasses on the tip of her nose and peered at me as I read.

Inside the folder were four creased pages of typing paper. Sentences formed from hacked words and letters were pasted on them. Each message began with the same salutation: "BITCH." The content varied after that. One letter insisted Galaxy keep her hands off, "my man." Another ordered Galaxy to quit messing around with what didn't belong to her. The third and fourth threatened to humiliate or kill Galaxy if she persisted in stealing another woman's husband. The language was crude, the imagery violent. There were no signatures or dates. Waves of fury rose from the jagged letters.

Galaxy lifted the eyeglasses from her nose and let them drop to her chest. "I received three more like this. I tore them up and burned the pieces at home."

"Same message, same style?"

"Yes. At first, I thought they were just crazy outpourings from a lunatic. But then the messages started making specific threats: times, places, body parts. So, I decided to save the most recent ones. I got this last night, which is when I called Smoke for help."

She shuffled the pages, putting a new sheet on top. Same lightweight paper, same ugly fury raging from shredded letters. "Look at this, it warns me against attending the faculty reception this evening."

"Any idea who sent these?"

Before Galaxy could answer, her assistant Nathalie popped around the door without knocking. "I'm out of here early, like we talked about, Dean Pindar. Don't forget you have that welcome back reception at the faculty club at five-thirty."

"I remember. See you in the morning, Nathalie."

"See you tomorrow. Good night, Mr. Rook."

When the door closed, Galaxy explained: "The faculty senate stages a big, boozy reception to welcome themselves back to campus at the start of the new academic year. I'm expected to say a few bland words and try to smooth whatever feathers got ruffled during the past twelve months. Academics hang onto grudges like jackals gripping that last bite of carrion. Vicious and brutal."

She shrugged, but without whimsy or nonchalance. The dullness in her eyes and the sagging lines around her mouth said she carried the toll of these academic resentments and skirmishes close to the heart.

"Which brings us back to these threatening letters, Galaxy. Something may go down tonight. But this resentment is older than yesterday. Or last month." I picked up a page and read its twisted message again. "Hanging onto grudges like jackals, you said. If anyone wanted to harm you or even scare you this way, it wouldn't be because of a new offense, some outrage from last week. This person sounds frightened as well as furious. The roots of this hatred go back years."

Sadness narrowed Galaxy's eyes. "Of course, you're right about the past. I don't want to think it's possible. Denial is a river and all that." Emotion splashed across her face in a wave of deep red. She held the clue to this mystery; my job was to poke until she was ready to share more.

As she opened her mouth to speak, the phone rang from her desk. "Sorry, got to take this one. The only person who calls me on a landline anymore is the president."

She sat behind her desk and punched at the flashing button on her phone's console. While she talked, I leafed through one of the books on the table. A private eye doling out privacy. If Galaxy wanted me to leave the room, she would have motioned toward the door as she started talking with her boss. But I could look like I wasn't prying.

The book was James Nakamura's prize nominee, *Hot Plate, Hot Type*. Below a glamour shot of the author, the text on the inside flap gushed his work was the definitive examination of the fierce newspaper rivalries that enflamed Chicago from 1920 to 1970. Not as sexy as I'd hoped. But then I wasn't the book's target audience. Maybe American Studies people lusted after old newsprint.

Rifling through the book's pages with one thumb flicking the edges, a sense of recognition nagged. I reversed the idle ramble and slowed to turn the leaves with care. Letters and words jumped at me. I knew them, but not in this form or order. Another riff with my eyes sharp, then again without focus, letting the pages ripple in a blur.

On the next pass I had the answer. This typeface and paper were the same as the chopped words pasted in the letters to Galaxy. Someone had torn apart a copy of this book to compose those threatening messages. Nakamura was the centerpiece in this academic drama. Would Galaxy admit to knowing more than she'd allowed so far?

After she finished the phone call, she circled her desk to return to the table. I didn't let her relax in her chair opposite me.

"You know who sent these messages, don't you?"

I speared one sheet with an index finger. She gasped. The challenge lowered my voice. "If you don't come clean, Galaxy, I can't help you. I'm wasting my time and yours if you won't talk."

I stiff-armed the table. "Spill the truth about James Nakamura. Or I quit."

# CHAPTER
# NINETEEN

Galaxy Pindar stonewalled. "What makes you think James is involved?"

Her eyes darted around the office, looking for refuge in her books, her statues, her bright textiles and photos. I didn't have a semester, or even a minute to waste on this coy academic nonsense. Shock tactics cut through BS, so I violated the book. I spread-eagled Nakamura's text, splitting its spine to flatten it on the table. Galaxy's eyes popped and she thrust a hand to stop the assault.

Pointing at a sentence, I explained my thinking. "Look at the word 'danger' in this paragraph. Its typeface is the same as the word 'danger' in the second message you received. And here. Another place where the letters from the words in this section have been chopped apart. They were pasted back together in a new order for the middle of your first message." Galaxy squinted at the pages through her red-framed glasses. When she blinked, I continued. "The 'T' and 'H' in the book title at the top of each page were used to spell 'BITCH' in your messages." I slapped the volume shut. "Nakamura is the key. So give it up."

Galaxy exhaled, the gust ruffling the pages of Nakamura's damaged book. She spilled the story. "Yes, James and I used to be together."

"What do you mean, 'together?' Precious won't cut it now."

She frowned then squeezed the indentations on the bridge of her nose. "Yeah, Okay. Back in college we dated. I was editor of the campus newspaper at Oberlin, he was president of the student senate."

"True love on the barricades, hunh?" I wiped the sneer from my lips, but it invaded my tone.

"I don't know if it was true love back then, but it felt real enough. We were pretty intense for a while. But then it faded. We broke up after graduation and went our separate ways."

"And you didn't stay in touch, for what? Three decades?" I frowned at this posh foolishness.

"Not really. We saw each other at conferences. Wrote a postcard or two. Then a few emails. But other than that, no, we didn't keep in touch. He got married. I didn't. I did field research in Nigeria. He worked in archives in the U.S. I published, he published. I got tenure on the East Coast. He got tenure on the West Coast."

I sighed. "And thirty years later you both land at Alexander. You as Dean of Arts and Humanities, he as chair of American Studies. File it under S for Small World." Academic romance was the same self-centered tripe the rest of us experienced. But with three syllable words.

Galaxy looked at her lap during my flip summation. Her lowered eyes and pink cheeks said she felt guilty. I threw a guess: "Maybe it wasn't a fluke. James ending up at this university. How did it happen?"

"Well, I didn't exactly encourage him to apply for the position. But I knew he was a top contender. So, when he came to campus for the interviews, I made sure the members of the search committee knew he was the strongest candidate. They put his name on their unranked list of three finalists and I gave my recommendation to the provost and president. James won the job fair and square."

Cynical reading was my specialty: "You put your thumb on the scale, that it?"

Galaxy bristled at my suggestion. How dare I suggest favoritism rather than sheer merit could win the day? Annoyance deepened the wrinkles around her eyes and she puffed up in her chair. "It was an honor to have a distinguished scholar such as James join our faculty. A feather in our cap that took Alexander's American Studies program to a higher level in national rankings."

Sure. And, if that high-ranking feather tickled her personal cap as well, so much the better. Win-win-win. Except somebody lost out in the transaction.

"You said he got married and you didn't. Tell me about James's wife. Maybe she's the one threatening you."

"Which one? He's been married three times." Galaxy dealt this shade with the right amount of salty homegirl snap, forcing a smile from me. She flipped her dreads again. Would she jerk her neck soon? "But I doubt it's them."

"Why not?"

"Candace works at a rainforest research center in Costa Rica. Pilar runs a bed-and-breakfast near Salinas, California."

"And who's the lucky contestant behind door number three?" I shook my head in mock horror at this thicket of academic entanglements.

Galaxy's throat shimmied as she suppressed laughter at my weak joke. Simple pleasure colored her face, making me warm inside too. "Well, that would be Reva. She was James's grad student. They got married eighteen months ago. Still in the honeymoon phase, right?"

"Some honeymoons go sour quicker than others."

The name Reva tickled a memory. A whiff of candied cherries drifted across my mind. Annie's perfume. *Rêves de la Plage, Dreams of the Beach*. I reached for Nakamura's broken book again. I flipped to the first page and read the phrases out loud.

"What do you make of this? It's dedicated to quote *The One* unquote. Then there's a line from Hamlet: 'I could be bounded in a nutshell and count myself a king of infinite space—were it not that I have bad dreams.' That tells the whole story."

"What story?"

A grin split my face; the solution seemed obvious. The crease between her eyes said the dean remained puzzled.

I explained: "James is saying the infinite space is Galaxy, right? And he would be your king, if not for the interference of those bad dreams. Which would be Reva."

Her honey-gold eyes popped with shock. "You're saying James dedicated his new book to me?".

"More than that. He pledged to get together with you if only he could get rid of his bad dream of a wife, Reva. I bet she didn't take that well. Once she scoped the dedication, she freaked out. You never read it yourself?"

"No, I didn't read the dedication. I read the manuscript in draft. But I didn't think to look at the book again after it was published. I guess I should have, hunh?"

"Damn straight. This is real world stuff here, not Ivory Tower make-believe."

Two clueless teens sending each other scribbled messages in the back of seventh grade social studies class. No wonder Galaxy and James kept missing each other for thirty years.

"I knew he liked me back then. Still liked me now, I guess. But I never knew he felt this strongly. Wow…I don't know what to say…" She trailed off, rubbing the cuticles on her fingers in slow assessment of the new orientation of her world.

I threw my best shot, hoping to unjam the sludge. "I'm not that good at relationship stuff. Lousy, in fact. I was a complete failure at it, according to my ex-wife. But you should talk straight to James. Tell him how you feel. Find out how he feels. Then decide where you go from there."

I wasn't going to go on a deep soul-quest with Galaxy. What would Annie say about me now? Would she'd think I'd grown up at last? Would she marvel to see I'd conquered the anger that destroyed our marriage? Would she rate me as hard as I still graded myself? Yet another thing I'd never learn now. I tucked this fresh sorrow into a backpack stuffed with regrets. My job was here and now.

Galaxy tried to clear a path forward. "Should I show James these nasty letters? I mean, the way Reva ripped up his book, the anger in that gesture speaks louder than her actual words. It's frightening."

"No. Not yet. See how it goes when you talk. Leave out the hate mail for now." I had nothing more. The Case of the Ardent Academics was closed and settled. The rest of the tough emotional slog was on Galaxy and her bashful suitor. Maybe those two crazy kids could work it out. Like in the movies.

I coughed to bring her back to earth. "You've got thirty minutes to get to your faculty reception."

"Wow. Time slipped away, didn't it?" Galaxy blinked the dazzle from her eyes.

"I can accompany you to the party, if you want."

"You mean for protection? Like a bodyguard?"

"Not a bodyguard." Dating university-style must be tougher than hippo hide. "But if you want the support, I'm glad to go along."

"No, I'll handle it. But thank you for the thought. It's gallant."

"Gallant? That sounds stuffy and old." I laughed at the image of me as a knight, striding through the medieval architecture on campus.

"Not old. But old-fashioned for certain. Anyway, now that I know where the threat comes from, I can keep an eye out."

Though the offer was genuine, I was glad she'd turned down my escort service. I wanted to get to Gerry Keith's office before the day was over. We walked to the door.

"You've been a big help, Rook. Thank you for cutting through the BS." She pressed a soft hand to my forearm. "Let's stay in touch. We're not so bad when you get beyond our stodgy campus ways."

Galaxy reached to turn the brass nob. A noise rattled in the outer office. She shrank from the door just as it blew open. A figure hurtled into the room. Howls blasted the dusty space. The attack's speed confused me. Black, purple, and yellow shreds of fabric and hair swirled. Galaxy fell to the carpet. Three blinks cleared my eyes. The storm resolved into a long-haired woman flailing at the dean with whirligig arms. The sight would have been comic if the shrieks hadn't been so eerie.

And if the knife flashing in the attacker's hand hadn't been so sharp.

I pulled the invader from Galaxy. She scooted toward her desk, beyond range of the attacker's blade. The woman and I swayed in a slow dance. I clamped both arms around her slender body. Her head lay against my chest, the blonde strands fanned over my black shirt like a cobweb. The pause was brief. She writhed in my grasp. Pounded her forehead against my sternum. Her thin shoulders shimmied until she freed one arm. She dragged her hand over my left cheek, a lover's touch. Then she clawed trenches in my skin. Pain darted from ear to chin. She bared her teeth, then spat in my face. Eyes popped, she raised the knife waist-high. The blade sliced my shirt. Next stop, my gut. I straightened my elbows to push her away from my body. But she leaned into my chest, her breath hot on my shirt.

"Reva! Stop it!" Galaxy crossed the room, shouting. "Stop!"

I turned my head. For an academic, she moved with lightning grace. The force of Galaxy's blow jolted the attacker's head against my chest. The blonde woman slumped in my arms, moaning. I lowered her limp body to the floor and looked up. Galaxy loomed above us, the wooden statue of the African mother clutched in both hands like a baseball bat.

Reva touched her damaged head. She stared at the blood dripping from her fingers. Smeared with red, an ugly switchblade fell from her fist and thumped on the carpet. I kicked the knife under the table.

"Galaxy, call the police. Now." I lowered my voice to command her attention.

Galaxy squeezed her lids, the eyeballs trembling. "No, I can't. I don't want…" She dropped the statue on her desk. It landed with a dull thud on the blotter. As if noticing the carved figure for the first time, she murmured, "Yoruba. Early twentieth century."

I needed the cool-headed dean not the dreamy scholar. "Galaxy, listen! Make the call. This is a police matter now. Call them. Or I will. When she comes around, she could attack you again."

I propped Reva against the base of the desk. Her blue eyes were unfocused. A milky film blurred the pupils. I crouched, pulling her shoulders toward me. I examined the wound on the crown of her head. Matted yellow hair hid the gash under a dirty clump. No fresh blood seeped through the straw; clotting had already begun. Strings of dull red drooped from her hair onto her back. She was concussed. Alexander's slugger dean had delivered a major league ding.

When I asked her name, Reva didn't answer. I tapped her cheek and asked again. Nothing. Was her silence guilt, muddle, rudeness, or all three? Or maybe Galaxy had knocked her clean into next week.

Galaxy called campus police. There were injuries, she said, but the threat was over. No one was seriously hurt. Squawking and screeching on the other end. A call from the dean incited frantic action from the local force. Alexander deans reporting physical violence on campus were rare occurrences. Good to know in case I ever visited campus again.

When I stood, Galaxy lunged at me with a wad of Kleenex, dabbing cuts on my cheek. "Reva got you pretty good. Put some iodine on the scratches when you get home. You're going to have quite a story to tell. Along with those war wounds." She took three swipes before the bleeding stopped. Two taps at my shirt smeared the blood into damp stains.

Another pass at my cheek. Her rubbing irritated the ripped skin and I winced. My face was scratched and so was my ego. But Galaxy's smiles were reward enough and took away the sting. And the embarrassment.

"This is James Nakamura's wife?" I looked at the slumped woman. "Fists of fury."

Reva's thin white hands jerked on the floor beside her hips. Her eyes pinwheeled from blue sky to muddy pond.

"Yeah. Never in a million years did I imagine little Reva had it in her. That was some old-school street skills right there." The glasses jiggled on Galaxy's chest as she chuckled. Grudging admiration tinged her speech along with a hint of nostalgia. "I haven't seen fighting like that since Hyde Park High back in the day. Skinny bitch knows how to cut."

Campus police burst into Galaxy's office within four minutes of her call. After ten minutes of assessing the scene and taking statements, two uniformed women officers escorted the wobbly Reva Nakamura to the squad car for a ride to the campus clinic. Two male cops stood at the round conference table to take Dean Pindar's detailed account.

Their interest in me faded once they determined I wasn't a member of the university community. They didn't need me. I didn't want to hang around. With a nod at Galaxy, I slipped through the muttering crowd gathered in the outer office of the dean's suite. I found the men's washroom at the end of the hall.

My hands shook and my knees vibrated as I pushed through the door. Air in the empty room chilled the damp gobs on my shirt and breezed through the rips in the cloth. Goosebumps prickled on my stomach. I leaned over the sinks, peering in the mirror. Stippling and hairline cracks in the glass blurred my view. I touched a finger to my cheek; it came away stained red. If anybody tells you academic life is for sissies, don't believe them. The blood smears reminded me of my other campus mission. I scrubbed my soiled hands, then headed for Gerry Keith's office in the Department of Anthropology.

# CHAPTER
# TWENTY

Escaping academic bedlam in the dean's office, I stumbled into the mellow sun of the quadrangles. I wanted to find the anthropology department fast. I was on the hunt and hotshot professor Gerry Keith was my target. Nathalie Kwan's directions were easy: I passed under the shadow of the giant arch, trooped due north, and found the Barstall Building after a fifteen-minute march. I didn't even have to ask directions from the campus cop who trailed ten paces behind me.

Nathalie had understated the ugliness of the pile. The glass cube was wrapped on four sides in red, blue, and yellow ducts and water pipes. Purple drainage spouts dangled from the roof at each corner. Matching purple metal railings bracketed the concrete steps to the front doors. The place was so ugly, I almost didn't go in.

I figured it was near quitting time, but the anthropology department office was still guarded by an admin assistant, a hulking black woman in a long green dress belted in a silky cord. She was Johnetta Ames, according to the nameplate on her desk. Chunky knots of hair tied with purple beads bristled from her head. She stared at my battle-scarred face and torn shirt when I asked for the department chair. She slotted her eyes left, then right like a nightclub bouncer. But when she spoke, lullabies wafted from her deep voice: "Dr. Keith stepped away for just a moment. Would you care to wait?" I guess some women go for the damaged rogue look.

There were no chairs in the space, only metal file cabinets and a wooden bench under the lone window. Floor to ceiling glass-enclosed cases framed the window. One display tower was filled with pottery and brightly feathered headdresses. The other featured weapons – daggers, guns, sabers, slingshots, clubs, and swords. Blocks of orange light from the setting sun pressed the carpet around Johnetta's desk. The bare bench looked stiff; sitting wasn't an attractive option. No need to seem aggressive so I didn't touch the desk, but I did lean into her space from my shaft of sunlight.

"Lots of sharp objects you've got there." I jerked my head toward the arms collection. "You hosting a war?"

She jiggled her cheeks at my thin joke and topped it. "Knives from Borneo and swords from Burkina Faso. Pistols from New Orleans, Anchorage, Monterrey, and Tokyo. Even a blow pipe for poison darts. From the Amazon, I think. Before department meetings, the chair tells me to seize all weapons." She reared her head and laughed at the ceiling. "He says it keeps tenure fights from getting wild."

"And you're the sheriff with the key, I hope?" I fastened my thumbs in my beltloops like a Texas lawman.

She grinned. "Nah, there's no keys for those cabinets. Lost 'em when we moved offices a year ago. Anybody wants one of them old things, they can have 'em."

I ambled to the nearest glass case and toggled the latch. When the door swung open the guns clicked against each other. Every weapon was bright and dust-free. "Nice collection," I said.

Stretching my fingers over the pistols, I felt a static spark leap from the steel to my skin. Gerry Keith had access to these guns. Would he use a weapon like this on Annie? I needed the police ballistics reports to confirm if slugs from one of these guns matched the murder weapon. I closed the door and returned to the admin assistant's desk.

Still no sign of Chairman Gerry. I had a hunch and I played it: "I'll visit the men's room while I wait."

Johnetta's smile said I was the brightest boy in class. "It's next to the elevator. Can't miss it."

The washroom offered a place to compose myself and assess the damage. Deep purple tiles and burnished copper surfaces contrasted with the glassy gleam of the rest of the building. I splashed water on my face. Cooling Reva's scratches would give me time to arrange my story before confronting Keith.

According to the mirror, I looked okay. Maybe wrapping up this little case, despite the violence, had smoothed the tension I'd been carrying for days. The harried hyper-alertness pinching my expression in the days since Annie's death was eased. I patted my cheeks with paper towels. Even the charcoal at the inner corners of my eye sockets looked brighter. I'd shaved the post-Annie stubble and shiny cheeks knocked a few years off my age. Thanks to Reva Nakamura's three nasty marks, I looked even younger. Like a punk after a schoolyard rumble.

"Rook, is that you? Hombre, you look like you just went fifteen rounds with Ali in Kinshasa."

Voice booming, Gerry Keith stepped from a stall. He stood beside me to rinse his hands in a copper basin. A navy sports jacket over black jeans gave him a formal air that the orange and green zig-zags of his tie were meant to counter. He loosened the knot to a rebellious drape and smoothed the flaps over his stomach. I grimaced, but said nothing.

He smirked at the mirror, red goatee bobbing, his eyes grabbing for mine. I waited for him to deliver the quip he had ready. "I trust the other guy looks worse than you."

His cackle prompted me. Did the whole campus know about the fight in Dean Pindar's office already? I wouldn't add details to the juicy story. "It was a pretty one-sided fight. But I made out alright. Thanks for your concern, Gerry."

Smirks bloomed into sneers. "Hey, de nada, pal. Us guys have to stick together. Especially when women get the upper hand. Speaking of which, I understand it was Reva Nakamura who stormed into Galaxy Pindar's office."

Maybe Annie had told him my mother was Mexican-American. Or maybe he'd figured it out from studying my face. Either way, Keith was slathering his version of south-of-the-border culture with a thick trowel.

Fishing for details, he clapped a damp palm on my shoulder. "Can you beat that? Nothing like an academic cat fight, is there? Two ladies, pregnant with the burden of degrees and intellect, mixing it up in public. Knives, nails, teeth. Reminds me of Henry Kissinger's old line about Ivory Tower battles: the hostilities are so fierce because the stakes are so low. I mean, *come on!* What sane woman would go to war over a beardless wimp like Jimmy Nakamura?"

Keith's sarcasm didn't deserve answers. I nodded, balled up the paper towel, and tossed it.

He didn't care if I spoke or not, and continued his nasty rant as though I'd agreed with him. "Right? I mean, have you met the man? And I use the term loosely. A lavender peacock on toothpicks, that's Jimmy Nakamura for you. *Maricón.*" Keith shook his head in mock horror. I thought James Nakamura looked decent enough; his appeal to female taste wasn't something I'd try to measure.

My silence gave Keith more room to crow. "Say, why don't you come with me to the faculty reception? I bet Jimmy's there right now, sucking up to some vice president, weaseling more money for his department. I want to see the look on Jimmy's face when he hears Reva attacked Galaxy. It'll be epic, hombre!"

Keith's eyes danced with glee. Next, he'd rub his hands like a ghoul in a silent movie. He raked fingers through his red curls to fluff them and finished the preening with a pass over his stylish whiskers. I frowned at the invitation and pivoted for the door.

Keith took the challenge, as I'd intended. He doubled down on his offer. "Hey, come on, dude. You're going to catch a cab on the avenue anyway, right? The faculty club is just across the quad. You've got to pass it to get off campus, so why not stop in? You'll be my guest. Come on, Rook. Take the sting out of your war wounds with a drink or two, why don't you?"

As Keith babbled on, the mellowness of my post-skirmish mood circled the drain. Anger I'd banked for eight days churned in my gut again. I'd never hit Reva Nakamura, of course. But the pent-up energy stoked by that one-sided contest burned in my fingertips. Pounding on chatty Gerry Keith might be a nice substitute.

I clinched my fists as I leaned on the bathroom door. Keith pursued me down the corridor, talking ninety miles an hour. My silence didn't daunt him. Some kind of lousy anthropologist he was. Ignorant was too gentle a word for this galloping oaf. With observational skills this dim, how'd he escape scalping by some fed-up local during his field research?

An hour ago, I'd told Galaxy Pindar I was forging my anger into something more productive. I hadn't wanted to scare her by using the term vengeance. But that's what I was after. Time to put words into action. I dialed the rage to a low simmer. A drink or two on Alexander University's tab was the ticket. I wanted more time with a gabby Keith. His loose talk might give me new clues into his relationship with Annie. Something he dropped might help me solve her murder. This was my opportunity to dig.

We'd reached the elevators. "Thanks for the invite, Gerry. I'll stop in for a minute, see how you academic types party."

Keith's grin broadened. He clinched his hand over my shoulder, like he'd greet a tribal elder. No doubt, he could blurt "Take me to your leader" in seventeen languages.

"Awesome! But don't get your hopes up too high, mi amigo. Faculty receptions tend to be pretty sedate affairs. Lots of posturing, not enough booze. Plenty of politics, zero authenticity."

Comfortable on his home turf, Gerry let his jerk flag fly free: "And despite all those affirmative action hires, bro, still too many sausages, too few ladies. No hot mamitas, I'm afraid." He rolled his eyes.

I shrugged to remove his hand, then poked the down button. "Warning noted."

# CHAPTER
# TWENTY-ONE

From the elevator, we walked through the glass doors and along a ramp onto the deserted quadrangle in front of the Barstall Building. The sun had dipped, stealing the Indian Summer and all those pretty girls who'd basked in its warmth. The last jeweled bars of light slid between the Manhattan towers, throwing stains of purple and ruby across the brooding trees.

Keith matched his loping strides to my slower pace. We cut the corner of a grassy triangle to meet a pebbled path. I wanted him talking. It didn't take much to get him babbling about his own accomplishments. A nudge was all.

"So, tell me about your new book, Gerry. I see it's up for some kind of prize?"

"Yes, the Blackistone Prize. That's the biggest scholarly award at Alexander. Categories alternate, so one year they give the prize for teaching, the next year for academic achievement in original research. Then for teaching again. This year it's for scholarship and I'm one of three finalists. Lovebirds Jimmy Nakamura and Galaxy Pindar are the other two. Can you believe that?"

I believed it, but Keith expected compliance, so I shrugged. "Yeah, pretty weird."

"Rigged, if you ask me. Mighty suspicious. How are they even in the running with me? Jimmy's research was in a microfilm repository, scrolling through reels of old newspapers, for God's sake."

Keith pursed his lips in disdain at this armchair investigation. In his telling, the dean had done even less.

"Sure, Galaxy went to West Africa a few times. But she did most of her work in the British Public Records Office and the Foreign Office archives in London. The dried-up old biddies in those libraries lugged the crumbling volumes to her, and Galaxy leafed through them wearing white gloves to prevent shredding the pages. How's that real research, I ask you?"

Keith's ears reddened. Pink blotches painted his cheeks, and his throat quivered with disdain. If apoplexy blew off his head, there wasn't a campus cop in sight to catch it.

Nakamura and Pindar could defend their academic credentials without my help. I wanted Keith to expand on his own field work. "Your research with the maids in Anniesha's company was different? How so?"

My question calmed him; the high color drained from his face, replaced by a sallow gloss. Lecturing was his favorite mode. With me as round-eyed student, he was happy to educate.

"You remember Sarah Anastos? Sally, right?" He wriggled his eyebrows until I nodded. "Cute kid. My lead research assistant. Between us, we interviewed almost three hundred individual workers in Miami. We spent thousands of hours in their homes, interviewing not only the maids themselves, but their families, husbands, neighbors, bosses, and customers. Using all that first-hand data, we built a 360-degree picture of the lives of those maids."

I scrunched my nose as if I could smell the stench of the ghetto rising around us. "Must've been tough."

"Not just tough, amigo. The work was tedious, grinding, boring. And sometimes what I did was dangerous. Those neighborhoods weren't the safest in Miami, you know. A slum is a slum, even with palm trees lining its streets. And those gals hung out with a pretty unsavory bunch of lowlife hombres."

I clutched my fists at my sides to contain the weight of undelivered punches. Blows straining to let loose on Gerry's smug mouth. His scorn for Annie's employees was breathtaking. But I let him go on. He was giving me information I could use.

"With a few exceptions, Anniesha's girls were on the up-and-up. Not smart, but decent and diligent. She screened all the girls and hired the best she could. But a lot of the people her girls hung out with were pretty dicey. You know, running drugs up from Latin America and the Caribbean. Money laundering, child trafficking, all the shit you read about. Those people were not the types you want to rub elbows with, if you value your life."

As the tired clichés dripped, he dropped his jaw in a mask of horror. Then he winked. Had Keith really spent time in Miami? Acid rising in my mouth threatened to choke me. I was one of "those people." I clamped my teeth shut and let him talk.

"But I had to do it, to get the research done. And to get it done right. That's the kind of risk Sally and I took every day. And that's why I'm so damn proud of what I accomplished in Miami." A few more boasts and Gerry Keith would inflate like a Goodyear blimp. I pictured him floating over the ivy-draped gothic towers, a dark blob merging with the dusky sky.

To stop him from launching into outer space, I tossed a softball. "Was your book, *The Dirty and the Clean,* based only on your research in Anniesha's company?"

"Mostly, but we used another cleaning company in upstate New York as a control group. An outfit run by that blonde woman, Pearl Byrne. Frowzy and dim. Classic washer-woman. You know the type: thick waist, potato-sack breasts, red hands, crow's feet. Did you meet her at the conference?" His mouth puckered in disdain as he picked at lint on his lapel.

I nodded. He plunged on.

"We did lots of interviews there too. Maybe almost two hundred. I forget exactly how many girls we interviewed up there. Plenty. Different kind of crowd from those Miami gals, I'll tell you. But that bitch Pearl

Byrne is one first-class liar. If she tells you something, you can bet the farm it didn't happen the way she claims."

The complaint against Pearl came out of the blue. What did the "washer-woman" do to him? Like the others, she was capable of protecting herself against Keith's attacks on her professional credibility. I let his smear slide.

I wanted to push him further on the academic award. There's nothing a jackass enjoys more than the sound of his own braying. So, I slathered compliments over his tender ego. "You got that Blackistone Prize locked down, right?"

He grinned. "If they evaluate it with intellectual objectivity, I'll win. No doubt in my mind."

"Nice load of cash. What is it? Five, ten thousand?" I knew the right answer, just like I knew Keith would enjoy correcting me.

"Oh no, it's *fifty* thousand." As he named the sum, Keith worked his fingers around his beard to erase the smile.

He wanted me to be impressed, so I whistled. "Do they give runner-up awards?"

Keith snorted. "No, dude. This isn't flag football where every kid gets a participation trophy. The winner of the Blackistone Prize gets the whole award – fifty thousand dollars. The others get nada. Zip." He popped his lips in juicy satisfaction.

"Will you share the winner's purse with co-researchers. Like Sally Anastos?" I knew the answer to this one too, but playing dumb worked like a charm.

The great man used simple words to explain the mysteries of academe to me. "Look, here's how it works: I'm the sole author of the book nominated for the Blackistone. The committee deliberates over the three nominees. If the committee selects my book, I win. And I'm the one who gets the prize money. Every peso."

I bugged my eyes and nodded, open-mouthed. "That's a boatload of cash, Gerry. Plus, lots of publicity and prestige." And Sally Anastos cut out of the whole thing. Did his adoring groupie know how Keith planned to horde the prize and the glory after his big victory?

"Yeah, this will be a definite boost for my academic career. Not that I'm slacking or sliding, obviously. But this recognition will put me at the front ranks of the field. I can write my own ticket from here on out, maybe even score an endowed chair out of it."

"What's that?" I had no idea a chair could be endowed with anything other than upholstery, so my ignorance was real.

"The university development office is talking with an extremely wealthy donor right now. I mean, *loaded*. Some Richie Richenstein with lots of money, tons of white privilege guilt, and an ego as big as Trump Tower. If they get that fat cat to agree to it, the anthropology department will establish a special faculty position for me with Richie's name on it."

Hard to tell whose condescension was bigger, the moneybag donor's or the self-satisfied jerk lecturing me.

Keith was on a roll, no prompt needed. "The donation is invested and the earned interest from it pays the salary of the professor who's appointed to the named chair. That endowment also pays all the professor's expenses for research, travel, support staff, equipment, graduate assistants, all that razzmatazz."

"An endowed chair is a pretty big deal, hunh?"

"Well, if a Tyrannosaurus Rex is a 'pretty big' reptile. Then yeah, an endowed chair is a 'pretty big' fucking deal. If I win the Blackistone Prize, I nail down the endowment too."

"Sounds like you got the prize sewn up, Gerry. Too bad Anniesha isn't here to celebrate your victory with you." Ice sharpened my words into stinging lances.

Purple rushed across his face. "Yeah, I'm sorry about that too. She was a great informant, a dear friend to me."

He blinked twice to soften his comments, make them more personal. He tried to squeak sounds an actual human being might utter. If he'd had a heart. Or a soul. The croaking noise didn't even come close. "She brought me into the Miami scene, showed me around, made me feel at home. Anniesha was a great gal. A wonderful gal."

I kicked a stone, watching dust spurt as it skipped across the path. More evidence about Keith's relationship with Annie might help the investigation. But it wouldn't help me. I touched a hand to my waist, just above the belt on the left side. A slow pulse, not quite pain, jumped in time with my heart. After twenty seconds the throbbing slowed, another ten and it disappeared. I lowered my hand and rubbed the damp palm against my slacks.

I stared at Keith. A shallow crease twitched above his nose. He realized I had a position in the equation too. Even if I was only a ghost from Annie's past. He eyed me, imitating empathy with a lizard's slow blink.

"Hey, look, amigo. I meant to ask you, how're you dealing with her death?" He licked at the corners of his mouth. "I know you were just the ex. Nothing current. But still, it could have hit you hard too. Even as hard as it shocked those of us close to her. Losing her like that."

His tongue gummed to the top of his mouth. He hocked saliva, the sound coating his words with phony compassion. This was the right thing to say, he knew from books. Keith didn't care how I felt. He lowered his gaze for a moment because he'd seen the gesture in a movie once. It was almost human.

My response was correct too. "It was a blow. But I'm doing alright, Gerry. Thanks for asking."

We both passed the manners test, our status as hypocrites intact.

He jogged both shoulders. Wind tangled the mantle of leaves above us, filling the silence with brittle rustling. The oak trees smelled parched, as if sand had replaced sap in their veins.

After a minute, Keith broke the hush. "You in mourning? For Anniesha?" He gestured at my black shirt, jacket, and trousers.

"This?" I passed a hand over my shirt front. "No, I wear black most days."

Relieved to land on safer ground, Keith hurried to turn the conversation. He ditched tragedy with a jibe: "You sporting a neo-Batman complex there, Rook? What are you, the Dark Knight of Lenox Avenue?"

I shook my head in mock sorrow. "No cape, no high-tech mansion, or English butler." Then, I bumped the banter. "And too poor to expand my wardrobe. But when my ship comes in, Gerry, the only thing you'll see me wearing is Hugo Boss and Armani. Maybe someday a fat cat will award me a Nobel Prize for detecting." I let my lips slide apart for the grin.

188

As we rounded a bend in the path, Keith increased our pace. "Yeah, sure, amigo, why not?"

He'd raised this topic, so my question was fair game: "You and Sally Anastos? Something going on there?"

Keith was back, the melancholy of past loss shed like a struck match. He grunted a wet laugh. "She's a fireball, huh? Lots of anger and muscle in that juicy little trap, I'll tell you."

I let my eyebrows jump: "Tasty for sure." Locker room banter always worked. Always.

Keith couldn't stop the ugliness. "Don't get me wrong. On a greatest hits list, Sally Anastos wouldn't make my top ten. Not even top twenty. A colleague nailed the description perfectly: he said Sally has Miss America tits and a Kentucky Derby face!" Keith's chuckle exploded into another snort. "But on a rainy night or a dull afternoon, the kid's got one of the sweetest muffs on campus. Desperation makes 'em juicy, right? Our Sally's a pathetic plodder. Never a champion, but definitely a contender."

As the bragging expanded, he forgot himself again. "But Sally's not in the same class with Anniesha. *That* gal's a whole different order of magnitude. Never seen anything like Anniesha. She's marvelous! First-rate! I'm talking kitchen faucet versus Niagara Falls!" He rolled his eyes, lips twisted in a grotesque leer.

*Done.* Communion ended. Gravel gargle would clean this bastard's filthy mouth. My next move was easy. Bickering squirrels on a branch overhead drew Keith's glance. I stepped sideways, swiveling my boot in a brisk arc. It clipped his heel. He grunted, then sprawled on the gritty trail. Two knees, two palms, and one chin hit the dirt. The squirrels hushed.

I stooped, clamped a hand on his elbow. I lifted him upright. "You okay, Gerry?"

He spit and dribbled. The squirrels chittered. I pulled a soiled tissue from my back pocket. He used it to brush gravel from his blood-specked palm. He dragged the chalky mess around his face. Then he dabbed at his stained pants. After ninety seconds of work, Keith looked fine. Except for the sand scattered through his red goatee. And the grimy smudge on his brow. And the dirt smeared in the hollow of his cheek. And the rip at his knee. The squirrels in the gallery clattered in cheery chorus.

I beamed the demure smile of a first semester co-ed. "That was quite a tumble, Gerry."

"Sure." Keith looked at me screw-eyed as he pocketed the filthy tissue. "No damage."

We limped a few steps along the path. A vine-covered heap of gray stone blocked our way. The structure had narrow windows on the upper floors and the notched roof-line of a castle. A heavy wooden door crossed by black iron struts continued the medieval theme. A dry moat jumbled with pebbles and weeds separated the building from the sidewalk where we stood.

Pointing at a low bridge which crossed the moat, Keith flung his arm wide, as if welcoming me to his own private fortress. "Here's the faculty club. A modest thing, but mine own." His voice blared like a trumpet. "Looks like the festivities are in full swing."

We peered through a large window which was divided into rectangles by black lead bars. I saw clutches of men in corduroy and tweed, bow-ties plentiful, vests stuffed to overflowing. The few women scraped their hair into low pony-tails and matched their somber sweaters to their slacks. Chandeliers cast yellow light on bald heads and waxy jowls. As we watched, everyone raised a glass to an unheard toast. White teeth flashed against the room's dark paneling. Either everyone was having a grand time. Or faking it in high style.

"It's been a long day, Gerry." I touched an index finger to the cuts on my cheek.

I let my shoulders sag. As if I was overwhelmed by exhaustion. Or grief. Or poverty. Or whatever hideous traumas he imagined were the burdens of my sorry ghetto life. "I'll take a rain check on the reception and head home."

"You sure? You're welcome to join us." He looked from me to the window and back again. Lines deepened around his mouth. He wanted to score points against James Nakamura and Galaxy Pindar. I was to be the gaudy bat for his assault.

But I wasn't playing the game. "Thanks for the invitation. Maybe another time."

We shook hands at the foot of the little bridge. I squeezed to grind the gravel into his palm.

Keith gasped then grimaced. Then he shook his shoulders like a boxer shedding an annoying opponent. As he crossed the moat, he wiped fingers on his pants. Smudges grew to black streaks under his oily touch. He pushed the heavy door of the faculty club and disappeared into the glare.

Darkness tinged with gold and pink collapsed in soft folds around me as I turned toward the edge of campus. A few paces beyond the faculty club, a uniformed cop stepped into line behind me. As long as I was at Alexander University – and Black – I'd never be alone. He escorted me with silent resolve until I slipped through the iron gates and beyond the campus walls. Gliding past the ivy, I saluted my dutiful companion. He tipped his chin, but didn't wave good-bye. Within a few minutes of reaching the avenue, I flagged a taxi for the short ride home.

Darting through the bustle of uptown traffic, Gerry Keith's callous words crowded my mind. He'd scraped my nerves raw, as if he'd dragged a fingernail over the scratches on my cheek. The man was a shrine to unlimited self-regard. The murder of *my* ex-wife was all about him. But he'd given me what I wanted, new leads. He'd pointed me toward the two women who could uncover how and why Annie had been killed. Her colleague Pearl Byrne and Sally Anastos, the elfin disciple, held the keys to solving my case.

# CHAPTER
# TWENTY-TWO

The evening of my campus skirmish, Brina turned first aid into a game, soothing my nerves along with my scratches.

Brina squinted into the mirror in my bathroom. "Iodine or ointment?" In her right hand, she held the dark little bottle caked on the rim with its dreadful liquid. In her left, she squeezed a tube of antiseptic. We leaned forward to examine again the three scarlet stripes blazed across my left cheek.

We were both dressed in cotton – a blue striped shirt over black boxers for me, a red t-shirt for her. This top didn't quite cover her lilac panties, a good arrangement. Smiles danced across her mouth as she stood beside me. Under her analytic gaze, I shifted from side to side, bare toes curling against the cool tiles. Herb the cat rubbed my ankles, purring like a lawn mower.

Brina traced a finger over the point of my collar. "You know, this blue shirt does something wonderful for your eyes. Where'd you get it again?"

She'd given it to me, of course. I said thank you with a kiss to the hairline above her right ear. And the nape of her neck. And her earlobe, right on the spot where whiffs of her amber scent lingered.

Brina joined Herb in purring. Then she unloaded another round of teasing. "This Reva-freak got you pretty good!"

"Well, I don't know…" I squeezed my eyes to block the reflection of my battle scars, but laughter bobbled my Adam's apple.

She insisted on showing off her expertise as she ran a finger over my flayed cheek. "That's natural nails right there. Acrylics don't leave marks like that!"

No dispute there, so I sighed and pointed at the iodine with an elaborate flourish.

She unscrewed the bottle, dipped a cotton swab into its clotted depths. "Going old school, hunh?" Balancing on tip-toes, she dabbed at the scratches until they were painted completely. I winced with more drama than the minor sting merited.

"Tell me again: how big was this Reva woman and how exactly did she take you down like this?" She kept her voice soft and sing-songy, to make sure I knew she was teasing.

I raised eyebrows and quirked my mouth. "Five-two, maybe three. One fifteen tops. But she didn't 'take me down.' I handled her all right. She was scrappy, true. And that switchblade was the real deal. But after Dean Pindar clocked her with a sculpture, I had no problem wrestling Reva to the ground."

We laughed at the improbable images cast by this thumbnail account of the latest case. First aid treatment complete, Brina led me by the hand to bed where we settled under the blue coverlet.

I leaned against the headboard and heaved a giant sigh. "And tell me about your afternoon basking in the special glow of Mr. 2-Ryght the hip-hop artiste extraordinaire. Was he everything you'd hoped he'd be?"

Brina screwed up her nose. "Naw, he wasn't all that. Short and kinda overdressed and underfed." She held her left hand about twelve inches above the coverlet.

"Scrawny? But flashy? Why am I not surprised? Lots of phony gold chains too, I bet."

"No, sir! Those chains were the real deal. I got close enough to check it out."

"That close, hunh? Did he smell good too?"

Brina landed a light punch against my shoulder. "You can joke, but that boy smelled like fame and money, lots of it. Like a green grassy meadow full of cash."

"He could bottle it and make even more. But how is 2-Ryght supposed to maintain his street rep if he smells like a leprechaun and looks like one too?"

Brina's giggling fit toppled her onto me, a development I encouraged with well-placed kisses. I'd hoped her story of hip-hop royalty's walk among the peasants was over, but she had more to say.

"The crowd was big and excited. Lots of jumping and shoving to get a look at the main attraction. You know that shoe store, how narrow it is. So, of course, they couldn't cram everybody into the place. Smoke told Daddy and me to stay outside and handle the crowd. While he went inside to keep close to the cameras and to the kid."

"And why am I not surprised. Smoke is the kind of joker who'd send a woman and an old man to do his job while he coasted on the glamour end of the show." The frown that snuck onto Brina's face wasn't pretty, so I backpedaled fast. "I mean… well… not that you and Norment aren't perfectly able to handle any crowd control…"

She'd heard a slight against her skills. I veered to an adjacent topic at whiplash speed. "Did you get any swag out of this gig? Or was the honor of serving His Majesty 2-Ryght payment enough?"

"Daddy got a pair of yellow-and-red high tops, signed by 2-Ryght himself. And mine are over there." She gestured toward the snow-glare white shoes toppled next to the refrigerator. "When you get to the office tomorrow, you'll see what's inside the box Smoke left on your desk. He picked them himself after I told him your size."

"Can't wait." This was in fact the end of the story. Or at least the last I could stomach listening to. "This day can't end soon enough. If I never hear of Reva or 2-Ryght again in my life, it'll be way too soon."

Brina agreed. She rotated in my arms so the red nightshirt lifted over her hips. Her kisses covered my eyes, my nose, and my damaged cheek, finally sliding down to my lips where they worked their healing magic for a good long time.

That night I was ready at last. I told Brina about Annie. I talked about our kiss, about the hope I'd found and lost the day she died. Brina asked questions, I stumbled through answers. She nudged and wept and laughed and chided. Brina's patience enfolded me, her steady refusal to pity or coddle me was the comfort I needed.

———————

Rustling of sheets awakened me near dawn. Brina tip-toed to the kitchen for a glass of water. Four sips, then she slipped next to me, pulling the sheets over her head. Snuffling dragged me from sleep's edge. I scooted toward the foot of the bed until my face was level with hers. Under the tent, I dropped a kiss against her damp temple. Pink sunlight filtering through the white cotton bathed her bare skin, casting a warm glow over the tears on her cheek.

"What's wrong, Brina?"

"Nothing."

"This nothing feels wet." I stroked a finger against her cheek. I kissed her eyes. "Tastes salty too."

"I'm just thinking too much. That's all."

"About Dreamie?"

She paused a beat. "About Anniesha."

Breath rushed from me. I rolled onto my back and raised a knee, lifting the sheet from our bodies. "What about her?" I figured Brina was jealous, still. But the depth of her anxiety surprised me. I'd thought she would absorb information about Annie, slot it into her data bank about me, and not dwell on the past. I had lots to process about Brina, even after all this time together.

Her soft profile stilled; her chin lowered to her throat. "Was she your first?"

"My first?"

"Girl. Woman. You know… When did you…? Uh… You know…" Her usual boldness had fled.

"Lose my virginity?"

"Yeah."

"Junior year of high school. Garnette Pace. Waitress who worked with my mother."

"She your age?"

"Eight years older. She was between boyfriends."

"Oh, I see." Little frown lines between her brows meant she didn't.

I whispered, the comfort aimed at her and my sixteen-year-old self: "It wasn't so bad. She needed something, I needed something. It all worked out."

"Did your mother know?"

"Mom would have killed me – and Garnette – if she found out. So no, she didn't know." I breathed a small sigh, ruffling her eyelashes. "We practiced 'Don't ask, don't tell' real early in our family."

"And Anniesha?" Her stumble over the name caused my throat to tighten. "How did you meet her?"

I sipped a gulp of warm air to ease my answer. "I met her the summer before junior year. My cousin Lolita owned a beauty shop. Every summer, Lolita hosted a family barbecue and that August she invited a new client, Annie's mother. Annie came too. A few weeks later, I got paired with Annie as my lab partner for first semester biology. She got an A; I got a B minus."

Brina chuckled. "And you started dating your study buddy then?"

"No, we never dated in school. Didn't get together until almost ten years later."

This time the sighs were Brina's. Cool pink air rippled against the sheet, eddying across my chest. To shake the goosebumps, I kissed her again. I was done with talking.

But she wasn't. "You've got to find them." Strong fingers dug into my biceps.

"Who?" I caught her meaning, but I wanted her to say the words.

"The people who killed Dreamie. And the ones who murdered Annie. You've got to find them. For all of us."

"I will."

Through with brooding. Until the next time.

_____

An hour later, my sheets wrapped around her bronze shoulders, her hair a gorgeous mess, Brina watched me prod the toaster and pour the coffee.

When she spoke, her voice was raspy and wistful. "I missed you, Rook."

"I missed me too." One cup full, I paused, the carafe dribbling coffee into the second.

"It's not over yet, you know." She was practical, realistic, and plain-spoken. Patching me up again, like always. Last night the healing was with iodine and tender kisses. This morning she used soft phrases to fix me. Just when I wanted to be romantic, she pulled from that brink. Did the Annie story reinforce her old doubts about me? Or did she distrust herself?

I wasn't going to probe. Not now. We'd moved along the path a bit. I'd take it for now. "I know. Not for a while. But I'm getting there."

As I lowered the coffee pot, Herb the cat jumped from the windowsill onto the chest-of-drawers beside the bed.

"You still hate Herb?" Her lips curved when I handed a cup to her. The smile dressed the worry in a coat of playful tease.

She glanced toward the cat's high perch. He was polishing his ears as he followed our conversation.

I decided I didn't want Herb to die after all. I took a sip, then announced, "Not anymore."

"He's glad. I'm glad too. We both missed you."

The cat hurled a yellow stare from the top of the dresser. His whiskers bristled in chummy satisfaction as he licked his tail. Herb had known I couldn't stay lost forever.

After we showered together, Brina headed to her own apartment for a change of clothes. Over the months, she'd imported a few items into the bottom drawer of my dresser: jeans, a red pullover, two embroidered blouses, a black bra, and some panties. But if she wanted to wear anything more formal, she had to return to her own place. Maybe the time was near to change those arrangements.

Soon after she left, a sharp rap at the door caught me off guard. With a damp blue towel still wrapped around my middle, I bolted to open the door. Had Brina returned to work on unfinished business?

No such luck.

# CHAPTER
# TWENTY-THREE

"You always greet your guests like this, Rook?" Smiles wreathed Archie Lin's round flat face as he surveyed my half-naked state. "Or you just glad to see me?"

He was decked in his detective best, a dingy brown suit with a faint khaki stripe. The eye-sore tie had swirls of tan, yellow, and army green which battled the moss-colored shirt. I was underdressed, but still better outfitted than Archie Lin.

"You've *got* to be kidding me." I pitched my words toward the ceiling. "Don't you have anything better to do than drop in unannounced on innocent citizens at ungodly hours of the morning? What kind of monster are you?"

"It's ten-thirty, Rook. Not exactly early for us working stiffs. You know, the kind with regular jobs. Anyway, I brought you breakfast." He waved a blue-checkered sack over his head as he barged past me to the kitchen. "So, cut your crying and put on another pot of coffee."

My stomach growled in approval of Archie's greasy bag. Two minutes to drag on jeans and t-shirt, another five to drip a fresh pot. I settled opposite my friend at the little round table between the sleeping nook and kitchen peninsula. Archie, full of unexpected manners, had retrieved a plate from the cabinet over the sink and arranged his gift doughnuts in an artful pyramid.

"I didn't know what kind you liked so I got two crullers, two whole-wheat, two chocolate-lovers' delights, and two pumpkin spice-flavored ones. For the season, you know."

"This is good, Archie, real good. Thanks for this."

Munching on a cruller, I brought the carton of milk to the table in case he wanted to lighten his coffee, which he did. Herb the cat insisted, so I poured a bowl of milk for him too.

"So, what's up? This isn't a social call." We were pals, the beer-and-peanuts kind. Not some suburban ladies' coffee circle, gossiping about the neighbors until the afternoon soaps came on. "You got something you want to tell me. Or something you want me to spill. Which is it?"

Archie shrugged, wiped pumpkin-orange crumbs from his mouth, and plunged in. "You're working a couple of cases right now we might have some details on. Stuff you could use, personal or professional. Either way, up to you. But I wanted you to get this info direct."

That gulp in his voice sounded ominous. I waved a chunk of cruller at him anyway. "What do you have?"

He gathered a full chest of air, then let it out in one swoop. "On that murder case involving your ex. You know we hit a brick wall. No leads on suspects came out of our inquiries with the Miami-Dade police. She wasn't Mother Theresa, but pretty near, at least by what her friends and colleagues say. Paid her bills, paid her employees, kept her nose clean, kept quiet around the neighborhood. Like I said, not a saint, but damn close to it. That was Miami…"

Here Archie trailed off and inhaled the other half of the pumpkin doughnut. Then he swallowed a big gulp of coffee. He was stalling, which meant the next part of his story wasn't so nice. Or it cut closer to home.

"Go on. You got more to say, don't you? What about the coroner's office? Didn't they come up with anything about the shooting itself?"

"Nothing about the shooting itself. She died instantly from a single .32 caliber bullet to the heart. Couple of cocktails, wine, and a seafood salad for dinner. The only thing that stood out was what she had after dinner."

Another long pause. This was like pulling teeth from a water buffalo. I didn't know who was going to get hurt more by the extraction, me or the buffalo.

"And?"

"And… Yeah, well, it turns out the guy she was with was that professor, Gerry Keith. You remember him? Anniesha and the prof got together after dinner. Not too long before she died."

It was my turn to take a gulp of coffee. And a big bite from my cruller. Archie's eyes were glued to a fascinating dollop of chocolate on his index finger. His mouth turned down and red stained his cheeks. This report from the medical examiner prompted fresh questions; he wanted me to answer without his having to raise them. But if he wasn't asking, I wasn't telling.

Misery seeped through me. I knew Annie and Keith had been lovers in Miami. He'd said as much during our stroll across campus. But I hadn't been sure until now that they'd kept up the affair. Now Annie's last hours played through my mind like a grainy silent film: booze, dinner, more booze, sex, a bullet chaser. If I'd stuck around that night, I could have protected her. I might have prevented her murder. My neglect didn't kill her. I knew that. But the more I chewed it over, the more this felt like my fault. Guilt for her distorted life crawled through me, dragging blame for her soiled death.

I set down the cup to avoid spilling the coffee. And to disguise the trembling in my hand. Archie, not as obtuse as he pretended, sighed in sympathy with my distress. He pulled a plastic zip bag from his pocket and laid it on the table. A long silver filigree earring clattered against the wood when I dumped it out.

"What's this?"

"You know what it is, dontcha?"

"Annie's earring."

He fingered a tiny tear-drop shaped hole in the star-burst array of coral. The silver framed an empty shadow. "You know where the missing piece is?"

"You know I do." I walked to the tall dresser next to my bed. I pulled a rolled gray sock from the bottom drawer. I retrieved the coral nugget I'd plucked from the carpet in Annie's hotel room. Seated at the table again, I dropped the chunk into its setting. It fit like a sun-kissed dream. I stroked an index finger once over the smooth surface.

"How'd you know I had it?"

"I saw you pick it up." Embarrassment soured his voice. "In her room, when we were checking it out."

"You didn't say anything."

He lifted his shoulders, then quirked his lips around an excuse. "Maybe you wanted a souvenir of her. Maybe you hoped it was a clue."

"It *could* have been a clue." Squeaky and high-pitched. Pathetic, but it was my truth, so I let the rest come out. "I wanted it to be."

"Yeah, I know."

"Maybe if the shooter had dropped it, maybe I could have found who killed Annie."

"That's what I figured you thought."

"Maybe her earring broke when she fought her attacker."

Archie's eyes narrowed in professional skepticism. "You saw the room, Rook. No signs of struggle. No overturned chairs, no lamps dropped on the floor. Sheets tossed from sex, not from any violent attack. Whoever killed her was no stranger."

Archie sighed again. I slipped the repaired earring into the evidence bag and pushed it toward him. That line of inquiry was done. Scrubbed, stamped, and filed. Archie's mug was empty, so I got up to do my host duties.

Pouring a fresh cup, I turned the conversation. "You got something else for me, Archie? You want another chunk of my heart today?"

I clutched fingers over my chest in mock agony. I had no leftover anger for him. But Archie's scant eyebrows puckered. He looked guilty again, so I knew the blows would keep coming.

"I don't know if this next bit cuts quite as close for you. But it does concern your extended family, so to speak."

"What is it?"

"On the skeleton found in the basement of that Strivers Row mansion, we got the M.E.'s report on the possible cause of death. It was a female, mid-thirties to forty."

"Yeah, I know. Norment Ross ID'd the remains. She was his missing wife, Jayla Dream. Dreamie. He reported her gone twenty-five years ago. So, can you determine if she died that long ago? Or is the death more recent?"

"Can't tell for sure, the body is decomposed so bad there isn't much to go on. Based on Ross's ID we checked with local dentists for records to compare with the skeleton. Nothing doing. There was a fire twenty years ago in that dentist's office where she used to work, so we figure her files musta went up in smoke along with everything else. So, nothing conclusive from that angle. But Gleason says it's possible she died around the time Ross reported her missing. Certainly, within the same year anyway."

I shook my head, then poked an index finger to arrange doughnut crumbs into a straight line on the table.

"She was wearing the same clothing Norment said she had on the last day he saw her. Doesn't prove anything. She could have bought new clothes during the interval. Maybe she just happened to be wearing the same jeans and sweater when she died. But the coincidence is hard to buy."

"Agreed. So where does that leave it?"

"Did the M.E. say what killed her? Or how she got into that hidden room?" I asked.

"Like I said, the decomp was so bad, lots of the usual evidence couldn't be determined. But he did say there were multiple broken bones. The pelvis and left femur were shattered. No damage to the skull, but broken vertebrae in the neck could be the cause of death."

"So, what do you figure, Arch? Was she beaten to death? Any clue from the nature of the breaks as to what she was hit with? Hammer, baseball bat, wrench, tire iron? Or did she fall and break all those bones?"

"Look, I'm giving you everything we got to go on. I asked Gleason the same questions you did. And I'm giving you exactly the same answers I got. We don't know nothing specific. If we knew, I'd tell you."

DELIA C. PITTS

"I appreciate you keeping me informed on this case. You know I do. It's hard when you've got so few facts. And when the feelings are still running so high."

"I know. You gonna share this info with Old Man Ross?"

I shrugged and chewed on my lower lip before I mumbled the answer.

"He took it hard when we went down to identify the body. Or actually, just the clothes. That was tough. They wouldn't let him see the remains. They said it was only a pile of bones anyway, nothing that could contribute to the identification. So, he had to leave with a look at her raggedy sweater and a pair of jeans with rat droppings all over them. That was a hard day. A hard day, Archie."

I reached for a napkin from the stack in the middle of the table. Archie didn't get to see me cry over Annie again. Once was enough. But it was okay if he knew the death of Norment's wife hit me too. A different way, but just as tough. I swiped the napkin across my eyes and touched it to my nose.

"Yeah, I know, Rook. I know."

I recovered my voice, the scratchy part. At the harsh sound, Herb swiveled his ears in my direction. As I talked, he bent his brows into a feline version of a frown.

"You asked will I share this new information with Norment right away. Maybe I'm wrong, but I'm going to keep it to myself. Until the time is right. Or until we get something more certain. Giving him a few scraps, without a big enough bite of the truth to sink his teeth into, is worse torture than knowing nothing at all."

"Right. I won't mention a word to him until you give me the go ahead." Archie locked eyes with me to confirm our agreement. Then his expression brightened as he looked ahead. "So, if you're not going to tell Ross, what *do* you plan to do?"

"I'm going to play my hunch on this, Archie. I've got an idea and I want to run it down. If my instinct leads nowhere, then we're back where we started."

"Sure. If your guess don't pan out, we're no worse and no better. But the case'll be a lot colder. You gonna keep me informed on what your gut leads you into?"

"I'll do my best. You've been straight with me. I don't know how this hunch plays out, so I can't make any promises upfront. Trust me to make the best choice for everybody on this one. Can you do that, Archie?"

He leaned forward, his chest pressing against the edge of the table. His pupils glittered like black foil between the lids.

"I can. Even if I didn't trust you, this Jayla Dream case is the coldest cold case we got on our board. Frozen solid. If we can erase it, we'll be obliged to you. Plenty."

We stood from the table and shook on our deal.

"Don't matter how you pull it off," he said. "You solve this one, I can live with a truck load of doubt."

Archie was a good cop, a better man. And the friend I needed.

———

Clark's Auto Body and Repair, four blocks from my apartment, was my first stop after Archie left. I didn't own a car, but Brina's battered Honda required frequent attention. Despite her fierce feminism, she was happy to let me handle all business related to car repairs. She pumped gas when forced to, but anything more complicated she passed to me. During two years of steady patronage, I'd forged a firm friendship with Clark "Superman" Kuo and the boys in the grease pit.

Today I wanted Superman's expert advice on the clues I'd harvested in the death of Dreamie Ross.

"How's it going, Mr. Rook?" Tarik Sims was the youngest mechanic in the shop, a muscular teen with shoulder-length black dreads under a red knit cap. He was short, so he'd double rolled the pants cuffs of his gray coveralls. He should have been in school, studying calculus or World War Two or Macbeth. But he'd fixed on an auto career, and his mother didn't complain about the good money he brought home. "No car for us this week?"

"Not today, Tarik. But I've got a question for Clark. He around?" Despite the up-flung garage door, trapped fumes of gasoline and sweet transmission fluid in the dark shop made my eyes water.

"Yeah, he's in the office, beating up a adding machine." The kid tilted his head toward the rear of the bay, then wiped a dirty cloth down the right side of his nose. "Go on back. He hates paperwork. He'll be glad to see you."

I swung under a lift where a yacht-sized Cadillac Seville dangled. Then around a sweet Ferrari, dragging my palm along its black curves. The bumper had a nasty dent and the left rear tail light was smashed. A teeth-grinding sacrilege.

I stopped at the vending machine next to the office door to buy two cans of Coke. Then I tapped on the pebbled glass and pushed with my shoulder. Clark Kuo was sprawled in a lumpy orange swivel chair, glaring at the screen of his computer. He wore the same stained gray coveralls he always wore. Oil smeared the red embroidered letters of his name above his chest pocket. Sweat plastered black strands of hair onto his head in a cross-hatch pattern. A pair of square black-framed glasses perched on his shiny scalp. His black eyes jiggled from side to side as his cheeks rose in a smile. A forest of black bristles thrust through his waxy skin. The growth made me regret not shaving before I left the apartment. When I parked a Coke next to the keyboard, my fingers jumped to my chin. Did I look as rough as Clark?

"Morning, Rook. Whatsa matter with your face there?" He seemed to read my mind's apology, although his tone was warm.

I shrugged, touching the tender scratches on my cheek. "Tough day at the university."

"You got worked over by some of them panty-waist brainiacs?" He popped the can and took a deep swig. "You losing your touch, my friend."

"Don't spread it around the neighborhood. I got a rep to maintain." I winked and he matched me.

"Mum's the word." He grinned, showing short white teeth below lots of gum. "You know, now I think about it, I bet you got beat up in a bar last night, hmm?" As our conspiracy unfolded, Clark's mouth widened. "Two against one, right?"

"That's it, Superman. Exactly." I nodded, punching a left hook as I sat down in the guest chair. "And they look a lot worse than me this morning."

The car man clapped grimy hands in approval of our fantasy slug fest. Clark leaned forward in his chair, getting down to business. "Whatchu got for me?"

I pulled a sheet of white paper from the printer next to his computer and smoothed it on the ledge sticking out from his desk. Then I reached a stack of dimes from my pocket. I sifted dust particles, lint, and little blue flakes from the coins onto the paper. Fragments of paint from Dreamie's sweater twinkled like dark stars on the white surface.

"Clark, I need your help. Can you identify these paint chips? I want to know as much as you can tell me about them."

He fastened the heavy black-framed glasses in front of his eyes. The lenses were smudged and blurry, but if Superman could see through them, who was I to complain? I opened my Coke and drank. He looked at my samples for a minute, then reared from the desk to pull the center drawer. He hoisted a giant magnifying glass over the paper, angling it from side to side.

"Hunh. These are tiny little bits. Ain't you got nothing bigger?"

"That's all I could collect. You recognize the color?"

He nodded. "From an old car, probably. Judging by the thickness and shine."

Clark balanced a sliver of paint on his index finger and brought the finger and magnifying glass closer to his face. "I can look it up on a database, PaintRef.com. It's got auto, truck, and fleet paint colors sorted by make and model going back almost a century."

With his left hand, the mechanic poked at the keyboard until he found the website. Then he looked at me. "You got to give me something to go on. Like a model and year you looking for."

I hesitated; I didn't want to prejudice the search. But my choice was clear. "Try Buicks, around 1992 or '93." I scooted my chair beside Clark's. In a single motion, we leaned toward the dust-streaked screen.

He scrolled over the array of paint shades on the Buick pages of the website. The colors were sorted into stacks by year, piled like tinted subway tiles down the length of the screen. Who knew there could be so many names for a simple color like blue? In 1992, the company listed four Buick blues: Neon, Light Sapphire, Medium Maui and Bright Aqua. But in 1993, the manufacturer's imagination exploded and the list lengthened: Medium Adriatic Blue, Light Teal, Medium Malachite, Medium Quasar, and Medium Sapphire Blue Fire Mist.

I was pumped for Quasar; the word rolled in my head with a fine rhythm. But after thirty seconds of study, Clark went a different route. "Your color's Medium Maui Blue. If I had to guess, I'd say from a Buick Royal. GM introduced the Royal sedan as a personal luxury car in 1973."

"When did production end for the Royal?"

"Not sure, early 2000's. Maybe '03 or '04." Clark set the magnifying glass on the desk, over a wet circle made by the Coke can.

"You think the name refers to the color of the sea. Deep cloudy blue? Like in a storm at night?"

"Sure. Why not? If you say so, Rook." Clark peered again at the fragments of dusky blue paint. "I'm seeing Star Wars myself." He shrugged. "This help you any? You working on a new case?"

"No, an old case. Twenty-five years old."

The mechanic steepled his fingers in front of his chest. "The past colliding with the present."

Sharp summary. Superman really did have X-ray vision. I nodded and gulped more soda.

Clark plucked the eyeglasses from his nose and rubbed them against his shirt sleeve. With a thumb, he flicked the paint fragment onto my sheet of paper.

"But you can't tell more than that, right? Confidential. Like a doctor. Or a priest," he said.

I shook my head and doubled the paper so the lint and paint flakes settled into the crease. Then I folded the leaf into a small square and stuck it in my pants pocket. I matched his summary with my own: "Old case, old car. New clue."

I downed the Coke, stood from the desk and shook Clark Kuo's hand. "Thank you, Supe. This is a big help."

"Sure thing. Next time bring that Honda your girl drives. It's due for inspection next month and those misaligned tires'll never pass."

I hit the street, hoping exercise would blow the vapors of motor oil, leather, and car wax from my lungs. I didn't need the headache inkling behind my right ear. As I trotted toward the office, I hammered out the angles of my hypothesis with every step. A brick wall and a blue Buick Royal sedan, vintage 1992, swirled in my dark thoughts. By the time I reached my desk, the theory and the headache were churning at gale force.

# CHAPTER
# TWENTY-FOUR

When I made the appointment to see Carolyn Wiley, I asked Allard Swann for the use of a private room. I wanted some place quiet where I could set Carolyn at ease, get her to relax as I tossed tough questions at her. I expected Swann would clear a parlor or an unused bedroom. But, when I arrived at the Memory Center the evening after my consultation with Superman, the director led me into his own office.

"Will this be all right, Mr. Rook? I know you said you wanted some place tranquil and private, so I thought this would be the best spot for you."

"I don't want to put you out of your own office. We can chat somewhere else if that's more convenient."

"As many times as you've helped us with Mrs. Wiley, I don't think we can thank you enough for all your assistance. Anything you want, Mr. Rook, you just have to ask. I've instructed Dalton to bring Mrs. Wiley to you as soon as you let us know you're ready."

"I'm ready now. But I don't want to disturb her routine."

"No, this is actually a good time. Carolyn has just finished eating supper. She usually remains downstairs for an hour or so after her meal for some TV before she's ready to be helped to bed. So, she should be quite prepared to visit with you." He wiped perspiring hands across his stuffed vest. "Well, then, if you're all set, I'll tell Dalton to bring in Carolyn."

Swann stepped from the room, leaving me to sink into one of the two heavy arm chairs that faced his desk. After a few minutes, the door opened and Carolyn Wiley fluttered in. She was dressed much as she always was, this time her shirtdress was green with cheerful orange piping and matching orange buttons down the front. An unbuttoned sweater in navy-blue covered her thin shoulders. Her snow-white hair was freshly trimmed, emphasizing her sharp cheekbones and deep-set eyes. I wondered what Dr. Swann and the attendant had told her about her nighttime caller.

Whatever they'd said, she recognized me as the son she missed so much. "Oh, Carl, how wonderful to see you again! I was so hoping you would stop by to visit with me."

Her brown eyes danced with joy; her mouth opened in a wide smile. She reached up to pat my cheek as she stepped around me. We settled onto a long sofa next to the black steel safe.

"They must be driving you like a mule at work these days. I'll speak to your supervisor tomorrow and tell him you need more time off. And they should let you leave the office at a reasonable hour. You're not a servant, you know. They need to treat you with respect, Carl."

"Oh, they're pretty good to me. No complaints at work."

"Well, that's wonderful to hear. Makes my heart glad to know you're doing alright. What do they have you working on, any big new cases? I know legal work is confidential. But is there anything you can share with me?"

Her son worked for a major law firm in Seattle, but I had no clue about the specifics of his assignments. I kept my replies vague to not disrupt the imaginary world Carolyn had constructed around me. The more she believed me, the more she'd confide in me.

"My cases are varied. Some big, some small. The clients are demanding, but I like the work. It keeps me on my toes and I never get bored." True of my private eye job. Maybe true for Carl too.

"Then that's just perfect for you, isn't it, sweetheart? Just what I always wanted for you."

"Can I ask you something?"

"Of course, darling. You can ask me anything you want. That's what mothers are for."

She entwined her fingers and settled them against her flat stomach. She looked at me with an open, eager expression. Guilt dripped like caustic acid into my chest.

"You remember that time there was a body, a dead body in the basement? What happened to it?" The transition was abrupt, even crude. But I hoped Carolyn would follow me without balking.

A wrinkle deepened between her clear brown eyes, but she didn't hesitate to reply. "Oh, now, Carl, I told you not to trouble yourself anymore about that. It happened so long ago. And we've forgotten all about it, haven't we? Best to leave such things lie, I think." She turned a watery smile on me and smoothed her thin hands over the skirt of her dress, pressing it flat against her knees.

The thread of memory was frayed, but I pushed on. "I'm trying to remember what happened. When I came home... I mean, I can't remember everything the way I want to. Can you help me remember what happened that night?"

I hoped I was wrong. That my guesses about what took place twenty-five years ago were misguided attempts to bring order to a twisted past. I wished Carolyn Wiley would look at me with sad disdain and reject my stories as fantasy.

But after a moment of consideration, she sank into the cushion. Her voice grew warm and milky, with that sing-song cadence mothers use to recite a bedtime fairy tale they've told over and over again.

"You were late coming home, like you always are. I hate it that you have to drive home from the office so late at night. It's quite hard to see after dark, especially in the rain. There was so much rain that night. You made it all the way home to our block safe and sound, when *Boom!* Just like a deer, that girl jumped out in front of your car." Imitating the impact of the collision, Carolyn clapped her hands together.

The sound shocked me, forcing my lips into a tight grimace. Moisture dried on my tongue.

Carolyn responded to the surprise on my face with the same soothing tones she must have used in the past. "Oh, Carl, don't worry. It's all right, darling. It's all right to be afraid. I know it startled you. You look just like you did when you got into an ugly fight at school, like a frightened and confused little boy."

"Where did I park my car?"

"Oh, that car! You loved that car, didn't you? Such a beauty. First one you bought with your own money. You called it your first-place trophy. Never knew a boy could love a mechanical thing the way you loved that blue Buick."

The grim pieces fell into place, so I rushed on before distraction overtook her jumbled mind. "But where did I leave it that night?"

"I told you to leave the Buick at the corner near the stop sign. No police ever come down our street after dark anyway. Why should they? Our block is so quiet, respectable and safe, you know. Never any trouble in our neighborhood."

"And when I ran to our house?"

"Your eyes looked just like they do right now, all wide and round. And your hair was sticking up all wild on your head. You looked just like those times you came home after school with your knees skinned and your shirt torn and your hair sprung every which way." She leaned forward, then stroked her hand above my left ear, smoothing the curls with a tender touch.

She continued, low and urgent. "I told you not to worry about anything. It would be all right, I said. We would take care of everything once we got her into the basement. You understood. You saw that I was right. So, together we carried her all the way from the street to the basement door."

"Was she bleeding?" I lowered my eyes. Heavy tears collected in the corners.

"Oh, no. Not at all. Not at all. She was clean and neat in her yellow sweater. She looked like a pretty little canary bird. Quiet, sleeping in your arms. I knew she wasn't, of course. But you weren't sure. I had to tell you."

"Then did we call the police to come get her?"

"Oh, no, darling, why would we do that? They couldn't help her, could they? No doctors, no police, nobody could help her anymore." Carolyn stroked the edge of my jaw, gently tugging at the bristles. "That poor girl was gone. I told you the best we could do was to lay her to rest in the back room in our basement. Keep her safe from harm there."

"So, we laid her in the back room?"

"Yes, she looked so comfortable there, didn't she? Curled like a sleeping child. I found a blanket to keep her warm and we covered her for the night."

"I remember crying." I blinked, releasing the teardrops to serve my purpose.

"Yes, you cried an awful lot that night, Carl. I held you in my arms all night, rocked you like when you were a pretty little baby. Just rocked all night, the two of us together. Like always." Her body swayed against me, acting out the memory. I felt her heart tapping next to mine.

"And in the morning, you drove your car away. I don't know where you put it. You were gone for a long time. Such a beautiful car, I know you were sad to see it go." She sighed as if feeling the loss all over again.

"And then we had to hide her."

"Yes, now you remember, don't you?" She patted my hand in approval. Her skin felt dry like feathers. The wispy touch sent shivers across my wrist. "It was you who suggested we drag those leftover bricks from the new patio out back. We brought them in little by little because they were so heavy. I carried one or two and you carried one or two. Until we had enough."

"The wall took so long to build. I remember that."

"Yes, you got angry a time or two at how slow we were going. You were always such an impatient little man, Carl. Always in a hurry. But I reminded you all good work takes persistence and careful attention. So, we had to take our time and do it right."

I pulled a finger along my lower lip, muffling my words. "But I don't remember putting up the drywall over the brick."

"No, you didn't do that, Carl. You don't know how to do that kind of handiwork. Never did." She smiled at the foolish thought, then ran fingers through her downy hair. "Remember my friend Helen Jessup?

She was always fussing and worrying about her son Tyrone because he couldn't get a job after school. So, I asked her if he could do some carpentry work around the house and she said yes, he knew carpentry. I paid Tyrone to come over every day after school to put in time finishing our basement."

I lifted my voice to a light and eager tone, like I relished the flood of memories. "He framed the rooms with two-by-fours and then put up the drywall and then all that painting."

"Yes, now you remember it, don't you!" She smiled in approval, drawing her palm over the nape of her neck, patting the thin strands. "Tyrone was slow at his carpentry work. A little slow-witted too, if you ask me. But I would never say such a thing to poor Helen, she loved that boy so much. And in the end, he did such a fine job, neat as a pin too. He complained a time or two about strange smells, but worth every penny I paid him. And to see how proud Helen was of her boy's work. Oh, Carl, it just made my heart sing to see her so happy."

I gulped down the bile. "And nobody knows."

"Yes, of course, Carl. Nobody knows."

Carolyn patted my hand again, stroking her frail fingers over the veins and tendons in soothing circular patterns. I felt the tension in my body dissolve as she touched me.

With our story at an end, she turned the questions on me. A gentle chiding tone entered her voice and her eyes narrowed as she studied me. "Now, you know you can't hide anything from me, Carl. A son can never hide from his mother. So, tell me, what happened to your face today? How'd you get those scratches?"

She pointed a wavering finger at my cheek and pursed her lips.

"I got into a fight at school, Mama." The name slipped out, natural and easy. Role-playing melted into reality in the gauzy theatre we'd created together. No regret clinched my throat, so I added the rest of my truth: "Just like before."

She clucked her tongue and frowned. "Those the same children who picked on you before?"

"Yes, the same ones." I remembered them; taller and bigger than me, pale faces tensed with grins as they circled, chanting my name.

*Shelba, Shelba.* Not Spanish, not English. An awkward name in every language. *Shelba.*

"Why didn't the teachers stop the fight?"

"They never saw us, Mama. We were on the other side of the school yard. The teachers couldn't see."

"Well, I'm going to have a word with Principal Conrad about this tomorrow. It's his job to protect every child. He shouldn't let those delinquents get away with such terrible mischief at the expense of the littler ones. Come here, baby, let me see it up close."

Carolyn tugged at my forearm until I knelt, facing her. With a gentle finger on my chin, she turned my head, inspecting my wounded cheek in the dim light of Dr. Swann's desk lamp. "Can you tell me what you were fighting about?"

Buried truth tumbled from my gut, spilling in old phrases onto her bosom. "I tried to protect a girl, Mama. But I couldn't."

"Well, the important thing is, you tried your best." She sighed through a thin smile.

"I wanted to save her, but I couldn't. I lost her, Mama. I lost her forever."

Carolyn pulled me toward her. I laid my injured cheek against the soft folds of her breast, inhaling lavender's powdery fragrance from her dress. Tender thumbs glided over my eyes, erasing hot tears. Fingers stroked my hair, winding through the curls. Low murmurs of solace and sorrow reverberated from her body to mine. Her tears slid past my ear as she whispered, "Baby, don't worry. Don't cry, my darling."

Maybe I should have been repulsed by Carolyn's uncaring response to the accident that killed Dreamie Ross. I knew her gentle attention to me now mirrored the loving support she gave her son then. Maybe I should have pulled away, rejected Carolyn's soothing embrace. But I didn't. I wanted her comfort. Needed the peace of her boundless love. Our losses blended without canceling one another. I knew about Carl; she knew nothing about Annie. I didn't say a word to dispel the brutal cloud of memories, hers and mine. I let the past, dear and callous, encircle us.

---

The next day, I called Archie Lin to my office. I outlined for him the events of the night Jayla Dream Ross died twenty-five years ago. I handed him the folded packet with the blue paint chips and told him about Clark Kuo's analysis. I showed him the pictures I'd taken of the keepsake Buick key fob in Carolyn Wiley's dresser. Her souvenir of buried disaster. The evidence fit, the cruel story gelled. But Archie doubted prosecutors would bring a manslaughter case against a seventy-six-year-old dementia patient. He said he'd contact Seattle police about interviewing Carl Wiley on his role in the deception that erased Dreamie's life and death.

After Archie left, I crept into Norment Ross's office to tell him what I knew. His lost Dreamie had been killed in a traffic accident, her death hidden for decades by careless people whose bloated egotism overrode decency or empathy. The old man didn't cry at the news. Neither revenge nor understanding was within his grasp.

After a quarter century, resolution was all he had left. At least I had given him that solace.

---

I waited to get home that evening before I phoned Carl Wiley in Seattle.

I wanted to be ready for the call. So, I prepared like a boxer for a title match. I stripped to my undershirt, unbuckled my belt, kicked off my shoes. I rotated my shoulders, loosening the muscles in my back and neck. I flexed my fingers until warmth surged from palms to nails. My stomach knotted under my lungs, so I chugged a Corona standing in front of the open refrigerator. The beer helped ease the knot a little, so I downed a second bottle. Herb the cat rubbed my ankles until I dumped a scoop of dry kibbles in his bowl.

Carl Wiley picked up on the second ring. I stated my name, no greeting or introduction or weather report. I told him how I'd rescued his mother from their former home.

The asshole tried to simper and sneer his way through excuses for his gross neglect. "What business is it of yours to interfere in the private matters of my family?"

"I made it my business when your mother called me by your name. Carl."

"You – you despicable interloper. You know nothing about my family. And you care nothing for my mother."

"If we're measuring care by the hour, then I come out on top, Carl."

"You stay away from my family."

"This is about my family too, Carl. About the people you broke with your reckless car ride twenty-five years ago."

I could hear the sharp gulp of breath. Then a cough. "What are you talking about?"

"Your mother told me how she helped you cover up the death of that young woman. The one you crushed with your precious blue Buick."

"You don't know anything. You're lying."

"I know enough, Carl. I found the body in the basement where you stuffed her. Your mother told me the rest."

Another violent intake of breath. Then smacking of lips. His voice cycloned to a shriek. "You – you vile imposter! I know your kind. You people are predators who victimize the elderly. You assume a false identity, pretend a fake relationship. You devise a phony intimacy to worm your way into her good graces. You're hoping to pry money from my mother, aren't you?"

"Fuck you."

"Stay away from my mother, understand? I'm warning you. Stay out of her life. If I hear of you visiting her again, I will get a restraining order against you. The police will dispose of you like the filthy con artist you are."

"Buy a goddamned plane ticket and visit your mother."

As we talked, I paced between the bed and the kitchen peninsula. With each pass, my bark tightened into a growl. But snarling wasn't enough. This bastard needed a beat down. I had no money to fly to Seattle. He didn't know that. But I had a head crammed with words. So, I dealt two fistfuls.

I said I'd be on the next plane to Seattle. I described what I'd do to his face when I landed. Spike his nose through the twisted vents of his brain. Break off his teeth at the gums. Jam his tongue down his throat. I wanted him scared shitless. I recited his work and home addresses. And the names of his law partners and clients. And the locations of his wife's art studio and their children's school. I threw in the names of his darling dog and cute neighbors. Carl Wiley thought he'd escaped his past by fleeing west. I wanted him to know I'd caught him. As I hung up, Carl's sloppy retching gurgled between his curses.

Words were good, but all that dammed energy had to explode. I tossed the phone on the bed. Then I punched a hole in the closet door. A quick right-left combo, with an uppercut finale. Splinters showered below the picture window. A dry gold heap, like straw.

The cat hissed, then slunk under the bed. Cuts on my knuckles popped red. I grabbed a dishtowel for my hand and snatched the broom from next to the sink. But thinking about the clean-up made me thirsty. So, I bought myself a drink from the Four Roses bottle above the refrigerator. No glass, no ice. Just fast gulps of smoky heat. The bourbon burned going down. Scraped my tongue like liquid shards. I sat on the bed and sprang for another round. The bottle dangled between my knees as I swallowed. On the white dishtowel, ooze from my knuckles dried to pink. I dribbled booze to clean the scrapes. A few drops. Not too much wasted on these little nicks. Then I gargled a heavy dose to scour my throat of the taste of Carl Wiley.

After the fifth round, the wood splinters on the floor looked nice. Brown, pretty yellow, tan. Spiky swirls like cool modern art. Herb leaped to his throne on top of the dresser. He stared at me, the shattered door, the splinters. Then me again. His eyes were golden disks of contempt. Scorn lifted his whiskers. So what? I didn't need him. The bourbon needed me. My full attention. Those pretty splinters could lay there overnight, piled on the memory of Carl Wiley. Herb licked his golden tail as I swigged round number six.

# CHAPTER
# TWENTY-FIVE

The next afternoon, my knuckles were still raw. Despite two scrubbings, my mouth still ponged with sour grit. Drilling above my temples had smoothed to a minor tick-tock. I was sober enough to leave the apartment. Almost fit for civilized company. Plunging into Annie's murder again hurt. But the pain cleared my head. Decades ago, selfish people had killed Norment Ross's wife. Maybe the same careless types had murdered mine. Academia seemed a fine place to hunt for swollen egos, so I headed to New York University.

Lounging around the bustling NYU campus was easy. But doing it without looking like a lunatic or a pervert was tough. The hangover made it harder. I should have shaved, but the stubble hid the scratches, so I took my hip tramp style downtown.

I wanted to catch Sally Anastos on her home ground, but not at her own apartment. I aimed to keep her off-balance, not defensive. My questions about her involvement with Gerry Keith, Pearl Byrne, and Annie could prove touchy. A relaxed and confident Sally would be more open if she felt she had the upper hand. Wounded and grieving was my pitch. Also my reality, but she didn't need to know.

A chatty assistant in the anthropology department told me their newest post-doctoral fellow liked to swim at the university athletic facility on East 14th Street most afternoons. According to Dana, the bloodhound in tan corduroy, Sally went by the more formal Sarah now that she had the Ph.D. tacked on her name. Sarah enjoyed swimming laps for an hour in the L-shaped deep-water pool. Dana recommended the stationary bicycles, treadmills, and elliptical trainers in the aerobic fitness room. But Sarah wasn't interested in improving her cardio health on dry land. Swimming was her jam.

The brute gray facade of the recreation center didn't give any cover for lounging in inconspicuous shadows. Square recessed openings sheltered the brass framed front doors and butted against the broad sidewalk. Winds hustled down the block, whipped into sharpness by the stark buildings and the metal awnings over ground floor windows. I flipped my jacket collar to fight the gusts. In front of the main entrance, a skinny tree with four brown leaves struggled from a square plot cut into the cement. I couldn't very well lean against the tree for long without drawing attention to myself. Or damaging the tree. So, I stood straight and motionless for ten minutes. My back was okay with the plan but my throbbing head, knuckles, and feet objected.

A cinderblock dressed as a university cop ambled by me. I'd had my fill of campus police; I didn't want to attract his professional curiosity. So, I bought an apple from a vendor in front of the Trader Joe's next to the rec center. Then I bought a cup of coffee from the near-by hot dog stand. I kept a close eye on the people exiting the building. No joy. Desperate to get off my feet and cover my surveillance, I took a chair at the outdoor café sheltered by the red awning labeled, "Five Napkin Burger." From this perch at the corner of the block, I had a clear view of the rec center front door. But a waiter with lime-green hair slanting over pasty skin insisted I purchase something from the menu. I ordered a cheeseburger and paid him upfront in case I had to leave in a hurry. Despite the restaurant's boast, I only used three napkins.

I was looking straight at the entrance, but when Sally Anastos slid from the building, I almost missed her. She'd pulled the hood of her purple sweatshirt close around her face, covering her red curls. Tight denims frayed at the knees and black lace-up sneakers with wedge heels were a perfect downtown disguise. A black nylon backpack was slung over one shoulder. She looked nothing like the sexy sprite I remembered from our first meeting in the bar of the Continental Regent Hotel.

I looked the same, however. Sally recognized me as soon as I stood from my table to intercept her. "You're Rook, aren't you? That detective boyfriend of Anniesha Perry."

She remembered that Annie's cleaning service company had my name. She knew I wasn't a boyfriend. Sally was sparring with me and put-downs were her weapon of choice. She intended to demean me or hurt me. I had to find out which.

"Ex-husband. And yes, I'm Rook. How're you doing, Sally? Or is it Sarah now?"

She had the decency to blush, but stood her ground. "What are you doing so far downtown? I thought your beat was Harlem."

"It is. But I wanted to talk with you."

"Me?"

"Yes, if you have the time."

She shivered, but didn't decline my invitation. The narrowed hazel eyes and twist to the mouth said she was curious about me. When she shivered again, I suggested we skip the windy patio and look for a table inside the burger joint.

My old friend the waiter tossed a raised eyebrow when I ordered another cheeseburger. But then I nodded at Sally and winked, letting my tongue peek from the corner of my mouth. I made him a collaborator in my imaginary pickup game. After pushing the hood from her head, Sally fished a pair of wire-rimmed glasses from her backpack. She scanned the menu then ordered a veggie burger and a ginger ale. It was too early for my usual four o'clock bourbon, so I settled for a diet Coke. Unprompted, my ally the waiter brought us a side order of onion rings to aid in the seduction he hoped was in progress.

Sally and I exchanged neutral notes about her new status as a post-doctoral fellow at New York University. She liked the loose hours, the lack of teaching requirements, and the access to library and technical support. She'd already completed an article based on her cleaning service research and submitted it to a journal for consideration. Her goal for the academic year was to revise her dissertation into a publishable book. By December, she planned to be in interviews for a top academic position, probably Ivy League. Harvard was hinting, Yale was flirting. She was sure she'd land an offer by spring. Sally's tone flattened when describing her colleagues in the NYU anthropology department. They were friendly but uninspiring.

I didn't care about them either, so I probed closer to my real target. "Nobody at NYU stacks up to Gerry Keith in the intellectual pizazz department?"

"Yeah, it would be hard to match him." Sally's eyes blurred as she sucked the ginger ale through a straw. "He's got more vigor in his little finger than the whole department down here."

Keeping the conversation on Keith was easy from there. Just drop a line and watch her bite. "I ran into him on the Alexander campus last week. I'm no expert, so you tell me: is it his ideas that are so fresh? Or is the pop in the style he delivers them with? Is it the steak or the sizzle with Gerry?"

She preened, polishing her curls as if the supposed compliments had been aimed at her. Chlorine wafted from her skin as she warmed under my smiles.

"Oh, I'd say both. Gerry pushes the envelope in the development of theoretical re-considerations of the intersection of class, ethnicity, and language. But he's dynamic as a speaker and a terrific writer too. Even if he wasn't saying anything truly important, you'd want to stop and pay attention to him. I don't know how he does it. He's genius."

Ga-ga for the great man. I'm no fem-libster, but Sally was sunk so low, it embarrassed me. Ride or die for real. When the burgers arrived, we devoted a few minutes of silence and several napkins to tackling them. I feared Sally would switch topics, but she refused to drop her hero.

"You said you ran into Gerry at Alexander? What were you doing up there?"

"Helping another prof sort out a little project."

"Private eye stuff?" Her lashes fluttered to contain the eyeroll of boredom.

"Right. But Gerry filled me in on that prize his new book is up for this week. What's it called again?"

Sally's nose scrunched as her mouth widened with pleasure. This was the chance to show off inside knowledge, so I let her drop details on the academic achievements of her idol. "It's the Blackistone Prize. For the year's top scholarly achievement. Gerry's got only two other nominees running against him, so his chances are strong."

"Yeah, he seemed confident of the win. He told me how he planned to spend that fifty-thousand-dollar prize money." Time to wriggle the hook until it lodged in her fond and foolish heart. "How much of a cut do you get, Sally? You were co-researcher. You must get some of the big haul, right?"

High color ran across her cheeks: she was sliced to the quick. "I...I mean...I don't know. I, uh... that's a lot of money. I never heard the exact amount. You sure it's the Blackistone Prize you're talking about?" Her eyes scanned the restaurant, looking for someplace to land other than my face.

"Positive. That's what Gerry was telling me about. He went on and on about the Blackistone Prize. How winning it would nail down his academic reputation as a world-class scholar. Plus give him all that money. He bragged hard and long about that grip. The man's pretty proud of himself and his achievement." I sucked at the coke and waited.

Sally crunched an onion ring, then reached across the table for the ketchup. She gave the bottle three whacks until it shot a puddle of sauce onto her plate.

I poked at the wound I'd opened. "Gerry said they announce the prize winners this Friday afternoon at five. You invited to the ceremony?"

"At Alexander? Friday? Yeah...um, yeah, I'll be there." She dragged another ring through the ketchup and took a bite before she spoke again.

"I put my heart into that research..., cockroaches and coke every-where..., all those people..., all the filth..." Her growl crept over the table in a soft monotone. She was speaking to herself, not me. Revisiting her past degradation, the present pushed aside.

I clunked my glass against a fork and raised my voice to bring her around. "Gerry said you did some of the research here in New York. Where did you go?"

She shook her head, clearing her mind to answer me. "Yeah, I went to Poughkeepsie, to interview workers at a cleaning service there. Run by a woman called Pearl Byrne."

"Pearl. I met her. Wasn't she the one who was supposed to speak on a panel with Anniesha at the business conference that day... that day she died?" The catch in my voice wasn't acting. Neither was the stitch in my gut or the ache in my chest. I pressed fingers against my belt to blunt the pain.

Sally caught the movement and I jerked my hand onto the table top again. I shoved a spoon under the rim of my plate. I'd wanted to raise the subject of Annie to see Sally's reaction. But I hadn't been prepared for how it would hit me. So, Sally's first response was to my pain, rather than her own feelings. She looked down to avoid my eyes and took a napkin from the pile next to the salt shaker. I could see her arm muscles flex as she twisted the paper underneath the table.

"Right. Yeah, Pearl was a co-presenter on that panel with Anniesha. I think they were going to speak about something to do with our research project." Her thin lips clamped to stem the tide of words.

I wanted to hear more. I leaned forward. "You mean, they were going to talk about the work you and Gerry did with all those maids in their companies?"

Sally snapped the next words, like a cornered lion tamer cracking the whip. "I guess so. How do I know what they were going to say? It wasn't my presentation, was it? I don't know anything about it."

These were the sharpest words Sally had uttered since we'd started eating. Annie's presentation meant something to her. Something uncomfortable or unsavory or dangerous.

"You didn't talk with Anniesha about her presentation that night after I left you in the bar?"

"Yeah, maybe we did. A little. Anniesha was ragging on about how exciting her talk was going to be. Pretty general stuff." Her eyes slotted left, copper-colored pupils filling the angles of her lids. "I really... I don't remember much -- I guess, details -- about what anybody said after the third drink, you know."

A slow hand ruffled the damp red curls at the nape of her neck. A tight smile stretched her lips. Pleading she was too drunk to remember was weak deflection. But Sally wasn't going to give me any more on that.

I shrugged and chomped on my burger. If she thought I didn't care, she'd relax. And if she saw I was a slob, she'd give me even more. Without swallowing, I changed topics through the ground beef. "Did Rick Luna ever come back to join you three for dinner?"

"That slippery piece of work? Yeah, he returned a few hours after you left. Caught up with us again after we moved on to dinner. That stench from his cologne was so strong, I could hardly keep my food down. Drugstore coconut and lime. Yuck!" Sally laughed and waved a hand in front of her nose. Her eyes sparkled again, inviting me to share her scorn for the boorish outsider.

I returned the smile, as if we were conspirators. "I know what you mean, he came on a bit strong, didn't he? But still, Rick was a pretty attractive guy. I could see why Anniesha was interested in him."

I was fishing and Sally bit with gusto. "Do you think she was involved with Slick Rick? I wondered about that when we were down in Miami. Obviously, she spent lots of time with him. He was vice president for marketing, so they had plenty of business reasons to be together."

"But also after hours? As far as you could tell?"

"As far as I knew, yeah, maybe they did." Sally looked doubtful as she cast her mind over the time she and Gerry Keith spent with Annie, Rick, and the others.

"Didn't you and Gerry hang out socially with Anniesha down in Miami? Hit the bars, clubs? The beach?"

"Not really." That sounded weak, so she rattled an explanation to puff her importance. "Well, obviously, I couldn't do that, since I was embedded as an employee inside the company. As you know, I worked as a maid in the cleaning service. That's how I collected most of my informant data. So, it wouldn't make sense for me to be seen in public as the social equal of the big boss. Gerry did spend lots of time with Anniesha at the office and after. But I didn't. Naturally."

"Naturally." I let my comment hang to take the sting out of what could have been a sneer. But I wouldn't let Sally slip off the hook now. I was on the track of information I wanted. "Come to think of it, that evening Anniesha did seem fond of Gerry. It looked like he felt the same about her. I was only with them a few hours, but I thought they clicked together. Like old friends or lovers or something. Warmer than business partners. Didn't you get that vibe too?"

Heat coursed up my neck. I assumed a red tint had reached my ears by the time I finished that speculation. Sally's signs of inner turmoil matched my own: her pale throat pinkened as I spoke about Annie and Gerry's involvement. Rosy splotches burst on her chest in the *V* of her unzipped sweatshirt. She touched her collarbone and then ran her fingers through her hair until the curls stood like spiked armor over her head.

"Maybe. I don't know." Sally lowered her lids for a slow beat trying to blot out the images racing through her mind. That raunchy slide show flashed pictures of raw sex featuring a man she desired and a woman she hated. The girl blinked again, then found her voice, a thin damp squeak. "Sure, they were close. I guess you could be right."

We both took swigs from our drinks. I prayed to the genie of bourbon that mine would transform into something hard and smooth. But my diet Coke resisted the magic spell. After a few more nibbles on her crumbling veggie burger, Sally flicked the whip again.

"So, you're saying you didn't know that Rick Luna returned to the bar later that night." Her half-smile was sly and the hazel in her eyes hardened into green as she pinned me. "You mean, you didn't hang around yourself? I thought you looked kind of interested in some Annie action too."

"Sally, I went straight home. Took the train uptown and dropped into bed before midnight. I was excess baggage at that point, and I knew it. You and Gerry and Rick were part of Anniesha's current life. I was just a sorry memory from her past."

Sally's eyes went soft. "No regrets?"

"Lots of regrets. Sure. But none I was in a position to correct." I shifted on the plastic seat and stared through the window to the deepening dusk.

Nostalgia. Or chagrin. Or regret. Whatever you chose to call it, the sentiment was dangerous. I knew war-seasoned soldiers who'd died when they let vague and bittersweet emotions replace hard calculation. Keeping your head in the here and now was essential to completing your assignment, solving the puzzle, staying alive. I knew what my regrets were; I wasn't fool enough to share them. But what regrets might Sally Anastos be keeping?

I'd let the silence linger for so long she charged into the void. "You loved her, didn't you?" A sigh, something akin to sympathy, sweetened her voice.

Pining was for fools. I knew, but I admitted to it anyway. I looked straight at Sally. "Yes."

"Still."

"Yes."

The syllable hung in the space between us, bare and mournful as a church bell. To muffle the sound, Sally offered a platitude. "Love's a funny old thing, isn't it?"

I didn't think it was all that funny, but I got her point. "You don't get to pick who your heart wants, that's for sure."

"No, you don't. You just love and love. No matter what." She hesitated, then added, "I'm sorry."

That whisper seemed like a non-sequitur, so I asked the obvious. "Why?"

"Just, oh…For nothing."

Hollowed out as we were, neither of us had much to say after that. The remains of the burgers lay in gray heaps among the wilted lettuce on our plates. We gulped the last of our drinks and rose to leave.

I dropped two twenties on the table next to the pile of demolished napkins. Doubling the bill would erase my waiter's disappointment that he hadn't been able to engineer a love connection.

As wind whipped the first chill blasts of fall, Sally raised her sweat-shirt hood and tugged it close around her face. I stepped forward and we shook hands at the curb.

I pulled her to my chest, forcing my words by the gusts. "Maybe I'll see you at the Blackistone announcement Friday afternoon. Annie ought to be represented. So maybe I'll show."

"Yeah, sure. I'll look for you Friday." Her promise blew away on the wind. "I need to get up there anyway to check on my brother. Make sure he's doing alright. George is a freshman at Alexander."

Darkness screened Sally's eyes. The lamplight's shimmer cast a sickly glow over her trembling chin. As she stepped from my arms, she stumbled over a crack in the pavement.

I clamped both hands at her waist to stop the fall. The blunt nose of a gun bumped my fingers. I pulled it from the kangaroo pocket of her sweatshirt. She gasped as I weighed it in my palm. The pistol was warm from her body and slick with the sweat of her hands.

I slipped it inside again. "You carry a weapon?"

"Obviously." Sally stuffed her fists next to the pistol, holding it snug against her stomach. "You really are a detective, aren't you?"

I'd earned the sneer, so I let it pass. "Why, Sally?"

"It's my dad's. He kept it next to the cash register in our restaurant in Bridgeport. When I moved to the city, he kept nagging me to take it. For protection, he said. But I always said no." She crammed space between each word, breaths chugging as she pressed her chin to her chest. "Then, in the last eight months, there were two break-ins, three muggings, and a rape on my block. I changed my mind. Now I carry it."

"You know how to use it?"

"Of course. My dad's unsophisticated and uneducated. But he isn't stupid. He wouldn't let me have his gun without lessons. He dragged me to a firing range every other morning for two weeks before he let me take it."

She thrust her head up. Shadows slanted across her brow. I couldn't see her eyes. Her lips tightened above the cinched knot holding her hood in place.

I wanted to keep her talking. "You haven't had to use it, have you?"

"No. So far, so good." She lifted the gun until its outline bulged against the thick fabric of her sweatshirt. "But I'm ready if I ever need to." I thought her voice wavered, or maybe it was the force of the gusts swirling around us. She said, "If I stay lucky, I never will."

Sally had minimal skills but enough knowledge to use the gun at close range. Did she have the guts to shoot when it counted? I wasn't sure.

When she raised an empty hand to me, I took it and leaned over her. "Then stay lucky, Sally."

"See you, Rook."

She drew her fingers from mine and pulled the sweatshirt cuffs until her balled hands disappeared inside the sleeves. As we separated, wind rattled the restaurant awning. Annie had been dead for twelve days.

# CHAPTER
# TWENTY-SIX

The morning after my hamburger with Sally Anastos, I returned to Alexander University. Her cult leader, Gerry Keith, was in my sights. Again.

Back to the eyesore Barstall Building. Dregs of early rain dripped from the red and purple ducts strangling the cement structure. But rain couldn't wash the ugly from the dreary facade. The university grounds crew had been at work. Whiffs of new-turned soil, fertilizer, and clipped grass met me as I walked the incline to the front door. The anthropology department office still bristled with weapons stolen from around the world. At her desk in the reception area, my second-favorite admin assistant, Johnetta Ames, wore a purple-and-gold checked wrapper on her head. A matching cloth draped over her shoulder. Maybe she had a skirt in the same material, but she was sitting, so I couldn't tell. She looked like a queen. Nothing lost by telling her so: "You look like a queen, Ms. Ames."

"Call me Johnetta, honey." The giggle bubbled through gold-plated fingernails. "What can I do for you today. You name it, you got it."

I unpacked flirtation skills I hadn't used since high school. Eyelash, lip tug, eyelash, smile. The heavy lifting produced details of her boss's location. "You hurry, you can catch the end of his lecture. Basement of this building, Bowl 3. Turn left when you get off the elevator. You can't miss it." Johnetta's grin widened. "You see all that sparkly light glowing through the classroom door, that's the sun shining out his majesty's ass."

Bowl 3 was a deep arena entered from the top. I slipped through the door and leaned against a padded wall at the rear. Fifteen half-rings of countertops curved around the windowless room. Students squeezed into purple swivel chairs fixed to the red desks. The stadium was full, maybe 150 undergrads tapping laptops with furious vigor. I counted four Black students in the crowd. The class was equally divided between the sexes, but males hung in the upper rows, eager women had seized the first seven rings of the bowl.

The focus of their energy was Gerry Keith. He circled the well of the arena, prancing behind a wooden podium which held his laptop. Three giant white screens framed his figure. The green shirt and black jacket and jeans set off his flame hair and beard. The room was still, the crowd riveted. At first, Keith seemed distant, as untouchable as the cold moon. I scanned the tense young faces below me, looking for cracks in the wall of attention. Nothing. But as the lecture continued, change took me. Keith seemed to expand, puffing warm breath against my face, filling me with his words. He was near me, around me; pictures in my head danced at his command.

Then a sigh rippled across the classroom. I exhaled too and looked around again. Keith's lecture was over. Without a glance at the stunned audience, Keith unplugged his laptop and slid it in a leather satchel. He pulled a purple cardboard box from the podium and ruffled through a pile of exam books stacked inside. Around me, students shut their laptops, hitched backpacks on their shoulders. They laughed and shoved as they clambered up the steps. I pressed against the wall. The crowd jostled past me through the door.

I watched a knife-thin white girl in a flowered dress and leather clogs speak to Keith. Her hair was gathered into a knot of brown strings and she shouldered a stuffed backpack. He shoved the box of exams into her arms. She climbed the stairs, the clomp of her shoes echoing in the empty bowl. Keith followed her, his steps silent like a cat's. At the top, he made no attempt to help her through the door. When I did, he glared at me. Her heavy backpack bumped my chest as she squeezed by.

In the hall, the girl turned toward the staircase. She toed the first step when Keith called out: "Devin, after you finish grading them, just leave them on Johnetta's desk. I'll pick them up tomorrow."

"No problem." Her squeak echoed in the stairwell as she vanished.

Keith shook his head. "They all talk like gum-chewing cows in some squalid dive, don't they? 'No problem!' Of course, it's no problem. She's my grad assistant, for fuck's sake. It's her *job* in this feudal system." He shot a crooked grin at me, then hiked his shoulders to invite me into the joke. "Peasants. Can't live with 'em, can't thrash 'em."

"Good to see you again, Gerry." I pushed from the wall, closing the distance between us. He backed a step.

"Glad you could catch the end of my lecture, Rook." He smelled of tobacco and menthol cough drops. "I saw you sneak in. You know, if you spend any more time on campus, the bursar will send you a tuition bill. This year, the charge is three hundred dollars per credit hour. A bargain at twice the price, don't you think?"

"Nice to catch your act."

He narrowed his eyes. The olive shirt made them greener than I remembered. Like blades of grass. Or pond algae. Mouth tight, he ditched the good humor: "Come on."

The students of Bowl 3 had disappeared, leaving the corridor empty. Keith and I walked beside a display of stark landscape photos. Utah, or maybe Dakota badlands. Past the elevators, Keith dropped into a chair made of foam blocks covered in purple suede. Aluminum pipes clamped the blocks together. He tilted his head toward the matching seat to his right. I took it. A square red steel table separated us. Keith parked his leather satchel on the table and rummaged inside it. He pulled out a pack of Marlboros, stuck one in his mouth, and fired a sleek Ronson lighter. No offer to me. Which made sense as we were sitting under a red-lettered sign: "No Smoking Please."

Two drags in silence. One silky stream spewed in front, the other jetted above our heads. My visit made me the aggressor, but I let the quiet eat at Keith. He bit after two more puffs. "This is stalking, Rook. I could call the police. A restraining order would be the next step."

"Feel free, Gerry."

"What do you want." Flat, with no upward lilt at the end of the sentence. "This stalking gets you nothing."

"If it gets me answers, I'm good."

"I doubt that. But go ahead."

"How did you come to be at the conference?" He knew the one I meant, the one where Annie died.

He crushed the back cushion, eyes fixed on the ceiling as thoughts jumped. "You know, I'm not sure. I believe Anniesha suggested my name to the conference organizers. I supposed she was eager to promote my new book. At any rate, I was invited to speak and I accepted." He leveled his gaze to meet mine and took a long pull on the cigarette. "I was thrilled to catch up with Anniesha again. She seemed as fresh and alluring then as when we first met in Miami." He curled his tongue over "alluring," as if it was a foreign term.

"You spoke with Annie the day before she died?" I knew the reports of Pearl Byrne and the hotel manager Brock Stevens. But I wanted the first-hand story.

"Sure. She phoned me in my room, said she'd be in the hotel gift shop. Of course, I came down to the lobby right away. No one ever says no to Anniesha. No one in his right mind." Lines softened around his beard. The wistful smile erased a decade from Keith's face.

"What did she want?"

Keith pulled the cellophane wrapping from the cigarette packet. He tipped ash into the tiny container. "To talk, she said. To reconnect. She suggested we have dinner. But I'd already made plans to meet Sally Anastos. Anniesha pouted in that imperial style she had when things didn't go her way."

He thrust his pink lower lip to imitate the expression. "A brief dark cloud flew across her face. Then she brightened, bubbling with a new idea. She invited Sally and me to join her for drinks in the hotel bar. She said we would let our dinner plans 'evolve' as the night rolled on. That's how Anniesha put it, *evolve*. Like something magical could happen for us if we relaxed into the flow."

"Magical," I echoed. But he didn't seem to hear.

"We might have said more. We would have, certainly. But that bitch, Pearl Byrne, barged in like a desiccated spinster determined to block everyone's fun." Keith snapped the insult through a jet of smoke. "Always nagging, always prying. That nasty woman pushed Anniesha to uncover things she never should have known."

"Pearl broke up your talk with Annie."

"Yes, we parted soon after that wretched hag arrived. Anniesha mentioned you would be joining us for drinks. Her ex. A private detective, of all things. She said we'd make a fun party of it. Fitting together all the pieces of her past. That's how she put it: a party for the past. Crazy lit, she said it would be. Exciting."

I wondered if Annie had been using me, hoping I'd be a shield. A form of security in the uncertain meeting with her academic friends. Or maybe she had intended for me to be a sword, a useful threat for an attack she planned to launch. Smoke curled before the sign over our heads, the gray plumes pinkening in the gloom. I dug elbows into my knees and studied a photo on the wall opposite. A harsh canyon draped with silver shadows.

I let the seconds creep. Ten. Twenty. "Who was she, Gerry?"

Keith tapped the packet and removed a new cigarette with his lips. "Whom do you mean?"

"The one you're so fucking angry with. Who the hell was she?"

He puffed his cheeks, then glanced along the edges of his eyes at me. He took the cigarette from his mouth. "You know, I was married once too. A long time ago." No more braying, this softer voice spooked me.

He sighed into the release. "Shawn and I married our second year of grad school at the University of Chicago. We met in a seminar on matrilineal systems in West Africa. We started dating October 5th, passed our doctoral qualifying exams May 13th, and married May 22nd."

"You remember the dates?"

"Yes, all of them. This was the brief, golden period when she was faithful."

"I see." I didn't, but debate would kill the story. He was whispering, so I did too. "But you got married anyway?"

"I didn't know about the cheating, not at first. And I thought I wanted it. Marriage, I mean. We were the golden couple. We were dazzling together. Beautiful geniuses. Everybody said it. The whole world was promised to us. So, we meshed our doctoral research agendas, planned our field work together, applied for grants together, lived seven months in that squalid hut together, hacking dust and wiping calamine lotion over our mosquito bites. We even contracted malaria the same week."

He lit the cigarette and inhaled. The ghost of a smile flicked across his mouth. "I wanted to preserve the golden moment we shared. The time when I had a loyal partner, a faithful wife. I truly did want it." Keith coughed, then licked his lips. "But I wasn't that lucky. She wasn't the woman I thought she was."

"How did you find out?"

"She told me. We'd planned to stay fifteen months in the field. After six, Shawn told me she wanted to go home. She wanted a different life. Not the one we were driving toward."

"So, you called it quits and both came home?"

"No. Shawn returned. I stayed and completed my field research. Alone." Keith sniffed; a deep drag on the cigarette covered the sound. "But she was right to move on. Absolutely. She was miserable and she would have made me miserable too. We divorced three months after I defended my dissertation."

"Not a complete wreck then." I kept eyes front on that silvery canyon. I could see Keith without shifting my gaze.

He fingered the lighter, stroking its slick curves. He set it on the table then tipped his head. He scoured my face, maybe looking for pity or even triumph. "Neither one of us crashed. We were pros, Rook. Meticulous, decent, even collegial. We launched our academic careers with great verve. Separate but equal, you might say. I had something to prove, so I pulled myself together and dived in." He expanded his chest and sighed little eddies into the smoke. "Winning is fine. But the best revenge is revenge. Always has been. Always will be."

That was his mission statement. I let it ride on the silence for a moment. "And where's your ex now?"

"Shawn died of ovarian cancer twenty-two years ago. I was only thirty-four years old." His voice was faint and clipped, all its public vigor sucked dry. He tapped the inch of ash into the cellophane.

At the far end of the corridor, someone opened a door to the outside. The rushing air sounded like an ocean swell. The figure disappeared into the sunlight. I raised my chin so Keith couldn't see wet glittering along my lids. "That's a tough one, Gerry."

"Yeah, her death hit me hard. Until that, I still hoped we had a chance. When Shawn died, I dug into my writing. I finished my third book and published two journal articles that year. I won tenure based on that work."

Keith snuffed the red cigarette tip between thumb and middle finger. His lips flattened, but he didn't wince. "You're good, Rook. Very good. What's your trick?"

"Trick?"

"Your technique, your methodology. How you make an informant divulge tough, personal details. The way you draw patterns and constructs from the intimate matter of someone's life. In a profession like yours, that trick must work wonders."

"No trick, Gerry. I listen. Then ask questions. And listen some more."

His voice thickened, nicotine roughing the sound into a rasp. "I didn't miss your little charade, Rook. You can't hide from me." He dropped the dead stub in the cellophane ashtray and crumpled it.

"What do you mean?" I shifted forward in the chair. My head and shoulders jutted from the shadows into the glare of the overhead spotlights.

"All these questions, these leading comments. You're hunting, aren't you? Stalking. Investigating your ex-wife's death." Trembling lips twisted into a sneer. "As if Anniesha still belongs to you. You're trying to claim her. Still. I suppose it's your natural instinct, a primitive compulsion driving you to protect her. Even now when it's too late. When you've lost everything. You still have a predilection to rush into the breach. A pathetic need to delve for evidence that might bring you some tepid solace. Give you some respite from your wretched burden of guilt and anger."

He stood, shaking his head. "I understand your miserable game, Rook. I truly do. But I'm warning you, dig too far, and you'll run into an iron deposit of painful facts. Truths you can't bear to uncover. Excavating will hurt. You will hurt."

Lecture done, threat delivered, Gerry Keith sniffed. He trained hard eyes on me. If I was the hunter, he refused to play the quarry.

I stood, arms clamped to my flanks, a stride forward until our chests touched. I didn't answer. He didn't care. No reply was needed. Keith retreated a step. He heaved his shoulders, as if shedding me and my pitiful troubles. He twisted his neck like a boxer, loosening muscles after the bout.

"I suppose we'll meet again, Rook." Thin pink lips trembled under his beard. He hoisted the satchel strap over his shoulder. "Next time, bring your tuition payment."

Lit by the overhead lamps, Keith strode down the corridor. At the far end, he shoved a door and disappeared into a classroom. I punched the button for the elevator to the first floor. When I reached the gravel path in front of the Barstall Building, I was still panting hard.

# CHAPTER
# TWENTY-SEVEN

Done with Gerry the Red, I took a cab to headquarters. I dug yesterday's triangle of tuna-on-rye from the top drawer of my desk. That, plus three swallows of coffee served as lunch. I phoned Pearl Byrne at her Poughkeepsie office. If she was Keith's nightmare, I wanted to talk with Pearl again. Her assistant Pam giggled when I gave my name. I figured she was twiddling her blonde curls for me. Pam said the boss was consulting with a client and would be gone for at least two hours. I left a vague message urging Pearl to phone my cell.

Instead of waiting at my desk for a return call, I stepped into the scant rain drops of a looming shower, headed to the Swann Center. Allard Swann had summoned me to his office, urgency crackling through his voice during our brief exchange. I hoped to see Carolyn Wiley too. An attendant ushered me into Dr. Swann's office, her mouth's tight clasp disapproving of the water I shed on the entry hall carpet.

Allard Swann didn't rise from his desk when I entered the room. He waved me to a chair and pushed aside folders to clear the surface between us. He didn't offer tea or lemonade. He looked at his watch twice before we ended the greetings. Perspiration shone on his brow and nose as he jumped to a formal speech. He sounded rehearsed. Swann's tone was curt, so different from the oily warmth he'd used the last times we spoke. Something big was up. Nothing good.

"Mr. Rook, I'm glad you made time to visit this afternoon. I have spoken by phone with Carl Wiley, the son of our resident, Mrs. Carolyn Wiley. He has put me in contact with attorneys who repeated the wishes he delivered to me directly." Darting eyes, rigid neck, plus shallow wheezing equaled worse than bad.

I stiffened my shoulders. "I figured they might reach out sooner or later, Dr. Swann. What did they want?"

"The attorneys have asked me to convey to you the following two points: First, you are to cease any contact with Mr. Carl Wiley. You should not call or communicate with him in any way. If you do so again, it will constitute harassment and Mr. Wiley will take appropriate legal action to stop you."

"Yeah, I'm not surprised. When I called Carl, our conversation didn't go so well. He sounded kind of peeved, come to think of it." I tried a smile, but dropped it when Swann grimaced.

I figured the next people contacting Carl would be the Seattle police department. They would follow Archie Lin's prompt about the unsolved death of Jayla Dream Ross. I had no control over official investigations on either coast. How the wheels of justice in Seattle and New York rolled was out of my hands. But I hoped those wheels crushed Carl Wiley to a fine powder.

Dr. Swann kept droning, his eyes raking a spot two feet above my head. "And second, you are not to visit or communicate with his mother, Mrs. Carolyn Wiley. At all. I've been instructed to prevent you from meeting with her here at the Swann Center. And you are not to speak with her by phone either."

I puffed, opening my lips so I didn't whistle on the exhale. I ran a fingernail along a crack in the edge of Swann's desk. No fresh quip or snappy response to his ultimatum. I'd been expecting it, but hearing Swann pronounce this stark banishment stunned me. Carolyn was attached to me, cared for me. She craved the attention of her son, real or imagined. And I'd been able to give her that. I was attached to her too. Even though she knew nothing of Annie's death, her soft words and kind touch had soothed my bruised heart. I needed her as much as she needed me. Keeping us apart felt unnecessary and cruel. But it did seem exactly like Carl to deepen his mother's unhappiness in this way. I'd never met the man in person. Our phone shouting match wasn't exactly a smooth introduction. But hiding behind Carolyn's skirts and using her infirmity to cover his own misdeeds seemed to be the pattern of his life. Anger churned in my stomach.

Allard Swann was just a man in the middle. The good soldier following orders, as the Nazis used to say. So, I squeezed the bile from my voice.

"Dr. Swann, do you think this is the best thing for Carolyn? Do you think I'm doing her harm by visiting with her? If you tell me you think it's best for her, then I'll stay away. I don't want to hurt her. Ever. But I need to hear it straight from you. Not from some tricked-out lawyers for her rotten absentee son."

"I don't know what to say, Mr. Rook. My hands are tied. I'm obligated to obey the wishes of the family in these circumstances. And Mr. Wiley's instructions are extremely clear. He doesn't want you around his mother anymore."

Swann studied his desk, rolling a heavy black fountain pen into a gutter between two stacks of note cards. Rain slapped the windows behind his shoulders. Minus the anger, Swann sounded as miserable as I felt.

"So, I guess that's that. I won't call, or come by, or write." I fastened both hands on the armrests of my chair, ready to hoist myself upright. "But if Carolyn asks about me, lie. Tell her I took another job. Say I had to move out of town. That's why I'm not around anymore. Can you do that for me, Dr. Swann?"

"Yes, I'll do that. If she asks, we'll tell her you've moved away." Swann hesitated. He swallowed, a soggy gulp which soaked his next words in regret. "But you have to understand, Mr. Rook, the way her dementia is progressing, it's possible she may never ask for you again. Or for her son. Both of you may join all the other faded shadows, lost forever in her past."

"Yes, I understand. Thank you for that." Acid curdled in my gut, clotting like rancid milk. I plucked at the knees of my slacks.

"No, thank *you*, Mr. Rook. You've been of service to us all."

I rose and shoved the chair backwards. I tipped my chin toward the square black safe near the sofa. "You keep valuables for the inmates in that?"

Swann flinched at my harsh term. "Yes. If the family requests, we store our patients' credit cards, documents, checkbooks, jewelry, phones." He eyed the steel vault like it might pounce. "Why?"

"You have a silver bracelet in there? Belongs to Mrs. Wiley?"

"Yes, that's right. A fancy hand-tooled chain with a heavy clasp. Really quite lovely."

"Return the bracelet to her, Dr. Swann. She misses it."

He gulped, then nodded, gaze sweeping the carpet. I'd done my best for Carolyn Wiley. Even if she'd never know it. I left Swann's office without another word.

The tight-mouthed attendant escorted me to the front door of the Swann Center. She stood guard on the rain-slicked porch until I reached the pavement.

———

I slogged the blocks between the center and my office. A dreary fog pressed around my head, erasing storefronts and faces, muffling the clatter of trains overhead and the pleas of vendors hawking purses and jewelry from curbside tables. The rain had ended, but the shower had dampened the sidewalks enough to send steam wafting around my ankles. Twice I checked my phone, hoping I'd missed the buzz of Pearl Byrne's call. No joy.

When I reached my block, I ducked into Zarita's, rather than sink into the dusty gloom of my office. Drinking in a neighborhood bar wasn't the same as drinking with actual friends. But the presence of familiar, if blotto, faces lent rough comfort all the same.

Jerome Stewart the bartender nodded at my entrance. He slowed his circular swipes of the gleaming brass counter, the swollen brown knobs of his knuckles flexing as he paused. He slid his dark eyes toward the rear of the room as I passed. Shoulders hunched, his gaunt neck disappeared into the collar of his shirt. The grooves around his mouth deepened as Jerome worked a toothpick between his thin lips.

I didn't want to hear what he intended to say. Sure, Jerome was a fountain of local gossip and neighborhood complaints. I'd gotten many useful tips from him over the years I'd drunk at Zarita's. He'd even hired me to rescue his punk son from several scrapes. But I wanted none of that, not this dismal afternoon. Eyes ahead, I glided past the three old fixtures hugging the bar and headed for my favorite booth in the rear. Jerome knew to bring a shot of Jim Beam dribbled over a single rock. If I wanted a second, I'd ask.

A thick silhouette in my booth arrested me with a cackle: "I figured you'd turn up some time, kid. Nice to see you again."

Smoke Burris sprawled in my seat. His dark face was shiny, his eyes buried in creases of good humor. A blue cloth driving cap was pasted to the back of his head. It matched the sharp blue stripe in his gray knit shirt. Grinning, he patted the table, his paw rattling the Michelob bottle and half-full glass in front of him. "Have a seat, Rook. Take a load off."

He'd startled me, but I refused to give that away. I clenched my jaw over a growl. "Thanks for the invite, Smoke." I slid onto the bench opposite him. "I thought you'd left town."

"That was the plan. But my client got side-swiped by true love. Some little Ayanna from the block got her claws into my boy 2-Ryght at the shoe store. You know how it goes: cute chick flips her weave, Dwayne swoons. Then little Dwayne does all the thinking. The boy switched his plans, delayed our departure until tomorrow morning. So, I thought I'd check out the old haunts. Cruised the nabe for a while, then I dropped into Zarita's to visit my favorite spot." He waved his eyes over the narrow stall like a king in his castle.

"This was *your* booth?"

"Sure, kid. Didn't the barkeep tell you nothing about the history of this place?"

"No. He didn't mention you."

"Maybe he didn't recognize me. You know, back in the day the bartender was a jive-talking old coot named Freddy. This new one, Jerome, he used to work the kitchen. He turned out a crazy good mac-n-cheese back then. Plus, his sloppy joes stuck to your ribs like nobody's business. Neighborhood famous, they was."

"Now the kitchen only serves cheddar cheese on toast. White, rye, or wheat."

"Jerome had a son, Spencer if I recall right. That boy was the image of his dad: black as a thundercloud, undersized, tetchy. Spencer would come to Zarita's every day after school and throw down in the kitchen right alongside Jerome. Awful good with a knife, that kid. I figured he graduate to a gun soon enough. Wonder whatever happened to Spencer?"

"Pence is in Vegas now."

"Up to no-good, I figure. No surprise. Only one way that boy was goin' to end up: a small-time hood and a big-time loser."

The burly detective stroked his moustache as Jerome set my drink on the table. The bartender's face was blank; if he'd heard us dragging his son, he didn't show it. Jerome drifted to his post, I sipped, and Smoke changed the subject.

"I been meaning to thank you for helping my cuz. Galaxy told me about your little dust-up over at the university." He eyed the scratches on my cheek and winked. "I hear you went three rounds with the bantam-weight champeen of the campus. KO'ed her but good."

"No, I just set the table. Galaxy batted clean-up." I'd perfected the art of mixing sports metaphors.

The bushy moustache jumped as he laughed. "My home girl still got some gangsta in her. Can't erase the ghetto, no matter how much schooling you swallow." Smoke flapped a heavy hand in the aisle. A minute later, Jerome re-appeared with another Michelob. I was still sipping, my bourbon less than half gone.

Smoke noticed my weariness. "Something eating you, Rook? You look poorly around the eyes, tight and gray. Like a eighteen-wheeler flattened you on the boulevard."

"I'm alright."

"Unh-unh, kid. That BS might work here in New York, where everybody's playing cute and working an angle. But I'm South Side born and bred. We call it out every time."

I didn't want to share the sting of the cruel setback with Carolyn Wiley. But I could let Smoke know what I'd uncovered about the death of his old boss's wife. "I found how Norment's Dreamie died."

Heavy folds over his eyes lifted. "What happened to her?"

"She was killed in a car accident twenty-five years ago. Her body was hidden in the basement of a house on Strivers Row."

"Christ Almighty! I'll be damned!" Smoke dragged a hand over his scalp, then down his nose. "All those years, Old Man Ross tormented himself about her disappearance. Fretting and wondering what he'd done to drive off his wife. Blamed himself for the hurt he caused little Sabrina. Poor man tortured himself with doubts."

Smoke sighed at the awful memory. He swiped his eyes and lips before speaking again. "You know how he goes for a haircut the nineteenth of every month? Never fails, Norment's at the barbershop the same day each month. Once, I asked Sabrina why he always goes that particular day. She said her mother disappeared on September 19. So, each month, Norment visits the barber on the nineteenth, grooming himself in hopes she'll return. Figure that! Twenty-five years, each month, regular like clockwork. Norment scratching at the past, picking 'til the scab crumbles and the flesh beneath jumps all raw and pink. Call it superstition or stunt, juju or prayer. I call it torture."

Smoke crumpled the paper coaster and dragged it across his nose. The wad left a streak of wet. He dabbed his moustache, then raised his eyes. "How'd they take it, when you broke the news?"

"It was tough. But they're coming around." My words squeaked thin and high, clattering like cheap metal. As if we'd crammed all our pasts in a dented cash box and chucked the key.

Narrowing his lids, Smoke noted the phony tin in my voice. "And you? You coming 'round? After your ex-wife got herself killed?" His blunt terms eased the bare facts.

I swilled bourbon over my teeth. "I'm working on it."

His eyes sharpened. "Working? Like investigating?"

"Yes."

"You find anything give an idea of who did the murder?"

"Something, but not enough."

"Spill, kid. It'll sort you out to talk through it."

Maybe Smoke was right. Or maybe the booze was doing its job. Or maybe I just wanted to talk. I took a gulp and plunged. "Fact one: Annie was with a man in her hotel room the night she was killed. Two, whoever shot her did it up close and without a struggle. She felt comfortable with her murderer. Three, she had dinner that night with friends, three people with access to guns. Four, those people stayed at the hotel overnight."

Misery blew through me as I sputtered to a halt. I downed the bourbon and leaned from the booth. Jerome caught my sign and scurried with a second shot. I dribbled it over the ice in my glass.

Smoke watched me take a good-sized swig before he responded. "But you left off fact number five: motive. What could make any of those people want to murder your wife?"

I shook my head, then twirled the glass until the brown liquor slopped to the rim. "I don't know. I'm missing the final piece. And I just don't know."

"You listen to Old Smoke, kid. One of those people got the clue. Maybe they know and they's holding out. Or maybe they's ignorant as my dog Daley. But for sure somebody's got the last piece to the puzzle. I don't know your case. But I do know people. How they think, how they act. Somebody's holding close a fact you need. You just got to pry some more and it'll fly loose."

Smoke gobbled the beer and smacked his lips over the foam on his moustache. He wasn't done giving advice. "Here's an old trick I use: draw a word picture for each of them. Two or three words max. That'll point you where to look for a motive."

He stared, I said nothing. He drummed fingers into the wooden table, then stared some more. I wasn't going to win the stand-off. The desire to talk took over, so I sketched Rick Luna. "The junior exec is ambitious, untested, but over-confident."

"Okay. You got something for the other two?"

"The prof is self-centered and revengeful." Gerry Keith was much more, but those words flew to mind first. "And his Girl Friday is devoted and desperate."

"Girl Friday?"

Thinking of Sally Anastos that way spiked acid in my already sour stomach. But I stuck with the image. "She's ride or die, like a loyal servant."

"Okay. That's a start." Smoke pumped his chin twice. "You talked it over with Sabrina?"

"No."

"That girl's a damn good detective. Got a fine brain in her pretty little head. You ought to share with her. Bring her into it. She could help, you know."

I had nothing to add. Silence was my best move. The man was primed to guess about my relationship with Brina, but I wasn't going to spill.

A hound with a bone, Smoke wouldn't let go. "Where'd you leave it with her?"

"Brina?" Playing dumb, or playing for time, I ducked his gaze. Guilt trickled through me, little drops of regret that my involvement with Annie was not a relic of the past, but a live concern plaguing my connection with Brina.

"Yeah, no clowning, kid. You know who I'm talking 'bout. You in something deep with Sabrina, ain't you?" He pinned me with a glare when I didn't answer. "You stringing her along? Or you in it for real?"

"I'm not stringing her along. I don't fool like that, Smoke."

"Then you been together long enough to know what you got to do, don't you?"

I shook my head, then sucked the ice into my mouth. "Marriage isn't in my nature." I cracked the cube and spit a shard into the glass. "Not anymore."

"I ain't said nothing about no marriage, kid. You hear me say anything about getting hitched?" Smoke's dark lip curled with mockery. "I'm talking about letting her know the score. That's what I mean.

Take it from this old player. Sabrina's no round-the-way girl. She's a serious woman. And serious women like to know where they stand with a man. They want to know they been chosen. Picked from the bouquet, so to speak. Plain fact is a woman – if she's worth anything – wants to be the one you choose. Dig me?"

Smoke's call to action stirred me. I felt the push, for sure. But in what direction? Annie was gone, I couldn't choose her. But was I ready to choose a deeper bond with Brina? Could we have something richer than anything I'd known with Annie?

"Got you," I said. I studied the bourbon draping the slivers of ice in my glass. We were so quiet, I could hear rain tapping on the picture window at the front of the bar.

Smoke tipped his bottle and emptied the beer down his throat. "Trust. Old Smoke got this right, kid. You either choose her. Or you don't. What's it gonna be?"

Coarse buzzing in my pocket saved me from answering. Pearl Byrne returning my call. I jerked my eyebrows at Smoke. He planted both elbows on the table, refusing to move.

I greeted Pearl, speaking low so she wouldn't detect the booze sloshing in my brain. She sounded tentative at first. After two minutes of generalities and poking to catch my mood, she asked how I was doing this week. I asked her the same. We agreed the shock was wearing off, but the sorrow remained.

A somber grimace curved Smoke's mouth as he listened. Maybe our misery pushed him. Perhaps memories of South Side manners surfaced at last. He hauled his bulk from the tight booth, fished two twenties from his pocket and slid them into the moist ring under his beer bottle. The big man clapped a hand on my shoulder and squeezed. When I nodded, he bowled along the aisle and out the door.

I told Pearl the reason for my call: I wanted to learn more about the contents of Annie's final presentation, the one she never got a chance to give at the business conference. "Were you two going to talk about the way you ran your companies? Your financing, strategic planning, expansion prospects, things like that?"

"Not exactly. I don't know how comfortable I feel sharing our talk now that Anniesha's gone." Her voice quivered, shrinking to nothing in the electronic distance that separated us. This reluctance might stem from professional courtesy. Or some other source.

"You sound hesitant, like you don't want to talk about this, Pearl. Is it because this information belongs to Anniesha and you don't have a right to share it?"

"Something like that, Mr. Rook."

She paused; I jumped to unblock the log jam. "You know, Anniesha always called me SJ. Everybody else just calls me Rook. I wish you'd pick one of those. The Mister makes me feel like I'm a hundred years old."

We laughed and she agreed to skip the formalities. "Okay, I'll go with SJ, if Anniesha did."

"Good, Pearl. Now tell me more about what you and Anniesha had cooked up for your presentation." I remembered Smoke's advice: Pearl could own that jagged bit of the puzzle. Even if she didn't realize she possessed the crucial piece.

We spoke for ten minutes. Not long, but enough for me recognize what Pearl knew was a bombshell. To detonate it with maximum effect, she had to deliver the message in person. And I needed to arrange a meeting for Pearl with the expert who'd best handle that fiery information: Dean Galaxy Pindar of Alexander University.

I knew why Annie had been murdered. I wanted to explode the puzzle to reveal who pulled the trigger.

# CHAPTER
# TWENTY-EIGHT

At five-twenty-five the next day, Alexander University's medieval towers dripped under damp skies. Low clouds dabbled mist over the Friday afternoon stillness as Pearl Byrne, Brina, and I crossed the campus. We had the gray puddles and gravel paths to ourselves. My usual police escorts had abandoned their posts, fled to dry barracks or coffee shops along with the student horde.

"It looks like a neutron bomb went off here." Brina's crack drew a wondering stare from Pearl. "You know, like a blast destroyed all the people, but left the buildings standing." She huffed a weak laugh as Pearl squinted and swung her head.

I offered snark without facts: "Students start their weekend partying Thursday night. Profs refuse to schedule classes on Friday." I shrugged. "Everybody wins."

Randolph Hall's glass doors were unlocked. Sour faces of the university's founding fathers peered at us from gold frames as we tramped to the staircase. All the pasty nineteenth century donors in these oil paintings wore suits of black or charcoal. Where was the bold pioneer in Alexander University's signature purple? My black trousers and jacket fit right in with this somber crowd. Almost. If I'd owned a lavender shirt, I'd have worn it. But I didn't, so I chose a blue one in honor of Pearl.

The second-floor hall was dim and quiet, an uneasy corridor of beige walls and scuffed oak planks. More tight-lipped portraits guarded the door of the dean's suite. I knocked, but no one answered, so I pushed in. Musty fumes rose from the old rugs in the outer office. No smiles from Nathalie Kwan greeted us when we entered. I was disappointed my favorite admin assistant had vanished, along with the rest of the Alexander staff. I'd hoped her warm welcome might calm Pearl's jitters and ease what was sure to be a difficult meeting.

We crossed the empty office, past the plush violet lounge chairs and the dark mahogany secretary's desk. The bookcase, with its bright show of academic power was still there, waiting for a new display to celebrate the winner of the Blackistone Prize. On the shelves, books by the nominated authors were mounded in three colorful pyramids. Above the bookcase hung the photos of the rival professors: Keith, Nakamura, and Pindar.

I glanced at the two women beside me. Pearl's cheeks were sunken and chalky, her pale eyes bulging. She wheezed as if we'd been running. Brina's nose and forehead glistened under a film of perspiration. A vein pulsed below her left ear. She licked her lips, gulped air, then licked again. Excitement drove them, mixed with a drop of fear. I wasn't immune to the tension: my stomach shot toward my chest as I rapped on the dean's private door.

Strong women turn me on. Mostly.

From an early age my mother, grandmother, and aunts taught me to respect their wise power. The older I got, the more I was drawn to strong women. But the sky-high energy of this meeting I'd arranged between Galaxy Pindar, Pearl Byrne, and Brina Ross set my nerves on edge. This was tinderbox territory. And I was flicking the matchhead with my fingernail.

After explaining my goal to Galaxy, we'd agreed to meet in her office Friday afternoon. She apologized for making the three of us travel to campus. She explained she needed to be near the conference room on the first floor of Randolph Hall. This was the location of the committee meeting which would decide the winner of the Blackistone Prize.

As both the dean in charge and a nominee, Galaxy needed to be on stand-by for the announcement.

We shook hands and the women circled, like boxers in a ring. Shoulders tense, necks stiff, no smiles, all business. I watched Brina and Pearl take in the complicated colors, patterns, textures, and artifacts of Galaxy's inner office. In Nathalie's absence, the dean brought us coffee and water from the kitchenette beyond the display case. Folds of her red and purple tunic rustled around black pants as she ferried cups and bottles into the office. While Galaxy set the table, the newcomers canvassed the space, scanning books, skimming papers, admiring photographs.

Pearl wore the same boxy blue nun suit she'd worn the day I'd met her. Maybe it was the only formal outfit she owned. A visit to the big city university campus deserved her best. She carried a white canvas sack with long straps, its weight butted her calf as she moved around the room. She drew a finger over the threads of the yellow tapestry on the round table. Then she dabbed at a dusty book on a shelf near the window. Would she pull out a handkerchief to polish the glass? Cleaning ladies never take a holiday.

At the far side of the dean's desk, Brina touched the forehead of the wooden mother-and-child statue Galaxy had wielded in my defense. She tipped it, looking for Reva Nakamura's bloodstains. Then she winked at me and flipped the hem of her red jacket. A Beretta Nano 9mm nestled in the waistband of her dark jeans. If Reva returned, I was well protected.

We settled around the table. The dean pointed Pearl to a seat next to her and I took the chair beside Pearl. Brina sat opposite me. I shifted to touch shoulders with Pearl, a nudge of solidarity and comfort. Sweetness lifted from her earlobe and brushed my face: Annie's perfume, *Rêves de la Plage*; tangy like cherries dipped in sugar. Pearl wanted Annie in the room with us.

I made the introductions, but urged Galaxy to lead the conversation. She didn't waste words on formalities. "Pearl, thank you for taking time away from your office." These were two professionals pressed to make the most of their short time together. Galaxy lifted a pad of yellow legal paper from a stack on the table. She ripped off the top page to reveal a clean sheet and parked her red eyeglasses on her nose. "For a business owner, every hour not at work means money lost, so I'm grateful for your visit today."

Pearl's smile faltered, but her words rang clear. "Not at all, Dean Pindar. The work is important. But Anniesha is more important. That's how I see it. I'm glad SJ could steer me in the right direction and get me to someone like you."

Brina's eyebrows shot up at hearing a stranger use such an intimate name for me. My shrug wasn't enough of a response; I'd owe her a fuller explanation later.

Galaxy's sip of coffee softened her direct language. "Rook has told me some of it. But I want to hear about your company from you."

Pearl leaned back in her chair, gripping a bottle of water. "I figure you don't really care to know too much about the cleaning business. It's pretty much what you'd expect." She sputtered to a halt and looked at me.

"Tell the dean about the people you hire, Pearl." I pushed confidence through a smile, hoping she'd relax into her story.

"I hire mostly women, provide them with equipment, uniforms, and cars and send them on assignments. The clients who contract with my company are homeowners, businesses, local government departments. Such like that."

Galaxy took a black ball point pen and scratched a few words on her yellow pad.

Pearl turned her round face toward me and drew the parallel to Annie. "We were alike in so many ways. She got her start just like I did: scrubbing floors and windows in rich people's homes for peanuts. She scraped and fought to turn that hard experience into a pretty fair business. Just like me."

Sitting beyond Pearl, I couldn't make out what the dean wrote, but I could see the capital *A* that punctuated her notes. Galaxy's precise speech and careful questions made the interview feel like a legal deposition. "And did you know Anniesha before?"

"No, I had no reason to. And no way to know anything about her company down in Miami. Our getting together was all because of Professor Keith. He did the introductions."

"So, Gerry Keith did his primary field research among the employees at your company. Just like he did at Anniesha's company in Miami? Is that how you understand it?"

Pearl's eyes narrowed and her voice contracted to a whisper. "Well, see that's the funny thing. Professor Keith only visited me in my office in Poughkeepsie just that one time. The next time it was the person he brought with him, that young assistant."

I filled in the name Pearl had forgotten. "Sarah Anastos? Sally. She's the one who came to see you with Dr. Keith?"

"Yes, jumpy little red-head in a black pants suit. That one. First, Sally came up with the prof. Then she came back three more times on her own."

"*Three* more times?" Galaxy was as puzzled as I'd been when I first heard that number. "Only three? I've read Dr. Keith's book and it details data collected at the so-called 'Blondie Cleaning Services' in Poughkeepsie from at least fifty different women interviewed over many months."

Pearl bit her lip at the challenge, but didn't back down. "Maybe that's in the book he wrote. But I was there. I can tell you for a fact Sally never came up to see me or my girls more than three times. And she worked slow. I know because I had to keep track of exactly how many hours she spent with each girl. So, I could pay them for the time, you see."

"How many of your employees did Sally Anastos interview?"

At this point Pearl reached into the cloth satchel on the floor at her right ankle. She pulled out a stack of papers and shuffled through them until she found the information she wanted.

"These are time sheets for each of my girls who put in claims after they got interviewed by Sally. Seven girls in total. Four of them interviewed for two hours; two of them interviewed for just one hour each. And one, Janet MacNeil, spent three hours. Janet must have been a pretty good source. Maybe that's why Sally spent so much time with her."

Galaxy looked up from her writing to nail this assertion. "So, you're saying, Sally Anastos interviewed only seven of your employees? And she spent a total of only thirteen hours doing it?"

"Yes, Dean. That's how I added it up. And that's how I paid out too. I sure wasn't going to cheat my girls out of their due. Fair is fair. Talking is just as much work as cleaning out a shower stall or mopping a floor, you know."

Behind her glasses, red threads popped in the corners of Galaxy Pindar's eyes. She was bone-rattling mad. She clamped her lips tight to get control of her words.

Brina spoke into the scary silence. "So, Pearl, did you ask Anniesha if something similar had happened at her company in Miami?"

"Yes, I sure did. When I found out she was going to be the keynote speaker at the business conference, I reached out to her. I knew she was the "Brownie Cleaning Services" company Professor Keith had talked about. But I'd never spoken to her direct. But when I saw she was going to be making a trip up here, I sent her an email."

Pearl turned to me. After I nodded, her blue eyes glowed with unshed tears as she continued.

"I thought we could get together, maybe have coffee or lunch. But Anniesha called me on the phone and we got to chatting. We talked a lot. About how it was to be a woman in business. How we made a go of it, how we handled the girls on our payroll. Competition, advertising, bankers, things like that."

Pearl twisted the straps of the cloth bag. Seeing the violence of her actions, she dropped the sack out of sight again and resumed.

"Anniesha was a real sharp professional and a first-class lady. But, you know, she was a regular gal too. She talked to me like a friend. I could tell she had education, maybe more than me. But she talked to me like I was worth something. I appreciated that. She was a real lady."

I took Pearl's hand and squeezed it twice. She was trembling, so I held her fingers as she gathered the threads of her story.

"When I described how the two professors did their work in my shop, Anniesha said they were the same at her place down in Miami."

Pearl reached into the bag at her side and drew out a tablet. As she fired up the device, she explained her plan. "We spoke several times by video conference call. I recorded them. I thought you might want to see Anniesha explain things in her own voice."

The screen flashed, Annie's face filling its frame. A white turtleneck threw a spotlight on her dark brown skin. Her fine chain of braided rose, white, and yellow gold hung around the high collar. Long black hair draped past her bare shoulders; pink hoop earrings glinted through the strands. Under thick bangs, the slant of her eyelids was outlined in blue pencil. Shiny pink lacquered her lips. Annie looked commanding. Beautiful. The strongest of the four women in the room.

Galaxy craned to view Annie. Brina rose from her seat to stand behind the dean. A river of emotions washed over me as I watched them. Galaxy jutted her chin forward, her eyes narrowing behind thick lenses as she concentrated. With the tip of her tongue peeking between her lips, the dean jotted notes on her yellow pad. Brina's breath clutched and rushed and caught again as the story unspooled. Tiny drops of perspiration dotted the frown line dividing her brow. Once she swiped at the sweat, then dabbed her fingers against her jeans. Brina kept her gaze on the screen, eyes wide, lips twisted as her teeth worried at the left corner of mouth. She wouldn't meet my stare as she absorbed Annie's account.

Annie's tone was brisk, without her usual warm drawl. The story was straightforward. She said she would have to dig to get the papers she had kept on the hours spent interviewing each of her employees. She said Professor Keith asked her to maintain a cuff account of the hours – informal notes on the back of an envelope – so he could pay each girl what was due them. "But he wanted it kept off the official company records, so it wasn't recorded as part of the regular hours each girl put in," Annie explained.

Though she hadn't stopped writing, Galaxy recovered her voice. Low, rough, and menacing. Lucky I wasn't the focus of her anger, I'd have burned to cinders where I sat.

"So, how many hours did Keith spend interviewing employees at the company in Miami?"

Pearl tapped the screen to freeze Annie's image and answered the dean's question. "I don't know exactly. Anniesha had that all written up. She told me it was twenty to forty hours he spent with about twenty women. That Sally Anastos spent time down there too, living in the neighborhood. But Anniesha said her workers told her Sally didn't do much talking with them, even on a social level. Kept pretty much to herself on the job and on the weekends too. Didn't go out, or visit, or socialize, or nothing. Just kept to herself all the time. Hiding out in her apartment. Scared or something, I guess."

"And did Sally Anastos spend the entire twelve months in Miami, as she claimed?" Galaxy's tone was frosty enough to snap the beak off a penguin.

"Not from what Anniesha told me. No. Sally wasn't down there a solid year. She'd fly in, work a little with one of the cleaning teams, and then disappear after a few days. Anniesha knew who was on each team, on each assignment, and for how long at each location. She told me she had proof of exactly how much work the two professors put into their research down in Miami."

Galaxy was terse in outlining the importance of Annie's information. "And she also had proof of how much time and effort they did *not* put into their research."

"Yes, Dean. She did." Pearl nodded and tapped the keyboard. "Here's what she said."

The tablet blazed again. Annie's bold eyes flickered as she leaned toward us. This time her voice had a metallic edge, like shears slicing through silk. "I'm going to show them, Pearl. Show them good. They thought they could pull a fast one. Use us in their little game of snob versus snob. But I won't be used. Not now. Not ever. And I won't let them use you either." The click of tongue against teeth made hairs rise on my neck. "Oh, it'll be a blast to see Gerry and his little side chick squirm, won't it? Their faces, puffing up like freaking pink frogs! Can't you just picture it, Pearl? I can't wait!"

Tears brimming, Pearl poked the screen. The smile on Annie's face froze, eyes tight with glee. Her voice stopped, one touch forever muting the past. My gut clenched; desire rushed, fresh as always. Guilt heaved too, glazed with anger. Bile slicked the crest of my tongue. Did Annie's pull grip the others? Did they want to claw through the screen to arrest the past too?

Behind me, Brina gasped. I turned to see her slam hand to mouth. But words escaped anyway: "She had no idea how serious this was. What she was planning. How it could devastate the careers those profs had built. Anniesha wanted revenge for being dissed. But she never imagined how deep the threat was."

Under Brina's wet glance, I gulped and shook my head. Nothing I had could break the silence. It went on for hours, years. When I winced at the gut pain, Pearl squeezed my hand tighter.

Galaxy asked the practical follow up. "So, what happened to Anniesha's report? The presentation she was planning to give with you, Pearl?"

"I've been wondering that myself. Anniesha had it all ready the day before. I saw her after she gave that keynote speech. She told me she had her presentation all set. Slides, graphs, PowerPoint. It must have been on a laptop or in one of those power sticks."

Brina, in her seat again, turned to me. "Did the police find a computer or thumb drive in Anniesha's room?"

"I asked. They said no. I didn't see one when we entered the room. But we weren't looking for a laptop."

An image of Room 1823, as it looked when Pearl and I followed the manager through that door, shimmered in my mind. The vision was clear. But I couldn't see anything except Annie's beautiful body. No bed or nightstand or chair. No suitcase or laptop. Just Annie, drifting in peace, terrible holes ripped through her breast.

"Then it must have been removed and destroyed by the murderer." Brina was the first to use that word. A grim reminder of the act that brought us to this point.

Galaxy's intervention was harsh, laced with bitterness that seemed as personal as mine, but for different reasons.

"Yes. This is academic fraud covered up by murder. Fraud at its purest. Keith and Anastos conspired to commit academic deceit. They fabricated information and presented the lies as truth. They forged data they claimed to have collected in the field from informants. They made up the names, backgrounds, histories, and interview responses for hundreds of informants to fill in the contours of their research. Plain and simple: they cheated."

"And Anniesha had the goods on them." Pearl said this with force, pride wringing sadness from her voice. She looked at the screen, smiled at Annie, then tapped it. Oblivion, in a dazzling blue wash of pixels, erased my past.

I squeezed her hand again. "Yes, she did."

Brina's crisp tone crackled with alarm. "But if Anniesha was in danger, doesn't that mean you could be too, Pearl? You know the same thing she knew."

"Maybe, I guess. I never thought about it. I didn't know why Anniesha had been killed. It never occurred to me the information she knew had cost her life. Or that what she knew, I might know too."

Realization contracted Pearl's eyelids until white showed all around her pupils. She stared at me, the only person she knew or cared about in the room.

I couldn't offer comfort. "That's exactly what the killer was counting on. That no one would ever figure out a motive for Annie's murder. That killing her was the single blow which eliminated both the knowledge and the person who held it."

I kept the rest of my thoughts to myself. The waste of Annie's death overwhelmed me again. I'd investigated enough murders to know sometimes people got killed because of a few tiny scraps of information. The victim could know something, or see something, or hear something that meant the end of the world to the killer.

Sometimes the victim might even know she possessed that nugget of insight. She could hold it up, turn it around, focus a magnifying glass on it. Even boast about it, the way Annie did. But without context, she could never imagine how crucial her bit of information was. And she couldn't conceive of how far a terrified fanatic would go to erase it. As I'd learned through painful experience, murder didn't take two to tango. Only the killer needed to know the information was of fatal value. Annie's had almost been a clean murder, one that erased the dangerous facts and the person who held them in a single blow. If not for Pearl Byrne's payroll accounts and her recordings of her conversations with Annie, we never would have known the truth.

I shuddered, sending a tremor from my body to Pearl's. She glanced at me, a frown line folding her brow. Then she squeezed my hand to reassure me as I had done for her a few minutes earlier.

"Don't worry about me, SJ. Nothing bad's going to get me. I'm too tough a bird to get into trouble."

"Nothing bad's going to happen to anybody. Count on it." I sounded more confident than I felt. Pearl looked relieved, so I tossed her a smile to seal my promise.

Galaxy Pindar had no patience with mushy reassurances. She lumbered to her desk. She punched at a cell phone lying on a stack of papers. Without introduction or apology, she snapped orders. She told someone he needed to hear from a new witness with key testimony about one of the books under consideration. She never used the term, but I knew she was speaking with a member of the Blackistone Prize committee. Academics are often accused of being vague, indecisive, and slow to act. Why decide today? When you can have three committee meetings about it this semester. And five more next semester. And submit a report at the end of the academic year after that? But fury driving her, Galaxy Pindar proved the exception to the rule: she moved fast.

When she hung up, the dean turned heated eyes on the three of us.

"Pearl, you come with me. A faculty committee is meeting right now in another part of this building. They need to hear your story. They need to know the background to Gerry Keith's field research for his book. After the committee, you go to the police."

Pearl gulped, her chin twitching. "Okay, Dean. If you need me. But I want SJ to come with me. Can he?"

"Of course." Galaxy was crisp as she stuffed her note pad into a tan leather folder. "Rook, the Blackistone committee is meeting in a conference room on the first floor. Both of you can come." She tilted her head to include Brina.

Her mouth squeezed into a tight O, Pearl looked a plea at me. I patted her shoulder as we stood from the table. Maybe the committee would boot me from the room when they listened to Pearl's story. But if she wanted me there, I was ready.

Galaxy led the way to the outer room of the dean's office suite. Sharing a nod, Brina and I stepped into flanking positions on either side of Pearl, forming a triangle of protection as we moved toward the exit.

But none of our security measures mattered in the face of a loaded gun.

# CHAPTER
# TWENTY-NINE

Sally Anastos prodded the nape of Gerry Keith's neck with her gun. As she herded him across the threshold into the dean's suite, she deepened her voice. Commands rumbled across the room.

At the four of us: "You, step back. Hands in front." Her stare raked across our line, vacant and cold. Did she even see us?

At Keith: "Stand over there. Next to him."

Gerry stumbled to my right. With the blunt nose of her Beretta, Sally arranged us in a broad arc. We were a captive chorus and she was the choirmaster. Did the formation suit her notion of status? Keith, then me, with Pearl, Brina, and Galaxy fanned on my left. Or was this the order in which Sally planned to kill us?

Hands clenched at my thighs, I focused on the wall over Sally's shoulder. No good challenging her with a direct stare. Defuse the situation, keep Sally calm. Connect her to us as humans, not aggressors or prey. Gerry Keith swayed, as if for a dance. At my left, Pearl shivered, fear seeping like rot through the room. Her whimpers would swell into groans if this stand-off wasn't resolved soon. Mewling might generate pity. Or provoke Sally into a sadistic attack.

Galaxy coughed. I turned my head. She launched daggers with her eyes: "What are you doing here?" Nonsensical and threatening, but it was her office. A dean in command, staring down the barrel of a gun.

"I brought *him* to you." Sally narrowed her eyes, then shifted her jaw toward Keith. He dropped his head until the red goatee brushed the knot in his tie. His hands twitched against his gray trousers. "You're the dean. You need the truth from his mouth."

"I've got the truth. Seen it. You – you don't need to do this…You…" Galaxy's plea spluttered to a gasp.

Sally laughed at the stumble. "You don't even know my name, do you?" The screech sliced the dank air. Galaxy stepped back, chewing her lip.

I spoke into the hollowed-out silence. "I know your name. Sarah." Maybe the formality would stitch her wounded pride. Restore her connection to us. "And you know me."

Sally swallowed hard. I slid my eyes to the left. Brina's hand twitched near her pocket. She wanted to grip the gun at the small of her back, a disastrous option. Matching firepower with firepower would end this standoff in bloodshed. I sent cautioning brain waves. We'd collaborated in crises before. Our ESP might work again. I tilted my head toward Brina with a quick warning. A flicker of eyelashes, nothing more.

But the subtle gesture ignited Sally's fury. "Don't move, Rook!"

She was dressed for her mission: black tights and shoes, a black shirt revealed ropey veins jumping along her neck. No earrings, her red hair spiked like a raptor's frill. Chewed skin flaked from her bare lips. She snapped at Brina: "Who are you?"

Muscles along Brina's jaw clenched, but she said nothing.

Sally filled in the gap. "You another of Gerry's little fuck buddies?"

The hard green of her pupils glittered with excitement. An animal musk rose from her body. This was exhilaration, the same release and triumph I'd seen in her face the morning after she'd murdered Annie.

Sally waved her pistol at Brina. "Over there, bitch." She pointed to a spot next to Keith. "He gets it first, then you."

Brina crossed in front of Pearl, then me. Sally jerked the gun again. Brina, wrists and knees flexed, stepped into place at Keith's right. Our circle contracted.

I wanted attention off Brina. I scratched my nail along a pants seam. The sound, like the rustle of a creeping rat, scurried across the room. Sally growled at me. "I know you don't have a gun. Don't do anything stupid."

I shook my head, but kept my eyes low. "Nobody's doing stupid, Sally. Not me. Not you. Everybody walks away. Nobody gets hurt."

"Too late for that." A laugh blurted from her throat. "And you know it. And *she* knows it too."

Sally whipped the nose of her gun from my chest to Pearl's. Tension contracted her finger.

"I... I don't know anything. I just clean houses. You know that, Miss. You know me. I'm just the cleaning lady." Pearl's stuttering appeal drew a gauzy veil over Sally's face.

Her gaze stiffened into steel when she turned to Gerry Keith. "But *he* knew," she snapped. She stepped into our tight circle.

The coward whined. "No, I... I didn't, ...not quite. Not really. No."

Red flooded Sally's cheeks at this babble of negatives. My fingers clenched and released. I wanted to slap Keith into silence.

Sparks darted from Sally's eyes. She waved the gun at her mentor. "You knew. Say it! You knew."

Keith flapped his hands in front of his chest. "Yes, alright," he said. "Yes, I knew. I knew you fabricated the data."

Brina sucked her teeth. Galaxy hissed contempt from the edge of the circle.

Sally ignored them. Keith was her target. "And you accepted it anyway."

Keith's chest swelled, rejecting the blame. He wagged his head. Blustering ego aimed a desperate dart at Sally's weak spot. "From *you*? You'd be *nothing* without me. I *made* your career."

Sally recoiled, her shoulders jerking. She stepped into the attack. "No, I made *your* career, Gerry." She railed against the professor she had loved. "And you accepted it. Like tribute from a vassal. You took it all."

His lips trembled. "No, that's not true. Not true." The splutter landed wet and futile in the hushed room.

Sally thrust the gun in a straight line. "Say it, Gerry. Say it here. Now. You used my research. You knew it was bogus and you used it anyway. Say it. Or I blast that stupid goat's beard off your face."

"Okay! Okay! Yes!" His eyes darted to the windows beyond the assistant's desk. First count in the indictment delivered.

But Sally wasn't finished. Next charge in the case against Keith: "And you slept with *her*. You abandoned me in that hell hole in Miami while you fucked your head off with… with *her*. Say it!"

Keith shook his head again. When Sally stepped forward, he clutched his chin. "Yes, all right. All right! Yes, Anniesha was… Well, she was someone I liked a lot."

Rancid tobacco floated as Gerry breathed at me. "I'm sorry."

Someone gasped. I squeezed my eyes. *Sorry.* A red tide pounded behind my nose. *Sorry.* Fourteen days since Annie's murder. Since these depraved freaks stole her life. Murdered my past. Cancelled my future. *Sorry.*

My eyes flew open when Sally's voice blared. "He knew I killed her. And he said nothing. He fucked her that night. Then me the next morning. He accepted her death. Like it was nothing. Erased. Like the phony data. She didn't count. She was just another sacrifice on the altar of his magnificent career."

Tears glittered on reddened lids. She turned toward Gerry, voice rising. "You knew. Say it. Say. It. Now."

"Yes, Okay. Yes, I knew. I guessed you shot Anniesha. You were excited that morning, buzzing and happy. Proud even. But I didn't know why. Not for sure." Drawing me into their orgy of confession, he muttered: "I'm sorry. I should have said something."

Pearl sobbed, the sound wet and distant, as if from a deep well. She swayed, bumping my shoulder.

All the anguish, the fury, and the sorrow burst from me. "You fucking bastard! You used Annie." I looked at Sally. "And her too. You used them like Kleenex. And what about Pearl? Were you going to erase her too?"

270

"No… I…" Wheedling, bargaining, maneuvering for his advantage, as always.

"Shut up!" My words.

Sally's move. She lowered her gaze to Gerry's mouth. Lined the gun barrel to track her stare. A smile flattened the elfin peaks of her lips. Slight pressure squeezed the trigger.

I leaned forward, blinking hard. Rage fouled my sight, cramped my voice: "It doesn't have to end this way, Sally."

She shook her curls; inhaled with a hiss. White sparked around dark pupils. Her eyes clawed at Keith. She had craved this ghoul's admiration more than honor or dignity. More than her own life.

"It does. And you know it, Rook. You know it. He deserves this."

Cold bit my fingers as acceptance washed over me. Let Sally rescue her pride. Take her revenge. Why not? This execution defined justice. Gerry Keith should die for what he'd done to Annie. To Sally. To me. Maybe a jury could find Sally guilty of his murder. I never would. A chill puff of air lifted the hair on my neck. My mind froze, my heart iced over. This stand-off would end as Sally wanted: Keith erased. I could live with that fatal outcome.

Except it didn't happen.

A sigh rippled beside my ear. Pearl dropped to the floor, eyes closed. Knees, belly, chest, forehead hit the carpet with soft thuds.

Sally yelped, her eyes bucking in surprise. She squeezed the trigger to kill Gerry Keith. I lunged at him, fists punching his shoulder. He fell against the desk as a shot split the air. When the buzzing stopped, no one screamed in pain. The bullet had gone astray.

No crying, no moans; the roaring ocean of talk meant everyone was safe. No need to get up, everyone was safe. Lying on the floor was easy, so I relaxed. Like in a movie, I watched Brina grab Sally's arm, forcing her gun up. Two shots struck the ceiling. Oily smoke drifted down. More shouts far away, but no crying. Brina stepped on red eyeglasses; they cracked. She was safe. Galaxy roared at a phone. Furious. She was safe. Gerry pushed my shoulder. Pulled his legs from under my heavy torso. Rude. But he was safe. I relaxed some more.

Four uniformed police rushed into the office, guns drawn. Loud squawking. I'd had enough of campus cops. These giants in long shoes stomped near my head. Their guns were huge; silly radios, cell phones, handcuffs, and badges dangled from wide belts. Sally's black shoes kicked in the air as she shrieked. I giggled. Voices bellowed in the shadows of the office, calling for back-up, for an ambulance. Who'd been hurt? Relax, everyone was safe. I focused on those big shiny boots. Like clown shoes, so funny. I couldn't see Brina. But I heard her voice above the others.

She screeched at someone, her voice snapping through the din. "Don't move. Don't move!"

I wasn't moving, my legs were too heavy to budge. She must be yelling at someone else. Maybe Sally was still struggling against the handcuffs. Maybe Pearl had awakened from her faint. She should chill. No one's hurt. Maybe angry Galaxy was threatening to bring the whole house down. Galaxy would make a fierce Samson. I giggled.

"Don't try to move." Brina repeated the command, this time in a gentle voice only I could hear.

Was she talking to me? She dug her fingers into my jaw to underline each word. I rolled my shoulder to loosen her grip. A tweak on my right side. The pain was so small it tickled. Maybe I'd pulled a muscle or bruised a rib when I fell on top of Gerry Keith.

Brina repeated her order as if I was a stubborn child. Her giant eyes were shiny. Funny. "Don't move. Stay with me, Rook."

I shook my head to calm the ocean roaring in my ears. Stitch in my side twinged again. Sharper pinch this time. A tweak, nothing I couldn't handle. I craned my neck for a glimpse of Brina, but I couldn't see her. She'd disappeared.

In her place, Pearl's moonlit face loomed into view. "Stay with me, SJ. Stay." Her breath was sugary like candied cherries. "Stay with me, SJ." Her voice melted into other warm, liquid tones.

My Annie's sweet face floated above me. *"Stay with me, SJ."* Her pink kimono flowering with rose-petal butterflies fluttered as she stretched her arms to me. *"Stay with me, SJ. Stay."* Long black hair lifted around her head as if raked by the boiling wind of a rollercoaster. *"Come home with me, SJ. Come home."*

From the pink cloud, Carolyn Wiley chirped in my ear, her smiling face drifting beside Annie's. *"Carl, stay with me. Stay here."* Wrapped in Dreamie's canary yellow sweater, Carolyn ran cool, slender fingers along my eyebrows. My cheeks. My lips. *"Stay with me, Carl. Stay here."*

A lovely old word, the first word, bloomed in my mouth: *Mami.* I didn't want Annie or Brina to hear me say it, so I closed my eyes. *Mami.* The pressure on my side pulsed, deepened. *Mami.*

Brina's voice cut through the roar. "Don't go, Rook. Stay with me."

I opened my mouth to tell her. *Of course, I won't leave you. Ever. I choose you.*

But my words were smothered by the fall of heavy black curtains.

# CHAPTER
# THIRTY

After five days of gray hospital gruel, the pepperoni pizza Brina smuggled to my room glowed like Technicolor heaven.

"You're looking better. I knew this would help," she said.

The red-and-green striped box was already seeping its life-giving grease onto the coverlet at the foot of my bed. Brina could argue with the nurses about that stain when they arrived for the start of the next shift.

"Nothing wrong with me that a slice of Luigi's pie won't fix."

I couldn't manage more than a few nibbles at one corner of the triangle. The spices overwhelmed me and nausea bubbled in my gut. But I appreciated her effort. As Brina scarfed down two slices, I made a show of munching.

"Mmm. Good stuff," I said.

"Glad you like it. You need to put on weight."

"Seriously?" I clutched the flimsy blue-checked gown around my waist.

"Seriously. Your hip bones are sharp as knives."

"Thanks. Way to kill my appetite." I returned the slice to the box. The pretext worked and Brina accepted the excuse without argument.

She spent most of every day at my bedside. She watched like a snapping turtle as the nurses changed the layers of padding and gauze on my wound. She haggled with the doctors over my intravenous antibiotics and pressed them to up the dosage of narcotics to ease the pain. She nagged the custodians to keep the room clean. She hovered when the nurses' aide gave me a sponge bath, then Brina dried me herself. Brina slept each night curled on a battered green sofa near the window of my room; she went home at noon to change into fresh clothes, but always returned by four-thirty for the night watch.

After the operation, everything itched. Every damn inch prickled like an army of beetles scurrying under my skin. But I could hold on: strict discipline was important to recovery. I resisted the urge to scratch at the stitches in my stomach, the catheter, the puncture sites for blood transfusions, the leads plastered on my chest for heart monitors, my oily scalp and prickly stubble.

There was only one important thing – the one true thing that mattered – everybody was safe. I knew because Brina told me so, her responses slow and patient each time I asked. Everybody's alright, nobody else got hurt, nobody died. I knew because I asked her each time I awakened. Everybody's okay. Everyone's safe.

I knew because, one by one, they all stopped by my hospital bed, steps muffled and voices hushed as though visiting a saint's shrine.

The first pilgrim to arrive was Galaxy Pindar. I heard her in the hallway negotiating with Brina for an entrance pass. I didn't feel weak; lying in bed all day hardly taxed my stamina. But I liked the fierce way Brina played gate-keeper, protecting my health against all threats.

When Galaxy made it past the sentry, she took a seat in the arm chair closest to my head. Ready to pounce, Brina perched in a metal chair near the door. I answered all the dean's stock questions about the nick to my liver, the blood loss, the damage to muscles in my flank, the surgery, the stitches, and the expected time of recovery.

Then it was my turn. "So, tell me. Who won the Blackistone Prize? The committee eliminated Gerry Keith, right?"

Galaxy snorted and rolled her eyes until her gaze rested on the ceiling.

"That bastard has already been booted as chairman of the anthropology department. The provost's considering other personnel action.

Suspension, early retirement, firing. If it'd been up to me, I'd have stripped Keith to his tighty-whities, stacked rubber tires around his neck, doused him in gasoline, and roasted him on the main quad."

I wanted to laugh. But I'd learned my lesson from early experiments: the wound blazed like a barbecue pit when I breathed too deep or laughed too hard. Not even the snug bandages strapped around my middle helped.

So, I kept my reaction to a sneer. "I'd pay to see that bonfire."

Brina growled. "I'd bring a canister of gas to the barbecue." She was extra blood-thirsty after my shooting.

Galaxy had the grace to look at her fingers entwined in her lap. But a smirk crossed her lips. "His publisher has withdrawn the book. They're suing for return of the fifty-thousand dollar advance they gave him. *The Dirty and The Clean* indeed." The dean snorted with force. "But to answer your question, it was me who won the prize." Galaxy beamed. It's hard to keep an academic ego down for long, even in the worst circumstances.

"That's good, Galaxy. Well earned."

"Thanks. I don't know if I deserved it. The whole thing feels so tainted. But I'm going to take the prize and do something of value with the award money."

"What's that?"

"I've got in mind donating the money to a primary school in Ile Ife, the old Yoruba capital I wrote about. I visit the school each time I travel there and I'm close with the head mistress. She can put the money to good use. New computers, desks, books, maybe even a science lab. That's what I'm thinking right now. I'll know more after I make a trip to Nigeria in March, during spring break."

Galaxy paused. A flush ripened across her cheeks. "And James has said he wants to visit Nigeria with me. He wants to see where I spend so much of my time and learn more about my research."

"That's good. Right?" I didn't have much to add, so I repeated my earlier words. My gut took the bullet, but my head seemed to fill with cotton after even a brief conversation. Energy seeped from me as Galaxy talked on. I blinked twice to stay alert.

"Yeah, it's a good thing. I don't know where it will all come out with James. But I'm going to give it a try." She reached into the brown suede briefcase resting at her feet and pulled out her phone. She slid a finger over its surface. "My cousin Smoke's blowing up my phone. Lots of messages asking about you. Hoping you recover soon."

"Tell him thanks."

"Smoke says you should never set foot on a university campus again. He calls it ghetto dangerous. But without the family feeling."

Galaxy flashed the phone's face at me. Cartoon cowboys and clowns danced through Smoke's messages. At the end of each phrase squatted emojis of brown poop.

"Point taken." Sleep dragged a fuzzy blanket over my brain. "Smoke speaks the truth."

She dropped the phone into her case with a laugh and fished out a slim envelope. "Cuz also reminded me I owe the Ross Agency for services rendered." She handed the envelope to Brina. "Smoke told me his hourly rates, so I multiplied by five and rounded up. I hope this amount is sufficient, Ms. Ross."

"Please, call me Sabrina." A pause to scan the lavender-tinted check. Then Brina's eyebrows jiggled. Just a little. "Yes, well, this is on the mark. Thank you."

Straight faced, she glanced at me, then raised her eyebrows again. But I couldn't manage more than a slow blink. I was fading fast.

The dean had one more item in her satchel. It was a huge greeting card with a purple elephant on the front. The animal had a yellow Band-Aid on its trunk and glittery stars circled a bright pink lump on its head. "I need to get going. But I didn't want to forget this."

She handed me the get-well card and pointed at the web of signatures inside.

"These are people you don't know. People who work for me in the School of Arts and Humanities. Faculty, staff, students. Nathalie – you remember my admin assistant – she had the idea for this card. To say how grateful we all are for your help."

I couldn't lean forward, so Brina took the card and placed it on the bedside table. The card meant a lot. More than the check. To avoid dissolving into mush, I tried a quip. "I was wondering about Nathalie. I felt guilty because I bled all over her rug."

"Don't worry about Nathalie. She made out like a bandit. For months, she's been nagging me to replace that filthy old carpet. So, you – with all your gaudy bleeding – gave us the opportunity at long last. New hardwood flooring goes in next week. Beautiful golden oak. Nathalie is thrilled as punch. All thanks to you."

"Call on me any time. Always happy to bleed out for a good cause." That was the last joke I could manage, my supply exhausted for the day.

Galaxy's lips relaxed. Her smile was reward enough. I sank into the pillows and lowered my lids. Galaxy must have left, but I didn't see her go.

As I drifted off, Brina settled into the arm chair at my side. She curled her feet into the cushion to join me in sleep.

---

Over the next days, my hospital room turned into Grand Central Station. Our landlady Mei Young and Jerome my favorite bartender visited. The construction crew chief, Darrell Peete, stopped by with greetings from his team. Archie Lin brought his wife Pinky Michel for a chat.

Archie told me the charges against Sally Anastos for killing Annie and shooting me were creeping their way through the legal system, one sludge-covered step at a time. When Pinky dragged Brina to the cafeteria for coffee, I asked about the case.

"Your crack team of snoops ever find Annie's laptop?" Loose ends bugged me. Even in my banged-up state, I wanted to wrap the investigation.

"Nah, I figure that crazy Anastos chick dumped it in the East River when she quit the hotel the next day." Archie shrugged, announcing case closed.

I shook my head. "Maybe not. A computer's valuable. Not some cheap throw-away for a poor kid from the sticks. Sally Anastos wouldn't toss it if she could find a better use."

"Like what?"

"Like give it to her kid brother. He started at Alexander this semester. Second one in the family to go to college. Sally could have kept that laptop, got it re-tooled at a computer shop. And given it to her brother."

"Makes sense. We'll check the university. Find the Anastos kid." Archie peered at me, then sighed. "You got to stop all this thinking, pal. You done your job. It's all past now. Let it go."

"Yeah, I'm working on it, Archie. Lying around here all day, I've got time to think. Letting go isn't what I do. But I'm trying."

"Try harder."

Archie pointed at my gown. He hiked his eyebrows and bent the index finger like a hook. NYPD's finest detective wanted to inspect the gunshot wound for himself. I lifted the gown. He tugged the bandages to open a gap in the swaddling on my right side. Then he plucked at the square gauze padding underneath. He leaned in for a closer view. An angry artist had painted my flank in sunset colors: orange, yellow, and twilight blue radiated from the incision. Stitches trekked like black zippers across the bruises.

Archie crumpled his eyebrows. "You said a nick." He repositioned the padding and pressed the adhesive tape to hold it against my skin. "That's a manhole."

"I lied." I shrugged, but got caught in a wince.

Archie clamped his jaw shut. A couple of tears balanced on the edge of his lower lids. It could have been allergies. Or out-of-season flu. But when he squeezed my knee and hitched a sigh, I decided to count it as something special.

Dr. Allard Swann's visit was short and melancholy. Trouble wrinkled his brow even before he sat. My damaged gut told me I wasn't the only cause.

After a few words of vague condolence, he gulped. "I don't want to contribute to your pain at this difficult time, Mr. Rook."

I waved off the apology and nodded for him to continue.

He squeaked through a coughing spasm. "But I thought you ought to know: Mrs. Carolyn Wiley passed away two days ago."

"What happened? You told me she was in good health." I struggled to sit upright. The pain in my stomach had nothing to do with bullet wounds.

Frowning, Brina shoved a third pillow behind me. I took two long breaths to calm the monitors which buzzed with my rising anxiety. When I settled, Swann continued, his fingers twisting like snakes in his lap.

"There's just no telling at that advanced age, Mr. Rook. Her son had made arrangements to fly Mrs. Wiley to stay with him in Seattle. Keeping her closer to him, he said." Swann had the grace to frown at the brute's sick claim. Then he rushed on. "So, we had her packed and ready to make the move. But on the ride to the airport, Carolyn slipped away. Right there in the back seat of the hired car. Just slipped away."

My fists clenched knots into the green cotton over my legs. "Was she happy to move out west?"

His eyes dropped to the rumpled bed sheets. Doubts pinged through my mind. But I checked those dark thoughts until Swann delivered his first-hand observations.

"I couldn't tell for sure. Carolyn never said much at all. Not more than a few words after that day she last visited with you." He screwed his lips to one side over the sour taste of these final images. "She was always such a quiet little bird anyway. But after you left, she seemed to draw inward and keep everything to herself. Not much more than a peep or two from her since you went away."

*Left her. Went away.* I glared to remind Swann he'd banished me. Against my wishes. Carolyn wouldn't have been alone if he'd let me continue my visits. Thinking of her last days squeezed a groan from my throat. "I didn't leave her, Dr. Swann. As you well know."

I rolled my head on the pillow to nail Swann's eyes with mine.

Had Carolyn wanted to stop living? To ease the chokehold of the past? Isolated, confused, scared; she wouldn't be the first person who'd willed herself to death. That hurt. But thinking of her trapped in a cell of domestic misery with her ungrateful son on the far side of the continent hurt even more. Death was a release for Carolyn Wiley. Maybe she'd welcomed the escape.

I clutched a hand to my stomach to make Swann think it was my wound aching. Not my heart. With that hint, he hurried away after a minute of thin good-byes.

———

Pearl Byrne trekked from Poughkeepsie to spend an afternoon. It was comforting to see her familiar navy-blue suit, the square skirt wrinkled across the lap from her train ride. She'd traded the block-heels for black sneakers with floppy laces and thick crepe soles. But her pale legs still looked lovely.

Her tears didn't help. In fact, they caused fresh pain in my chest. The duty nurse hustled to my room after I triggered some over-sensitive monitor at the nurses' station. I waved off her frowns and mumblings about the machine's beeps. I told Pearl to stay as long as she could.

Pearl unsnapped her purse to pull out a crumpled white sheet of paper. She read a dry email message from Rick Luna. Ricardo Luna, Chief Executive Officer, as he signed it. He managed six words to wish for my recovery. And twenty-five more to invite me to the grand opening of Rook Cleaning Service's newest office in Hialeah. I guess after our phone condolence swap, Ricky was feeling generous. His control of Annie's company was secure now. He could keep the name she'd given it. That soothed my heart. A bit.

Brina asked Pearl about the cleaning business. At first, I figured the questions were just politeness. But as the exchange deepened, the two women talked boss to boss. They leaned forward in their chairs, knees touching, faces near, as if they were exchanging breaths. They drilled into finances, networking, client services, and marketing. When they hit employee management, I closed my eyes. They talked on.

A question about Annie lifted the veil of sleep. I kept my eyes shut, pretending to doze.

Brina wanted to know what kind of person Annie was: "How did she build her business from scratch?"

Pearl's response was sharp: "She was a natural leader. She could have been a great teacher or a champion coach. Anniesha knew how to motivate, how to guide. How to award the gold stars or snap the ruler. When she demanded something, her people never said, how? They asked, how much? Then, they delivered double."

The voice slowed as Pearl sighed. I wondered if she was crying, but I didn't open my eyes to see. This was woman-to-woman talk. I wasn't invited.

Softness cushioned Pearl's next words. "I thought about her so much these last few weeks. Trying to figure her out. Anniesha wasn't perfect. Not even near. She was selfish and reckless; greedy and short-sighted too. Is vengeful too harsh a word? Maybe, but that's what comes to mind. Her judgment of people was clouded. And that's putting it kindly. She liked what she liked. And wanted who she wanted. Anniesha was full-speed ahead, consequences be damned."

Pearl shuddered to a stop. Brina whispered, "Annie raised trouble. She broke the rules and charged after the life she wanted. She was disruptive."

"Disrupter. Yes, that's her exactly." Pearl gritted out the words. "You think it's why that poor girl shot her? Because she couldn't be Anniesha?"

"Maybe so. Not envy or fear. Despair."

"I guess we can't know for sure about Anniesha. Now she'll never get to speak for herself."

"No, not for sure. Not ever," Brina said.

Her sigh let me raise my lids, as if I was returning to consciousness. I blinked, shifting my gritty eyes to take in the two women. They squeezed hands, smiled at me, then pressed back in their chairs, releasing the connection.

With me awake again, the talk dwindled. A few minutes later, Pearl rose to leave. She called me SJ and patted my hair. She squeezed me until the shredded muscles in my stomach protested. Her sudsy vanilla scent curled around me. I clung to her and pounded her square back as hard as I could. She was a link to Annie I didn't want to lose.

When Pearl left, Brina settled on the bed. She draped her arm over my shoulder and laid her head against my neck. Her knees pressed behind my thighs. I dozed again, this time drifting through clouds of pink butterflies and dented blue Buicks. I wrestled with guns, twisted silver bracelets clamped on both wrists. Fluttering pink wings whipped the odor of musty decay with candy perfume into a blizzard circling my head.

I yelped and started upright, sweat stinging my eyes. Brina squeezed my arm, then stroked my hairline. "Hey, baby, hey. It's all right, you're all right. Wake up, you're safe."

I leaned against the pillow. She lowered her head. Her braids rubbed my cheek. I thought of the tangled strands in these cases: Annie, Dreamie, Carolyn. Fear and desire plaited with frayed old threads of carelessness, revenge, and unruly love. I burrowed my head into the pillow, searching for a cool spot. Face pressed against my neck, Brina slept after a while. Then I did too.

---

On the day before my release, Norment Ross dropped by for another round of gin rummy and straight talk. I won the card game, but as usual, he did most of the talking.

"You put a big ole country scare on us there, partner. The little bit left of my hair turned whiter than a Klan rally waiting for you to come out of that surgery."

"Sorry, Norment. Didn't mean to give you such a fright. Won't happen again."

He beamed at my feeble pledge, then launched into another story. "I been shot a few times myself over the years, of course. Not everybody greets the numbers runner like he's Santa Claus, you know. And then there was that time I tunneled into all the dirty deeds Ava Bunton and Dax Miles were up to when Old Man Bunton was out of town. All three of them lying, deceiving, no good hypocritical jackasses took pot shots at me. You know, after all these years, I never did figure out which of 'em finally clipped me."

Norment's grin broadened and his eyes danced in his shiny face. Was this another of his fables? But then he lifted the hem of his gold corduroy pants to show me a small black crater in his right calf.

He tapped a long index finger twice on the bullet hole as I let out a whistle. "Were you hospitalized?"

"For a tiny little termite hole like this? Naw. But it did lay me up for three weeks. Got the Blue Cross insurance for the agency after that. You're covered as an employee because of that. We all got medical now."

He leaned back in the green chair, swinging his bullet-pocked leg over the upholstered arm. He was wearing the new yellow-and-red high-top sneakers Smoke Burris had donated to the Ross Agency fashion cause. The rapper 2-Ryght would be proud.

"You know, that's how me and Mei Young got together." Norment hadn't finished with the shooting story. "After I got hit, she toddled up from the Emerald Garden kitchen every day to see me. Started bringing a sandwich to my office at noon to save me the trouble of staggering to the restaurant. Best sandwiches I ever ate. Chicken roasted perfect, sliced thin, touched with homemade mayo. Just right. Those sandwiches, plus her famous green tea potion fixed me up quick."

"I never knew how you and Mei Young got together."

"You might not guess it, but that little gal can be quite a conversationalist when she wants to unwind and let her hair down. *Quite* a conversationalist." Norment's rich voice melted to sweetness. He prized Mei Young for many things, not just her flair with mayonnaise.

"Mei came along at just the right time in my life. There's no substituting for Dreamie, of course. But I've arrived at a good place after all this time."

Norment's huge head swung to the left, taking in the jagged line of skyscrapers framed by the window. From this height, the surging city looked quiet, its vibrant colors dabbed to a rosy brown in the autumn haze. Like an old souvenir postcard mailed from the past.

When he continued, Norment's voice was sharper. Like his message.

"You don't never move on from that one big wound. The one great loss. From the life you might have led if she were still here. But what you do get is a solid chance to untangle those dreams of the past from the reality you're in now."

He looked me in the eye as he switched from reflection to command. "Son, you got a chance to escape the past. Make a new, better version of your life. Now. If you've got the guts to do it."

The challenge was unmistakable. I nodded to show I'd absorbed the lesson he'd shared. I didn't try to form an answer. Annie was gone, Dreamie too. The future Norment pointed to didn't scare me now. I could face it head on. Getting shot had cleansed me, rinsing away the debris of fond memories and the rubble of old regrets. The past could serve as prologue to my future, if I let it. Silence flowed around us in that hospital room, soothing and deep. I drifted on its stream for a moment, out of respect for the women we'd lost. And the better women we'd found.

Then, as he often did, Norment switched subjects with a jolt. "You hear any more about that jacked-up little girl who shot you? She was some kind of loco fiend is the way I figure it."

My sentences crawled: "Norment, that's not fair. Jealousy and ambition twisted Sally until she couldn't see a way out, short of murder. She broke under the pressure. When she cracked, she caused a lot of suffering." A weak defense. But then I wasn't Sally's attorney.

Norment's face squeezed in rage. "On the way down, Sister Nutjob got plenty of help from that sack of shit, Keith. Just a pissant little man who believed the big-time stories he heard from his own pecker."

My heart raced. Drops of sweat slid down the back of my neck as anxiety rose with this rant. The old man meant no harm, so I didn't call him on it. It was important for him to get this anger out of his system now. Maybe I needed the release too. But as Norment continued, the sleepless hours ahead taunted me. I'd pay the price for these musings.

"You're *waay* too kind, son. That Anastos chick was flat out cray. Like I said to Brina, little white girl went insane in the brain with all that fancy education. It was more juice than her poor system could handle. Well, now she's cooling her heels waiting for arraignment. No bail for that cocoanut. One thing for sure, she'll get a Ph.D. in cuttin' and cussin' from the fine perfessors at Rikers university long before she arrives in court. Think she'll plead guilty?"

"She might. Or might not. Depends on how tricky her lawyers get about her mental state."

Norment huffed, ready to dive into damning lawyers and their slick ways. But I tossed a question nearer to both our hearts. "How's Brina taking all this? I see her here in the hospital every day, but she doesn't talk about how she's feeling. Mostly to keep me calm. But she's holding a lot inside."

Norment reared back in his seat. He stretched long legs to rest his feet on the bed. He steepled his fingers and touched them to his lips twice.

"Sabrina's like the hide of a yearling deer: tough, strong, but soft and tender too. Folds like a blanket, but she don't never rip nor shred. That's the best way I can describe her, soft and tough."

His eyes shimmered under a brilliant veil of tears as he continued. "But you're right to worry, 'cause she took it hard when you got shot. She said seeing you cut down in front of her was the worst shock she ever experienced in her whole life. The way she cried that night like to slice me in two."

"I don't know what to say. I mean... I feel guilty somehow. Like I..."

"Aw, don't be a blamed fool. None of it was your fault. None of it." He blinked, then lowered his eyebrows. "Except for the part where you thought you'd play some idiot cartoon hero. *That* was you acting the moron, for sure."

Norment quirked his mouth into a half-smile at the picture of me as a comic book champion. I wriggled my feet to draw attention from the heat rising to my ears. But the old man wasn't done with me yet.

"Now comes the next test. Don't flunk it. You gonna keep acting the fool now? You gonna try to take care of yourself at home after you get out of here tomorrow? Or you gonna accept when Brina offers you to come to her place for a while?"

"I...I mean, she hasn't asked me. I don't know..."

He stuck a long finger straight at me, poking the air with force. "And *that's* what I mean by playing the fool. I'm telling you, she's *gonna* ask you. And you better get straight in your head what the answer is. Else you risk causing lots more harm all around. Don't be a moron. You got me?"

"I got you, Norment. Thanks for that. For everything."

---

The next night when I left the hospital, Brina raised the subject, just as her father predicted. But in such a roundabout way, I almost missed it.

After Miguel the nurse delivered the discharge papers, he helped me button a denim work shirt over my chest and step into gray sweatpants. Then he disappeared in search of the wheelchair required to cart me to the exit.

I sat on the edge of the bed while Brina stuffed my t-shirts, underwear, and socks in a duffel bag. When she stowed the toothbrush, I asked about the health of my pet. "How's Herb doing?"

"You've been laid up here for ten days and you're just now asking about your cat? That's some kind of responsible, Rook."

I didn't match her eyeroll, but I returned the smile. "I had a few other things on my mind. And anyway, Herb's cool. He's a resilient kind of cat."

She tucked a plastic razor into the duffle. "Since you ask, Herb is fine. I brought him to my apartment the night you went into surgery."

"And how'd he take *that*?" I shivered in mock horror.

"About like you'd imagine. First, he spit, then he scratched. Then he hid. Then he sulked. And went on a hunger strike."

"Sounds like the Herb I know. Did he ever come around to the new set up?"

"After three days of nonsense, Herb decided he'd give the food at my place a taste. No poison, so he started eating regular. Each afternoon, when I'd come home to feed him, I'd find Herb sleeping in a different spot: the window ledge, then the sofa. The bookcase, then the arm chair."

Brina ragging on the yellow monster brought a painful laugh to my belly. I coughed once, then smiled to erase the frown on her forehead. I waved my hand to encourage her to continue the story.

"Yesterday, Herb made it to my bed. He curled between the pillows. When I came in the door, he looked at me with a fierce frown, like an emperor disturbed from his beauty sleep."

I recognized my feline avatar's role in this negotiation. I smirked, no teeth, like a cat would. "Herb knows what's good for him and sticks to it. He's a smart cat."

"Yeah, he is." Brina grinned and folded the last t-shirt. She zipped the duffel and tossed it to the floor. "I'll pull the car around to the entrance. See you in a few."

Miguel pushed my wheelchair through the hospital's sliding front doors. He parked me at the curb as Brina steered her Honda around the traffic circle. A brisk northern breeze ruffled across my face, the first chilly hint of a new season. Exhaust fumes blended with cool fresh air to send a rash of goosebumps racing along my neck. When she arrived in front of me, Brina jumped from the red Civic and popped the trunk. She grabbed the duffel bag from my lap, threw it into the trunk, then unzipped it. Miguel hoisted me into the shotgun seat, leaving me to my fate.

Brina dragged a black sweatshirt from the bag. She walked to the open side door and tossed the shirt in a high arc. It landed on my head. I pulled the sweatshirt over my face, twisting it until I got the left arm through the sleeve. The damage on my right flank wouldn't allow me to raise that arm above shoulder height. So, I let the empty sleeve hang over my chest like a limp scarf. Pathetic.

After watching my contortions, Brina eased the trunk closed. She slipped behind the steering wheel and looked at me along the curve of her eyes. She reached across me to tug at the seatbelt.

When she clicked the buckle into place, I sighed. "Back where we started this whole ride, aren't we?"

"What do you mean?"

"Me, damaged goods, wrecked and unable to fend for myself. You, fixing me. Again."

"Is that how you see this… this whatever we've got here?" She waved her hand between us.

"Yes."

"Fix you? You think I'm looking to repair you, be your caretaker? Like I get a kick out of patching you up? You think I have some kind of Nurse Nancy fetish or something?"

"I don't know. Maybe." I gulped, then jumped in with both feet. "I can't figure what you see in me. Or what you get from me."

She gathered a big breath, ready to shout. But then her voice dipped to a murmur. "What I get from you is joy. It's as simple as that. And as complicated. You calm me when I'm edgy. When I'm brittle, you brace me. So, that's it: I need the joy."

She hunched her shoulders, then shook her head. When she raised her eyes, she captured mine. "I'm sorry I didn't let you know that before. I should have. But I'm lousy at a lot of things. Like trusting and opening and sharing. Losing a mother will do that to you. But there it is."

I laughed softly. "You're talking to the champion of ducking and deflecting here. Losing a father will do that to you."

"No hope for us, then. We're a matched pair." She smiled though a sniffle.

I tapped her chin with my thumb. "Yep."

"So, what's it going to be?" She gripped the steering wheel in both hands, tendons in her knuckles popping. She looked straight ahead, like she was afraid of what I might say. "Do I drive you to your own place?

Or do you come home with me? I told Herb you'd be around to see him, if that influences your answer."

I scratched my ear. "Like I said before, Herb is one smart cat. Smarter than me. I'll follow his lead. Curled between the pillows on your bed sounds like heaven." She chuffed and I laughed too.

I tugged her hand from the wheel and raised her fingers to my lips. I wanted her to feel my answer as well as hear it: "Sabrina Ross, I choose you."

As I spoke, she tilted her head. In the crisp twilight, a smile lit her face. After a moment, she glanced at the surging traffic. We pulled into the lane for the ride home.

Thank you for reading *Murder My Past*, the fifth book in the Ross Agency mystery series, featuring private detective SJ Rook and his colleagues.

I want to express my deepest gratitude to diligent readers Cheyanne Boyd and Carol Brett who scoured an early draft of the manuscript for *Murder My Past*. They unearthed inconsistencies, cross-checked characterizations, and flagged holes in my plot. Their insights shaped the final manuscript in numerous ways. In our conversations, these readers were generous and supportive. I also thank my tireless editor, Sarah Monsma, who displayed all the best traits: she was as determined and meticulous as Rook, while delivering helpful suggestions with the kindness and humor of Brina. Sarah is the best editor a writer could wish for. Any remaining faults in this book are mine alone.

The previous books in this contemporary noir series are *Lost and Found in Harlem*, *Practice the Jealous Arts*, *Black and Blue in Harlem*, and *Pauper and Prince in Harlem*. All are available in eBooks and print. If you enjoyed reading them, please consider leaving an honest review on Amazon and Goodreads. When you write reviews, you enliven the book community. Other readers will appreciate hearing from you. Further adventures of Private Eye Rook are explored in several short stories: "The Killer," was published in *The Chicago Quarterly Review*, Vol. 31. Another story, "A Deadly First," was published in the holiday crime anthology, *Festive Mayhem*. To learn more about these novels, stories, and my other writing, visit my website at www.deliapitts.com . You can also follow me on Instagram at deliapitts50 and on Twitter at @blacktop1950.

Sorting fact from fiction takes on deadly urgency for Rook and Brina in the upcoming sixth novel in the series, *Murder Take Two*. When Rook is hired to guard the set of a hot television show filming on the streets of Harlem, he expects his toughest challenge to be fending off star-struck fans. But the private eye's brush with Hollywood glamour quickly turns dark when the death of a top TV executive writes a grim finale to the production. The flashy murder throws Rook into a twisted struggle with a secretive killer whose motives are hidden in plain sight. A second death, a seductive star's tragic past, and Rook's own unspoken desires complicate the search for the killer. *Murder Take Two* will be released in 2022. Read on for a sneak peek at the first chapter of the next Ross Agency mystery, *Murder Take Two*.

# MURDER
# TAKE TWO

A Ross Agency Mystery

# DELIA C. PITTS

# CHAPTER
# ONE

A brick, wrapped in tin foil and tied with a silver shoe lace, exploded the pane of my office window at dawn. Dirty glass shrapnel plunked on my desk. The block bounced off the sofa's arm, landing in a pile of glittering shards.

I was sitting at my desk, regretting I'd added the empty calories of fake French vanilla creamer to my third cup of coffee. My stomach cried that real sugar or honest bourbon would have been a better choice. When the brick hit, I lurched in my chair, knocking the file cabinet behind me.

On this chilly Thursday morning, boulevard traffic was hustling. As I struggled to right myself, I could hear delivery vans and garbage trucks rummaging in the dire April sunshine. The brakes of a bus moaned. I was awake because I'd hardly been to sleep. My job protecting a Hollywood TV crew filming in Harlem had wrapped at three-thirty in the morning. First call was scheduled for eight. My office was closer to the set than my apartment, so I'd spent the sliver of night dozing on my leather couch. Deflated corduroy pillows had etched little grooves in my cheek. I was waiting for the creases to subside before running a razorblade over my face.

The night hadn't been a total waste. I'd put the time to good use, carving up my desk. When the brick hit, I'd been bent over the oak in a gray fog of half-dreams, chiseling the hell out of my name. I worked with care; using an old hunting knife to carve *Shelba Julio* into the dark surface had taken me the better part of two years. Private eye jobs paid the bills, sure, but those gigs interfered with my blooming career as an engraver. This morning I'd been chipping at my name for an hour when the brick landed. I'd just started on the *ROOK*. All caps. That brick jerked me from a beautiful groove. The knife bucked in my fingers, carving a naked divot from my ego project. The three-inch steel blade gashed a brutal trench through the slope of my favorite letter. Now the rough-hewn *R* staggered like a drunk ladder.

Banging against the metal file cabinet tore the cobwebs from my brain. The brick toss was gaudy and juvenile. Vandalism tinged with old-school flair. But efficient, like a mallet to the temple.

I pressed the button on the knife handle, sheathing the blade. I slipped the weapon into the desk's shallow center drawer and stood. My puffy eyelids itched; waves of vanilla coffee tilted in my stomach. Blocks away, an elevated train shrieked an insult at nobody in particular. My head throbbed in sympathy. Thanks to the brick, cool air jetted through the star-shaped hole in the glass.

Careful to avoid shredding my fingertips, I lifted the brick from the glass heap. I flicked the silver shoelace, but didn't pull it. Tied under the lace was a sheet of white paper, gleaming pure against the shiny foil. The page was thick and expensive, like the perfume it was doused with. I'd read the love letter in a minute, but first I wanted to catch the guilty clown who'd wrecked my window. And my morning.

Cradling the brick, I crunched to the window. I looked through the web of cracked glass to the roof of the grocery next door. Fumes of rotten flowers and bruised fruit pulsed on the updraft in the narrow gangway. A slim figure tip-toed along the roof edge, arms outstretched for balance, head silhouetted against the gray clouds. Snub nose, soft lips sucked for concentration. Black tufts formed a ragged Mohawk. Yellow sweatshirt bagged over spindly torso. I recognized the brick-slinger:

Randall Blunt, a twelve-year old neighborhood hotshot climbing the rungs to career criminal.

I started to shout his name. Then clamped shut again. I was pissed, but startling Randall into a fatal plunge was a step too far. I was a private eye, sworn to protect lives, not end them. Randall needed help, not another boot in the ass. I rushed for the door. I could cut off the kid's escape in the alley behind our building, if I ran.

Run was a loose term. A roadside bomb in Iraq had destroyed two toes on my left foot, gifting me a dull ache, survivor's guilt, and a permanent limp. I jogged through the empty outer office of our detective agency, along the hall, and down the stairs to the rear entrance. I counted on surprise: I figured Randall would retreat to his sister's place or the local boxing gym. The quickest route to either was by the alley.

I punched through the rear door to the outside. A deli occupied the first floor of our building. The fatty stench of sausage, butter, onion, and garlic fluttered across my face. Smashed produce boxes were stacked waist-high next to garbage bins along one side of the narrow cement court. At the end of the yard, I eased open the gate in the chain-link fence and waited for my quarry. Metallic clanking marked Randall's trip down a fire escape to the alley. When he crept by, I sprang, grabbing the hood of his sweatshirt.

"Randall, my man. How're you doing?" I twisted the spongy cloth until the boy's throat bobbled under my fist. "Out early on a school day, aren't you?"

"Mr. Rook. I – I didn't see you!" His eyes bulged, the brown pupils swimming in pools of white. Sweat popped across his nose. A nice face, sweet even. Rich brown skin over baby features, large gap between the two front teeth. Chocolate and nougat on Randall's breath was Snickers, not the breakfast of champions. The lower lip tremble could have been fake. But no one was that good an actor.

I held the brick to his face. "You saw enough to toss this through my window." The white paper flapped in a sudden gust.

"You…you were inside? I didn't know. I swear… I didn't mean to hurt nobody."

"Not hurt, kid. You just dinged my pride." I relaxed my grip on Randall's collar, but didn't smile. He staggered a step. I jerked him vertical. "Who put you up to this?"

"I ain't telling." He straightened to his full four-foot-ten and squared his scrawny shoulders. "I'm no snitch, Mr. Rook."

"Sure, kid."

I grinned and nodded. We agreed on the code of the street: secrets demanded silence. My left hand still on the boy's neck, I pinched the paper with my right thumb and index finger. I shook it loose from the shoelace. The brick plunked to the pavement between us. I unfurled the page and scanned it. "How much did she pay you to deliver this note?"

Randall's eyes bugged. He gulped over a whisper, "You *know* her?"

"Of course. She's my boss. She signed the message, see?" I waved the paper, but didn't let him read it.

"No disrespect, man. But that butch with the pushed-in face is your *boss*?" Randall kicked at the brick. The tin foil split and we watched pink chunks tumble through the rip. "I thought you worked for Old Man Ross at the detective agency."

"I do." Off his frown, I explained. "Opal Cunningham is my temporary boss. Just this week."

As an operative with the Ross Agency, I corralled petty disturbances around our Harlem neighborhood. I dug up criminal records, nabbed thieves who preyed on scatterbrained relatives, or traced runaway spouses and skip-artist business partners. Assignments weren't always safe or clean. Or even sane. The work stretched my imagination, tested my grit. I helped people and brought home a few hundred bucks a week. The trade was fair: straightforward jobs for low-key clients. Good work, no frills. Ordinary laced with miles of tedium.

But this week in April was different. A welcome taste of excitement and glamour after a bleak winter. I was hired muscle for Zenith Metropole Entertainment, a production company filming an episode of their hit TV show, "Undaunted," in our neighborhood. My job was to keep three-way peace between fancy Hollywood invaders, star-struck tourists, and rowdy regulars from Harlem's streets. Tomorrow would be my last day.

"I saw you hanging around the set all week, Randall. Scrounging errands, picking up extra coin." I pressed the kid with a twist of his collar. "So, Opal Cunningham asked you to do this little job?"

Maybe he was tired; maybe baffled by the mystery of adult ways. Whatever his reasons, Randall sighed, then spilled: "Yeah, she asked me if I knew you, where you worked. I said sure. She handed me the brick, wrapped like a friggin' birthday present with the note tied on it. And her funky perfume all over it." He sniffed, then paused for the perfect beat. "And she told me to throw it in your window."

"Why not deliver at the front door, like a regular letter?"

"Nah, Opal's a stone freak, man. She's off-the-chain wild. Said I had to chuck it. Window open or shut, didn't matter. I had to throw it."

"Dramatic effect," I said. I'd seen enough theatrics from the Zenith crowd over the past four days to earn a degree in acting.

The boy shrugged and raised two flattened palms. "I don't know nothin' about no drama. Or no effect. But she did pay me ten real dollars. And she promised I'd get another ten after I done it." He looked up, water twinkling on his lids. "Now, you gone and *wrecked* it. And, I don't get my ten dollars." The wail was heart-wrenching. Almost.

"Wrecked? You're the one who broke *my* window, remember? I ought to call the cops."

"No, don't do that, Mr. Rook." The boy squirmed, but I tensed my grip.

Nobody in this neighborhood wanted the police involved. Ever. So, I escalated my threat: "Or maybe I'll buzz your sister, see what she thinks about your second-story act."

"Oh, no! You can't tell Kara! She'll *kill* me."

I knew his big sister from the local basketball courts. Kara was twenty-four and tough as cement. "I'm counting on it."

Randall's huge eyes scraped my face in search of mercy, but I stiffened. I could have pouted, but that would have been over-the-top.

"Look, kid. Here's what we'll do. You want me to keep your secret, right?"

The boy nodded. "Please."

"I'll do it. Your secret's safe. But here's the deal. You get to school, stay clear of the boulevard today, and I'll make good on your money. Deal?" He lips pursed, he dipped his chin. I fished my wallet from the back pocket of my jeans and pulled a bill. "You said ten? Here's five."

Randall nodded again, eyes wide and shiny. "Thanks, Mr. Rook. You're a straight-up dude." He stuffed the cash in a pocket. "I hope you don't get in no trouble with your boss over this."

"Don't worry. I'll square it with Opal. And tonight, I check with your sister to see if you made it to school." I had no intention of leaking our secret deal to his sister. But to keep the menace going, I lowered my face to his and delivered a squint-eyed glare.

His lip dropped. "Ah, jeez! I didn't do nothing wrong… Nothing *real* wrong." Randall scratched his scalp as a new thought passed under it. "Say, you working on the TV show like that. You know those big flash stars, right?"

"Not exactly." I stood tall and bobbed my eyebrows so he'd know the modesty was false.

"But you know 'em *enough*, don't you?"

"Enough for what?"

"Enough to ask that hot babe Vicky for her autograph." The boy sucked the gap between his teeth like a grizzled player. Vicky Joyce, the show's lead, was a break-out star. An Instagram goddess with a million followers. *Personality Magazine* had named her "Sexiest Woman on the Planet."

I'd never spoken to her. "You mean Vicky Joyce."

"Yeah, *her*. That chick is sex on a stick! Piece of ass force tears to your eyes." Lines quoted from his older running buddies, no doubt. Imitation lust gleamed through Randall's long lashes. "You know her?"

I'd never met her. "Sure, kid. I know Vicky." The white lie could polish my neighborhood rep.

His eyes bugged in wonder. "Can you get me a signed picture of Vicky Joyce? I'd boost rank in my crew if I scored that. You can hook me up, right?"

"I'll see what I can do."

"You're the straight-up bomb!"

"Beat it, kid."

"Dope!" Snapping a salute, Randall skipped away.

"Yeah, sure. Dope."

Five paces from me, he turned, flashing a cell phone. He snapped me holding the letter chest high. "Now I got proof I did the job," he crowed. "I show this to Opal, she'll pay up too. I can earn twice off this one gig." The little hustler was violating our secret deal already.

Randall grinned at the prospect of double-dipping, then tapped his temple to brag on his smarts. A poke of his sneaker scattered pebbles and tin cans as he disappeared down the alley.

I smoothed the white paper against my thigh. As humid spices pummeled my nose, I read its message again: *"Rook – Believe Me. My Murder is No Fake – Opal Cunningham."*

Like I said, dramatic effect. I crumpled the paper and shoved it in my pocket.